STONES *River*

STONES *River*

A Novel

Book I of
The Sentinel Heart Trilogy

M. F. JONES

FIELDWOOD
BOOKS

Cover design and Interior Formatting: Damonza Studio

Fieldwood Books
P.O. Box 289
302 Northgate Mall Drive
Hixson, Tennessee 37343-9998

Copyright © 2025 by M. F. Jones
ISBN (ebook) 979-8-9918200-0-4
ISBN (paperback) 979-8-9918200-1-1
ISBN (hardcover) 979-8-9918200-2-8

Library of Congress Control Number: 2025903535

To Doug

"Bold, cautious, true, and my loving comrade"

-Walt Whitman, *Drum-Taps*

Somebody's darling, somebody's pride
Who'll tell his Mother where her boy died?

- Refrain of the popular Civil War song
"Somebody's Darling"
Music by John Hill Hewitt (1864)
Words by Marie Ravenal de la Coste

Author's Note

I grew up in Massachusetts with Southern parents, and on my family's yearly trips down south, my Georgia cousins often teased me to the point of tears by calling me a Yankee. I didn't know what that was, only that they made it sound like a shameful thing. When I was twelve, my mother suggested that I was at last old enough to read what, for her and other white, privileged Atlanta natives, was a sacred text: Margaret Mitchell's *Gone with the Wind*. I was enthralled by it, and, naively, I sympathized with the Confederates, rather than with the Yankees so vilified by Mitchell and my cousins. At that age, I had no real comprehension of slavery.

My interest in the Civil War receded until the early 2000s, when my husband, a professional trumpeter, began playing with an 1860s-style military band. The group performed at historical sites and major Civil War re-enactments, and I went along, dressed in period-appropriate clothing (which made me heartily grateful that women no longer have to wear corsets). One night, at a commemoration of the Battle of Gettysburg, I walked around the vast Union campsite and was struck by the authenticity of the scene, which evoked the romance of an earlier time. The idea came to me: What if a young woman participating in an event like this wandered away from the settled area of the camp and met a handsome young man with whom she felt an instant connection—only to learn that he was the ghost of a Civil War soldier? In that moment, this book was born.

Research for the novel opened my eyes to what I had never understood in my preteen infatuation with *Gone with the Wind*: Many of those who claimed that the Southern motivation in the war was to protect

"States' rights" meant, primarily, the right to profit from the free labor of enslaved people, without which the Southern agrarian economy, and the lifestyle so idealized by Margaret Mitchell, would collapse.

My fictional hero, Lemuel Sanders, joined the Confederate army, but, having grown up in the mountains of eastern Tennessee, had never witnessed slavery firsthand and had no commitment to it. Like many young men of the time, he went to war seeking imagined adventure and glory, and to protect his home from invasion. His best friend fought for the Confederates and so Lem did too, but he could as easily have supported the Union cause. His part of east Tennessee was split, as evidenced by the fact that my mother's two grandfathers, both from that region, fought on different sides of the conflict.

I now live in Tennessee, near the Stones River National Battlefield. I pray that our beautiful state and our country will never again know the pain and loss suffered by my characters and by the real Civil War soldiers and their loved ones on whom this story is based.

M. F. Jones
October 2024

Contents

PART I: SENTINEL IN THE FOREST

Chapter 1: Encounter. 3

Chapter 2: Bombshell 10

Chapter 3: Demon or Deliverer? 18

Chapter 4: The Mission 23

Chapter 5: Outsider. 30

Chapter 6: Life Stories 38

Chapter 7: Romance Versus Reality 44

Chapter 8: Mortal Musings 56

Chapter 9: Turtle Dove. .62

Chapter 10: Phantom Kiss 72

PART II: SEEING THE ELEPHANT

Chapter 11: Rebel 79

Chapter 12: Liberation. .85

Chapter 13: Acts of Mercy 93

Chapter 14: Brother Foe. 103

Chapter 15: Fleeing the Elephant. 110

Chapter 16: Repentance. 119

Chapter 17: Wilderness Rite. 126

Chapter 18: Battling Bands 132

Chapter 19: Destiny at Stones River. 137

Chapter 20: Silent Anguish 144

Chapter 21: Confession .149

PART III: THE SEEKER

Chapter 22: Dead Letter 161

Chapter 23: The Indifference of Strangers 169

Chapter 24: Restless Spirits 180

Chapter 25: The Bitter Cup 189

Chapter 26: Mothers of Soldiers. 196

Chapter 27: Some Little Room for Hope 202

Chapter 28: Portal to Paradise 210

PART IV: IMMORTAL HOME

Chapter 29: Looming Shadow 223

Chapter 30: A Land Full of Graves. 231

Chapter 31: Pay Dirt 240

Chapter 32: Without Honor 248

Chapter 33: Belle of the Rebel Ball. 256

Chapter 34: A Time to Mourn 262

Chapter 35: Unearthing. 270

Chapter 36: Gift of Comfort 276

Chapter 37: Love Token. 282

Acknowledgments 289

BONUS: Chapter 1 of *Soldier's Joy*, Book II of
The Sentinel Heart Trilogy 291

About the Author. 301

PART I

SENTINEL IN THE FOREST

ENCOUNTER

THE CAMPFIRE POPPED, sending bursts of orange sparks spiraling up into the ink-blue sky. Beyond the reach of the firelight, the neighboring cornfields and the surrounding forest guarded their secrets in their dark depths.

Jessie Gibbs took off her wet apron and hung it on the clothesline stretched between two tents. She carried her wooden-and-canvas folding stool over to the group sitting around the fire, opened it, and sat down.

Pete DiSpirito's voice rose above the murmur of other conversations. "Guys, how do you know when you're getting in a little too deep with this re-enacting business?"

"How?" was the obliging response.

"When you see a beautiful woman in a bikini and you think, 'Hmmm, wonder what she'd look like in a hoop skirt?'"

Amid the chorus of guffaws and hoots, across the circle Jessie caught his gaze, and he gave her a wink, the firelight dancing in his dark eyes. The wink surprised and warmed her, making her feel as though they shared a private understanding, but she knew that was just Pete's way, friendly and easygoing with everyone.

Pete played tenor horn, and his sixteen-year-old son, Ben, was principal cornet in the Civil War-style band whose members had gathered for this weekend campout to plan the coming summer's schedule of performances. Jessie played the piano for the group when they did indoor concerts, accompanying soprano Becky DePew in the sentimental, old-fashioned songs that had cheered Civil War soldiers, and their families and sweethearts. At outdoor events and training encampments like this weekend, Jessie also helped fellow cook Abby Newcomb feed the ten hungry bandsmen and whoever had come along with them, and shared the cleaning up. It was hard, hot work, especially when dressed in period-appropriate clothes as the band members always were at their official gatherings. Now Jessie flapped her long skirt, soaked from washing the large iron cooking pots, in a futile attempt to dry it in the humid air.

Jim Bryce, the band's conductor, rose from his stool beside the fire, got everyone's attention, and ran down the next day's schedule: Reveille at 6:00 (groans); inspection of uniforms and kits. ("Stash the cell phones, plastic lighters, and wristwatches, folks. New guys, get authentic eye-glasses as soon as you can, and old guys, you have no more excuses. And just a reminder—no sunglasses. Only syphilitics wore sunglasses in the 1860s. I want everybody looking excruciatingly correct at Gettysburg in three weeks.") Marching practice would occupy the morning; the band, which usually performed seated, would be leading the Confederate troops in a parade onto the battlefield at the upcoming re-enactment of the 144th anniversary of the July 1863 Battle of Gettysburg. "And those of us who missed marching band in high school need to make sure we don't trip over our feet," Jim said.

"Or smash our teeth in with the mouthpiece," someone added to a general shudder.

Jim then went over the program to be performed at the Carter House in Franklin the following weekend. "Jess and Becky, I've got you down to close the program with 'Somebody's Darling.'"

"After that one there won't be a dry seat in the house," baritone horn player Les Spraggins joked amid more groans. Tuba player Ed Forte, laughing, leaned over and gave Les a shove that nearly knocked him off his stool.

Jessie laughed too, but the truth was, "Somebody's Darling" was the saddest song she knew, about a young man, mortally wounded, carried into a battlefield hospital in his last moments. Whenever Becky sang the lines, "Somebody's darling, somebody's pride, who'll tell his mother where her boy died?" there were always audible sniffles among the listeners.

After Jim finished, people began to rise and say good night, tired from putting in a full day at their jobs, packing and hauling their gear, driving to Murfreesboro from wherever they lived, some as far as two hours away, and setting up camp. With a tug of envy, Jessie watched Abby heading with her husband JJ to their tent, which they'd set up a little away from the rest. They had left their three-year-old son with Abby's mother for the weekend, and Jessie imagined them savoring this rare chance to be alone together, quietly making love in their cocoon of canvas and soft bedrolls.

When Jessie had joined the band two years earlier, after getting her master's degree in music education and returning home from the University of Tennessee, she had hoped that a side benefit would be meeting someone and having an intimate relationship. But so far it hadn't happened; all the men in the group were married or coupled, and her hopes of finding romance at the larger events had likewise come to nothing.

The night was still and placid; no sound of the mechanized world intruded on the music of crickets, the rustling of foliage. "I'm going to take a little walk before bed," Jessie said, getting to her feet. "It seems pretty safe around here."

"Just holler if you see any Yankees," someone said.

"I know y'all would protect me." Manly rumbles of assent followed her as she went to her tent and took a lantern from its hook over the entry flaps, lit the candle inside, and began walking away from camp.

The campsite was on farmland just west of the Stones River National Battlefield, owned by the uncle of one of the bandsmen. She held her skirt up above the roughly mowed swath of stubble running between the large cornfield on her left and the forest on her right, beyond which, she knew, was the boundary of the national park.

The crickets were louder here. She walked past the edge of the cornfield and entered a wooded glade. The faint flickering glow from the lantern and the light of the half-moon helped her navigate over the uneven ground. The woods gave way to a clearing with a large flat-topped stone at its center. The place appeared untouched by humanity except for the remains of an old snake-rail fence. Jessie sat down on the stone, placing the lantern on the ground beside her, and savored the beauty and serenity of the night.

Nothing of the modern world marred the tranquility of the immediate environment. The only sounds nearby were the murmuring of leaves stirring in the slight breeze, the scratchy chorus of insects rising and falling, and the snap of a twig as an unseen creature—its light noises reassuring her that it was only a small animal—moved through the woods. In the distance she could hear the whoosh of traffic on Interstate 24, but she could make herself believe that it was the rushing of a river.

Movement among the trees to her right caught her eye. A figure came into view, a man, swathed in a blanket. She leapt to her feet, adrenaline sparking to the end of every nerve.

"Evenin', ma'am." He raised his floppy, beat-up, wide-brimmed felt hat. With his other hand he clutched the blanket closed in front. His skin was darkened with dirt or soot, making the whites of his eyes look very bright. As she took in the details of his clothes, Jessie's heart rate slowed, her breathing calming. Not a vagrant or a homicidal maniac after all, but a re-enactor, a fellow "living historian," dressed in the motley uniform of a Confederate soldier. In the opening at the top of his blanket-cloak she could see the collar and wooden buttons of a tan or gray jacket. Beneath the blanket hem the baggy legs of his trousers stopped short of his ankles, bare above worn, brogan-style shoes.

"I'm sorry if I scared you," he said.

"I was just surprised," she said. "I didn't expect to meet anyone out here. We're camped right over there." She gestured in the direction she had come from, hoping to convey that help was close at hand if he should try anything. "My band."

"A musical band?"

"Yes. We play music for the troops."

"I'd sure like to hear that."

"You definitely will when we rehearse tomorrow."

"That'll be real nice. It's been a long time since I heard some music." He seemed strangely solemn.

There was a silence, then Jessie asked, "What's your unit?"

"Company I, the 37th Tennessee Infantry Regiment."

"Where's the rest of your group?"

His gaze darted to her face, then fell to the ground. "They're nearby."

But where? she wondered. There were none of the usual sounds of laughter, loud male voices, or axes thumping on firewood, no scent of woodsmoke, no firelight flickering through the trees.

"So you're the lucky one who pulled picket duty?" she asked with a smile.

He didn't smile back, only hesitated a moment, then said, "Yes, ma'am. That's right."

"Is there something going on at Stones River this weekend?"

"Pardon?"

"I wondered if there was some event happening at the national park that we hadn't heard about."

"No, ma'am, I don't know anything about that."

He was only a little taller than her five-foot-six-inch height, maybe five-nine, and he seemed to be about her age, in his mid-twenties. And now that she was looking at him full in the face, she saw, beneath the grime that shadowed his skin, that he was strikingly handsome. His bold eyebrows and the planes of his roughly shaven cheeks and jawline were definitely masculine, while his large, dark eyes and finely shaped lips would not have been out of place in a woman's face.

Good-looking, for sure, but a little slow on the uptake. Or, possibly, shy—strange though it seemed for someone as attractive as he was to be socially awkward. That thought put her more at ease; Jessie could certainly relate to shyness.

"My name is Jessie Gibbs," she pressed on.

"Pleased to meet you, ma'am. I'm Private Lemuel Sanders."

"Well, now that we know each other's names, you can stop calling me ma'am. It makes me feel so old."

"Well, all right then, Mrs. …?"

"Miss." No anachronistic *Ms.* for this role-playing.

"Miss Gibbs," he said.

Sometimes re-enactors, in addition to dressing the part, tried to emulate the manners and diction of the nineteenth century. And, in fact, some units required that their members stay in character for the whole event. Maybe Lemuel's group was like that. Maybe his real name wasn't even Lemuel, which seemed as antiquated as Hezekiah or Jabez; maybe he was actually a Kyle or a Brad. She was glad her group confined their efforts at authenticity to clothing, instruments, food, and equipment. Yet for the moment, she was willing to play along.

"So Mr. Sanders, when do you go off duty?"

"Not for a while yet."

"If you're free tomorrow, come by our campsite, you and your friends. We're here all weekend. You can hear the music up close."

"Thank you for inviting me. How many are with you?"

"Our band has ten members, but as usual there're other people along."

"Do you play in the band?" He was looking at her intently.

"I play the piano at indoor concerts, but when we travel and camp out, I and another girl do the cooking."

"Lady cooks!" He gaped at her. "Your boys have it good. We have to do for ourselves, when we get rations. Which is not too often."

"Just hardtack and salt horse, right?" she said teasingly.

"We feel lucky when we get hardtack and salt horse," he said. "Parched corn is more like it." He smiled at her broadly for the first time. That smile—bright, straight teeth, a deep dimple in his left cheek, and a shine in the eyes that held hers—made something strange happen in her chest: a leap of excitement, a plummeting, like doom.

The moment was broken when from across the field came the notes of "Taps" played by Ben on his bugle. "I'd better get back," Jessie said. "I have to be up at dawn to fix breakfast. Musicians are a hungry bunch."

"I sure liked talking to you, Miss Gibbs," he said. "Will you come again?" His tone, his gaze when she met it, held an earnestness, even an urgency, that was both flattering and puzzling. Her sister Lou Ann often told her, "You'd be really pretty if you'd do something with yourself." "Like what?" Jessie once asked her. "You know," Lou Ann explained, "put on some makeup, get some sexy clothes. And you need to learn how to flirt a little. You're too serious. You have to play the game."

Jessie resisted; she'd feel like a fool or an imposter doing most of those things. And the kind of man she hoped to attract would not want to play games.

So far, however, she had not met such a man. Until, maybe, now. Her heart quickened. "You'll be here?" she asked him.

"Yes, ma'am, I'll be right here."

"All right, Mr. Sanders. If you're not free to come over in the daytime, I'll come back after supper. I'll bring you some of our food."

"I wouldn't want you to go to any trouble—"

"It's no trouble."

"Well, thank you. You be careful now, walking back by yourself."

"I know the way. It's not far."

"Good night, Miss Gibbs."

As she began walking away, she could not stop herself from glancing back at him.

The clearing was empty. The woods were dark and still.

CHAPTER 2

BOMBSHELL

HE DID NOT appear at her group's campsite the next day. During the morning rehearsal, Jessie kept looking over toward the path she'd taken the night before, hoping to see him and some of his comrades coming from the direction of the cornfield, drawn by the music. He really had seemed to yearn for music.

She replayed in her mind their brief conversation. The awkward, halting words hadn't signified much. It was the intensity of his gaze and the brilliance of his smile that she kept recalling, each time with a little jolt of wonder and excitement. No man had ever had such a powerful, immediate effect on her before. And it seemed he felt something for her too.

Then she checked herself. She knew nothing about him. He might be married, or otherwise unavailable. No sense setting herself up for disappointment.

Right after the supper dishes had been washed, as several of her bandmates dealt out a card game and others chatted around the fire, Jessie slipped away from the encampment, carrying a large piece of cornbread which she'd buttered and spread with honey, knotted in a clean muslin dishtowel.

After ten minutes or so, she arrived at the wooded glade and passed through it into the clearing marked by the flat boulder.

"Mr. Sanders?" she called.

He emerged from amid the trees. "Evenin', Miss Gibbs." There was that bright smile again, and as before, it caused a little leap in her chest.

He was still wearing his blanket, clutched closed, and she wondered if he could possibly be cold on this over-eighty-degree night. His skin was still streaked with what she assumed must be black-powder soot from firing his musket. In the last light of day, she noticed details of his appearance that she hadn't been able to make out the night before. His eyes were an unusual amber-brown, and his hair, which fell long and waving below his hat, was dark blond.

"I brought you something," she said. "Some of my homemade cornbread with honey and butter."

"Well, I'll swan," he said. "That was right nice of you. But I don't want to take it with my hand so dirty. Would you just set it down on that rock there and I'll have it later? Thank you kindly, Miss Gibbs."

Jessie smiled. "My grandmother is the only other person I've ever heard say that."

"Say what, ma'am?" He did not seem to be able to dispense with the courtesy.

"'I'll swan.' She's from East Tennessee."

"That's where I'm from, too," he said. "Beulah."

"Really? My grandmother's from Caton's Forge. Your next-door neighbor, so to speak. Maybe you know her, or some of my relatives."

"What are their names?"

"My grandmother's married name is Marshall, and her maiden name was Garner."

"Seems like I did know folks by those names," he said. "But not to speak to."

She wondered at his use of the past tense, as if he had been away from home for a long time.

He gestured to the rock. "Will you set a while?"

She sat down beside the wrapped bundle of food. "Won't you sit too? I don't see any officers around to yell at you." Once again, she noticed the lack of noise or activity in the immediate vicinity.

"No, I reckon they're all off taking their ease, like always." He lowered himself to the ground in front of her, being careful to keep the blanket closed, and crossed his long legs. The trousers pulled up, revealing thin, sockless ankles, the skin streaked with dirt.

"It's beautiful there in the Smoky Mountains," she said. "Whenever I have some free time, I go stay with my grandmother. She has a big front porch with rocking chairs, and I can sit there for hours just looking out over the mountains and valleys. It gives me such a feeling of peace."

"Me too," he said. "I loved it."

Again, she wondered at his use of the past tense. "You don't still live there?"

He was looking down, frowning a little. "No, ma'am. I haven't been there for quite a spell." After a pause he raised his eyes, and she felt a thrill as their gazes met. His expression brightened. "What-all did you do today?" he asked.

"We rehearsed in the morning. Did you hear us?"

"Yes indeed. It sounded so nice."

"And I and my friend Abby cooked the three meals and cleaned up."

"What did you fix to eat?"

"Sausage gravy and biscuits for breakfast. Vegetable soup for dinner. Beef stew for supper with the cornbread. Lemonade and fruit shrubs to drink."

"My land!" He looked at her, wide-eyed. "That sounds like the kind of fancy cooking my mama would do on a Sunday."

"Well, I wouldn't expect guys alone to go to all that trouble," Jessie said. "Y'all probably just poke a bayonet through a piece of bacon and stick it in the fire."

"We never get bacon. We used to get pork belly sometimes, but mostly it was pretty near spoiled. One time my friend Jeremiah and I caught a squirrel and cooked it over the fire. It was good to have fresh meat, even if it was just a few bites."

He sounded so convincing. Jessie said, "What do you do for fun? When you're not on picket duty?"

"I liked wood carving. My granddaddy learned me how. It helped me pass the time in camp."

"Don't you still do it?"

"No, ma'am."

When he said nothing more, she prompted, "What did you make?"

"I got pretty good at making finger rings, with little vines and flowers all around them. Some of the other fellows asked me to make them for their sweethearts. I didn't mind doing it."

Jessie had seen wooden rings like that in museum displays. He must have too. He really had the diction, the mannerisms, and the details of his persona down pat. But she was beginning to wish they could relate to each other without role-playing.

"I finished a toy not too long ago and sent it to my little sister," he went on. "It was a right interesting puzzle to make. It had a square cage that I hollowed out, with a little ball inside that rattled around loose, and a chain on one end. I had me a time, getting that ball round and smooth without breaking the little cage, and getting the links of the chain to hang loose of each other." He shrugged. "It's kindly hard to explain..."

"It sounds really intricate. How did you think to make something like that?"

"When we were down in Alabama, we passed an old fellow setting outside a store, carving, and he showed me what he was making."

"I bet your sister loved it," she said. "How old is she?"

"Fifteen."

"What's her name?"

"Polly." His voice was warm. "I promised her a bonnet. I wasn't able to get one for her before ..."

"Before?" she asked.

"Before I came down here," he said, and fell silent.

Something seemed to have made him withdraw into himself. This conversation was baffling—by turns warm and easy, but then with these strange moments of distance.

She tried to change the mood. "What do you do in real life?"

"In real life?" He looked perplexed.

"What work do you do?"

"I worked on my pa's farm. I reckoned I'd find something else to do when I got back home."

"But you changed your mind?"

He shrugged, looking uncomfortable. Afraid that he found her curiosity intrusive, Jessie decided to tell him a little about herself. "In addition to playing the piano, I'm a school music teacher and the organist for my church."

"Is that so?" He looked at her with interest. "I'd sure like to hear you play."

"Maybe you can sometime. I'd like to play for you." Her cheeks warmed at the boldness. She was glad that the blush was concealed by the now full darkness, the moonlight muted by a thick cloud cover.

It was time to go; she picked up the lantern and stood. He rose too, adjusting the blanket.

"We'll be leaving after breakfast tomorrow," she said, hoping he would take the cue and ask how to get in touch.

"Where're you going on to?"

"Oh, just back home. Back to work tomorrow."

He didn't seem to register her answer. His eyes searched her face with that same intensity. He was close; close enough that it almost seemed he might lean forward and kiss her. In the concentrated focus of his gaze, Jessie's pulse quickened.

"Will you come back before you go and say goodbye?" he asked.

"Yes, but where's your camp? How will I find you?"

"I'll be here."

"You will? Don't you ever get a break?"

"If I'm not right here, I'll hear you and come."

"It'll be around eleven, noon at the latest."

"It doesn't matter when you come. I'll be here."

"Well, then, I'll see you sometime tomorrow morning. Good night, Mr. Sanders."

"Good night, Miss Gibbs. I sure enjoyed visiting with you."

She gave him a smile that, she hoped, conveyed all that she could not quite find the words to say.

IT WAS RAINING the next morning. When the breakfast dishes were washed and the tents and equipment loaded into the cars, Jessie set off swiftly along the path that led to the clearing in the woods, worried that Lemuel Sanders' group might have left early because of the weather.

The glade was empty and silent when she approached. "Mr. Sanders?" she called out.

And there he was, coming out of the forest, still wrapped in his blanket. "Lord, Miss Gibbs, you'll take a chill in this rain."

"I don't mind," she said.

"I'm so glad you came back." Once again, there was that urgency in his expression that she did not understand—almost pleading.

She was concerned at how drawn he looked. He was handsome, still, but in the bleak daylight his skin was pallid, his lips a grayish color.

"Aren't you and the other men going home today?" she asked.

"No, ma'am."

She was puzzled. "Don't y'all have to go back to work tomorrow?"

He looked away a moment, frowning. As she waited for his answer, Jessie became aware of something strange. The rain was pelting down now, dripping from the stiff brim of her bonnet, soaking through her shawl and weighing down the hem of her long dress.

Lemuel was standing in the rain as well—and he remained perfectly dry. The heavy drops left no dark splotches on his hat, or on his blanket, or on the dusty leather of his brogans.

A dart of alarm shot through her chest. She took a step back and he stared at her, the entreaty in his eyes naked.

"Mr. Sanders," she began, and could not think of how to form a coherent question. Finally, she brought out, "Why aren't you getting wet in all this rain?"

"Well, you see, Miss Gibbs," he began. "See, I've been trying to think of a way to tell you…"

"Tell me what?" She watched him, something still and cold gathering within her.

"I wouldn't do anything to upset you. You're so pretty, and so nice to come see me."

She waited, hardly able to move.

He went on. "What I have to tell you is … there was a fight here—"

"Yes, the Battle of Stones River."

"Is that what they're calling it? Well …" He looked away again, rubbed a hand over his mouth and chin, then said quietly, "I was killed in that fight. They buried my body here. And so here I have to stay." With an obvious effort he brought his eyes back to meet hers, his expression apologetic.

Jessie lifted her skirts, abruptly turned, and began to walk quickly away.

"Oh, wait," he said. "Please don't go."

Somehow, he was again standing in front of her, startling her.

"Mr. Sanders—Lemuel—whoever you are, we can cut out the play-acting now. I don't think this is the least bit funny."

"I'm not play-acting, honest I'm not." He reached his hands out, palms turned up to show that he meant no threat. The motion made his blanket fall open. Jessie gasped at the sight of what he had been so careful to conceal—a slash in the fabric of his short tan jacket was surrounded by a dark red stain, and through the gash in the cloth she saw a large wound like a crimson mouth in the exposed pale skin of his abdomen.

Her knees gave way and she swayed. His hand shot forward and she saw it close over her arm; yet she felt no pressure, no touch of solid flesh, only a stirring agitation of the air. There was something strange about his nearness. Electricity seemed to charge the atmosphere around him, like the tingling energy that lightning-strike survivors reported feeling before the bolt hit them. In addition, there was a barely audible sort of humming vibration.

Recoiling in horror, she whispered, "What *are* you?"

"Oh, please, Miss Gibbs," he said. "Please, don't be scared away, let me explain. I can't leave here, and you're the first person I've talked to since—"

Suddenly regaining her ability to move, Jessie bolted from the clearing, running blindly through the forest glade, along the cornfield, and past the empty campsite to the parking area. Safely locked in her old van, she drove with reckless speed, bouncing along the rutted farm road, glancing into the rearview mirror, fearful of what she might see. The rear window framed only the deceptive ordinariness of the rain-washed landscape.

CHAPTER 3

DEMON OR DELIVERER?

JESSIE TOOK A break from her job at her father's plumbing supply company where she was working part-time over the summer to supplement her modest teacher's salary. She walked outside with her cell phone and sat down at the picnic table shaded by a tree, where employees often went to eat or smoke. There was no one there at the moment. The day was warm and sunny, and a little stream burbled a short distance from where she sat, but she hardly registered her surroundings.

She was shaky from agitation and exhaustion. She had not managed more than a few hours' restless sleep since coming home from the encampment two days earlier. Memories of her conversations with the handsome, mysterious soldier kept circling in her mind, along with questions. What was he? He was not a mortal being, that seemed clear from the way he stayed dry in the downpour and from the ghastly wound which looked real. She remembered feeling only the charged air instead of the hand that had closed over her arm—to do what? To help steady her, or to try to draw her close for some dreadful purpose?

Was he a ghost? Did ghosts really exist? Fearful of what she would find, she had done an Internet search about what the Bible and Christianity, the faith she'd grown up in, said about spirits. The findings disturbed her; ghosts, more than one article said, were actually demons disguising themselves as dead people, emissaries of the devil. The spirits of Christians who died did not stay on the earth, but went straight to either Heaven or Hell, the authors firmly asserted.

Lemuel Sanders did not seem at all demonic. He was shy, earnest, and had appeared sincerely regretful for upsetting her.

Jessie knew she should probably ask her pastor, John Brinton, what he thought. But she felt sure of what he would say, something like, "Put it behind you. Pray about it. And don't try to see him again." She did not want to put herself in the position of having to disobey someone she had always respected so highly.

Because going back to see Lemuel Sanders was just what she was considering doing, though it frightened her.

Now and then a fleeting, ironic thought crossed her mind. Wasn't it just her luck that when she finally met a man who seemed to be everything she wanted and who appeared to be strongly attracted to her, he would be... whatever he was?

She opened her phone, scanned the contact list, and pressed the office number for Dr. Becky DePew. As a professor of American history at Murfreesboro's Middle Tennessee State University, Becky took every opportunity to share with her bandmates her encyclopedic knowledge of the Civil War.

"Is there a way to find out about individual soldiers who were killed at Stones River?" Jessie asked her after the initial pleasantries.

"Anyone in particular you're looking for?"

"A private named Lemuel Sanders."

"Confederate?"

"Yes, the 37th Tennessee Infantry Regiment." Jessie hoped she remembered his unit correctly. Feeling that some explanation was necessary, she went on, "He was the relative of some friends of my family, and when they heard I was into Civil War history they asked me to see if I could find out any information about him."

"Well, you could try the Visitor Center at the battlefield. Or the Internet. And I'll be glad to do some looking myself."

"What if he was killed and buried with no identification?"

"That's very possible," said Becky. "Tragically, that was the case for hundreds of thousands of Civil War soldiers."

"That many?" Jessie was shocked.

"I read the statistic that as many as forty percent of all the Union soldiers killed, and an even larger percentage of Confederates, were unaccounted for. All their families knew was that they never came home."

"My God. I can't even imagine how heartbreaking that must have been. Left in suspense forever."

After the call ended, Jessie phoned the Visitor Center at the Stones River National Battlefield but was told that they did not have complete casualty lists of all the soldiers for the reason Becky had stated: thousands of dead soldiers were unidentified.

"Many of the graves in the National Cemetery contain multiple remains," the man explained. "Of course, your Confederate soldier wouldn't have been buried in the National Cemetery."

My Confederate soldier, Jessie thought with a strange pang of pleasure.

Her own online search delivered such a welter of confusing information that she quickly gave up.

Late that afternoon, as Jessie was in her apartment heating up some leftover campfire stew for dinner, her cell phone rang. It was Becky.

"I found a record of that soldier you asked me about. There's a website of Tennessee Civil War regiments and soldiers. Private Lemuel Sanders was in Company I of the 37th Tennessee Infantry Regiment, Army of Tennessee. That company was raised from Sevier and Blount counties."

That, Jessie thought, all squared with what he had told her. Becky went on to say that the 37th Tennessee did fight at Stones River on both December 31, 1862 and January 2, 1863. However, there was no record of Lemuel Sanders' death.

"Well, thanks, Becky. That's at least something to tell the family," Jessie said. "Some place for them to start trying to find out what happened to him. Would you please send me a link to that website?"

When the call ended, her heart was beating faster at this evidence that the lonely soldier in the forest might indeed be who, and what, he said he was.

JESSIE DROVE to the Pine Bridge Church to put in her practice time on the organ. It was the church she had grown up in, a nondenominational Protestant congregation. A year and a half earlier the organist and choir director, Miss Lucie Stiles, Jessie's first piano teacher, had retired, and Pastor John Brinton had offered Jessie the position.

The summer before that, Jessie had been hired as the assistant music teacher at Murfreesboro's Westwood Elementary School, so with the stipend from the church job she was earning enough—to her great relief—to afford to move into a place of her own. Since finishing grad school two years earlier with a load of student debt, she had been living with her parents in her old bedroom, feeling thrown back in time and as though none of her achievements counted for anything. Desperate to begin life as an independent adult, Jessie found a small one-bedroom apartment in a down-at-the-heels complex that seemed to be a waysta-tion for people who hoped not to be there long—the recently divorced, the not-yet-coupled.

Entering the church, she breathed out a deep sigh. The peaceful interior always soothed her with its pale gray walls and white woodwork, golden oak pews, and brass chandeliers and sconces. The piano stood on one side of the chancel, and an electronic organ on the other. Jessie had first performed on this piano when she was seven. Everybody had always made a fuss over her talent and encouraged her, although few in the congregation knew the first thing about music beyond country and pop songs and old-time hymns. Still, they had made her feel like a prodigy.

Up until her junior year of high school, she'd had dreams of becom-ing a concert pianist, until her piano teacher—a professor from Middle Tennessee State University—gently set her straight about the enormous financial burden of attempting such a career. Jessie's father's business was modestly successful, but she and her sister would need to finance their own education; there was no money for anything extra. Not on that scale, at least.

The professor advised her instead to pursue a career as a music teacher and seek out performing opportunities at the same time.

The light in the church sanctuary was fading. She switched on the lamp on the organ. Her plan had been to keep practicing, play local concerts and recitals, and ultimately move to a city with a thriving classical music scene. But it was turning out to be nearly impossible to put in the hours of practice necessary to keep her skills at a high level. She was just too tired and distracted at the end of the working day, whether at the school or at her summer job. And as for finding performing opportunities, she had no idea how to begin, and her lifelong shyness made the prospect even more daunting.

So, two years after completing her master's, here she was, teaching third graders how to play the recorder, accompanying a chorus of piping little voices in "Oh! Susanna," and playing church services and free or low-paying Civil War concerts. It was not the musical life she had dreamed of.

She roused herself to practice and adjusted the stops on the organ for the Bach prelude she was planning for the coming Sunday. As she did so, she recalled the soft voice of Lemuel Sanders: *I'd sure like to hear you play.* And his face rose vividly in her memory.

If he truly existed (and over the past few days, the doubts had returned about that, and also about her mental stability), and if his situation really was as he'd portrayed it, then shouldn't she try to help him? How awful to be stuck there, all alone, for 144 years.

This was a rationalization, she knew. She had to admit that she wanted to see once again those gold-brown eyes shine at the sight of her, and watch that smile spread over his face.

Suddenly, in a life that had begun to feel predictable and stuck, this mystery had opened up. Though it might be crazy, though she might be putting herself at risk, she had to explore it.

CHAPTER 4

THE MISSION

JESSIE PULLED HER van into the parking area, switched off the ignition, and sat still, momentarily unnerved by the solitude and the silence that was broken only by the ticking of the cooling engine.

At least it was not yet dark; on this late-June night it would be light until nine or so. Even so, she took her candle-lantern. She stepped out of the van and closed the door behind her as quietly as she could, wondering just whose attention she was afraid of attracting—the bogeyman? Haints? The man with the hook, of childhood slumber party legend? It made little sense to fear any of these imaginary menaces when she had come on purpose to seek out a ghost.

She locked the car and made her way toward the campsite. In the dusk, it looked forlorn, the grass tamped down from the tents, the firepit black and lifeless. Hurrying past the cornfield, she moved through the stand of woods and entered the clearing with the flat boulder. There were the remnants of the little bundle of cornbread, now just a few torn shreds of cloth. Her heart was pounding, its throbbing making the fading light of the day pulse in her vision.

"Mr. Sanders?" she called out softly. The sound of her own voice was unnerving. "Lemuel Sanders?"

There was only silence. She waited, tense, a sick dread spreading within her. He wasn't here. Maybe he never had been? Maybe she was losing—had already lost—her mind, and had somehow dreamed up a romantic apparition?

Or maybe—and this thought brought a pang of fear—it *was* some kind of demonic trickery that had lured her back here.

After a few more minutes of anxious listening, straining to see into the shadows within the woods, she sighed and turned to go back to her car.

"Miss Gibbs?"

Her heart gave a jolt. She whirled around to see him moving from out of the trees. In the twilight, she again saw the grayish pallor of his face beneath the soot, the deep red stain visible on the rough, butternut wool of his jacket. He didn't trouble to hold the blanket tightly closed anymore and just grasped the top to keep it from falling from his shoulders.

"I thought you weren't here," she said, happiness and relief vying with an instinctive wariness.

"Where would I go?" he asked, his tone teasing.

"I have no idea. I don't know anything about you. I've been wondering if you were even real." She was surprised by the heat that surged into her tone.

He was looking at her closely, suddenly serious. "I know this all must seem strange to you," he said. "I thought sure I'd scared you so bad I'd never see you again. I'm sorry for that. I'm mighty glad you came back."

"I was scared," she said, "but I don't think you mean me any harm."

"That is true, Miss Gibbs. I give you my solemn word that I would never do anything to hurt you."

They stood and regarded each other for a moment. The tension eased within her and at last Jessie let herself smile at him.

His expression relaxed into an answering smile—the bright teeth, the dimple, the lurch in her chest. Motioning toward the flat stone, he said, "Will you take your usual seat, ma'am?"

"Thank you, kind sir." She lowered herself onto the rock. "There's room enough for two."

He sat down beside her. A slight tingling stirred the hairs of her arm nearest him.

"Who ate your food?" she asked.

"Big old raccoon," he said. "I let him be. At least somebody got to enjoy that fine-looking cornbread."

"So you can't eat?"

"No, ma'am."

"Or touch things, or move things?" She remembered his hesitation to take the cornbread from her.

He shook his head.

"And I can't touch you," she said.

"I reckon not." He held out a finger, black with dirt or gunpowder, its nail chipped and stained. Fearfully, hesitantly, yet compelled, she tried to touch his fingertip with her own. She felt only a sensation like a mild electric shock, and her finger passed through his.

She pulled her hand back, startled. He gave her an apologetic smile. Then his gaze dropped. "You look … different tonight, Miss Gibbs."

"I do?" She thought about it. "Oh, right. My clothes are different." She glanced down at her close-fitting jeans, sneakers for walking through the rough field, and a short-sleeved purple T-shirt with a fairly low U-neck, the thin cotton knit skimming the curves of her breasts, waist, and hips. She realized that he might be embarrassed by what must seem to him shockingly revealing garments. He was clearly avoiding looking at her.

"I guess it must look really strange to you," she said. "This is what women—ladies—wear in the twenty-first century."

"The twenty-first century?" He looked dumbstruck. "What year is it?"

"2007."

"Great goodness alive! I had no earthly idea." He shook his head, trying to absorb the implications. "That means … my mama and papa are gone. My brother and sister too, and their children, and their children's children …" His expression was agonized.

"I'm so sorry, Mr. Sanders." Jessie realized it must feel to him like losing his entire family all at once.

"Thank you, Miss Gibbs." He stayed quiet, and she kept a respectful silence.

"Would you like to be alone?" she asked him.

"Oh, no," he said. "No, indeed, I've been alone so long, it's good to have company. It's just hard to get used to knowing it's been that much time. And that my family's all passed on."

"It must be a terrible shock," she said.

Then, making an obvious effort to change the mood, he looked at her sidelong and said, "Why were you dressed like you were from my time, before?"

"It's kind of a long story."

"I don't have any place to go." His smile was rueful.

"Well, you see," she began, "a lot of people today are very interested in the Civil War."

"That's my war?"

"Yes, didn't you call it that?"

"No, ma'am, we just called it the fight. A time or two I heard it called the War Between the States."

"Well, people are still fascinated by it," Jessie said. "They study all about it in books, and they have events and campouts where they try to live and dress like people of your time did. That's what we do, in our band. We wear dresses and uniforms from the 1860s and play on antique instruments from that time. Lots of other people even act out the battles, with uniforms and horses and guns and cannons. Not using real ammunition, of course."

He shuddered. "I declare I don't know why anybody'd want to do that."

Comprehension dawned. "That's why you were so surprised at the idea of lady cooks in camp. You thought the war was still going on."

"Yes, ma'am, that's what I did think. But why do folks want to do such a thing?" he said again, looking troubled.

"For adventure, I guess," she said. "Some of us want to go back to a time when things seemed simpler. And we also do it to honor people like our ancestors by trying to experience some of what they—what *you*—did." It suddenly hit home that she was actually talking with someone who had lived through the events she had studied in history books, and that she and her bandmates worked so hard to understand and faithfully interpret. She looked at him, awed.

He took off his hat and the dark-blond hair, flattened around the crown, curled on his forehead and fell in waves behind his ears to the nape of his neck. He rested his hat on his knee, and she studied his hand. With its prominent veins and tendons, and long fingers with knuckles that looked slightly swollen, she found it hard to believe that such a strong-looking hand had no physical substance.

"I can't say I understand all of what you're telling me," he said, "but the part about honoring us, that's nice. That makes me feel like what I did wasn't for nothing."

"Mr. Sanders, does that wound hurt you? Are you in pain?"

"Aw, no. It looks bad as anything, I know. I'm sorry you have to see it. But no, it doesn't hurt. I'm past feeling—things of the body, I mean."

"Is there anything I can bring you? Do for you?"

He was quiet for a moment. "There is one thing," he said at last, tentatively.

"Tell me and I'll do it if I can."

"Well, the reason I stayed here is that I couldn't abide the thought that my family might not ever know that I got killed. And where I was buried. I know if they did, they would bring me home, or at least come to see my grave and pray over it. Only, nobody ever did. And all the other boys buried with me, what must their folks have thought, to never hear from them or see them again? Thinking about that made it so I couldn't rest. I've been watching and hoping for somebody to come along who could help me."

"How many are buried here?"

"Six others besides me."

"And you've been standing sentinel here for 144 years?"

"From what you tell me, I reckon that's right."

"Like being on eternal picket duty."

He laughed softly. "Funny way of saying it."

She struggled with how to tactfully ask the next question. She dreaded the answer. "Do any of the other men who're buried here share picket duty with you? I mean, are they here now, like you?"

"No, ma'am. Just me, for some reason."

"How lonely for you. You said I was the first person you'd talked to. Nobody came here? All these years?"

"Oh, a few folks came, raggedy men and young'uns seeming like they were lost or something. I tried to talk to them but they got scared and ran off."

"And then I came along," she said, "dressed like I was from your day. That must have gotten your hopes up."

"Yes, ma'am."

"Well, I'll try not to disappoint you. How can I help?"

"It's prob'ly too much to ask." He took a deep breath. "But if you could find my people—" he corrected himself, "the ones who are living now, and bring them to this place, and if you could let folks know about the other boys buried here, and if a preacher could bless this grave proper-like, then I could go home to the Lord in peace."

Jessie inwardly reeled. How could a shy introvert like herself really do all that? If his family had stayed in the Smoky Mountains, as so many old mountain families did, she could look for them when visiting her grandmother. But how many cold calls would she have to make, how many strangers would she need to talk to—and what could she tell them? As for the blessing of the grave, her pastor might be willing, but first the site would have to be identified as a burial ground, and how could she possibly make that happen?

Her mind spun.

He said, "Don't worry, Miss Gibbs, if you can't do it. I know it's a lot."

"I don't know how much I can do, but I want to help you, Mr. Sanders. The reason I came back was that I felt sorry for you, being here all alone for so long."

"Bless you for that." The emotion in his eyes made her breath catch. She had to look away.

A train whistle sounded from the Nashville/Chattanooga tracks that lay about a half mile to the east, a reminder of the real world going on outside of this glade. "I should be going," she said. She took a box of matches from her pocket, lit the candle inside her lantern, and stood.

He rose too, put his hat back on, and turned to face her. Once again, there was a moment that seemed to yearn toward an embrace, or a kiss, or a touch of the hand.

Instead, their eyes held and they shared a smile that acknowledged some mutual understanding. It filled her with a strange elation.

As she began walking away, a thought occurred to her, and she turned to face him across the clearing. "When I come back," she said in a playful tone, "should I wear my long dress again, the one from your time? Would you be more comfortable?"

"Then you will come back?"

There was no longer any doubt that she would, drawn by the promise of intimacy with a man, however different this might be from her imaginings, however charged with risk. And in a life that had felt essentially stalled, she now had a purpose, a mission—to help him go to his final rest.

All these thoughts whirled in her mind, but she only nodded.

He broke into his dazzling smile. "No, ma'am—Miss Gibbs," he said. "I'm used to twenty-first century ladies' clothes now. In fact, I'm right partial to them."

CHAPTER 5

OUTSIDER

THAT SHE WOULD go back to see Lemuel again was certain. Still, Jessie persuaded herself to be cautious and sensible by letting several days pass. But as she went about the routine of working in her father's office, taking care of everyday chores, practicing in the evenings, all she thought about was Lemuel Sanders.

Not that there weren't ample opportunities for distraction in the huge amount of preparation to be done for the band's upcoming trip to Gettysburg. A commemoration of the 144th anniversary of the battle was taking place the weekend of July 6, two weeks away, and several thousand re-enactors were expected to participate. The band had been hired by the organizers to march the Confederate troops onto the field, and to play at the Confederate ball on Saturday evening.

Jessie finished sewing the new dress she had made for the occasion, a pretty pink-and-white-striped cotton, and sorted out the other components of her wardrobe, making sure they were all clean and mended. She and Abby conferred about food for the weekend and made up an enormous list which they split in half. Jessie's trip to the grocery store took more than an hour and yielded six full bags. The other members of the group would chip in their share of the cost.

On Sunday, July 1, she went to have dinner with her parents and load her van with the kitchen equipment and camping supplies they let her store in their backyard shed. Amber-tinged evening sunshine was streaming down when Jessie arrived at the tidy white split-level house where she had grown up. In her childhood, the neighborhood in south Murfreesboro had been rural and quiet, but now shopping malls and multi-lane highways surrounded it, and at night all the stores and streetlights sent up a glare that muted the stars.

The mellow sunlight made the colors of her father's meticulously tended gardens glow—lilies in various shades of yellow, russet, orange, and pink; brilliant purplish-pink coneflowers with bronze centers; other flowers and bushes, lush and green, whose names she did not know.

She carried the potato salad she had made up the short flight of stairs to the kitchen. Her mother was working there, standing at the stove.

"Hey there, sugar," Betty Gibbs said. "You can set that right over there." Almost fifty, her mother still had a trim figure which she showed off this evening in pink Capri pants and a sleeveless pink, white, and green striped shirt. Her shoulder-length, graying light-brown hair was pushed back with a green headband.

Jessie kissed her mother's damp cheek and caught the scent of floral perfume. "Whatcha got cookin'?"

"Summer squash and onions, okra and tomatoes. Daddy's barbecuing chicken on the deck. Lou Ann's coming too. I asked her to bring dessert."

Jessie leaned against the counter and watched her mother lift lids, stir, and adjust the heat of the burners. As they exchanged light chat, Jessie felt a tug of longing. She wished she had the kind of relationship with her mother that would allow her to confide at least something of her confusion over the situation with Lemuel Sanders.

However, she had learned over the years that any attempts at discussing intimate feelings made her mother close up. *Mama*, she imagined herself saying now, *I've met somebody. He's a soldier, from the next town over from Ganny's. He's handsome, polite, the nicest, most attractive guy I've ever met. But there's this one problem …*

Impossible.

Her mother interrupted her musings, handing over a stack of paper plates, plastic cutlery, and napkins. "Let's go out on the deck. Keep your daddy company."

Jessie's father was standing at the grill, overseeing the barbecuing of the chicken pieces. He wore a white bib apron printed with acid green smiley faces. The Marine Corps tattoo on his tanned forearm made the ridiculous garment even more incongruous.

"Nice outfit," Jessie teased him.

"I asked your mama for an apron, and this is what she gave me," Frank Gibbs said, leaning over and kissing his daughter. "I think she's trying to make me into one of those 'new men' I see on the TV."

"No, sir, I like my old man just fine," Betty said, giving him a one-armed hug around the waist, a plate of appetizers in her other hand.

Jessie's sister came through the sliding doors from the living room, still wearing scrubs from a shift in the ER and carrying a gym bag and a plate covered with plastic wrap.

"Hey, stranger," Jessie said. Their lives didn't intersect often. Lou Ann's active social schedule rarely included her older sister. Not that Jessie minded—Lou Ann's hard-partying friends were not her type. They favored bars where the walls and floor vibrated from the powerful bass, and people had to shout and shriek with laughter to be heard over the din. It made Jessie's sensitive musician's ears feel assaulted.

Jessie did envy Lou Ann her easy success with men. Since high school, her sister had never been without a boyfriend. She had a knack for getting guys to fall for her, breaking up with them when they got serious, yet usually still managing to keep them as friends.

Over dinner, Lou Ann said, "Whoo, what a crazy day. We had a car wreck, a kid who blew off a finger with a firecracker, another kid who water-skied into a dock and broke his leg. Everyone was okay, thank God. I'm so glad I get the Fourth off. I sure don't want to be in the ER when people start drinking and racing around in cars and boats and handling explosives." She took a long swallow from her beer can.

"What are y'all doing for the holiday?" Jessie asked.

Frank said he was going fishing with Cleotis Thompson, his business partner and closest buddy. The two men had served together as eighteen-year-old Marines in Vietnam, and whatever they had experienced there had cemented their friendship, unusual between white and Black people in the South in that era. Their wives were also good friends, and the two couples, her mother said, were getting together for a barbecue at the Thompsons' on the evening of Independence Day.

"If you girls aren't doing anything the night of the Fourth," her mother added, "come on over and join the picnic."

"Thanks," Lou Ann said, "but I'm going to the Nashville Speedway with Darren and Brenda and Tommy. They're having fireworks after the races."

Jessie could only imagine the volume level of that event. She explained that she and Abby would be getting their supplies organized for the Gettysburg trip and then having dinner together. The truth was, she planned to go see Lemuel Sanders. The thought caused a little burst of excitement in her chest—inward fireworks.

"Gettysburg's a heck of a long drive," her father observed.

"Close to 500 miles," Jessie said. "But I'll have company. Two guys from the band, a father and son, are coming along with me." Pete DiSpirito had called to ask if he and Ben could ride with her. He offered to share the driving and expenses. She was glad not to have to make the trip alone, though she wondered if it would be a strain having to keep up a conversation with near strangers for eight to ten hours.

"They let you camp out and play your music and do all that battle business there in the national park?" Frank asked.

"No, on a farm ten miles away. There's lots of space there for the Yankee and Confederate encampments, the battlefield, and a village with tents for shopping and lectures and presentations."

"What do y'all do all day?" Betty asked.

"Well, cooking and cleaning up after three meals takes a lot of time," Jessie said. "Then we rehearse, and if there's any free time, we go to some of the talks and demonstrations. The big deal is the battle on Saturday. The band leads the Confederate parade onto the field and plays during the re-enactment. Believe it or not, bands did play on the battlefield during the Civil War."

"To me it sounds like a total nerd-fest," Lou Ann said, crunching a celery stalk stuffed with pimento cheese.

"Yeah, you'd go crazy," Jessie said. "For one thing, you'd have to do without your cell phone for an entire weekend."

Lou Ann grimaced at the thought.

"You should come sometime, Daddy," Jessie said.

"I might just."

"And Mama?"

"Oh, no, honey, camping's not for me. I like my bed and my hot shower. And my dishin' machine." They all smiled at the term, coined by Betty's mother, Jessie and Lou Ann's beloved Ganny, a woman who liked living simply with as few modern appliances as possible.

"Your mama goes for the finer things in life," Frank said to Jessie, looking at Betty affectionately.

As twilight gathered, the neighborhood was filled with the sounds of people enjoying the beautiful summer evening. The clear sky above the rooftops was deepest blue, and a few bright stars had begun to shimmer amid the currents of rising heat.

Somewhere a fusillade of firecrackers went off. Jessie wondered what Lemuel Sanders would think as people all over town commemorated the holiday with official and improvised pyrotechnics. Would it make him anxious, remind him of the noise of battle? It was painful to think of what he must have suffered in the war. Her mind traveled across the night to the glade in the forest some five miles away. She imagined the darkness sifting down amid the trees, and the solitary watcher keeping his vigil in the clearing. What did he do, all alone? Did he walk around, or just sit still and absorb the sights and sounds? Time didn't matter to him, he had told her. After all, he'd had nearly a century and a half to learn the patience of timeless waiting.

Betty's chair scraping on the deck startled Jessie back to the present. She rose to help clear the table.

"Sorry I can't help y'all," Lou Ann said. "Before you called, Mama, I told Darren I'd meet him at The Roadhouse at nine."

"You're not going to have any of your brownies?"

"I tested them before I came. Just to make sure they weren't poison. Thanks for the good food." To Jessie she added, "Have fun at the war." Soon the throaty growl of her car speeding off, along with the thumping of her stereo turned up to maximum volume, came through the open front windows.

"That gal drives like she's running from the law," Frank observed, opening the cooler to get a fresh beer.

In the kitchen, as Jessie and her mother worked together to put away the food and load "the dishin' machine," they sang together, as they sometimes did out of a shared love for the old Southern gospel songs. Betty on melody, Jessie on harmony, sang "I'll Fly Away" and "Down to the River to Pray." Times like these gave Jessie a rare glimpse into her mother's heart. They also offered evidence that she had not been switched at birth with another baby in the hospital, an idea she'd sometimes considered. It was clear where she had gotten her natural feeling for music. That made it all the more frustrating that Betty had little appreciation for, or interest in, the classical music that Jessie loved.

"Y'all sound pretty," Frank called from the den, over the sounds of a TV baseball game.

With the kitchen work finished, Jessie and her father went out to the storage shed to pack her van with the equipment for the weekend—her tent; the five large coolers, the cooking grates and pots; and the wooden, rope-handled storage boxes that Abby's husband, JJ, had made to hold the group's utensils and dishware, spices and seasonings, towels and aprons.

"I meant what I said," her father said. "I might like to come with you sometime to one of these campouts. The history part of it sounds interesting to me, and I always did like camping. Let me know about the next one."

"I will," she replied, warmed by the thought of spending time with him, just the two of them, as they hadn't managed to do for years. He had been an older father, thirty-three when she was born after a childless earlier marriage that didn't survive his return from Vietnam. He had doted on his little girl and taken her with him on his weekend rounds to the hardware store and the barbershop, the convenience store and sometimes the liquor store (though he made her wait outside in the pickup truck while he went in there).

Those times of closeness had waned as she discovered music in third grade, began taking piano lessons, and spent every spare hour not occupied by schoolwork or chores in practicing and exploring the musical possibilities of the piano.

As she handed her father the boxes and bundles from the shed to put into her van, she was preoccupied. This evening had highlighted once again the puzzling differences between herself and the people closest to her. Where had her compulsion to make music the center of her life come from? She thought about how her family found meaning and purpose: her mother from keeping a picture-perfect house and caring for her husband; her sister from giving her all to take care of patients and then feeling free to just blow off steam in her spare time; her father from the satisfaction of providing for his family, even if the work of running his plumbing-supply business might not be especially fulfilling in itself. He found enjoyment in his marriage and family, his friendship with Cleotis, and peace in spending quiet hours fishing and caring for the yard.

Why, for her, did music have to be so isolating, so all-consuming? Why couldn't it just be something she was content to do to enhance an ordinary life? Jessie knew the answer to that, if she was honest. The idea of an ordinary life—never being anything more than a public school music teacher and amateur musician—felt like failure.

But now, with Lemuel Sanders, another path was opening before her, and it was surely extraordinary. And thrilling. And scary.

Frank gave her a close look in the yellow light from the shed. "Are you feeling okay, sugar? You don't look like your usual perky self."

"I'm fine, Daddy. Maybe I just haven't been getting enough rest."

"Well, I'm sure it's nothing a few nights sleeping on the ground with a couple hundred snoring men won't cure," he said with a wink.

CHAPTER 6

LIFE STORIES

ON JULY FOURTH, Jessie got everything ready for the trip the next day, packing a carpet bag with clothing and toiletries, collecting sheet music in case there was a piano at the Confederate ball, cooking two big pots of beef stew to heat up on the campfire on Saturday. She had a little of the stew for dinner but was too excited and jumpy to eat much.

As the sun began to set, she dressed with special care in a gauzy shirt over slender black jeans, dangling silver earrings with purple stones, and a mother-of-pearl barrette clasping back the top of her hair while the rest of it flowed down over her shoulders and back. She thought about putting on some makeup and decided against it; in Civil War times, she'd been told, cosmetics were only used by harlots, and Lemuel Sanders might be shocked.

With her heart pounding and breath short, she hurried to her van and drove the eight miles to the farm and the encampment. If she met someone who asked what she was doing, she'd say she wanted to look for some lost item at the campsite. Why she would undertake such an errand at nine o'clock on a Saturday night, dressed as if for a party, she hoped she would not have to explain.

"I'M GETTING READY to go to one of our Civil War events," Jessie told Lemuel. "It's up in a town in Pennsylvania called Gettysburg. There was a terrible battle there, in July 1863. Now people come every year to commemorate that and honor the dead."

They were sitting once again on the rock. The air was still; the lights from the city tinged the low cloud cover with a pinkish glow.

"I'm glad we're not forgot," he said. "Who won that battle?"

She was silent, trying to think of a tactful way to tell him of the loss. He spared her the need, nodding grimly.

"And the war?" he asked.

She just shook her head, and he gave a deep sigh.

"Mr. Sanders, do you mind if I ask you why you fought?" Jessie said. "People today say the main reason Southerners fought was to defend their right to have slaves. But there weren't many slaves in East Tennessee."

"That's true," he said. "Nobody I ever knew had slaves. I hardly ever saw any colored people. The reason I joined up was because the Yankees were fixing to invade us. My best friend Jeremiah Walker worked in the dry goods store in town. I'd go see him there, and the fellow who ran the place, Mr. Leland Berry, told us Abe Lincoln called up 75,000 soldiers to come lick us Southerners. Then the Yankees went and burned up some bridges in East Tennessee. I felt like I had to do something to defend my home."

"I can understand that."

A strong breeze rose up and stirred the leaves on the trees and bushes. Lemuel's hair and clothing did not move. "When Jeremiah told me a Rebel company was forming up near us," he went on, "and he and Mr. Berry were going to join up, I decided I would too."

In the silence that followed, he stretched out his long legs in their rough woolen trousers. She glanced at his bare, slender ankles, then at his profile. He was looking down, his expression pensive.

"To tell you the truth," he said at last, "the real reason I joined up was to go against my father. I'm ashamed to say it."

"You didn't get along?"

He shook his head. "When I was little we did, then when I was seven he got trampled by a horse. It broke his leg and his hip, and it never did heal up right. I think it hurt him bad all the time. He always walked with a hitch. I reckon the pain made him cross. I hardly ever saw him smile."

"I'm sorry."

He shrugged. "Most of the time I stayed out of his way, or tried to, but he was always after me to do something or other on the farm. And nothing I ever did was right."

"What about your mother?"

"Oh, Mama." His voice softened. "She was good and kind. Smart, too. Book-learned. She used to be a schoolteacher before she married Pa. Her pa ran a newspaper in Dandridge. She taught me how to read and write." Then he gave her an apologetic grin. "Seems like I'm trying to make up for all those years of not having anybody to talk to. You sure I'm not wearing you out?"

"I'm sure." Jessie smiled back at him. "Tell me more."

"Well … like what?"

"More about your family. You said you had a little sister. Polly."

"You remembered!" He looked at her in surprise.

I remember every word you ever said to me, she thought but didn't say. "Did you have a brother?"

"Yes, ma'am, my older brother Caleb, two years older than me."

"Did he fight too?"

"No, he went to live out west before the war, him and his wife. To the new state called California. I never saw him after that."

Jessie wondered, but did not ask, if conflict with their father had also caused his older brother to find some way to get far from home.

He told her about his paternal grandfather, who came to live with the family to help out after his father's accident. "He was like the father I always wanted. Everything you want a father to learn you, he showed me. Carving, like I told you, and how to recognize animals by their tracks and tell birds by their songs, how to build things."

He was quiet for a moment.

"He taught me how to shoot," he went on at last. "When I was little, I always hated to hunt. I hated killing animals, but we had to, for food. Pa called me a shirker, but Granddaddy knew how I felt. He took me out to the woods to shoot at targets on trees, over and over, till I got to be a real good shot. 'That way your kills will be clean,' he said, 'and the animal won't suffer.' After that I could do what I had to do."

"Maybe as a soldier too?" Jessie ventured.

He shrugged and made no reply, and she worried that the question had been tactless.

"Tell me more about your grandfather," she said. "He sounds like a fine man."

"The best I ever knew. Just as patient—I never heard him say one mean word." He gave a soft chuckle at a memory. "He used to play the banjo, and I'd sing and play the spoons. We made us some music."

"Oh, do you like to sing?"

"I love to."

"I do, too," said Jessie.

"And you said you played the piano. I'd sure like to hear that."

"Well … it'd be a little hard to carry a piano out here."

"Reckon so." He laughed.

"And you can't leave here." It was a statement, not a question.

"I don't know if I could," he said. "I never thought to."

"No, I guess you wouldn't want to risk not being here if somebody came along who could help you."

"That's right." He looked up at her from under his brows. "And somebody did come along. Somebody real nice."

She felt heat stealing up her neck and was grateful for the darkness. "Do you mind if I ask, were you married, Mr. Sanders?"

"No, ma'am, I don't mind, and I wasn't. I had a sweetheart, Louisa. We were going to get married when I came home. What about you, Miss Gibbs?"

She shook her head. "I'm not married, and I don't have a sweetheart."

"I can't hardly believe that. A pretty little thing like you."

Nobody—other than her father—had ever called her a pretty little thing. It made her feel bold. "You, sir, are a silver-tongued flatterer."

"I'm just speaking the plain truth."

The smile they shared was interrupted by a distant booming. He flinched and straightened up, suddenly alert. "What's that?" he asked. The noise went on and on, probably the finale of a big public fireworks display somewhere nearby.

"Today's the Fourth of July. That's the sound of fireworks. Did you have fireworks?"

"Oh, yes, ma'am, I saw them a time or two." He looked embarrassed. "It sounded to me like cannons."

"Ah." She studied him, sobered by this reminder of what he had been through. "Brings back bad memories."

He nodded.

Something caught her eye. "Look!" she said, pointing. Flowers of color were blooming, then fading, in the night sky, just visible above the treetops. Like fountains of light the fireworks rose, dispersed, and fell in sparkling fragments.

"Aren't they pretty," he said, watching them. Jessie's gaze was drawn to his face, the reflections of the colors shining in his eyes, tingeing his skin.

All was quiet at last, except for the breeze rustling the limbs of the cedar forest around their clearing. "It's so peaceful here. But I really should be going," she said with regret. "I have to leave early tomorrow, for Gettysburg."

They stood up and faced each other. "Will you come back again?" His eyes searched hers, gleaming.

"I will. It won't be for a few days, till I get back from Pennsylvania."

"Time doesn't make any difference to me," he said. "Just so long as you come back."

"You're not in a hurry for me to try to find your family?"

"I waited this long. I can wait a while longer."

She nodded. "Well, when I do come back, I want you to tell me your whole story—if you don't mind," she added, thinking of her father, who always evaded her questions about his wartime experiences in Vietnam.

"I don't mind. But it'd take some time."

"That's all right."

"I'll just stretch it way out, so you'll have to keep coming back."

If I had my way, you'd make it like the thousand and one nights of Scheherazade, she thought, but only smiled at him in reply. As she walked away, her long hair swinging against her back, she felt his gaze following her.

CHAPTER 7

ROMANCE VERSUS REALITY

PETE DISPIRITO TOOK a sip of coffee from a takeout cup as Jessie steered the van through the early morning traffic on I-40. "We had an ulterior motive for wanting to share the drive with you," he said.

"Oh?" Jessie glanced over at him. He was a good-looking man, probably in his mid-to-late thirties, with straight black hair that he wore fairly long, dark eyes, and a black mustache. She had opted for the comfort of jeans and a t-shirt for the long drive. Pete and his son Ben were dressed in their Civil War clothes: gray woven woolen trousers; homespun, band-collared shirts with wooden buttons; white canvas suspenders; and brogan shoes with metal taps that had clicked loudly on the floor of the McDonald's where they'd stopped first thing that morning for breakfast.

"We have something we want to ask your help with," Pete went on. "If you're not too busy. Ben, tell Jessie about your project."

"I've been talking with Mom and Dad about going to music school for college," Ben said.

"That's next year, right?" Jessie asked, catching his eye in the rearview mirror. She could not help smiling at how uncomfortable he looked, sleepy-eyed and tousle-haired at this early hour, wedged against the door by gear piled beside him on the back seat—there had been no room in the cargo space, what with all of Jessie's kitchen supplies.

"Yes, ma'am." His Northern parents had obviously taught him the manners of a good Southern boy. "So I need to make an audition tape to send with my applications, but I need an accompanist. I hoped maybe—well, could you be my accompanist?"

"Sure. I'd be glad to."

They discussed the timetable; applications would be due in December, so they agreed to begin working together in the late summer. "We can rehearse at my church on nights when nothing's going on," Jessie said.

"I'll ask my trumpet teacher about good pieces," Ben said.

"We'll pay you for your time, of course," Pete said to Jessie.

"Oh, no," she began, but Pete insisted, and she put an end to the uncomfortable topic by saying they could talk about it later on.

As they drove on, Ben fell asleep. The interior of the van was chilly— the antique air conditioner had only two settings, frigid and torrid—and the only way to regulate the temperature was to turn it on and off. She switched it off for a while.

She felt that it would seem callous not to ask Pete about his wife, though she was afraid that it might cause him pain. Andrea DiSpirito was suffering from advanced breast cancer. The previous summer, Jessie had seen her for the first time at an event at the Stones River National Battlefield; Andrea sat in a folding chair, watching her husband and son play in an outdoor concert. Despite the warm weather, she wore a sweater and had a fleece blanket draped over her lap. The bright sunshine emphasized her pallor and the unnatural shine of her reddish-blonde hair, obviously a wig. A few weeks later, at the next band rehearsal, Jessie overheard Pete telling some of the group that Andrea had been fighting cancer for a few years; first in her breast and now, unfortunately, it had spread. Jessie had asked Lou Ann what that meant and Lou Ann shook her head.

"Not good. With metastatic breast cancer, she'll be lucky to make it five years."

"What's your wife doing this weekend?" Jessie asked Pete now.

"Her good friend came to stay with her," Pete said. He gazed out the window and Jessie thought he might not want to talk about the subject anymore. Then he said, lowering his voice though his son was clearly oblivious, "I really considered not going on this trip. Things aren't going well."

"I'm so sorry."

"Thanks, Jess." He sighed. "Anyway, Andie insisted that we go. She knew how much Ben was looking forward to it. And I guess she wanted me to have some time off from being a caregiver. It's hard to leave her, though…" He left the rest of the thought unspoken. "She'll be really happy to hear that you're willing to work with Ben."

"I'm glad," Jessie said. She focused on the road as an eighteen-wheeler cut in front, a little too close for comfort. Thinking that he might welcome a change of topic, she asked, "How did you two get involved with the band?"

"Jim Bryce's law firm sponsored the high school baseball team," Pete said. "When Jim heard Ben play the national anthem at a game a year ago, he asked Ben if he'd be interested in joining the band. Ben's been nuts about the Civil War since he was little. He really wanted us to do this together. But I wasn't so sure."

"How come?"

"Well, to my Long Island and Brooklyn relatives, I'm definitely wearing the wrong color. And, not to offend you, but I wasn't sure whether we'd be getting ourselves involved with a bunch of Lost Cause fanatics still fighting the war."

Jessie suppressed a grin at his rapid-fire delivery. "I'm not offended. I wondered about that too, when Abby first suggested I join the group. After all, my daddy's best friend is Black. Maybe you've seen the bumper stickers on some of the cars at events, 'Heritage, Not Hate.'"

"I have seen those."

"I hope I'm not being naïve, but to me that's the attitude of the people in the band."

Pete nodded. "I think so too. Still, at some of the big events I've noticed a certain…"

She finished the phrase that tact seemed to be preventing him from completing. "Redneck contingent? For sure, it exists."

"But, yes, the guys—and gals—in our group are cool," Pete said. "Everybody's careful about authenticity and all, but nobody takes themselves too seriously. And, you know, they all seem pretty open-minded. Nobody raises an eyebrow about Becky and Deb." Becky DePew's partner, Deb Farris, an officer with the Nashville mounted police force, sometimes came to local events, bringing her horse "Big'un." "And Ben and I have enjoyed learning about history together, firsthand," Pete went on. "It's been good to have a way of staying connected to my son—" Again he lowered his voice, though Ben was still sleeping, "during a time when most boys want to have as little to do with the old man as possible. And Andie puts up with us practicing together at home. She even says she likes it." He drank the last of his coffee. "All in all, it's been a positive thing. A welcome distraction from reality."

Considering the reality he was facing, Jessie could well imagine that.

DARKNESS WAS GATHERING by the time they arrived at the huge Confederate encampment occupying several forested acres of the farm outside Gettysburg. The Yankees had their own camp on the far side of the enormous field that would be used the next day for the recreated battle.

The campsite was divided into sections allotted to the various Confederate generals. Jessie, Pete, and Ben located a small wooden sign that marked General Maney's section—their own—parked the van, and followed a path into the forest, greeting strangers who were setting up tents and unpacking supplies. Finally, they found their unit's campsite, and Becky DePew offered to help them unload the van.

As Becky walked behind Jessie, carrying one of the ice chests, she asked, "Hey, Jessie, did you ever find anything more about that soldier you asked me about—Lemuel Sanders, am I remembering right?"

A shock ran through Jessie at the mention of his name, so matter-of-fact and casual. "No, not yet."

"I have a colleague who's writing a book about Stones River. He's been on sabbatical, but when he comes back in the fall, or if I see him before then, I'll ask him how to find out more information."

"Thanks, Beck. That'd be great."

By nine, Jessie had set up her tent. Abby Newcomb and her family had arrived, and together the two cooks organized the kitchen area: two wooden folding tables under a large canvas fly, near the fire ring. All the ice chests and food storage bags were crammed into Jessie's tent, since there was no room in the Newcombs'.

Before bedtime, Jessie took a candle lantern and headed off to the "sinks"—a row of plastic porta-potties set up near the other conveniences, a communal woodpile and a tanker truck full of drinking water, that the event organizers had provided. As she walked along the dirt road, the woods rang with the sounds of mallets driving in tent stakes, axes splitting firewood, and occasional bursts of laughter. No radios, no cell phones, no generators, no visible or audible technology of any kind spoiled the illusion of an earlier time. The scent of woodsmoke from scores of fires filled the air. Now and then through the humid evening atmosphere drifted the sound of a drumbeat, or the shrill music of a fife. Horses and mules tied among the trees near drinking troughs snorted and pawed the ground and whinnied, or just stood with their heads hung low as they dozed. Candle lanterns gleamed among the trees and the light from campfires leapt up and played in the forest canopy.

It was a romantic scene. Jessie wondered what Lemuel Sanders would think of it. She imagined walking along with him, asking him about the authenticity of the living arrangements, the equipment, the uniforms.

Then she thought of the camera in her cell phone. She had decided to keep the phone with her over the next few days, muted and hidden, and surreptitiously take some pictures to show him.

AT FIRST LIGHT, the encampment began waking up. Amid the dawn chorus of birds, voices echoed among the trees and buglers sounded "Reveille" from all around the forest.

Jessie rose and got dressed in her various layers. Experience had taught her to put her socks and boots on before her corset, since once she was laced in, it was very difficult to bend over to pull up hose and tie shoes. When she had first donned the full regalia, she had felt trapped and unable to breathe; she was used to it now but still found it hard to believe that women of the past worked and cooked and took care of children and endured the heat of summer while wearing such confining garments. But, as Abby had once told her, a corset was the only way women had to support the bust—brassieres weren't invented until the turn of the twentieth century.

With her new pink-and-white-striped dress buttoned on, and a gray apron tied around her waist and pinned to her bodice, Jessie knotted her hair into a bun and tied on a kerchief, then stepped out into a warm, muggy morning.

It had rained a little during the night, and a haze of humidity was suspended in the air. The ground was damp and muddy in spots. The blue sky visible among the leafy treetops promised a clear day; the afternoon was sure to be a hot one for cooking over an open fire and re-enacting the battle in heavy wool uniforms.

Several more tents had been set up in the unit's campsite since she went to bed the night before. Stan Trabue, one of the tuba players, had already revived the fire and put on a big pot of coffee.

"Mornin', Cookie. You're lookin' mighty pretty." Stan smiled at her, plump cheeks pushing up antique square-framed glasses. His white beard—Lincoln-style with no mustache—contrasted with the ruddy complexion of someone who spent most of his time outdoors on his farm and in a job with the Highway Department. "This brew's about ready."

"Thanks, Stan, I can always count on you," she said.

The smell summoned other early risers from their tents. "One of the pitfalls of setting up camp after dark," Tim Stebbins announced, scratching his side, "is that I pitched my tent right in the middle of a patch of poison ivy. That stuff is all over my uniform."

"Aw, just douse it with some kerosene and set it on fire," Ted Klein said, and then in a broad Southern drawl he added, "That's how the boys did it."

Abby Newcomb appeared, tying on an apron, and helped Jessie bring the breakfast supplies from her tent. As Abby cracked eggs into a large crockery bowl, Jessie sliced bread and scooped butter, jam, and apple butter into period-correct small wooden and ceramic containers.

Pete came over and volunteered to cook the bacon. "Anybody else hear those guys a few campsites over, singing 'Sweet Home Alabama' at two in the morning?" he asked as he crouched down, poking at the strips with a long fork.

"I slept right through it," Jessie said, taking large containers of orange juice and milk out of a cooler.

"If they do it tonight," Pete said, "I'm going to have to counter with 'New York, New York.' And no doubt reopen the hostilities."

Tammy, the new girlfriend of drummer Luke Delmotte, asked if she could help.

"Thanks." Jessie handed her an apron. "Pour the drinks into these, please." She handed her two large stoneware pitchers. "And don't go anywhere near the fire with your hoop." The rule was, no hoop skirts in camp for safety reasons; Jessie and Abby wore corded petticoats that they tucked between their knees when cooking over the fire. Tammy was wearing a costume—that was the only word for her synthetic taffeta off-the-shoulder gown with an extra wide hoop—and Jessie shuddered at the thought of how that material would go up in a flash.

When everything was ready, Ben sounded the meal call on his bugle.

As the troops lined up with their tin plates in hand, Jessie snapped a quick picture of the table with its load of steaming food.

Afterward, the band headed off to the parade ground to rehearse, and the women stayed behind to clean the breakfast pots and begin preparations for the midday meal. Jessie, Abby, and Tammy sat on canvas stools at the tables under the shade of the tent fly, chatting as they chopped vegetables for the soup. It was peaceful in the woods, with the sounds of music and laughter from other campsites and the rays of the early sun slanting down between the trees, gradually dispelling the mist. Now and then, soldiers walked past and tipped their hats to them, another aspect of this hobby that Jessie found entrancing—the observance of the lovely courtesies of the past. She looked at the men in their clean uniforms and thought that none of them were as handsome as Lemuel Sanders, sooty and unkempt though he was.

Like water running over rock, incessant thoughts of him had carved out a channel in her mind which had already grown so deep that it drew large portions of her conscious awareness and many of her dreams into its flow. It was as useless to resist as to try to block the downhill rush of a mountain stream at full flood in springtime.

She took out her phone and snapped some pictures to show him: a group of soldiers at the next campsite, sitting around on logs, one demonstrating how to play a drumroll; Abby and Tammy chopping vegetables, while at their feet Joshua built a fort out of sticks. Jessie passed the phone to Abby and asked her to take a picture of her, standing by the cooking fire with her large cast-iron ladle beside the pot of soup.

WITH DINNER SIMMERING away on the grate, the women walked down to watch the band rehearse. Joshua marched along behind them, carrying his "musket," a gun-shaped piece of smooth-sanded, stained, and varnished wood, made by his daddy. His mother carried a wooden portfolio, also made for her by her husband. "I portray a female sketch artist," Abby explained to Tammy. "That would have been a completely unconventional role for a woman back then, but my character's a free spirit. I travel with the army and draw camp and battle scenes and sell them to *Frank Leslie's Weekly* or *Harper's Magazine*."

"Cool," Tammy said. "Luke has been telling me how realistic all this is."

Jessie recognized the pleasure Tammy got from saying his name. "We try," she said. "What do you do? In the twenty-first century, that is."

"I'm a customer service manager at Horizons Bank," Tammy said. "That's how I met Luke."

Jessie knew that he worked as a loan officer there. She had no knowledge of, or, honestly, interest in banking, so could only come up with, "Do you like your job?"

"I do. I really like meeting new people."

Jessie wished she shared that fondness; it would make her task of finding Lemuel's relatives easier. Or possible, even.

Drawn to the sound of music, the three women and Joshua found their group playing while standing in an open field next to the large, well-appointed encampment of General Lee's Army of Northern Virginia. Nearby, soldiers marched and turned in formation, and they practiced presenting and shouldering arms. Abby stood with her portfolio propped on one hip and supported by her left hand. With the other, she boldly sketched the scene with a stick of charcoal.

Careful to avoid being observed, Jessie took a video of the band and then of the soldiers as they went through the steps of loading their guns and firing—though they just pretended to fire during this drill; they were saving their blank ammunition for the battle that afternoon. She had never paid close attention to the military maneuvers before, being much more interested in the civilian aspects of the Civil War era—music, crafts, clothing, food, and domestic life. But gun handling and troop formations had taken on new meaning now that she knew someone whose life had actually depended on mastering all these techniques. Watching the soldiers tear open the cartridges with their teeth, push them down into the barrels of the guns with their long ramrods, replace the ramrods, and insert a firing cap, she wondered if it really could have taken so long. The whole process seemed to leave the soldier defenseless for some twenty seconds.

Was that how Lemuel had died, frantically trying to reload his gun while a Yankee took a shot at him?

"Jessie?" Abby said.

"Hmm?"

"Everything okay?"

"Yes, why?"

"You groaned."

"I did? Guess it was one of those fleeting thoughts, here and gone in a split second."

THE SUN WAS still high and hot at five o'clock when Jessie, along with Abby, Joshua, and Tammy, took up a post along a split-rail fence bordering the huge field where the battle would shortly be re-enacted. Jessie took some still shots of the lines of blue and gray forming on either side, the horses prancing, flags waving, and cannons gleaming. She snapped a few pictures of the grandstand, packed with what looked like a few hundred sunburned people in shorts and tank tops with binoculars and cameras around their necks, day-trippers who had come to see the exhibits and watch the engagement.

From a distance behind her came the strains of the band and the beat of the drums, and Jessie's pulse quickened. Soon the musicians came into view playing "Dixie," sunlight gleaming on their antique brass instruments. Jim Bryce led the parade in his officer's uniform, marking time with his gold drum-major mace. Behind them marched ranks of a few hundred soldiers in Rebel gray and butternut, some in tailored uniforms, some in authentically motley attire, like Lemuel's. Flag bearers waved the Confederate battle flag and the flags of their states; horses and cavalrymen brought up the rear. Far across the field, at the top of a hill, the Federal troops were approaching, as numerous as the Rebels. It was an impressive sight, a much larger turnout than Jessie had ever seen before.

The band halted and formed ranks on the edge of the battlefield, playing a quickstep. Cannon fire exploded, signaling the beginning of the battle, and Jessie stealthily switched to video mode and aimed her camera at the spectacle of the two armies marching toward each other through a thickening pall of musket and cannon smoke. Infantrymen fired and reloaded their guns, several falling in a pantomime of injury or death. Cavalrymen galloped in close formation on amazingly fearless horses. Horse-drawn, canvas-covered ambulances crisscrossed the field, doctors and nurses jumping out to collect the most severe "casualties," some of them probably genuinely felled by heat exhaustion in woolen uniforms in the ninety-degree weather. Bugle calls rose above the din of the fusillade, and an announcer narrated some of the troop movements over a loudspeaker for the benefit of the spectators in the bleachers. Still the band played on, as, improbably, a band had played during the actual Battle of Gettysburg.

Jessie tucked the phone into the pocket of her skirt and watched. She wondered what Lemuel would think of the pictures, and whether he would be willing to tell her about his experiences. Or would he deflect her curiosity about his wartime ordeal, as her father always had whenever she asked him what Vietnam had been like?

LATER THAT EVENING, after all the supper dishes had been done, the bandsmen, who had an inexhaustible appetite for making music together, set up their wooden music stands with candle holders on either side, lit the candles in their glass globes, and sat on stools to give an informal performance. The candlelight diffused in the evening haze, surrounding the musicians with an ambient glow.

People wafted out of the woods and sat on stumps or on the ground to listen. Jessie half-hid behind a tree to take a video, unseen, of Pete and Ben playing side by side. Andrea DiSpirito would undoubtedly enjoy seeing her husband and son in action.

Between the numbers, Jim Bryce gave short talks and answered questions from the now-sizable audience, to give the musicians' lips a chance to rest. "Some of the most popular songs of the time were quite melancholy," he said. "The soldiers would get so homesick hearing them that they would be tempted to desert. So bandleaders turned the songs into upbeat quicksteps—like this next one, 'Ever of Thee.'"

Jessie wondered how many young men, hearing such jaunty tunes, were deceived into thinking that the war would be a jolly romp, and rushed to enlist. And how many, hearing them after they'd been in battle, and had possibly been wounded and lost comrades, felt a bitter irony.

But people back then were much less cynical than today. They believed in things—God, honor, the righteousness of their cause, whichever side they fought for. Maybe these tunes lifted their spirits with reminders of home and loved ones and happier days, the things they were fighting for. Maybe the music recharged their hope and courage, filled them with a sense of the exalted, perhaps even of the divine. All her life, music had affected Jessie that way, as nothing else could.

Except, she was beginning to think, love.

CHAPTER 8

MORTAL MUSINGS

AFTER BREAKFAST THE next morning, Jessie busied herself with putting away the bacon, butter, and eggs in coolers, leaving out bread and jam, a chunk of cheese, and a bowl of fruit, all covered with a clean muslin cloth, in case anyone wanted a snack. With free time until an afternoon rehearsal and an evening performance at the Confederate ball, everyone had gone off to visit the exhibition area or the booths of the various vendors of Civil War merchandise. She had thought herself alone in camp and had been enjoying the peace, singing softly as she worked. Suddenly, the flap of a nearby tent opened and Pete came out, looking pale and rumple-haired.

"Morning, Jess," he said. "I wondered whose pretty voice that was, weaving its way into my dream. What time is it?"

"A little after nine. Want some coffee? There's some on the fire there, though it may be kind of burnt."

"That's how the boys had it." He massaged his temples with the thumb and fingers of his right hand.

"I don't think the boys had coffee. Not our boys, at least. Boiled burnt peanut shells was probably more like it."

"I'm truly grateful, especially this morning, that we don't have to be that authentic," he said. "Back in a minute." He headed off through the woods.

When he returned, he went to the jug of drinking water and poured some into his hands, then splashed it on his face. He took a tin cup from the kitchen table and filled it from the charred coffee pot steaming on a grate over the fire.

He lowered himself carefully to sit on a canvas camp stool. "Todd Farman brought along some good bourbon, and I hung out with a bunch of the guys after you left and Ben went back to our tent. I'm afraid that as the night wore on, I was moderately overserved."

Jessie smiled at the euphemism. "How about some bread?"

"It'll either kill me or cure me. I may have had a touch of heat exhaustion after the battle yesterday. It was incredibly hot on that field, wearing all that wool. And then the Jack Daniel's on top of that …"

She cut a slab of bread, buttered it, and handed it to him, placing a jar of homemade plum jam on a stump beside him. He held the bread in one hand and the coffee in the other, seeming intent on remaining very still.

Jessie went into her tent to get vegetables from the ice chest for the noontime soup. She sat down under the canvas tent fly and began peeling and cutting carrots.

Pete took a small bite of the bread and chewed it reflectively, then followed it with a sip of coffee. Then with bleary eyes he looked at her from under a thatch of hair, still damp from his face-splashing, that had fallen over his brow. "Do you ever get any time off at these events, Cinderella?"

She laughed. "Abby's got the cleanup after dinner, so I'll go hear a lecture about ladies' fashions of the Victorian era. After that there's a Civil War wedding, so maybe I'll stay for that too. I'm afraid y'all are going to have to fend for yourselves for supper—just sandwiches and pickles and fruit."

Pete nodded. "Sounds fine. For those interested in food."

"I'm sorry you feel bad."

"I have only myself to blame. Eating something seems to be helping. And the coffee is quite eye-opening."

They sat quietly for a while.

"Everyone seemed to enjoy the music last night," Jessie said. "Ben's really good."

"Thanks. I think he's got talent. But it's nice to have an expert opinion."

She shrugged, embarrassed by the compliment. "Wonder if he'd like to accompany Becky and me sometime on some of our songs?"

"Cool idea," Pete said. "I've never known Ben to pass up a chance to play. Since he was nine, he's lived and breathed the trumpet."

"I fell in love with the piano early on too."

"That's what it takes to be really good, starting young. Trying to learn an instrument at thirty-six is an uphill battle."

"You do fine."

"I know enough to only play the notes I'm sure of and lay out on the others. But if it's a C or a G you need, I'm your guy."

They laughed, then subsided again into an easy quiet, the only sounds Jessie's knife thumping on the cutting board, the snapping of the fire, the songs of birds, and the distant shouted commands of officers drilling their troops.

Pete got up and poured himself more coffee, then stood by the fire, looking at her. It made her a little self-conscious. "Are you a Tennessean, Jess?" he asked.

"Yes, on both sides, from way back. And you're one of those exotic specimens—a native New Yorker."

"Yep. Brooklyn born and raised."

"What brought y'all to Murfreesboro?"

"The publisher I worked for in New York bought Broadworth Press—do you know them? A religious publisher in Nashville. They needed an editor in chief. Andie and I thought it would be a good place to raise our son, especially after 9/11."

"Oh." Jessie was sobered. "If you don't mind my asking, did you know anyone who died?"

"Not personally," said Pete. "We lived right down the street from a firehouse in Brooklyn. Those guys were so friendly to Ben. They'd always wave to him, and if they weren't busy, they'd let him sit on the engine and put on a hat. That firehouse lost eight men."

"How terrible." She waited a moment in solemn, respectful silence, then stood. "I need to put the rice on and start the stew. Excuse me while I get things ready."

"I'll help you," Pete said.

"No, sit and relax. You don't feel good."

"The Tylenol and coffee are kicking in."

She gave him some onions and green peppers to chop. He sat down in the shade of the tent fly. She went into her tent, brought out the brown rice, and measured it and water into one of the large cooking pots.

With the rice pot covered on the fire grate, she brought over the large stew pot and set it on the table beside them, adding water, spices, and a couple of large cans of black-eyed peas.

As they continued to dice the vegetables, she asked him about the books he was editing. "One of them," he said, "is going to be a big seller, I think. It's called *Portals to Paradise*, and it's a collection of true accounts by people who have died, gone to Heaven, and come back. They give detailed descriptions of what Heaven is like."

"Do their accounts agree with each other?" she asked.

"Pretty much," Pete said. "Brilliant light, and loved ones waiting to greet them, and ethereal music. Those all seem to be common themes. I would really like to believe that what they say is true."

"You question it?"

"I don't question that *they* believe it. I was raised Catholic, and I do believe in God, but somehow, well, I'd give anything now to know that there's a life beyond this one—and that I'll see Andie again there." His voice remained steady. He kept his eyes focused on the movements of his knife.

Jessie struggled to find the right words. Pete spared her the need by continuing to speak in a musing sort of way. "Sometimes I wonder if people who have near-death experiences—or, in the case of the people in this book, *actual* death experiences—are just experiencing an overload of some shock-activated or pain-blocking chemicals in the brain. And I wonder if the afterlife as religion portrays it is just a metaphor for the fact that our spirits, and the matter of our bodies, blend into the vast soup of other energy and matter, and so in that way we have eternal life. I don't *want* to believe that. I wish I really could believe in the resurrection of our individual selves, and reunion with our loved ones in a better world, and all that stuff I learned in Catholic school. But my rational mind wants proof."

Jessie looked down at the stalk of celery she was cutting. She felt sorry for this man who was facing his wife's death. It would be a kindness, wouldn't it, to tell him what she had discovered—that the spirit does survive after death, with personality, memories, individual essence intact?

Yet she wasn't ready to speak of it with anyone. Pete might think she was crazy. Even worse, a skeptical reaction from this intelligent man might shake her own faith in her sanity and in the relationship that had become so important to her.

"I've had those questions too," she said. "I don't think our rational minds can answer them." She rarely talked about her spiritual beliefs. They were too personal and complex to put into words, and such talk often made other people uncomfortable. But the open way she and Pete had been conversing made her feel free to add, "Only faith can."

He was looking at her with a thoughtful frown, but he didn't seem to be focusing on her, just letting his eyes rest on her face while he wrestled with his inner preoccupations. "At this point my faith needs some kind of sign," he said.

Then, abruptly, he flashed a smile at her. His dark brown eyes slanted down a bit at the outer corners, which lent his expression a slightly melancholy aspect even when smiling. Beneath his black mustache his teeth—the two top front ones slightly overlapping—gleamed white. *He is a very handsome man*, she thought, and then inwardly chided herself for having such an inappropriate thought about a married man whose wife was probably dying, for heaven's sake.

"Boy," he said, "not only do you have to sit here and slave away while everybody else is out enjoying themselves, you also have to listen to a guy with a hangover blathering on about the afterlife."

"I like talking about these things. I'm not very good at small talk. Guess that's why I don't get asked out on many dates."

Pete let out a short bark of surprised laughter. "You're really funny, Jess, and that's impossible to believe. I suppose that answers my next question. I was going to ask if you're with someone."

"There is someone I care a lot about." It felt momentous, liberating, to finally admit it aloud. "But he's far away. And there are … other obstacles."

"Ah. That's too bad. I'm sorry."

"Thanks."

Looking down as he cut his onions and green peppers into precise squares, Pete said, "Thanks a lot for listening to me, Jess. This is the first time I've been able to talk about some of this stuff. I don't really have any confidants, beyond Andie."

Caught off guard by his openness, all Jessie could think of to say was, "I'm glad if I could help." She stood up and dumped the vegetables into the pot and Pete did the same. Jessie moved to pick up the pot, but Pete rose quickly, hefted it, carried it over to the fire, and set it on the grate.

She took off her apron and picked up the drinking water bucket. "Time for a refill."

"I'll be glad to do that," Pete said.

"Next time," she said. "Keep the fire going, okay?"

Glancing back as she walked through the woods, she saw him sitting on a log beside the fire, stirring it absently with the long iron poker, and she had a piercing sense of his loneliness.

CHAPTER 9

TURTLE DOVE

"I BROUGHT YOU some pictures. I thought you might like to see what one of our Civil War events was like. You can tell me how wrong we got everything."

Jessie and Lemuel were sitting together on the blanket she used as padding under her bedroll at re-enactments. It was a beautiful night, lit by a bright slice of the waning moon. She had returned from Gettysburg late the evening before, and throughout the day had barely been able to sit still at work, jittery with excitement at seeing him again.

"I sure would like to see that," he said. He sat with his own blanket draped over his shoulders, legs crossed, hands hanging over his knees. The lantern burned beside them. The fields were loud with the scraping of insects, and every now and then an owl called out nearby.

Now that she was here, Jessie felt relaxed and in no hurry to take out her phone and start scrolling through the pictures and explaining them. It was good just to sit with him, savoring his charged nearness.

The owl hooted again.

"He's saying *Who cooks for you, who cooks for you-all*," Lemuel said. "Granddaddy told me that. He knew the songs of all the birds."

They sat listening for the owl again. The only sound was the distant, rushing torrent of traffic noise from the Interstate, and the melodious chord of a faraway train whistle.

"I specially loved the turtle doves at home," he said, looking down, fingering the frayed hem of his blanket. "They seemed so gentle, and their call sounded so sad. When they came back every year, you knew the winter was gone and soon it would be sunny and warm, with everything blooming again. One time they built a nest in my window, up in the loft where I slept, so I could get right up close to the mama bird a-setting there on her eggs. She came to trust me and wouldn't fly away. She would just blink her bright little black eye."

He raised his gaze to hers. His expression was shy but earnest. "You're like that turtle dove," he said. "A pretty little gray-brown bird. You're not scared of me. You don't fly away. And when you come back, every time it's like the springtime." And then he added tentatively, "Jessie."

She did not look away. Her words rushed out. "I want to come back, Lemuel. When I'm not with you, I think of you all the time."

"Sweet turtle dove." They sat still, letting darkness and silence absorb the confessions they had just shared.

Then he said, "I'd be glad if you'd call me Lem. That's what all my friends called me, and my … Louisa."

"All right," she said. "Lem." She savored the strange sweetness of speaking his name.

A jet roared overhead on its approach to the Nashville airport. The moment was broken. He looked up. "Jessie, what *is* that? I've been wondering about those things."

"It's called an airplane. As many as a hundred people, maybe more, ride inside it, and fly all over the world. Like birds."

"Help my time," he said incredulously, and she smiled at the old expression, another one her grandmother used. "A hundred people. It 'pears too small for that."

"It's way up in the sky, that's why. They fly about six miles above the land."

"Good night! What keeps it up there?"

"It has very strong engines."

"Did you ever ride inside of one?"

"Yes. Once."

He shook his head. "Jessie, I declare I don't know why you want to spend your time with me. You know so much and have done all these things, and I haven't seen or done anything."

"Lem, how can you say that? You've been to *war*." On impulse she added, "And I think you're the handsomest and most interesting man I've ever met."

He peered at her as if searching for signs that she was teasing him.

"I mean it," she said.

He ducked his head, gave an embarrassed shrug. "Well, thank you for that."

"And, I think, the bravest."

"Ah." There was bitterness in the sound. "I hope you'll still think so when you know my whole story."

"I know I will."

She took out her phone. "Now, let me show you these pictures. I know you had photographs in your day, but we have them in color now. We can take photographs that move and have sound, too."

"You don't say." As he moved closer, she heard the humming vibration that always seemed to accompany his nearness, and she felt the tingling agitation of the air.

She brought up the first picture. "This was our camp. You can see here, through the woods, the other campsites. There must have been maybe fifty different companies camped out around us, each with ten or twenty members. And we were just the Confederates—the Yankees had their own camp a mile or so away."

Lem stared at the pictures with keen interest, commenting as she scrolled through them. "Everything looks so clean. Everybody has shoes. We didn't have tents. No, never—only the officers did. We slept under blankets. Yes, indeed, it sure was cold. Sometimes I woke up with snow all over my blanket, or soaked through from the rain. Would you look at that food! My land, we would have thought we'd died and gone to Heaven to see a table like that. Oh, there you are with your stirrin' spoon. If I saw a lady cook like you in our camp, I probably would have ran away and hid. I would've been too ashamed to let you see how filthy I was. I feel ashamed now."

Jessie shook her head. "Don't be ashamed. I meant it when I said you're the handsomest man I ever met." She reveled in the new freedom to express her feelings.

They looked at each other and their eyes held. No one had ever looked at her with such fervor. It both thrilled and disconcerted her. Dropping her gaze to her phone she said, "Do you want to see some more pictures?"

"Yes, indeed."

"Here are some of the moving ones." She showed him the video of the soldiers loading their guns.

"I'll swan."

"Is that how you did it?"

"Pretty much," he said. "Except most times we were layin' down or trying to hide behind a rock or tree with Yankees shooting at us. All these fellers look so calm. Sometimes we'd be so nervous we'd forget we'd already put in a cartridge and ram in another one. Or two. Then the rifle could blow up."

"Oh. How awful. I hope these pictures don't bring back bad memories."

"No, Jessie, they're right interestin', but it's kindly hard to believe anybody'd do all this for fun. Show me more, if you have them."

"Well, here's the battlefield. And they had these seats set up so people could sit and watch."

"Look at all those folks. What'd they do with their clothes?"

She laughed. Shorts and tank tops probably did look nearly naked to him. "That's how a lot of people dress in the summertime these days."

"Do you?" He glanced at her.

"Not too often. I like to be more covered up."

"Hmmm," was all he said. She pushed the play button to run the video of the battle. "There were more than 10,000 people re-enacting that fight."

He watched the screen, frowning. "It's interesting," he said at the end.

"But not like the real thing."

"Oh, no. No, indeed. Nobody would want to make a picture of the real thing. Or show it to anybody else." His tone was grim. He said nothing more, and she was afraid that she had spoiled the mood by reminding him of all he had been through.

"Lem, I have one more picture to show you. I think you'll like this one." She played for him the recording of the band's rendition of "The Bonnie Blue Flag."

His face brightened. "That was one of my favorite tunes. I wish I'd been there. Maybe you and me could've had ourselves a dance."

The warm night breeze blew her hair across her face, and she swept it back. His hair did not stir.

"I wish I didn't have to go," she said.

"You'll come back soon?" he asked, his eyes searching hers.

There was no longer any pretense of resisting what everything in her yearned for. "Tomorrow," she said. They stood and she bent down, gathered her blanket, and picked up the lantern.

As she walked away, she looked back. He was standing in the gloom of the clearing, watching her go, a dark figure shrouded in his blanket; and seeing him from afar, she had a sudden, jarring realization. *I am falling in love with a man who's dead.*

The irony was that no one had ever made her feel more keenly, exhilaratingly alive.

AND SO BEGAN their idyll. Night after night, she returned to spend as many hours with Lem as she could. It always had to be the nighttime, since by day she had to work and take care of all the routine business of life. Too, being out of the glare of daylight and away from any reference point in the ordinary world enabled her to forget about the strangeness of their situation.

Jessie didn't let the weather deter her. On rainy nights, she brought a poncho and draped it over tree limbs to make for herself what Lem called "a little hidey-hole." Even when thunder boomed and lightning slashed the sky, she still made her way through the field and forest, apprehensive until she was with him. But then, in his presence, she felt—however irrationally—completely safe. Lem sat beside her exposed to the rain, but as she'd seen before, never getting wet or windblown. It seemed that the environment didn't affect him; neither, it appeared, could he alter it even so much as to pick up a stick or move a branch. She hadn't yet seen him pass through anything, as ghosts in movies and books did, and when he sat, he looked as though gravity was anchoring him to the ground, just as it did her.

She was tired a lot of the time; when she'd last seen her mother, Betty had said, "Are you all right, honey? Your eyes look like two holes burned in a blanket." Jessie reassured her mother that she was fine, just hadn't slept well the past few nights. She dragged herself through her days—fortunately the summer office job didn't take much brain power. Sometimes after work she went home to take a quick nap. Then at around nine, as it was getting dark, she would get in the van and drive out to their meeting place, her heart pounding with expectation, all her senses quickening at the thought of their reunion.

Something had to give, of course, and it was her piano practice. At first, this made her guilty, then she began to feel a certain defiance. She had always put her music before everything else, but what had the hours of solitary servitude to the keyboard gotten her? She had been starved for intimacy with a man and now that she was beginning to have it—although of a kind she never imagined—everything else paled in importance, even the one thing by which, since the age of nine, she had always defined herself.

What that said about her commitment to her art and professional career, Jessie would not think about now. This love was fated not to last. She had promised Lem that she would find his people. She would have to begin that search before long; school would be starting again in early August. But, most of all, she knew it would not be healthy for her to stay in this strange, heightened, unstable state for too much longer.

And when she did find his relatives, there would be nothing holding Lem to this earthly realm. He would go to his rest, and she would never see him again.

The piano would still be there after Lem was gone, and she would figure out then what it meant to her.

THEY TALKED ABOUT the changes in the world since the mid-1800s. Lem was endlessly curious, and often stricken nearly speechless with amazement.

"We have machines," she told him, "that do all kinds of farm work, and machines that let us talk to people far away."

It was a windy, cloudy evening. The flame of the candle inside the lantern rocked now and then as a zephyr of air penetrated the enclosure. Lem was lying on his side, beside her on the blanket she had brought, leaning his head on his hand, looking up at her. She took out her cell phone. "This camera I showed you the other night is also what we call a telephone. It sends a signal through the air and somebody else's telephone receives the signal and we can talk to each other, miles away. Listen." She dialed the number of the church, turned on the speaker, and held the phone toward him as the voice of Pastor John Brinton announced the church's hours. Lem looked at the device with a mix of mistrust and curiosity.

"We have machines that clean the house and wash clothes and dishes," Jessie went on, putting her phone away. "And machines that take the place of horses and wagons, and go very fast on the roads. Today you can go from Beulah to Knoxville in half an hour."

"Used to take us half a day."

"We even have machines, sort of like that airplane, that have carried people to the moon. People have walked on the moon."

"Oh, now, Jessie," he protested. "You're making fun of me."

"I'm not, Lem!" She laughed. "I know it sounds crazy, but it's true."

He sat up, crossed his legs, and was quiet for a few moments, appearing to consider. "Life must be easy, with all those machines to do all the work."

"Too easy," Jessie said. "We don't get enough exercise from our daily jobs. So we have machines that make us run or walk or lift heavy weights to build our muscles. Those machines don't have any other purpose but to keep us from getting fat and weak."

She was aware of motion beside her, and when she looked over at him, she saw that he was shaking with silent laughter. "How in the world does a machine make you run?" he asked.

She described a treadmill to him and thought that he would fall over with hilarity. As they laughed together, her heart felt light and warm.

Then she went on, "People don't really know what to do with the free time all these machines give us. And they're always comparing themselves to other people and thinking they need more and more new machines. And another problem…" she said, straining with the effort of rendering these ideas accurately in terms he could understand, "is that scientists say the heat from all our machines is warming up the whole earth and sky. And the waste products from all those engines are making the earth and water and air dirty. All that heat and dirt is changing the weather. Storms are getting worse, the ice that used to cover the top and bottom of the earth is melting, and animals who live there are losing their homes. If it keeps on the way it has been going, someday water from the melted ice will cover up cities that are built on the coast."

"I'm right sorry to hear about that," he said. "Especially about the poor animals."

Another time, she felt the need to tell him some of the positive things that humanity had achieved in the past century and a half. "People live longer," she said. "So many sicknesses that killed folks back in your time have been eliminated, or we know how to make them much less severe. It's common now for people to live into their eighties."

"I wish my granddaddy could have lived till his eighties," he said. "He died when I was fifteen. He was sixty. Old, but not that old."

"I'm sorry, Lem."

"Thank you, turtle dove."

"My grandmother's eighty-four," Jessie said. "She seems like a person in her late sixties. Doctors can do all kinds of things now to help people live longer."

"Seems like all they did back in my time was make folks die quicker." He shivered. "I think us soldiers were more scared of doctors with their saws and knives than we were of getting shot to death. One time, me and some other boys came up to this old farmhouse that was being used for a hospital. We could hear hollering from inside like somebody was getting slaughtered, and out back we saw this pile of arms and legs, all swole up and black and green. It plumb turned us inside out to see it. And smell it."

"I can imagine," Jessie said. "Surgery was a terrible thing back in your time. They didn't know how to control infection and prevent pain the way we do now. But now, doctors can do things like take the heart or kidney or eyes from a person who just died and put them into the body of somebody else who has a sick heart or kidney or eyes—and that person will live a long life or be able to see again. Doctors have machines that let them take pictures of the insides of people's bodies. They can even look into a mother's womb and see if there's something wrong with her unborn baby. And if there is, and they can fix it, they can do surgery right then and sew them both up again, and when the baby is born in its proper time it's completely healed."

"Merciful heaven," Lem said.

"Women don't die in childbirth nearly as often as they did in your day."

"That's a blessing, sure enough. I had a cousin died in childbirth."

"And women can choose when to have babies, or not to have babies at all," Jessie ventured.

"There's a machine for that?" Lem asked, with a spark of mischief.

"Well, not exactly." She hesitated, wondering if she dared broach the subject of sex with him. She forged ahead. "Doctors have figured out ways to prevent pregnancy until a couple wants it. People don't have to worry that they'll get a baby if they're not ready. So it's changed everything about the way men and women behave with each other. There's not much mystery between the sexes anymore."

"It was sure a mystery to me," he said, looking down.

"I wish we could have back some of what you had in your time," she said. "Some of that modesty, and imagining, and longing. And the excitement and the joy, when you could finally give yourself completely to the one you love."

He said quietly, "I never did get to do that."

"I'm sorry, Lem." She was momentarily sobered by the thought of all the experiences he had been denied, all the promise of his young life cut short.

"Did you?" He looked at her warily, as if dreading her answer.

She considered what to say, balancing the desire to be honest with him against her sense of what, as a man of his time, he could possibly understand and accept. "I've never had that kind of love, no." It was the essential truth. In college and graduate school, testing her new freedom and trying to become a liberated artistic woman, she had slept with her two boyfriends. The experiences had fallen far short of the complete, ecstatic merging with another person that she wanted to believe possible, that she longed for.

His expression relaxed. "I hope you don't mind me saying it," he said, "but I'm glad to hear that."

CHAPTER 10

PHANTOM KISS

"Now **tell me** about you, Lem," she said, the next time they were together.

"Like what?"

"Well, start with your childhood."

He told her about growing up on the farm and a dog, Pal, who was his constant companion and best friend and brought him his first grief when Pal was killed by a panther—or, as he pronounced it, a painter—when Lem was six. He told her about the awful day when he and Caleb came home from school to find their mother, white-faced, rushing to them from the barn saying that they had to turn right around and run the four miles back to town to fetch the doctor because a horse had hurt their father badly.

"You told me he never healed right after that," Jessie said.

"That's right. He had a bad limp and an even worse temper."

He described his schooling during the winter months in the little schoolhouse an hour's walk from his home; he told her about the Baptist church he and his family attended, and how his boredom with the endless sermons gradually turned to eagerness to go to worship not, he admitted, because of any increase in piety, but because it gave him a chance to look across the aisle at the pretty girls in their Sunday best.

One of them had looked back at him. That was how he and Louisa began their courtship, he told her.

"What was she like, Louisa?" Jessie asked.

"I don't rightly know what to say." He thought for a moment. "It's hard to describe another person, isn't it?"

"It is. What did she look like? What kinds of things was she interested in?"

"She was little, with big green eyes and light-colored hair. She loved animals, same as me, and she liked reading, like my mama. And flowers."

He paused.

"Did she live on a farm, like you?"

"No, she was a town girl. Her pa was a doctor, like his pa before him—Louisa's granddaddy. It was old Doc Rabb who came to take care of Pa that time with the horse. It was a far piece to walk to their house from our farm. Mrs. Rabb would sometimes invite me to stay the night. I'd sleep in the bed with Louisa's little brother, Henry. That was like trying to sleep with a sack of fighting cats."

Jessie laughed at the image.

He and Louisa had courted for a year. He went on, "Saying goodbye to her was one of the hardest parts about going to war. But there were things I had to prove about myself before I could feel like a fit husband."

"What things?"

"Well, that I was brave. And my pa always told me I was a shirker and a dreamer who couldn't do anything right and wouldn't amount to anything. I thought being a soldier would let me show him that he was wrong. And show me too." At that he gave a brief, soft, derisive laugh.

When she asked him what was funny, he said he'd talked enough about himself and wanted to hear about her.

Jessie found it hard to talk about herself. Words didn't come easily; music was the way she felt best able to express herself.

Fair was fair, though. "I grew up here in Murfreesboro," she told him. "Though I spent a lot of time in the Smokies, visiting my grandmother in Caton's Forge, right near where you grew up. I love it there."

"I do, too." Then he corrected himself. "Did."

When she didn't continue at once, he urged her on. "I have a sister," she said. "She's twenty-one, five years younger than me."

"So that makes you twenty-six."

She nodded. "How old are you, Lem?" It felt like a strange question, because in one sense he was over a century and a half old.

"Twenty-two."

"Ah." Four years younger than she—yet for a man of his time, twenty-two was probably the equivalent of thirty in the present century, a time when a person was expected to support himself and marry and begin raising a family.

"You were telling me about your sister," he said.

"She's a nurse who works in a hospital taking care of people who have been in accidents or have come down with sudden illnesses." That was how she thought to describe the emergency room. "My mama and I aren't very close. We love each other, but we can't talk about things in any kind of depth. My father and I are closer—though come to think of it, there are important things we don't talk about, either."

"Like what?" Lem asked.

"Daddy was in a war in a place called Vietnam. It's over on the other side of the world, south of China. I think it was one of the most important parts of his life and I always wanted him to tell me what happened to him there, but he never would. Or could."

"War isn't something that ladies and gals can understand," Lem said. "I didn't write to my mama or my sister or Louisa about most of the things that went on in the army. I didn't want to worry them."

Jessie didn't feel it was the right time to tell him that these days women served as soldiers, even in combat. All she said was, "I think my daddy also doesn't want to remember the war himself."

Lem nodded. "That's prob'ly true." Then, when she said nothing more, he looked at her.

"What do your mama and papa think," he asked, "about you being gone every night?"

"They don't know about it."

He gave her a questioning look.

"I don't live at home with them," she said. "I have my own place."

"And you live there all by yourself? Is that safe?"

"Oh, yes, it's safe," she said. "Most people—men *and* women—my age who aren't married move out of their parents' houses, and if they can afford it, they live alone. People of my time are very concerned about their independence."

"Isn't it mighty lonesome?"

"It can be lonesome," she said. "I hope I won't have to live like this forever."

They were quiet for a moment. Then he said, "I sure wish things could be different."

"I do, too." She hoped they were talking about the same thing.

"Jessie, I don't feel right having you come here every night on my account."

"Oh? Do you want me to stop?" It chilled her to think that she might have misread him, that he might be impatient for her to get on with the business of looking for his family.

"Oh, Lord, no," he said. "It makes me so glad when you come. It's just that I don't feel right taking all your time when you ought to be finding yourself a husband."

"I'm leaving that in God's hands," she said. "Right now, I want to make the most of whatever time we have together."

"Well, thank you. If I had my way, you'd never go away."

They looked at each other, a long, searching gaze. The night seemed to go still. Everything faded from her awareness except his eyes—which held, in this moment, no hint of shyness.

"Lem," she murmured, "can you kiss me?"

He moved closer to her on the blanket and drew his face close to hers. The humming vibration grew louder. She closed her eyes and felt on her lips a stirring of the air that carried within it little tingling shocks. He had no scent.

She opened her eyes and looked at him, his face so close, his lips parted, eyes heavy-lidded. She raised a hand to touch his cheek. Her fingers passed through his beard-stubbled, soot-smeared skin, as if through a holographic image, and there was that electric disturbance of the air.

She drew back, unnerved but trying to hide it. "I've never wanted to kiss anyone more."

"I'm sorry, darlin'," he said. "I'd give anything if we could."

"What are you, Lem?" she asked him. "Are you a ghost?"

"I don't rightly know," he said. "I always thought ghosts were evil. And I don't think I'm evil."

"No, I'm sure you're good."

"I'd just say, a spirit."

She sat, weighing her next words, not wanting to say anything to make him feel bad. "It doesn't matter. I want to be with you. Our hearts can touch each other, even if our bodies can't."

"I'm glad you feel that way, Jessie. I want you to be happy here with me. I couldn't abide for you to leave me alone."

The words pained her to speak. She had to remind them of the truth. "Sooner or later, Lem, I'll have to, to find your people."

"Yes," he said. "But don't go just yet."

"I can't. I haven't heard your story. Tell me about your regiment, your friends, the places you went. Tell me what happened to you."

"All right, turtle dove." His face was grim as he said it.

PART II

SEEING THE ELEPHANT

CHAPTER 11

REBEL

THE GOODBYES HAD been the hardest part.

He had taken his leave of Louisa at her house on the day before the October 1861 date when he was due to join his company. She had said she could not bear to see him off and say their farewells in public.

Mrs. Rabb came to the door, her face a tight mask, and he couldn't tell if it was because of disapproval or sorrow. "Come in, Lemuel," she said. "I'll call Louisa."

"Thank you, ma'am." He waited in the front room, looking out the window at the porch swing where he and Louisa had often sat in the evenings while her parents occupied this room. Dr. Rabb would be absorbed in reading—or acting like he was—and Mrs. Rabb in sewing, the couple occasionally exchanging quiet words. Lem likewise spoke softly to his sweetheart to avoid being overheard.

Light footsteps rushed along the corridor and Louisa entered the parlor and shut the door quickly, leaning against it, hands behind her back. She wore a yellow dress with a white apron tied over it. She had flour on her nose, which made him both want to kiss it away, and cry. She stood looking at him, eyes a blazing green surrounded by red rims and shining with tears.

Then she rushed across the room and, to his shock, threw herself into his arms, pressing the length of her body against his.

His head spun and his knees went weak. For most of their year-long courtship they had only held hands. He'd dared a few kisses. Now her arms were tight around him and his arms encircled her back. He held her close, as he had wanted to for so long, feeling the stays of her corset, and her small bosom pressing against his ribcage. She turned her face up to his and their lips met. Her mouth was loose and wet with grief, her breath rushing hot between her lips.

"I love you, sweet Louisa." The words burst from him, unrestrained. "I'll be true to you. God willing this fight will be short and I'll come back home to you soon, and you'll be my wife and we'll be so happy."

"Don't forget you're taking my heart with you," she said, pressing her face into his neck. "You have to keep it safe, by keeping yourself safe."

And then, with a last tight hug and a kiss, she released him. "Oh, please, go now!" she said in a strangled voice, and he left the house, the warm wind cooling the wetness on his cheeks, whether her tears or his own, or both, he didn't know.

THAT NIGHT at the supper table his father, Jacob, finally spoke, following several days of wordless anger after learning that Lem had decided to join the Secessionists.

"So you're off to play soldier." Jacob's fork clinked on the plate as he scraped up the rest of his beans as if inflicting punishment on them.

"I'm just trying to do my duty, Pa," Lem said. In truth, he couldn't wait to get away from the daily drudgery on the same patch of land he'd spent his whole life tending. He wanted to see new places and be with new people, and above all, do as he saw fit away from his father's constant nagging and criticism. Those were his reasons for joining the army—rather, he would have to admit, than any devotion to the

Southern cause that shopkeeper Leland Berry was always talking about, which Lem couldn't really say he understood all that well.

"Duty," his father snorted. "Duty to that passel of traitors. And you might think some about the duty you owe your father. But it's plain to see neither of my sons care a thing about me. One boy gone clear across the country, the other skedaddling off leaving me to break my back trying to keep this farm going by myself."

"Jacob, please," his mother, Ruby, said. "Let's try to make Lemuel's last night at home a peaceful one."

"There you go again, taking up for him and paying me no mind."

"My dear husband, you know that's not true."

"Don't make it sound like it's his last night *ever*, Mama," Lem's little sister Polly said.

"Of course not, sweetheart, I only meant last night for a while."

"When I come back, Polly-wolly-doodle," Lem said, "I'll bring you a pretty bonnet like the girls wear in the big city. With feathers on it."

"That'd be nice. You have to bring it back your own self, not send it. And you have to come home to stay." She looked at him and bit her lip, as her golden-brown eyes reddened and filled.

"None of that, now," Lem said tenderly.

"Well, I wouldn't want to ruin this little farewell party." Jacob pushed back his chair and stood up. To Lem he said, "You keep your mind on your business. Don't go getting yourself hurt in this fool fight. I need you back here."

"No, sir, I sure won't, the good Lord willing." Lem made his tone as cold as he could. Jacob nodded and limped outside into the darkening evening.

That, as it turned out, had been their goodbye, father and son.

His father had been nowhere to be found when, early the next morning, the time came for Lem to leave to join his company. Jacob had taken the wagon, which caused Lem some anxiety—the unit was to assemble in the town of Tasman, some ten miles from Lem's hometown of Beulah. Too far to walk and get there in time.

His mother and sister stood with him, fretting by the roadside. Then their neighbor, Thomas Smoots, appeared in his old cart pulled by a dusty mule. He stopped, and when Lem explained his plight, Mr. Smoots offered to drive them to Tasman and then "carry Miz Ruby and the little gal back."

On the way, Mr. Smoots quizzed Lem about the war and the army. Unlike many of their neighbors and fellow church members, who had become noticeably colder to the Sanders family, Mr. Smoots did not seem to disapprove of Lem's joining the Rebels. He just expressed curiosity. Lem, however, was in no mood to chat. For one thing, Mr. Smoots' questions made him acutely aware of how little he really knew about what he was getting into. For another, he was so nervous that his stomach was cramping, making him fear he would have to ask the old man to stop by the woods.

Soon, conversation subsided. Lem glanced back to see his mother with her arm around Polly, holding her close, her face sorrowful. His heart clenched at the knowledge that he was making them both suffer, and for a cause his mother disapproved of as much as his father did. She had asked him, when he first announced his decision, what his reason was, and with her usual gentle firmness expressed her belief that slavery, which the Confederates were fighting to preserve, was a great evil. When he tried to explain that protecting his homeland was his sole motivation, his words sounded hollow to him and, he was sure, to her as well. But she accepted his answer with loving forbearance—more than he felt he deserved. She did not question him again.

A small crowd had gathered in front of the Tasman courthouse to wave off their young heroes with flags and handkerchiefs and flowers. Other people watched balefully from doorways, windows, and benches—Union folks, Lem figured.

The leaves on the trees were gold and crimson against a brilliant blue sky. It was a beautiful day for an occasion that, to Lem, seemed as somber as a funeral. He could tell from the smiles and jokes of his fellow recruits and their families, however, that the general mood was eager anticipation.

One of these new soldiers was Leland Berry. Tall and thin, with receding hair, the thirty-year-old Leland looked every bit the shop clerk whose days were spent out of the sun, doing nothing more strenuous than hauling down bolts of fabric, lifting barrels and boxes, and measuring out coffee and sugar. He grinned at Lem, who nodded in reply, unable to summon a smile, almost sick as he was with nerves and dread at parting from his family and his sweetheart. Suddenly, he was overcome by doubt that bordered on panic.

Jeremiah and his parents seemed to feel as Lem did. His friend huddled with his mother and father, looking down at the ground with his hat hiding his face. His mother was holding a handkerchief to her eyes as his father stood with one arm around her waist, his expression grave.

The captain, a gentlemanly young man in a fine gray uniform complete with gold trim, gave an order to the first sergeant, who yelled for the company to form up. That was the signal for the men to take leave of their families, friends, wives, and sweethearts.

Lem turned to his mother. Ruby's brown eyes were red and shining; her face was set in the tight-lipped scowl that she always wore when fighting strong emotion. She hugged him tight and murmured in his ear, "God bless you and keep you safe, dearest son. Conduct yourself like a Christian. Write to us." She drew back, still grasping his shoulders, and fixed her gaze on him. "Write to your papa. Lemuel, you must know that he really does—"

"Form ranks!" shouted the sergeant again, and Polly threw her arms around Lem, shaking with sobs, preventing him from learning whatever his mother had meant to say.

He couldn't speak and only kissed the top of his sister's head. Her blond hair smelled like leaves after a rain.

Ruby pried Polly's arms from around him and led her back to the wagon. Lem turned away, breathing deeply to master himself as he walked into the group of recruits.

Jeremiah kept his head bowed to hide his face, and from time to time he dashed at his eyes with the sleeve of his gray wool blouse. Lem caught a glimpse of Jeremiah's mother sobbing in her husband's arms, seeming near collapse. He had to look away.

The men lined up, laughing self-consciously as they bumped into one another and tried to sort out who should stand where. Finally, they were settled, and the captain addressed his new soldiers and their families. He told them that the cause of protecting their homeland and fighting for Southern rights was the most sacred one they would ever know. He asked Almighty God to bless them all. He thanked their families for sacrificing their loved ones. "A sacrifice only for a time, God willing," the young captain said. "I pray every one of us will come back soon, in victory and in glory."

Rumbles of agreement swept through the crowd, along with muttered insults about the Yankees' ability to fight, sly references to the Northerners' parentage, and boasts about how many Yankees one Southerner could lick. Then the sergeant ordered silence.

The captain turned and took his place at the head of the company. "Forward, march!" the sergeant called. The drummer began beating his drum and the bugler sounded a call. The men began marching as best they knew how, trying to synchronize their shuffling footsteps with those of the people around them.

"Goodbye, goodbye," everyone cried out, and waved their flags. Some of the girls ran forward and scattered flowers on the dusty road before the marchers. Out of the corner of his eye, Lem saw a man who was leaning in a doorway glower, then spit onto the ground.

Little boys stared in open-mouthed awe at the sight of the soldiers in their homemade uniforms. *They think we're bound for glory*, Lem reflected. *I would have thought the same thing at their age.*

And then the question arose in his mind, impossible to suppress, making his throat ache: *Will I ever see this place, these people, again?*

CHAPTER 12

LIBERATION

GLORY, LEM QUICKLY found, had little place in a soldier's life. The new recruits spent hours every day drilling, marching, being schooled in military discipline, and shown how to load, fire, and clean their guns. Those guns were a sorry collection, scrounged up from Lord only knew where—flintlocks, smoothbore muskets, squirrel guns, most of them so old and balky that they seemed like they'd be useful only as clubs in hand-to-hand combat.

The instructional sessions and camp duties still left the soldiers with vast amounts of free time to fill, and the time hung heavy on their hands. Some of them played cards or games like mumblety-peg, often wagering some of their meager earnings. Telling bawdy tales was another favorite pastime. So was sleeping the idle hours away.

Fights sometimes flared up out of boredom. Soldiers from the middle and western part of the state looked down on the East Tennesseans, suspecting them of being not quite loyal to the Cause. "Y'all Yankee fellers," the other men sneeringly called them, or, "You mountain gals." Jeremiah, whose quick temper and fists made up for his small stature, often got into scraps in defense of his compatriots' loyalty and manhood.

Lem chose to keep his head down—literally. He carved. He blessed his late grandfather for teaching him how to handle a knife.

85

Concentrating on the close work of paring and shaping wood allowed him to shut out his surroundings, giving him the illusion of solitude, which was a nonexistent commodity in the army. Solitude had always been a hunger in him, something he sought in the woods and fields at home whenever he could get away from his chores and his father.

He sat for hours fashioning spoons and forks and little animals. One day, some of the gamblers asked him to carve dice. Lem had been raised to believe wagering was a sin and so only reluctantly obliged with some wooden cubes, telling the men to burn their own dots on them as they saw fit. Then he got the idea to make a finger ring. He worked on it carefully, sizing it to fit the tip of his little finger, managing to trace a pattern of delicate flowers and vines all around it. With a rough rock he smoothed the inside so that it would not irritate tender skin. The finished ring pleased him. Some of the other men admired it and asked Lem to make similar ones for their sweethearts or wives. Soon Lem had enough commissions to keep him constantly busy, and found his carving getting more and more precise. He would not take any pay for the rings. He was glad for the pastime.

He mailed the best of the rings to Louisa. She wrote to him to tell him that it fit her fourth finger on her right hand, and she wore it on special occasions, taking care for it not to get damaged, thinking of him with love. He kept that letter in his shirt pocket, close to his heart.

He wrote letters to Louisa, to his parents together (never, as his mother had entreated, to his father alone), and to Polly. Paper was scarce and when he ran out of space, he would turn the letter over and upside down, and write between the lines, finding in the filling of pages a way to push forward the heavy weight of time.

In late December, the regiment, as part of William Carroll's brigade, marched northward to Kentucky to join Brigadier General Felix Zollicoffer's forces. They made their way from Knoxville through the Cumberland Gap, a grueling passage over rough, mountainous terrain. Freezing temperatures in the nighttime made good rest impossible. Issued only a thin blanket and a rubber sheet, Lem and Jeremiah, like most of the other soldiers, shared their bedding and spooned together, trying unsuccessfully to stay warm. But sleep was fitful. The next day, a few exhausted men fell out of the line to drop beside the road. Lem was shocked when an officer on horseback yelled at two soldiers who broke ranks to help a fallen comrade. The officer wouldn't hear their excuses and raised his whip to them, threatening them with a flogging and making them rejoin the march. Lem glanced behind at the man lying in the frost-covered weeds beside the road, still as a corpse, no one tending to him. He had never in his life witnessed such callousness. *And him one of our own*, he thought.

He learned to doze while continuing to put one foot in front of the other. These moments of shallow slumber brought vivid dreams of home. Going out on a summer morning, breakfast of buttermilk and cornbread filling his belly. Striding along at first light down the hillside in front of his family's cabin, spying a mother bear and her cub, or some deer or turkeys gliding through the tall grasses a little ways away. Seeing the sun slowly spread light over the mountains, their undulating flanks covered with the thick pelt of dark green forest. Pausing in his work to admire a hawk in flight, or to watch the shadows of clouds pass swiftly over the mountains, or just to listen to the silence. Coming back after his day's labors to see his mother standing in the doorway, welcoming him home, her smile radiating love. Washing off before supper at the spring near the house, using all the cool water he wanted to cleanse himself of the sweat and the dirt of the day. Entering the front room to the rich smells from pots simmering on the fire; sitting down and eating his fill of his mother's good cooking while his little sister chattered with her usual sweet silliness, and Mama tried to keep the atmosphere pleasant as his father forked up his food in brooding silence. Climbing at last up the steep stairway to the loft to lie down gratefully on his corn-husk mattress, pulling the quilts over himself, his last sight a wash of stars across the black sky framed by the small window above his head, his last sound the reassuring noises of his family settling in below for the night—safe, together.

To wake from such dreams was agonizing—perhaps crashing into the man in front of him as the line of marchers abruptly stopped, or finding himself shivering on the ground wrapped in his thin blanket amid the snoring and coughing of his fellow soldiers. He felt hollow at his center, physically ill with loss. *This is what being homesick means*, he thought. He never knew before. It really was a sickness. And inevitably, the thoughts would follow: *Why did it take this to show me how dear my home and family are to me? Why did I ever leave them?*

He treasured the memory of Louisa's passionate farewell. He relived it over and over at night lying on the cold, hard ground, and on many a day sleepwalking on the march. After a while, like the writing gradually fading on a letter too often handled, the remembered images and sensations began to grow indistinct and evoked only a dim echo of their original power. Still, he clung to them because they were all the sweetness that his life as a soldier held.

THE 37TH ENGAGED in a few small skirmishes, over before Lem had a chance to get involved. As the months passed and they saw no major action, they began to grouse. "Dang war's gonna be over without us getting a chance to show what we're made of."

"What do they want us for anyway, show ponies?"

"Pack mules, more like it."

Lem was deeply divided about the prospect of actually fighting. He dreaded it, and at the same time felt that almost anything that would break the monotony of marching or loitering in camp would be welcome. And he did feel an urgent need to settle the question of whether he would be as courageous, even noble, in battle as he hoped he would be.

For the present, the only quality required of him as a soldier seemed to be brute, mindless endurance as he and his comrades tramped onward to a destination and purpose only the officers knew.

Army life called into question just about everything Lem had always believed about himself. Did he think of himself as pious? Most nights he was so exhausted from marching and boredom that he lay down on his blankets and went to sleep without praying. Did he consider himself a loving son and brother, and a devoted future husband? He had trouble thinking of things to write to his mother and Louisa and his sister; his life at present with its filth and harshness and crudeness, the casual, even gleeful, acceptance of sin he saw everywhere around him in camp, was utterly foreign to anything women could understand. He listened to the way some of the other men talked about women, the things they said that they had done with them, and he felt that his love for Louisa was as fragile as a flower being trampled by hundreds of marching feet. He began to feel subhuman, dirty, and lice-ridden as an animal, and he wondered if army life would make him permanently unfit for gentle society.

Food became an obsession as the rations, always meager, dwindled away until some days they disappeared altogether. Like all his fellow soldiers, Lem grew thin and easily fatigued, and was further weakened by constantly cramping, watery bowels. In midsummer, passing by corn plants ripe in the fields, Lem could not resist taking part in a raiding party, stuffing several plump ears under his jacket. Later, he roasted the ears in their husks in the fire, then stripped them and gnawed the parched, dried kernels with a desperate hunger that took no heed of how their toughness made his teeth and gums hurt.

He and Jeremiah managed to catch a squirrel one day. Lem knocked it out of a tree with a stone and Jeremiah grabbed it while it was still stunned and dashed its head against the ground.

"Poor little thing," Lem said. "I'm sorry, but if we don't get something to eat we're going to perish."

"He understands. Don't you?" Jeremiah said to the squirrel he was skinning. To Lem he said, "You always did have a soft spot for the animals. I remember when we went hunting and killed that possum, and you cried when you saw it had babies."

"Well, shoot, I was only ten."

"And when you knocked down Vern Hatcher for throwing stones at that sick old dog."

"I can't abide meanness."

They cooked the squirrel over the fire, and it made about two good mouthfuls for each of them. They sucked the bones clean. "I'm ready for the next one now," Lem said.

"Keep your shirt on," said Jeremiah. "Them two others ain't ready yet. But that cornbread looks purt' near done." Lem noticed that since joining the army, his friend had slipped into habits of diction that would have horrified Jeremiah's proper mother and likely drawn the disapproval of his educated postmaster father. Probably trying to fit in with the other privates, Lem thought—for the most part a bunch of raw backwoods boys that made the two of them look like city swells. Lem himself had relaxed into a slang that his former schoolteacher mother would have taken him to task for—though it was the way his pa naturally talked and Mama, loyal wife that she was, never corrected him.

"I see those peas and bacon are boiling good," Lem fantasized.

"The okry might could use a few more minutes."

"Don't forget to leave room for the pie."

Now and then, a foraging party would bring back a shoat or chicken or pumpkin. Lem's conscience troubled him about taking part in stealing sustenance from a Southern farm family like his own, but hunger overcame his scruples. Why did the army not feed its men? The allotted scant measure of cornmeal, a brew of burned grain that passed for coffee, and chunks of rancid sowbelly with the hair still on it, couldn't keep men in marching and fighting trim. How could they be expected to defend their homeland in a state of starvation?

No one seemed to have an answer to these questions.

THERE WAS ONE THRILLING event. At the end of August, the soldiers of the 37th and the other companies in their regiment were to be sent from Jackson, Mississippi to Memphis, Tennessee by rail—Lem's first time riding a train.

He stood transfixed, pulse quickening, as the enormous black locomotive, its bell ringing slowly, lumbered toward the crowd of soldiers milling alongside the track. Spouting huge puffs of white steam and black smoke, the engine's bulk shook the ground. Lem felt it reverberating in the deepest part of his chest, making his heart quiver. As it passed, he saw the engineer, away up high in a little window. In the rear, a colored man, shirtless, his dark skin shining with sweat, was feeding the beast, throwing coal from the tender into the red-glowing firebox.

With a loud squeal, the train stopped. A hot metal smell filled Lem's nostrils. The engineer climbed down from his perch and walked around with a long-spouted can, pouring something shiny onto the rods between the wheels.

The orders came to board and the soldiers climbed up into the wagons. Lem looked around the inside of the car, the floor strewn with hay, a water bucket with a dipper in one corner, and what must be a piss bucket in another. He hoped no one would confuse the two. The interior was windowless, with big open sliding doors. Daylight shone through the cracks between the planks of the walls. There was just enough room for each of the forty or so occupants to sit with his back against a wall or to curl up on the floor. Most of the soldiers sat or lay down, exhausted from a long march that morning and hours of waiting in the hot sun. Jeremiah stretched out and pulled his hat over his eyes.

Lem wanted to be fully alert for this new experience. He claimed a spot near the open doors. He remained standing and peered out to see a few officers beside the train, looking up and down the track. One of them at the head of the train called something to the others and the men jumped up into the cars. The bell began to ring again, and two loud, wavering wails of the whistle made the hair stand up on Lem's arms. There was a great squeal, then the car gave a lurch and a bang, causing him to almost fall out of the doorway. He grasped a long metal bar beside the door and steadied himself, holding on tight as the train rolled forward, slowly at first, the tempo of the engine's chuffing rhythm increasing along with its speed. Black and white smoke poured from the smokestack, billowing high into the sky. Faster and faster the train went until at last it was fairly flying through the brown fields.

Lem stayed in the open door, the hot wind blowing through his hair and pressing against his face as the train hurtled forward, rocking from side to side. So swiftly were they traveling that a pair of horses in an adjoining field, running full out, rapidly fell behind. One continued to prance along, shaking his head defiantly, and the other stood, looking dejected. Incredulous laughter bubbled up inside Lem's breast and burst forth unheard amid the din and the clatter. He threw back his head to watch the heat-bleached sky rush by.

For the first time, he had the sense that life could be immense and fast and unrestrained. He felt something in him rise to meet the challenge of such a life. *This is the reason I left my home.*

He lay that night still beside the open door, reluctant to sleep and miss a moment of this wonder. He marveled at the way the moon sped along with the train.

CHAPTER 13

ACTS OF MERCY

ONE COOL SEPTEMBER night, Lem and Jeremiah were spreading out the bedding they shared. They had marched all day and arrived somewhere in the woods of northwestern Tennessee. Nearby, a man everyone called "Preacher," because of his habit of constantly reading his Bible in free moments, was tending a roaring campfire.

A tall, stout, bearded man came over and lit a corncob pipe with a stick from the fire. He stood smoking and his eyes fell on Lem and Jeremiah. He said, smiling snidely, his lips glistening amid the curls of his black beard, "You young fellers seen the elephant yet?"

The two friends exchanged glances. Neither wanted to answer and risk being mocked. Lem finally said, "I don't rightly know what you mean."

"Aw, you know. That big ol' fire-breathing, red-eyed, murdering elephant," said the bearded man. "Don't tell me you ain't seen him yet. He and his kin are a-stomping around ever'whar nowadays."

Preacher looked up from his place by the fire and said, "He means have you been in battle yet. Have you been under fire. That's what it's called. Seeing the elephant."

"Oh," Lem said.

"No, we ain't," Jeremiah said.

"Well, you won't forget it when you do," said the man, walking away. "That is, if you're still around to remember it."

Several days later the unit, marching onward, came upon a clearing in the woods where all signs indicated that the elephant, or a herd of them, had been on a rampage there. Some dozen bodies dressed in Union blue lay around the destroyed campsite, amid flattened tents and bloodied blankets, looted rucksacks and overturned cooking pots. The attack must have been recent because the campfire was still burning, a coffee pot incongruously steaming on it, and the corpses' blood was still red. There didn't appear to be any Yankees left alive.

These were the first of the enemy that Lem had seen up close. He had only seen one dead body before, his grandfather. His heart, or his stomach, was in his throat; he didn't want to get too close to the bodies out of a combination of respect and revulsion.

His unit mates didn't seem bothered by either emotion. They jostled one another to get some of the real, hot coffee—a luxury they had not enjoyed in months. Others rummaged in the tents for food. Still others began stripping the bodies of useful pieces of clothing and equipment. Lem was shocked, but when he thought about it, those men were past needing any of their things, and the Southerners certainly had no equipment as fine. Some of Lem's fellow soldiers didn't even have shoes.

A strangled whinny sounded from the woods to his right. Lem followed it into the trees and drew a sharp breath when he saw a horse weakly flailing, trying to get up, a hole torn in its throat. He drew near to the animal and walked around out of the range of the hooves. He looked at the terrified huge brown eyes, the wound pumping out gouts of blood.

"Don't you worry, feller," he said softly. "It's all right now. Don't you fret." He patted the bony forehead, the velvet muzzle. Then he stood up, took a cartridge from his box, tore it open with his teeth, and rammed it into his rifle. He replaced the ramrod, inserted the firing cap, took aim at the white blaze on the horse's forehead, and pulled the trigger. The explosion echoed through the woods.

"What the hay-ul?" he heard someone yell.

"It's just me, Sanders," Lem yelled back. "I thought I saw something moving in the woods. But it weren't nothing."

"Sanders, you damn fool, like to start a firefight," a voice yelled back amid the racket and commotion of pots being overturned and tents being ransacked.

Lem knew he would be charged twenty-five cents for the cartridge and punished, or at least made to do extra duty for firing without orders, but he didn't care.

Just then a low voice came from a thicket nearby. "I say, Mr. Sanders …"

Lem spun around. A man in a Yankee officer's uniform lay in the bushes on his back. He had fair hair and a blond mustache. His face, ghastly pale, was thin and refined.

Quickly, reflexively, Lem moved to pull out the ramrod from his rifle. His mouth was dry, his hands shaking.

"Go ahead, load your gun," the man said, gasping. "I would be grateful if you'd do for me what you just did for that poor brute."

Lem drew nearer to the man. It was then he saw that the right side of the man's groin was a ghastly mass of mangled flesh, blue cloth, and bright blood. God help him, wounded right in his privates.

"You see?" said the man. "It's over for me. So won't you hasten the end of my suffering?"

Lem swallowed hard to keep from retching and dropped to his knees beside the man. "I can't do that, sir," he said. "It's one thing to put a poor animal out of his misery. But only God can take a human life."

"A strange viewpoint for a soldier. Aren't we soldiers in the business of taking lives?" croaked the man, his agonized gray eyes meeting Lem's. "And I'm your enemy."

"I haven't been in battle nor took any lives yet," Lem said. "Killing a man in cold blood … no, I couldn't. And you don't seem like my enemy." He pulled his canteen from behind him and removed the cork. "Here, take some water. I'll stay with you for as long as I can."

He lifted the man's head and helped him drink.

"I haven't much time," the man gasped after a small swallow. Greasy-looking sweat glazed his chalk-white skin. "I want to ask you to do me a great kindness. Write to my wife. Letitia Perrin, Stockbridge, Massachusetts." He spelled it.

Lem had nothing to write with. He concentrated hard, repeating the name, the town.

"Please write to her and tell her… I love her and I love our children," Perrin said, his speech halting. "Tell her I died a Christian, doing my duty to my country. Tell her to let my parents know that I have always honored them. If you could tell her where I fell… maybe she could have my body brought home. How sweet that'd be to me, to be back home forever."

That talk of home moved Lem deeply. He said, "I promise I will." He rested his hand on Perrin's shoulder and sat quietly with him as his breathing slowed. The Yankee's eyes closed; the pauses between his breaths grew long, making Lem wonder each time if the end had come—then with a shudder the next breath would be drawn.

Sounds from the camp had ceased; his unit must have moved out. Just as Lem thought that he had better get going before they left him behind, spasms shook the officer and his breathing stopped.

Lem stood and looked down at the soldier for a while longer, but there was no further movement. He whispered the Lord's Prayer, then walked quickly back through the trees. He could just see the dust of his retreating regiment rising from the road in the distance. He ran until he reached the end of the line and fell in with the marchers.

"Thought you'd deserted, Sanders," said one of the men.

Lem said nothing. He trudged on, pondering what he had just experienced. It was the first time he had witnessed a human soul crossing over into eternity. He had seen only death's aftermath—the Yankee corpses in the camp, his grandfather laid out in the front room of his family's cabin, having died while Lem was away from home taking corn to the mill.

He thought about the striking change in the Yankee officer's face, just seconds after death. The skin was waxen, the jaw fallen, making the formerly intelligent face look slack and stupid. The staring eyes were blank, robbed of the keenness and urgency that had burned in them before.

The soul, Lem thought, *must be a mighty powerful thing.*

He trudged on, letting his attention dwell on the dull sound of hundreds of footfalls so that he would not have to think about what he had just seen. He repeated the name that the man had entrusted to him: Mrs. Perrin (he'd already forgotten her first name), Stockbridge. He made a mental note to help him remember, *livestock going over a bridge, Massa—tooshets?*

THAT NIGHT IN CAMP, he asked Preacher if he had writing supplies. Although writing a letter was the last thing he wanted to do, he did not want to risk forgetting Mrs. Perrin.

"Where do you reckon we were today, where that Yankee camp was?" he asked Preacher as he took the paper.

"We passed by the town of Clarksville about an hour before we got there."

Lem thanked him. He sat on a rock, in the blue dusk that was loud with the twittering of roosting birds. Then he wrote:

Dear Mrs Perrin,

I have the sad Duty to tell you that I was with your Husband when he died today, somewhere north of Clarksville Tenn. Although I am a Soldier on the other side please believe me that I had nothing to do with your Husband's death. I met him after he was Mortally wounded in an attack by men who had ran off. He asked me to write and tell You he died a Christian for his country and that loving thoughts of You and your Children were in his heart. He also wanted you to tell his Parents that he honored them. Your Husband seemed like a brave and good man. I am glad that I could give some comfort to his Last moments and send you his Parting words. I am very sorry for your Loss. I pray that God will comfort you. I hope that you will be able to find his Mortal remains and bring them home. He said he did so want to be home.

Sincerely,

Private Lemuel Sanders

Company I, 37th Tennessee Inf Regt

Confederate States of America

That night, he couldn't sleep. Finally, Jeremiah turned over and said, "What's the matter, graybacks biting? You're fidgeting so much I can't get to sleep. And you done took all the blankets."

"Sorry," Lem said. "Say, Poke …" It was his nickname for his friend, dating from when they were about nine and Jeremiah had come running up to him at a church supper saying, "Lem, come on, let's go get us some of that good *poke* meat," which, the way he said it, had struck Lem as funny. He had teased Jeremiah and called him Poke Meat and now just Poke.

"Yeah? Reckon you want to keep me up chitchatting now." Jeremiah sighed and flipped onto his back. He put his arms over his head, looking up at the sky. "Well, shoot."

"Did you ever see anybody die?"

His friend turned to look at him. "No, did you?"

"I did. Today in that Yankee camp."

"Was that a Yankee you shot?" Jeremiah raised up on one arm, his eyes bright in the dusky light.

"No, a horse that was dying. I just couldn't stand to see him suffer, so I had to shoot him. Then this voice came out of the bushes and it was a Yankee officer laying there. He was bad hurt, and he asked me to put him out of his misery."

Jeremiah lay back down. "But you didn't?"

"No, I couldn't. I stayed with him till he died."

"Where was he hurt?"

"The worst place you can think of. Shot right in the privates."

"Good Lord."

"He told me his wife's name and address. I wrote a letter to her. Didn't look like there was anybody else left alive who could do it, so the poor lady might've never known what happened to her husband."

"Dang," said Jeremiah. "That was right nice of you to write to her."

"Well, I couldn't say no to his last request. Even if he was the enemy."

They were silent for a while.

"It'd be a shame to get shot in my privates," Jeremiah said solemnly. "Before I get to use 'em."

"Amen to that," Lem said.

Then, overcome with a sudden sense of absurdity, they burst out laughing. They hooted with mirth. Someone nearby told them to shut the devil up, people were trying to get some sleep. They tried to quiet themselves, but for the next little while one or the other would shake convulsively and then they'd start up again, choking with stifled laughter tinged with a note of something desperate.

ONE EVENING IN mid-September, two soldiers came from a nearby camp to socialize. They were part of Brigadier General George Maney's brigade. Like Bushrod Johnson's brigade, of which the 37th was part, the unit these men belonged to had been ordered to support General Braxton Bragg's campaign into Kentucky. The aim of this operation—if the information passing among the soldiers was accurate, which was never a given—was to win that wavering state's support for the Confederacy.

Lem sat near the campfire among a large group of his fellow soldiers eager to hear the visitors' news. There was still enough light left for him to continue working on his latest carving project, a chain of four loose links with a little rectangular box attached to one end. He was making the box into a cage. It was intricate work, to hollow out the wood inside the cage's delicate bars, leaving a small lump inside that he would shape into a ball that could roll around freely inside the cage. He had been greatly impressed to see a similar device being fashioned by a man sitting outside a barbershop in Tuscumbia, Alabama, and he had decided to try his hand at making one himself.

One of the visiting soldiers was a young man with a pale face and a receding chin. He sat on a stump, smoking his pipe, and he seemed content to let his friend do all the talking. The other soldier looked to be in his late thirties, a tall and lanky fellow with a broad face, sparse black hair on his head but bushy red-brown sideburns that spread over his cheeks and joined in the middle of his upper lip in a thick mustache, below which his small, pursed mouth looked a little prissy.

There was nothing prissy about his words, however. He told about the aftermath of the battle at Shiloh church, in which his regiment had fought the previous April. He had been shot in the shoulder, he said, and treated for several days in a barn that had been taken over as a hospital near the battlefield, where he could observe the events that followed the fight.

"Wounded men were left lying on the field for days," he said. "And a week later there were still hundreds of men, dead and bloated and laying in the mud. Wild hogs and buzzards were eating the dead bodies. Words can't describe the smell. I knew if I didn't get out of there soon, I'd catch some awful disease just from breathing the air. My shoulder wasn't healed—it still isn't right—but I hied on out of that hell on earth."

"God almighty," said one of the men in Lem's company. "How in the name of heaven could they let them lay there so long? The wounded men especially."

"What else could they do?" said the visitor. "There must have been,

I don't know, looked like thousands of bodies. The gravediggers were working hard as they could. But they couldn't work fast enough to beat the hogs." Someone handed him a flask and he took a long pull, wiped his mouth with the back of his hand, and shook his head.

Lem had set down his carving. "How could they dig that many graves?" he asked.

"Graves, boy?" The visitor snorted a mirthless laugh. "Trenches and pits is more like it. Just long shallow ditches, and they shoveled the bodies in and covered them with a little dirt. No markers."

"How'll their families ever find out where they died?" Lem persisted. "Or even *that* they died?" All eyes turned to him, and he wondered if it was a stupid question that would make him a target for mockery.

No one in the circle around the fire seemed inclined to mock him. The other men looked back at the visitor, who shook his head. "Reckon an officer or one of their friends would have to write to their folks. That'd be the only way. But boys, if I told you the half of what I saw…" He took another sip of whiskey. "I saw men blown to bits. It happened so quick you couldn't tell who they were, and you sure couldn't tell afterwards. They just disappeared. There wasn't anything left of 'em. Not a speck."

Lem had heard all he could stand. He rose and went over to his pile of bedding and belongings. He wrapped his work in progress in a cloth to protect it, then put it into his haversack.

He walked a little way from the camp and sat on a rock, gazing out over the landscape of southern Kentucky toward the Cumberland Gap. Before him stretched a vista of mountains nearly as rugged and dramatic as those at home, bathed in the glow of the setting sun. He only dimly registered the beauty of the view.

He was deeply troubled by the soldier's story. Of course, he knew that killing and dying and maiming were part of war, but somehow, he had imagined that these grim realities would be accompanied by the proper observances befitting human dignity. He had trusted, for instance, that a wounded man would receive prompt medical treatment. He had expected that, if death should be inevitable, it would be marked by at least some fitting rituals: sorrowful tributes from the soldier's comrades, the gathering up of the soldier's personal effects to send to his family, the writing of letters to the relatives about how and where their young hero died and relating, perhaps, his last words. The body would be removed and conveyed to the soldier's home so that his family could bury it in their graveyard and visit the gravesite and decorate it lovingly for all the years to come. At the very least, the fallen soldier would be respectfully buried on the battlefield with a marker and perhaps a map to note the place so that it could be found later and the body brought home.

Never had he imagined that someone could just vanish entirely. Or lie wounded on the battlefield for days, suffering and maybe dying from neglect. Or witness the dead bodies of his friends and comrades being eaten by wild animals. Or simply be shoveled into a shallow, unmarked trench with other corpses, like so many slaughtered cows.

This war was terrible in ways he had never dreamed possible.

CHAPTER 14

BROTHER FOE

As the soldiers marched on into the fall, northward into Kentucky, the effects of a long and unbroken drought made their lives even more miserable. The sun beat down mercilessly; the air was thick with the dust scuffed up by hundreds of feet. The men looked as if they were covered with ash, their eyes reddened, grit crunching between their teeth. All the watercourses had dried to a trickle; ponds, streams, and lakes were surrounded by cracked earth. Thirst became an obsession. Sometimes a day would go by with nothing to drink, and when the soldiers came to a pool or a stream, they would fill their canteens with a muddy sludge and suck up the water that rose to the top. Some men dropped to their knees and scooped up handfuls with heedless greed.

Drawing a cup full of brackish liquid from a pond, Lem inspected it and saw tiny creatures squirming. "We wouldn't let our animals drink this at home," he said, pouring it out, and a man filling his cup beside him nodded.

"True enough. But reckon if we boil it up and throw some of that so-called coffee into it, we won't notice how bad it is."

Though agonizingly thirsty himself, Lem saw how soldiers who were desperate enough to drink the water without boiling it first became violently ill.

As the army entered the small town of Perryville in early October, the inhabitants came out of their houses and stood beside the road, crying, "At last! Our deliverers! Thank you! Hurrah for Jeff Davis!"

There were some civilian men among the onlookers and a few of the marchers taunted them. "It's all very well to thank us, but what's keeping you fine fellows from putting on a uniform and helping us protect *your* home?"

And other, kinder soldiers advised the townspeople, "Best be clearing out of here, folks, likely a big fight's coming."

The 37th and some other regiments set up camp outside of Perryville. Lem was assigned to picket duty that first night. It was dark as the inside of a cow, and unexpectedly cold compared to the infernal daytime temperatures. He stood concealed in a grove of trees beside a small road, shifting from foot to foot, keeping moving in an effort to stay warm. Goosebumps contracted his skin as the chill air penetrated his rough-woven blouse and trousers.

"Pssst. Johnny Reb." It was a whisper from within the woods across the road, and it made the hair stand up on Lem's scalp. He lifted his gun.

"Don't shoot!" the other man said. "I'm only a picket like you. I don't mean you any hahm." That was the way he said it, in a flat Yankee accent. He stepped out of the bushes, appearing ready to dive back undercover if Lem showed signs of aggression. He was short and stocky, with a thick black beard, dressed in the dark coat and light trousers of a Federal, his kepi looking sharp. Lem felt like a scarecrow by contrast in his filthy pants, grimy woolen blouse, and worn-out shoes with no socks.

The two men looked at each other warily through the gloom.

"What's your name?" asked the other.

"Sanders."

"No fooling! I'm Saunders. Edwin Saunders."

"You don't say," Lem said. "My Christian name's Lemuel. Where're you from?"

"Franconia, New Hampshire." There again was that funny pronunciation, New *Hamp-shah.*

"Long way away."

"You?"

"Beulah, Tennessee. How long have you been in?"

"Since the beginning."

"Seen a lot of battles?"

"My share," Saunders said. "Bull Run, Fair Oaks, just a few weeks ago a nasty bit of work in Maryland. Town called Shahpsburg."

"You come through them all."

"Thank God. How about you?"

"I been in the army going on a year and we haven't been in a real fight yet. Just a few little set-tos, but they were over before I could join in."

"I'd call that pretty lucky," said Saunders. "From what I hear, we'll be seeing action soon. Everybody on our side's getting ready for a big fight, tomorrow or the next day."

"I heard tell of that."

The two men were silent for a moment, pondering this solemn prospect.

Then they began talking of their lives at home. Saunders said he worked in a bank; he was married, with a young son. "Daniel. He's just two. I miss him something terrible," said Saunders. Shyly, he opened the top button of his frock coat and showed Lem a large silver medal on a chain. "St. Christophah," he said. "It shows him carrying the Christ child. I wear it to remind me of my own boy." He gave a soft laugh, tucking the medal back inside his coat. "With any luck, maybe it'd block a bullet."

Lem had never heard of a St. Christopher. He was touched by the warmth in Saunders' voice when he spoke of his son. He wondered if his own father had ever spoken that way of him.

"How about you, Lemuel?" Saunders asked. "What work do you do? Are you married?"

Lem told him that he worked on his family's farm and had a girl back in Tennessee whom he couldn't wait to marry when he returned.

Saunders asked Lem if he wanted an apple. His unit had camped in an orchard a few nights before, he said, and filled their knapsacks with the fruit. They'd all eaten so many they had "the shoots," he said.

Lem laughed at the term. "We got the shoots from eating nothing," he said. "They're starving us. I'd be glad to have me some supper."

The other man was close enough that he could have stepped forward and handed Lem the apple. But it was as if there was an invisible barrier in the road between them that both men were hesitant to cross. Instead, Saunders tossed the fruit to Lem, who caught it. Saliva flooded his mouth. He bit into it. It was cold and tart and sweet.

"Tastes mighty good, thanks," he said. He did not throw the core away, but ate it—seeds, stem, and all. Anything to fill the void inside. "Wish I had something to give you."

"It's all right," said Saunders. "I'm just glad to have somebody to talk to, to pass the time."

For the rest of their watch, they compared notes on conditions in their respective armies. They sounded much the same, except for food. The Yankees were very well supplied, it seemed. Real coffee and sugar, and yes, the same hardtack and "salt horse" as the Rebels got, but regular rations at least. And, Saunders admitted, foraging parties had availed themselves liberally of the "hospitality" of the farmers they passed on their way south.

Lem went silent at this, wondering if his family had been among the "hosts."

Edwin must have sensed a cooling; he said, "I'm sorry, Lemuel, I shouldn't have said that. Those are your people."

"Well, war's war, I reckon," Lem said.

"No hahd feelings?"

"Nope."

At midnight, Lem heard his replacement thrashing through the undergrowth. "Hey, Edwin, best hide yourself. I hear my relief coming."

"Nice talking to you, Lemuel. Stay out of trouble in the fight, all right?"

"You too. Get back home to that boy of yours."

On his way through the woods back to the encampment, Lem pondered how it could be right to have to kill such a friendly, harmless man as Edwin Saunders—a husband and father—as he would have to if they met in battle.

When he crawled under his blankets, Jeremiah was asleep but stirred when Lem lay down beside him. "What time is it?" Jeremiah mumbled.

"Late. Midnight. Say, Poke, I think we're fixing to see the elephant tomorrow or the next day."

"How do you know?" Instantly wide-awake, Jeremiah turned over and looked at him.

"I was talking to a Yankee fellow just now. He was in the woods across from me standing picket for his side. He said everybody in his camp's getting ready for a big fight sometime in the next two days."

"You talked to a Yankee?" Jeremiah's eyes widened. "You didn't fight him?"

"No, he seemed like a peace-loving kind of fellow. He gave me an apple to eat. We talked about our families."

"Hmmm." Jeremiah rolled away, looking up at the sky.

"What do you reckon it's going to be like?" Lem mused. "Being in a fight?"

"I don't know. After all this time, part of me wants to find out. I just hope I don't up and run. Or benasty my drawers."

"Mine couldn't get any nastier."

They lapsed into a thoughtful silence. At last, Lem said, "If either of us get killed, let's promise to tell the other one's folks."

"I promise you," said Jeremiah.

"I do, too," Lem said. "I see now that it would be pretty easy to get blown up or buried somewhere without anybody at home ever finding out about it." *Or eaten by hogs, or left to rot on a battlefield,* he thought. Like the men after Shiloh. Jeremiah had been off somewhere during the visiting soldier's recitation and Lem hadn't had the stomach to tell him about it.

"I promise you," Jeremiah said again.

THE NEXT DAY, the mood in camp was restless, anxious. Word spread that the Yankees were nearby and that there would be an engagement soon. As the day passed without orders to move, the soldiers occupied themselves as best they could.

Lem and Jeremiah walked into the little town near their encampment. There was not a sign of life in the buildings lining the main street. No one came out to cheer this time. No faces peered from behind windows, no dogs barked. Lem tried the door of a small white church, but it was locked. The inhabitants of Perryville seemed to have fled.

The men tried to distract themselves from thoughts of the approaching conflict. Preacher read his Bible. Jeremiah organized his cartridge box and container of firing caps and cleaned his gun to a shine. The gamblers played at their dice and cards. Other men busied themselves by sewing papers printed with their names and home addresses into their clothing. Lem whittled, making nothing, just reducing each stick to a pile of shavings at his feet, then he'd pick up another and whittle some more. Now and then, he glanced up at the hazy blue sky stretched over the rolling terrain. It looked serene and unperturbed.

He considered writing a letter. He thought about his mother's parting words. *Write to your papa. He really does…* And then his sister had interrupted with her tearful goodbyes. What had his mother been fixing to say? *He really does…* what? Need you to help him on the farm? Well, Lem knew that; his father said it often enough, when he wasn't complaining that Lem never did anything without having to be asked over and over. Which, Lem had to admit, had considerable truth to it. Yet his mother had seemed to signify something else. Could she have been trying to tell him "He really does care about you, underneath it all"?

As his knife bit into the dry wood and carved up ivory-colored curls, Lem searched his memory for evidence of his father's affection or concern. He could remember only his own dogged efforts to get his father to smile or to talk about anything other than the most immediate task at hand. Lem had always wished that the two of them could go fishing or build things together or share activities that he saw other fathers enjoying with their sons, and that he himself had enjoyed with his grandfather. Or even laugh together; he'd seen fathers and sons do that too. But his father was always silent and distant, preoccupied, probably, by the lingering pain of his old injury, which must have been inflamed by the toil of every day. After a while, Lem had given up.

That night, the moon was full and brilliant. Once again, the temperature plummeted after the intense heat of the day. Lem lay under his blanket washed by silvery moonlight, tense and wakeful. Jeremiah must have been similarly preoccupied, because although Lem knew he was awake, his normally talkative friend said not one word.

Later, or maybe early the next morning, there was a distant booming. Lem stared up at the clear sky. No storm clouds obscured the glittering stars.

The battle had begun.

CHAPTER 15

FLEEING THE ELEPHANT

OCTOBER EIGHTH DAWNED clear and cool. Just after sunrise, once again a thunder of cannon fire set the men's nerves on edge.

Around eleven, the orders came for the soldiers to leave their belongings behind, take their weapons, form up, and move out. The drummer beat the long roll, a sound as yet unheard by most of the members of the 37th—the call to battle. The bugler sounded "Attention," then "Assembly." Lem and Jeremiah looked at each other.

"Well, reckon this is it," Lem said.

"Yep." Beneath its new growth of patchy light-brown beard, Jeremiah's face looked pale, his features set in an expression of grim resolve.

The order was to form up in echelon. Lem took his place between Jeremiah and a man named Amos Brower, from Maryville, who had a bad stutter but played the harmonica sweetly. Lem wondered if he would ever hear him play again.

The 37th, along with the other Tennessee units in Johnson's brigade, marched forward through the rolling countryside, autumn-brown and peaceful under the placid blue sky. Lem glanced down at his feet and saw a tiny orange butterfly frolicking among some dusty yellow and purple wildflowers. It might be, he thought, the last peaceful sight he would ever see. His throat contracted in a dry spasm, his breath came fast. His hands on his rifle were wet.

The Confederates went over a rise and saw below them a white farmhouse and a barn beside a sluggish brown creek running low between mudbanks. Several Yankee soldiers, unsuspecting, were filling their canteens from the creek. Lem's heart went still, and his breath caught at the sight, on top of the opposite hillside, of hundreds of bluecoats advancing, flags whipping in the hot breeze, their cannons aimed right at the approaching Rebel lines.

"Forward, men, double-quick!" came the command. The Confederates began running toward the Yankees in the creek, who had begun shouting and scrambling out of the water or fleeing down the creek bed. Lem focused on the white, vulnerable-looking legs of one enemy soldier whose blue pants were rolled up to the knee for wading. The man was scrambling up the bank of the creek when a shot struck him in the back, and he threw out his arms and toppled into the water. It was the first violent death Lem had ever seen.

There was no time to absorb the shock. As the first wave of Rebels met up with the enemy, the firing, bludgeoning, and stabbing began. Then the day was shattered by a deafening blast from the cannons.

The noise seemed to shake the earth, and a high-pitched, keening yell burst from hundreds of throats. Lem realized from the aching in his own throat that he was yelling, too, although he couldn't hear himself over the din. As he hurtled forward with his comrades, following the first line of Confederates up a small hill, shells screamed overhead. One exploded in the middle of the first rank of soldiers, sending a rain of gore and hot iron fragments on some of the men. The shrieks and howls of agony made Lem's legs go weak. A man to his right doubled over, vomiting.

Jeremiah had run ahead. Lem spotted Leland Berry sprinting along at Lem's left, his awkward, knock-kneed gait that of someone not much used to running. Suddenly, he reeled backward, his hand to his throat, blood spurting through his fingers. He fell back, down the hillside, and the man behind him tripped over him and went down too.

My God, thought Lem, *my God*. Teeth clenched, he ran forward, his breath coming in ragged gasps as he clambered up the slope. The day's brightness was obscured by a spreading pall of smoke, and the murk seemed to have entered his skull, confusing his thoughts so that only stray, random impressions registered in his awareness with unnatural clarity. A sharp double glint came from somewhere on a far hillside to his left—someone looking through field glasses? A gray-clad soldier sitting down, cradling another soldier in his arms, frantically patting his face, urging him, "Tom, Tom, get up, we got to go on." Lem could see, from Tom's pallor and the blood spreading over the breast of his jacket, that he would not be getting up ever again.

Jeremiah was nowhere to be seen. The disordered line of men of which Lem was a part had descended into a small valley and then began climbing another, taller hill toward the Yankee line. Lem became aware of the frantic exertions of gun-loading going on around him, men pausing to rip open their cartridges, the furious motion of ramrods catching the dim sunlight that filtered through the battle smoke.

I better shoot, he thought. He groped in his cartridge box, halted, loaded his gun, and tamped the charge in with the ramrod. He raised the weapon and sighted along a line of Yankees, fixing his gaze on a man with a large brown beard who was loading his gun, shouting something to the man next to him. Lem held his breath to still his gasping and steady his hands—then something made him raise the barrel slightly so that he was aiming clear above the enemy soldier's head when he fired.

He ran forward, mindless as a stampeding animal in a herd, stopping and loading again and firing, taking care not to hit anyone as two realizations emerged from the fog within his mind: He was not going to be able to bring himself to shoot a man, and so he had better find other ways to be useful.

He began picking up weapons from fallen soldiers, loading them and passing them to the men ahead of him. He pulled some wounded men out of harm's way, dragging or carrying them behind a stone or a tree, until an officer came up beside him, grabbed his arm, and hollered into his ear above the din, "Leave them boys be, soldier, and get the hell back in the fight."

He ran on with his comrades until he came to a group of Rebels crouching behind a stone fence, rising up from time to time to shoot.

"I'm out of ammunition!" one of the shooters yelled.

"Me too," said another voice. "Anybody got some to spare?"

"I'll go find us some." Lem stood and ran into an open field, crouching low to try to make himself a smaller target for bullets which whizzed past him like enraged hornets. All kinds of discarded treasures were strewn on the ground—photographs and knives, the little sewing kits that the soldiers called "housewives," letters and prayer books. And everywhere were bodies, some twisted and broken as if flung down from a great height, others looking as if they were napping in a placid field on a summer afternoon, still others reaching out toward passing legs for help, or struggling to rise.

He dropped to his knees amid a group of dead bodies and with shaking fingers took off their cartridge belts and cap boxes. A sharp pain stung his upper arm; he looked down and saw that the sleeve of his blouse was torn, a bloody stripe scored into his skin.

He sprinted back to the stone fence to deliver the supplies, then made several more scuttling forays onto the field to get more ammunition and weapons. At one point, he picked up a fallen man's rifle and accidentally grasped the barrel, which was searingly hot and burned his fingers. But he hardly felt it.

A lieutenant who had been kneeling and firing from behind the fence turned and braced his back against the rocks, scrawling something on a piece of paper. "Who'll take this message?" he yelled.

"I will," Lem said, and crawled over to him.

"Find an officer and give him this," the lieutenant shouted into Lem's face, spraying him with spittle and rank breath. "Tell him we need reinforcements here."

"Yes, sir." Lem took the piece of paper and ran back in the direction from which they'd first come.

He found a colonel on horseback and gave him the paper, pointing towards the fence line, though little could be seen through the pall of smoke. Then, momentarily uncertain what to do, he looked around him, hunched over, hearing the whizzing of bullets and the shouts and screams as they found their marks. The urge to just lie down and hope that the battle would pass over him was strong. Lem forced himself to resume his self-appointed task.

The lines of men had fallen apart; there was no order anymore, just small groups and individuals advancing up the hillside, dodging the horses and men who were fleeing downhill away from the front lines. A red sun was sinking beneath the battle smog. Bayonets caught the crimson glare, looking as if they were tipped with blood. The fighting must have been going on for hours. It felt as though both an eternity had passed—and no time at all.

The crest of the hill was in sight. Through the smoke, Lem could see the brass cannons gleaming, spewing fire as they discharged. His ears were stunned by the roar.

There was another poor man curled on his side just ahead of him, a Confederate, barefoot. He didn't respond when Lem shook his shoulder. Blinded by smoke and his own streaming sweat, his breathing rasping from his throat in little involuntary grunts, Lem gathered up the contents of the man's ammunition containers. He glanced up to see several Rebels brawling with bluecoats only about fifty yards away near the crest of the hill—a melee of fleshy thuds and grappling, blood spurting, bayonets glinting. For a moment, like a shaft of sunlight piercing through a break in storm clouds, strains of music penetrated the hellish din. It sounded, insanely, like a brass band. Could the Yankees possibly have a band playing during this inferno? Or were his ears playing tricks on him? Then once again, the booming of artillery, the shouts, and the crackling of muskets overwhelmed all other sounds.

A horse ran toward him, riderless, panic-stricken, trampling some of the fallen men. Lem jumped to the side to get out of its way and stumbled over a body, apologized, and then realized that he was apologizing to someone with only half a face. Struggling to his knees, dazed, revolted, he saw a chaplain kneeling beside a soldier. Bible open, one hand resting on the injured man's head, the brave parson was murmuring a prayer. As Lem watched, transfixed by the sight of such selfless courage, at that very moment the preacher lurched forward, clutching his abdomen. He toppled onto the fallen man and lay still, and Lem saw blood pouring down over the man beneath, while the Bible fell from the preacher's hand, its thin white pages riffling in the hot battle wind.

Lem retched. The revulsion and terror he had been fighting to suppress all day suddenly overcame him. Mindless, desperate, he stood up, whirled around, and let himself be swept down the hillside amid the throng of wild-eyed men fleeing from the conflict, rushing to the rear.

He ran across the creek, past the white house and the barn—now a smoking black ruin—back toward the town until he came to a thicket out of range of the combat. He threw himself down and lay there, sucking in air, his heart ready to explode. Then he turned on his side, lying amid the branches, overcome by sickness, shame, and exhaustion.

The fighting went on into the darkness. Finally, the shrill notes of bugles pierced through the chaos, sounding the call to fall back. Gradually, the shooting and cannonade subsided. Men came limping toward Lem's shelter to find their own spots in the bushes.

Lem sat up, conscious of a raging thirst. He drank some hot, foul water from his canteen and looked around for Jeremiah. Among the thousands of soldiers milling in the gloom, most unrecognizable with black powder, filth, and blood obscuring their features, there was little hope of identifying his friend.

The moon rose, illuminating the carnage on the hillside and around the creek. It looked like the end of the world, like the judgment day of the damned. Fires burned here and there; trees that had been decapitated by cannon fire stood blackened and jagged. Bodies lay everywhere. Lem saw a kind of swarming, a slow churning on the ground like the squirming of maggots on a carcass. It was, he realized, the writhing of wounded and dying men. Through the ringing in his ears, he could hear their groans and cries.

A sergeant came over. "Go make yourselves useful, you slackers. Go get our wounded boys off the field."

Lem rose and with a small group of searchers and stretcher-bearers went back up the hill, looking for injured Confederates. White handkerchiefs tied to sticks signaled a truce as both sides engaged in this gruesome task. Still, a stray shot now and then felled one of the rescuers. Lem was so exhausted he felt beyond fear. One part of his mind bitterly reflected that a Yankee bullet would be good enough for him, after his failure to do his duty and kill the enemy, and then his panicked flight from the field like a scared dog.

As he moved among the bodies and the debris of broken wagons, abandoned weapons, blankets and shoes and haversacks, Lem blocked out all thoughts. He searched for men who were still alive, calling out to the litter bearers when he found one. As he pulled corpses off injured men trapped underneath, he prayed that he would not see faces he knew—Jeremiah's, or Preacher's. Then he came upon the black-bearded man who had taunted him and Jeremiah by the campfire with his tale of the murdering, fire-breathing elephant. He lay pallid in death, his eyes wide open with two little moons shining on their sightless orbs.

"Poor devil," Lem murmured. "That old elephant stomped you good, didn't he?"

As he lifted the wounded, it began to penetrate through his misery and exhaustion that these were suffering, terrified fellow human beings, many in their last moments—not just a dead weight to be hefted and handed off to the litter bearers. So he tried to say a kind word to each of them, and to those who could drink he handed canteens and flasks that he picked up from the battlefield.

"You're all right," he told a young boy, sixteen if that, whose right arm looked to be attached to his body only by some strands of muscle or sinew. The boy's eyes were darting from side to side, unseeing. He was quaking. "Doc'll patch you up fine," Lem said, and hailed some passing stretcher-bearers.

"Looks like you'll be going home, lucky dog," he said to another man, who was groaning as he pressed his hands to his split-open abdomen to try to keep his guts inside.

"Naw, it don't look too bad."

"That's right, Papa's right here. You rest now."

AFTER SEVERAL HOURS, Lem's group was relieved by other men bearing lanterns and torches. Lem made his way across the fields toward the town, found the previous encampment, and located his belongings where he had left them in what seemed like another life. He spread out his blankets and lay down. Alive. He had never felt so keenly alive, so aware of every physical sensation. His ears continued to ring with the echoes of gunfire beneath which he still heard screams. The swollen tide of his blood pounded in waves against the inside of his skull and outward into his every extremity, pulsing in his burned fingers, throbbing in the place on his arm where the bullet had grazed. The tang of gunpowder borne on the chilly night air filled his nostrils. Thin scudding clouds across the face of the moon, stars winking and disappearing behind the rapidly moving veils, all were more beautiful than he had a right to behold.

He drew in a deep breath and expelled it in a cloud of life-warmed fog. How could he have lost his nerve so badly? Why had he been unable to fight like the brave men he'd seen all around him?

Motion beside him. Jeremiah kicked open his bedding and flopped onto it. His face looked as if it had been tarred.

"Oh, thank the Lord," said Lem, sitting up abruptly.

His friend turned over, presenting him with his back. "I don't want to talk now, Lem. I just want to sleep."

It was cold, and after a while Lem moved onto his side and spooned together with Jeremiah for warmth under their thin blankets. The moans of wounded soldiers who had been carried or managed to walk back to camp made sleep impossible. In his own weakness and exhaustion, Lem wished that they would just shut up—and that gave him another reason to despise himself, his lack of charity.

Sleepless though he was, Lem pretended unconsciousness when Jeremiah began shaking from something—an attack of nerves, or suppressed sobs, or a terrible dream. When the tremors had subsided, as if in an involuntary motion of slumber, Lem sighed deeply and let his left arm flop over Jeremiah's breast in a loose embrace. It gave him, at least, some comfort.

CHAPTER 16

REPENTANCE

IN THE EARLIEST hours of the morning, while it was still dark, there was a commotion in camp. There would be no extended rest for the weary men, it seemed. Nor would there be food. By order of General Bragg, the army was to retreat immediately.

Lem and Jeremiah rose and gathered up their bedding and equipment. Stumbling, mute, past exhaustion, the Confederates began trudging the ten miles north to Harrodsburg. A gray dawn turned pink, and the sun came up over the horizon. Lem and Jeremiah walked behind some of the wagons bearing the wounded. The screams as the wagons lurched over the rutted road would have been terrible to hear if Lem had been able to feel anything. Drops of blood that fell from the wagons lay like bright jewels quivering on top of the dust, the dry earth being too hard to absorb them at once.

The soldiers passed a Yankee corpse propped against a fence, dark blue frock coat and light blue pants soaked with red. Flies swarmed, drawn to the blood. Someone had posed the body with its ankles crossed. The soles of the bare feet were pink and tender from being protected by good strong Federal shoes that were now giving comfort, no doubt, to some grateful Rebel. The prankster had cocked a hat over the corpse's face and stuck a corncob pipe in its mouth and put the arms up on the lowest fence rail in an attitude of leisurely repose.

"Hey, there, Billy Yank," some of the passersby called. "Nice morning for a nap, ain't it?"

Lem glanced at the corpse, then quickly averted his eyes. Then something about the figure drew his gaze again—the thick black beard, the portly middle. A large silver medal on a chain lay against the white shirt that showed in the open collar of his coat. Lem wrenched his eyes back to the dusty ground in front of him, willing himself to reject the notion that there was anything familiar about the man. The only thought he did acknowledge was that the person he had once been would have been shocked by such a desecration of the dead.

He was no longer that person. Barren of emotion, he trudged on.

THE MARCH from Perryville to Harrodsburg was grueling, the terrain steep and overgrown with brush in places. It wasn't until the exhausted soldiers had set up camp and slept for a while that Lem and Jeremiah finally spoke to each other. In the mid-afternoon, Lem approached his friend, who was sitting on a rock a little way from where some soldiers were heating their meager rations over a campfire. Jeremiah's face was still black with gunpowder. His eyes were unnaturally blue in irritated, reddened rims.

"Are you all right?" Lem asked him.

"I'm here." Jeremiah shrugged.

At that moment, a man from Company G of their regiment, a rough fellow named Stokely, walked by. He was a foul-mouthed gambler at cards who had been punished a few times for drunkenness. "Hey, Sanders," he said, jeering. "Whar'd you run to? When I saw you skedaddling off, I said to myself I just knowed them East Tennessee boys couldn't take a little heat."

Before Lem could respond, Jeremiah startled him by jumping up from his rock as if it were on fire. His five-foot-six-inch skinny frame was quivering with rage, his fists clenched and unclenched by his sides. "Shut up, Stokely, or I'll shut you up."

"Yeah? I'm scared. Everybody knows y'all Yankee fellers won't fight."

"I'll show you who won't fight, you son of a bitch." Jeremiah lunged forward. Lem leapt up and grabbed him by the upper arms. "Don't," he said. "He ain't worth it."

"And where were *you*," Jeremiah yelled after the retreating, laughing Stokely, "when my friend here was picking up our wounded boys till midnight last night? You just go to hell. And stay out of my way."

"Poke, I declare I don't know what's gotten into you," Lem said, shaking his head. "You went off like a regular firecracker. And just a-cussin'!"

"He made me mad."

"He's right, though," Lem said. "I did skedaddle."

"What d'you mean?" Jeremiah resumed his perch on the rock. Lem sat down on the ground, cross-legged, unable to look at him.

They had never kept secrets from each other. In a low, shamed voice Lem told Jeremiah about being unable to shoot anyone, aiming over the Yankees' heads, busying himself instead by scavenging ammunition from fallen soldiers and loading weapons for other men.

"I did stay in the fight till sundown," he said. "Then I saw a parson kneeling beside a dying feller and reading the Bible to him, and then that preacher got shot. He fell on the man and his blood gushed all over him. It was the worst thing I ever saw. I felt like if God could let that happen to a holy person like him, then what in the world was going to happen to me? So I ran away. Like some white-livered coward. I can just hear what my father would say."

"Some people just aren't the killing kind," Jeremiah said.

"It makes me a pretty sorry soldier."

"I reckon we both of us feel pretty sorry today. For different reasons."

Something in Jeremiah's voice drew Lem's attention away from his own inner turmoil. He looked up at his friend. "How'd it go for you yesterday?"

"I purely disgusted myself," Jeremiah said.

"How come?"

"I went wild. I started firing like a madman. All I wanted to do was kill, kill, kill. Everything I saw was red, like my eyes was full of blood. Whenever I'd drop one of them bluecoats, I'd laugh and whoop and holler. I couldn't get enough o' murdering." Jeremiah shook his head. "I looked into a man's eyes and saw him beg for mercy and I shot him in the face. I was like hell's worst devil." A tremor passed over him, and he pressed a hand to his mouth as if about to be sick.

"Well, you can't blame yourself," Lem said. "What else have we been drilling and training for but to kill?"

"That may be, but it sure seemed wrong to like it so much."

Preacher had been squatting close by, near the campfire, seemingly— as usual—preoccupied with his own thoughts. He stood up and said, "Sanders, the sergeant ordered me to go for wood. Would you give me a hand?"

"Yes, sir," Lem said, finding it impossible to address this dignified older man in any other way though, like him, Preacher was only a private.

With hatchets and canvas sacks, they headed into the woods. Lem looked around, anxiously alert for signs of Yankees, but the forest was quiet. He noticed for the first time that it was a beautiful October day, scarlet and gold foliage blazing against a blue sky, making him remember the day of his departure from home—could it possibly have been only a year ago? It seemed a great mystery that such a peaceful scene could exist in the same universe as the field ten miles away, clogged with the wounded lying in agony, and the dead, bloating under the beating sun.

They began gathering up the loose branches on the forest floor, breaking and chopping the ones that were too long to fit in the sacks. Lem kept glancing around nervously, as if enemies might suddenly materialize from amid the thin tree trunks.

"I couldn't help overhearing some of what you and your friend were talking about back there," Preacher said. Lem had never been this close to the man before, had never looked full into his face. Preacher wore an old no-color felt hat crammed down on his head. Under its brim a few graying sandy wisps of hair escaped. His eyes were surrounded by wrinkles as if from years of squinting, with unruly eyebrows above them. "Was this your first fight? It's Lemuel, isn't it?"

"Yes, sir," Lem said to both questions. "And your real name?"

"Tippin. Virgil Tippin."

"Pleased to meet you. Formal, like," Lem said, and they shook hands.

Preacher picked up his sack again and went back to work. "Baptism by fire. It's never what you expect."

"You've been in fights before?"

Preacher nodded. "Yes, I fought in the Mexican war."

Lem didn't know anything about that but didn't want to betray his ignorance. "Are you a preacher?" he asked.

"No, just a student of God's word."

They worked in silence for a while. Then Preacher said, "Do you read the Bible, Lemuel?"

"Not too often, sir." Lem didn't want to admit that the true answer was *never*.

"Well, God promises us in his word that he will be with us in all our trials. We can call on him for help and he will give us strength." He picked up a hatchet and chopped a large, thick branch into small sections and put them into his bag. "All he asks is for us to obey him."

"How do we know if we're obeying him?"

"By following his commandments."

Lem thought about this. He tried to remember the ten commandments. The first one that came to mind was, "Thou shalt not kill."

"But, Mr. Tippin," he ventured, "aren't we going against the ten commandments if we kill?"

Preacher kept on loading lengths of wood into the bag. "In the case of a just war, it's different. Just look at the Bible. It's full of killing and violence, but in the name of God. Our cause is righteous; the Yankees invaded our homeland, so you could surely call it a just war. No, the sixth commandment is talking about wanton murder." He paused then and looked at Lem. "The important thing to remember is that if we sin and ask God's forgiveness, he will give it freely. But if we are unrepentant, then we can't expect God to help us. Do you understand?"

"Yes, sir. I think so. Thank you."

Lem thought for the rest of the day about what Preacher had said. It gave him hope to think that God would give him strength if he asked for it. He had heard such statements before, of course, but they'd had a hollow ring when delivered from the safety of the pulpit and in the affected tones of the preacher at home. Now, in the aftermath of one battle and probably in the face of another, spoken with simple sincerity by a veteran of many fights, they had new meaning.

He pondered the idea of killing, that it could be just if the cause was righteous. It went against everything in him, but he vowed that, if he should be in another battle, he would do his duty and trust in God's protection.

What Preacher said about sinfulness troubled Lem. Maybe God would withhold his aid because Lem was a sinner? He thought about his failings. Cowardice, of course. Stealing the corn from farmers' fields and partaking of stolen meat and vegetables. Thinking lustful thoughts while listening to some of the other men talking about women.

Worst of all, it occurred to him now, was that he had gone against the commandment to honor his father. He had harbored bitter feelings and treated his father with cold avoidance for a long time, to punish him for not being the warm and affectionate parent that Lem wanted him to be. He had been a reluctant worker, adding to his father's trials the burden of constantly reminding him about chores that needed to be done. And then Lem had abandoned his father to fight in this folly of a war. In truth, with the Confederacy drafting men since the previous April, he would have had to go anyway, but he could have given his father some seven months' more help on the farm.

Lem asked God's forgiveness for all that, and he resolved that when he saw his father again, he would ask his forgiveness as well. Perhaps he would even write to him and tell him he was sorry.

At the idea of finding the right words, and setting them down on paper, his spirit faltered. Maybe, though, he could try doing as Preacher had suggested and call on God for help.

That night before sleep, he prayed that God would show him a way to make amends to his father.

CHAPTER 17

WILDERNESS RITE

LEM'S BRIGADE MOVED back through Kentucky, southward into their home state.

On a chilly gray afternoon in late November, they were passing along a road that somehow seemed familiar. The road led through a town, past a brick church with scaffolding around its blackened, white-painted wooden steeple that Lem remembered seeing some months before and thinking it must have been struck by lightning. Further down the main street he saw a sign on a building that he had seen the previous summer and meant to point out to someone, but at the time none of the dull marchers around him had seemed interested in conversation. *Vester Payne, Surgeon*, the sign said; Payne, Lem had thought at the time, was a good name for a surgeon. He remembered amusing himself as he trudged onward by pairing familiar names with appropriate occupations: Rule, a schoolteacher; Sales, a shopkeeper; Cutter, another surgeon, or maybe a tailor—Taylor, too, of course; Robb, a thief; and so on. The exercise had given him a few minutes of distraction from the heat and tedium.

Now, as they continued along the road that led up and down through rolling fields stubbled with cut corn plants, the sense of having been here before intensified. He remembered that farm with its yellow farmhouse and red barn, the black-and-white cows in the pasture, and he recalled looking at this leaning, run-down split-rail fence beside the road and being glad that, whatever hardships his present life might hold, at least for now he was spared the tiresome, endless job of splitting rails and building and repairing fences.

The line came to a standstill, probably as usual for reasons that the soldiers in the rear would never learn. After an hour of waiting, permission came down for the men to rest for a while. The marchers took off their bedrolls and stacked their arms, then sat or lay down. Those who had shoes took them off to give their feet an airing.

Lem looked over toward a thick forest, its gray, leafless trees like skeletal hands stretching into the flat white sky. He stood and approached Jeremiah, who was lying down, leaning against his bedroll, reading one of the pamphlets that some missionaries had been handing out to the soldiers as they passed through a town the previous Sunday. Jeremiah laid the pamphlet face-down on his chest at Lem's approach and Lem saw the title, *Soldier, Why Do You Swear?* He couldn't help smiling.

"What?" said Jeremiah.

"What you're reading."

"Oh." Jeremiah looked at the cover. "Well, it was either this or *Prepare to Meet Thy God* and I didn't like the idea of that."

"I don't blame you," Lem said. "Poke, come with me?"

"Where?"

"To those woods over yonder. There's something I want to see. We can get water while we're there."

They asked permission of the nearest sergeant, and soon were making their way toward the woods, the canteens of several of their fellow soldiers draped across their bodies, clattering as they walked.

"Where are we going?" asked Jeremiah.

"This way, I think," Lem said.

"You know this place?"

"I believe so."

"All right, make me guess." Jeremiah trudged through the corn stubble toward the edge of the woods. "Is there water where we're going?"

"Like as not."

They walked on and entered the silent forest. They passed through the trees until at last they came to a clearing. There, just as Lem had suspected, were the remnants of an encampment; weathered canvas tents moldering into the ground, a few stray pots and canteens, a blackened fire ring. What commanded the two men's attention most were the bones and human skulls scattered around the clearing.

Jeremiah picked up a knapsack. "USA," he said. "Lem, is this the same Yankee camp where we were last summer?"

"I reckon it is."

"And they just left all these bodies laying here?"

"Or animals dug them up."

Lem walked away from the clearing, heading in the direction he remembered from a few months before, apprehensive about what he might find but needing to see.

He saw the skeleton of the horse first, a few shreds of dried flesh and hairy hide still clinging to the white bones. There was the skull, shattered by his bullet. He crouched down, looking for the lead ball, but didn't find it.

Reluctantly, he looked to the side, to the thicket, and his heart sank to see the remains of the Yankee officer. His clothing had been reduced to scraps of blue and white cloth and dull brass buttons by foraging animals. His skeleton had been dismembered below the waist, some of the leg bones carried off, but his torso, arms, and head remained intact. His skull tipped to the side, jaw sagging, eyes hollow sockets. The bones were mostly picked clean.

Jeremiah came up behind him. "Is that him? That Yankee officer you told me about?"

Lem nodded. "I wonder if his wife ever got my letter. I couldn't tell her much about where to find her husband's body. I would write to her again, but I can't remember her name or the town. What a terrible thing, him just left to rot away like this."

"You did all you could."

"I wish we could bury him now."

"We don't have a shovel. And we ought to find water and get back. But … should we say a prayer or something?"

"I wish Preacher was here. I don't know what to say."

"Maybe there's something in this little book." Jeremiah took out his pamphlet and leafed through it. "Well, we don't know if he swore, but he prob'ly did some other kind of sinning, so maybe it'll do."

They took their hats off and Jeremiah read, "'Soldier, are you a prodigal son of our great and good Father in Heaven? Then, arise and return to him. Make confession, vow to conquer your sins and end the pern-, pern-, pernicious habit of swearing, and let your lips express only praise to him. Assuredly, he will meet and embrace you; put the robe of righteousness upon you; and there shall be joy in the presence of God, as well as in your heart.'"

They said Amen and stood in uncertain but respectful silence for a few moments. Then Lem said, "Rest in peace." And they put their hats back on and went back through the woods in search of water.

DECEMBER 15 FOUND the 37th camped on farmland east of Knoxville. Lem and Jeremiah yearned to take the short trip into the mountains to see their families, but furloughs were not being granted. That didn't stop many of the soldiers—the ranks of their regiment had grown noticeably thinner as men, starved and disillusioned, deserted. Lem's honor would not allow him to do that, tempting though it was. Also, he had heard that relatives of deserters were often punished by army search parties, sometimes injured or even killed. Nothing would make him risk that for his parents and little sister.

One afternoon, a mule-drawn wagon rattled up with sacks of mail. There was a package for Lem containing a letter from his mother and a jacket she had made. He opened it and read her words:

My dearest son,

I hope this letter and Christmas present will reach you. Father and I and Polly pray that you are safe and well and that God will keep you in His care.

Your account of the battle in Kentucky caused us great anxiety to think of you in the midst of such danger. We are relieved beyond words that you and Jeremiah escaped without injury. Dear Son, I can only say that it does not seem a failing to be unable to kill another human being. I have never been able to imagine the gentle boy we raised doing the killing work of a soldier. Do not think for a moment that we judge you harshly, dear, or consider you less than courageous.

Neither Papa nor I would presume to advise you on how to conduct yourself if you should be in future battles. But we do feel bound to say that we hope you will not try to prove yourself brave in a way that leads you to act rashly. You must do your duty, of course, but do not deliberately court danger.

Lem raised his eyes to survey the open field where the regiment was camped. On this warm, sunny afternoon, some of the men were playing a ball game in their shirtsleeves, shouting and laughing, their voices carefree. Beyond the field, the mountains rose in the southeastern distance, purple-gray. Among them was cradled his home. He thought of the psalm he had often heard in church, something about wishing to have the wings of a dove and flying away to be at rest. He could imagine no sweeter or more comforting rest for his troubled spirit than to be in his home, among those who loved him.

Three days after Perryville, he had felt the need to write a long letter to his parents, telling them about what had happened in his first battle and unburdening himself of his shame at his failure of courage. Now, he wondered, did his father really share his mother's acceptance? Or was she just saying that he did, to spare Lem distress?

He turned his attention back to the letter:

Now to happier subjects. Lemuel, I know this jacket is a little short but I could not get more material. I hope it will fit you all right. Louisa asked if she could add something. You will find it inside the left side, to wear near your heart.

He looked under the flap of the jacket and found a small white cross worked in wool, knitted, he guessed. He glanced around and, seeing that nobody was watching, he lifted it to his lips and kissed it, breathing deeply to try to catch a hint of Louisa's floral scent.

He read on:

Louisa showed me the ring that you carved for her and Polly received that fascinating puzzle, with the ball inside the little box and the loose chain links. I found it under Polly's pillow when I straightened her bed the other morning. She misses you so. I can't imagine how you could conceive of and fashion such intricate carvings. You will have to give us a demonstration. Oh how I hope that it may be soon.

Papa and Polly add their dearest love to mine. Jed would too if he could. He whines by the door sometimes and I know he misses you. God protect you and comfort you and strengthen you. Write to us when you can. We will think of you with love on Christmas, as always.

Your devoted Mother

He folded up the letter and put it into the pocket of his broadcloth shirt, something else to keep close to his heart.

CHAPTER 18

BATTLING BANDS

Christmas dinner for the regiment was cornmeal mush and some nearly spoiled fatback, and coffee that was more bitter burned grain than coffee, and a few sips of whiskey from a flask that one of the men passed around.

Amos Brower brought out his harmonica and there was carol singing that started out bashful then gained in strength. Lem and Jeremiah joined in, Lem singing harmony on some of the songs, for which he received some approving thumps on the back.

Then the mood grew reflective.

"Excuse me, Preacher," someone said.

"Yes?" came the quiet voice from somewhere unseen in the darkness.

"Would you kindly bring over your Bible and read us something about Christmas?"

The tall form emerged from the darkness. Virgil Tippin sat down on a stump near the fire. Someone brought out a stub of candle, lit it, stuck it into the hollow top of a bayonet, and held it up to illuminate the pages as Tippin began reading aloud the Christmas story, with the Bible's old-fashioned language that Lem had always found so hard to understand. Tonight, though, Preacher's solemn tones lent a church-like atmosphere to the gathering that Lem found comforting.

When Preacher finished, some of the men sat in silence. Others drifted off to lie down and sleep. Lem suddenly felt a strong impulse to write to his father. He wrapped himself in his blanket and sat near the fire, and he thrust the bayonet that still held an inch or so of candle down into the not-yet-frozen earth. He took a piece of paper and a stub of pencil from his haversack and sharpened the pencil to a point with his knife. Then he began to write:

Dear Father,

I have not wrote to just you before so you will probly be Suprised to get this letter. But it is Christmas Eve and my Heart is heavy with thoughts of how I have disapointed you as your son. I wanted to write and try to make things Right between us. If this War spares me to come home I Promise to help you however I can.

He sat in thought for a moment. If he'd had another sheet of paper, he might have thrown this one into the fire and started over—he feared he was saying too much and at the same time not saying enough. But he had no more paper, and he didn't want to stop now and lose his nerve. He pushed on:

I always wanted for us to be Frends and do things together. Maybe if I help you more we can. I will try to lighten your Load. For some reason tonight I am recolecting when I was little and cut my Chin so bad. I remember Your face and how scared it looked, but your Words were joking like you didnt want to make me Scared. and then when you had to put the Firewater on the cut I could tell it hurt you to hurt me. After the big Fight we were in at Perryville that I wrote you and Mother about I had to go around picking up our Wounded. I tried to talk to them the same way you talked to me then, to joke a little so they wouldnt know how Bad hurt they were.

Where in the world, he wondered, had that memory come from? He had been about five; he and his brother Caleb were roughhousing in the barn and Lem had fallen down and gashed his chin on a filthy shovel that stood beside the door, used for mucking out the mule's stall. Blood gushed from the wound and Caleb's eyes grew huge, then he turned and ran from the barn shouting, "Paaaaaa! Lem's hurt!"

Jacob came running and when he caught sight of Lem's bloody chin, his face went so white and shocked that Lem, scared, began to cry more. Then his father came over and picked him up, sat down on a hay bale, and held him. He took out his bandanna and carefully daubed at the wound, looking at it closely, and said, "Now, what's there to cry about? It's just a little cut. What'd you hurt yourself on, boy?"

"The shuh—the shovel over yonder," Lem had sobbed, pointing to it, and Jacob looked over at it, and Lem saw a grim set to his father's face as he surveyed the filthy, rusty implement. But the expression that Jacob turned back to him was rearranged into a reassuring smile.

"Well, we're going to have to give that mean old shovel a licking, ain't we? Tell you what. I'm just going to clean you up a little. It'll smart some but you're a big brave boy, ain't you? You set right here while I get me some of the firewater I keep out here."

He went back to the storeroom and came back with a dusty glass bottle full of some clear liquid. Taking Lem back on his knee, he uncorked the bottle. Lem now knew the liquid must have been moonshine. Jacob tilted Lem's head up and poured the firewater liberally into the wound to flush it out. It burned ferociously and Lem howled with pain. Jacob then wetted his handkerchief with the whiskey and pressed it tight against the cut as he rocked Lem and began softly singing. "*Fox went out on a chilly night, prayed for the moon to give him light, for he'd many a mile to go that night before he reached the town-o, the town-o, the town-o, had many a mile to go that night before he reached the town-o.*" He sang several verses as he kept the handkerchief pressed to the wound until the bleeding stopped and Lem gradually calmed. After he sang Lem's favorite verse, the last one, about how the fox family, eating the stolen goose, "*never had such a supper in their life and the little ones chewed on the bones-o, the bones-o, the bones-o,*" Jacob got the mule out of his stall. They rode into town, where old Doc Rabb put some medicine on the cut and stitched it closed while Jacob held Lem and told him what a brave boy he was.

On the way back, his father said, "One thing, son. No need to tell your mama about the firewater. Let's just keep that between us, man to man, all right?"

"Yes, sir," Lem said, proud that the day's ordeal had elevated him to manhood in his father's eyes, though he did not understand why the firewater was such a secret.

The cut healed up fine. The only consequence of the episode was a small scar on the underside of his chin. He fingered it now thoughtfully.

That must have been just before his father's injury changed everything. How strange that he had only now remembered that incident after all these years.

Lem sat for a while longer. The candle burned down and guttered out. By the light of the fire, he put the last words to his letter:

I Pray I will see you again Father and be able to ask your Forgiveness for not being a better son to you. I will try my hardest to be better and do Everything you ask me if the Good Lord lets me come back Home again.

Your son Lemuel

The next day, before he could think better of it, he put the letter into the mailbag.

THEY MARCHED ON, southward. The weather was cold, and a freezing rain pelted the soldiers and soaked through their clothes. Jeremiah had developed an awful cough that kept him, Lem, and everyone nearby up every night. Lem felt sorry for him, but sometimes, desperately tired and craving escape from the horrific images of battle, he had the crazy thought that it was a good thing he had no pillow. Because if he did, he'd be tempted to put it over his friend's face to shut him up.

On December 30, they camped outside of Murfreesboro, joining several other regiments massed there. It was cold and miserable, still drizzling rain, but fires were forbidden because the Yankees were nearby.

That night, borne on the chilly air came the sounds of a band. The soldiers looked at one another in disbelief as they recognized the Yankee songs, "Rally 'Round the Flag" and "Glory, Glory Hallelujah." The music sounded unnervingly near.

Then, from closer by, another band began to play, answering the Yankee one with Rebel tunes like "The Bonnie Blue Flag" and "Dixie." Despite their cold and anxiety, the men smiled as the bands played back and forth, trying to outdo each other in cheerful musical warfare.

Then the Yankee band started to play "Sweet Home." And the Confederate band joined in. Smiles faded, heads lowered. Some voices sang along softly. Huddled, shivering under his blanket, Lem heard a few sniffles.

Soon enough, he knew, the musical accord would turn into the violent clash of battle. It might be that this was to be his last night on earth. If death came, he wondered, would he be brave? Since he had tried to make amends with his father, would God accept him into Heaven?

He reached inside his jacket and fingered the little white cross.

CHAPTER 19

DESTINY AT STONES RIVER

THINKING THAT LEM might welcome a break from his story, Jessie brought her guitar out to their meeting place one evening in late July. She also brought her small tape recorder.

He came to her as she was spreading out the blanket. "Now what-all have you gone and brung?" he asked, as she set down her instrument case and opened it on top of the blanket. "Why it's a git-fiddle. You know how to play that?"

"A little," she said. "I wanted an instrument that was a little more portable than a piano. I thought we could sing together. And look." She took the tape recorder out of a canvas bag. She pressed the record button and spoke a few words, then rewound and played it back. Lem's eyes grew wide.

"It's sort of like a camera for sounds," she said. "Say something, Lem. Talk here." She pointed to the microphone.

"I feel like a fool talking to a little black box," he said. She rewound the tape and played his words back to him and he laughed. "I'll swan."

"This way I'll have your voice with me always." She tuned her guitar. What songs would they both know? She thought hymns might be a safe bet. "I'll bet we still sing some of the hymns you sang in your time. How about 'When I Can Read My Title Clear'?"

"I know that one," he said.

She turned on the tape recorder and started playing and singing. He joined in. His voice was a clear, strong tenor. On the second verse, she began singing harmony while he held the melody perfectly. Their eyes met and held in the intimacy of shared music-making. On the third verse, it was clear that he had forgotten the words. She mouthed them to him, and he picked them up a half-second behind her, which made both of them smile as they sang.

"That was mighty nice," he said when they finished.

She rewound the tape and played the song, and he laughed, shaking his head in disbelief.

"You sing so pretty, turtle dove," he said when she had finished.

"Sing me one, Lem?" She pressed Record on the tape player.

"Well, let me think." He drew himself up to sit and adjusted his blanket around his shoulders. "All right, here's one. My granddaddy used to play this on his banjo."

He closed his eyes, tapped a rhythm with his hand on his thigh, and began singing, "Shady Grove, my little love, Shady Grove I say. Shady Grove, my little love, I'm bound to go away. Cheeks as red as the blooming rose, eyes of the prettiest brown, you are the darling of my heart, stay till the sun goes down …"

She knew the song but didn't attempt to accompany him, just sat watching and listening as he sang in an unaffected tenor with little lifts for emphasis at the ends of the lines. It was the traditional style of Southern mountain singers, and it awed her to hear the authentic music of a bygone time.

When he had finished the song, he said, "It should be 'eyes of the prettiest gray,' but that wouldn't fit the rhyme." He looked at her significantly.

"You have such a nice singing voice."

"Well, I don't know about that, but I always did love singing.

Sometimes in camp while I was working, somebody'd tell me to shut up and I wouldn't have even knowed I was singing. It was just my natural expression."

"Mine, too," she said. "And playing the piano. I can say things in music that I can't say any other way." She put her guitar away and snapped the case shut. She turned off the tape recorder. "I wish I had thought to bring this with me before, so that I could have your whole story to listen to." As she put the machine carefully back into the bag, she thought back over the many nights she had sat beside him, entranced, appalled, and moved as he poured out his tale, as if the telling of it relieved him of a great burden.

"Oh, why would you ever want to hear all that again?" He shook his head, his lips compressed.

"Because it would be a way to keep you with me forever." She could not look at him, feeling near tears. She busied herself with taking out her notebook and pen. "I want to take the names of your family and friends so when I go to my grandmother's I can begin looking for your people. But when I find them—" she decided to say *when*, rather than *if*— "do you want to meet them? To have them see you?"

He pondered this for a moment. "No," he said at last, "I don't believe I do. I don't want to scare them. Or to have them see me this way, all dirty and bloody. No, Jessie, it'll be enough to know they're here and that they know what became of me."

He told her his parents' names, Ruby and Jacob Sanders. His fiancée, Louisa Rabb. His aunts and uncles, and the towns where his relatives lived.

"Then there's my best friend, Jeremiah Walker. I wonder what happened to Jeremiah," he mused, looking suddenly grave. "He was with me … that last day."

She closed the notebook and looked at him. "Do you feel like telling me about it?"

He shrugged. "Why not. I told you everything else."

HE WOKE TO a rustling around him. It was still dark, but the men were silently, urgently moving in the pre-dawn gloom, whispering to one another. "Get up, boys," someone said, hitting Lem's feet. "We're fighting this morning."

Lem and Jeremiah jumped up, gathering their equipment and readying themselves to follow orders.

Just as daylight was beginning to tinge the horizon and filter through the chill mist that shrouded the landscape, a young major said in a low, intense tone, "All right, men, move forward, quiet as you can. Don't let them hear you coming. Give them hell and God be with you."

Their unit fell in behind some others, two long lines of men creeping soundlessly across a field. Jeremiah was convulsed with trying to stifle his coughing in the crook of his arm so as not to give their advance away. Lem's heart was beating so wildly that his vision pulsed bright and dark. *Yea, though I walk through the valley of the shadow of death I will fear no evil for Thou art with me, Thy rod and Thy staff they comfort me*, he prayed silently. He remembered no more of the psalm, just kept mouthing those words over and over.

They passed through a forest, and there was a moment's pause as the front lines halted. Between the men ahead of him, in a clearing past the trees, Lem glimpsed soldiers in a Union camp going about their early morning routines. He could hear the soft murmurs of their conversation. He even caught the strong, enticing scent of their coffee.

Then the nearest Yankees began to laugh and exclaim, "Would you look at all them critters runnin' out of the woods. What's come over them all?"

Then someone else shouted, in a high, alarmed voice, "Rebels, that's what! There's Rebels coming through the woods!"

Then the Confederates burst out of the forest with the ungodly shrieks that were their battle cries.

In the melee that followed, Lem caught only fleeting impressions—a half-dressed man fighting off his attacker with his suspenders looped down around his waist and his pants sagging down over his drawers;

another flinging boiling coffee from the pot on the fire into the face of an advancing Rebel. A late sleeper crawled bleary-eyed out of his tent to see what was going on. His jaw dropped and he popped back inside like a groundhog into its hole. It would have been a comical sight under other circumstances.

Lem grasped the arm of a Yankee who had picked up a log from the fire and was about to strike a Confederate in the back of the head with it. He hooked his foot around the man's leg and toppled him, then tore the canvas cover off a tent and threw it over the man, tangling him up long enough for Lem to escape.

He stayed near Jeremiah as the Confederates ran across an open field away from the Yankee camp, toward the forest. Riflemen from the woods ahead picked off men around Lem, but there were no Yankees visible to shoot back at in retaliation. He kept glancing to his side to make sure his friend was unhurt.

The Rebels entered a thick cedar forest with low-growing branches that snared the soldiers' legs, tripping them. The overgrowth trapped the gun smoke and combined it with the morning mist into a blinding fog. But Lem didn't stumble. His vision seemed to be abnormally sharp so that through the gloom he could see the emerging forms of the enemy. Time, too, seemed to have slowed; he loaded his rifle with no haste, and when a blue-coated soldier jumped from behind a tree, poised to shoot, Lem took aim, pulled the trigger, and felled the man. There was no time to reflect on his first killing of another human being. All he thought was, *Thank you, Granddaddy, for learning me how to shoot to kill clean.*

He felt no panic or even urgency as he ran on through the forest, all the while keeping Jeremiah in view. The same powerful feeling he had experienced on the train had surged up in him once again. He felt invulnerable. He kept shooting with a calm control, more often than not hitting where he aimed. There was no satisfaction in killing, only in knowing that he was at last doing his duty, proving himself to be brave and capable.

The Yankees turned and ran, and Lem and his comrades pursued them out of the treacherous forest and into a cotton field. The dry brown plants still had some blooms on them, and seeing men reach down to grab the puffy white fibers and stuff them into their ears, Lem did the same, slightly muffling the din. From time to time, the enemy soldiers halted in their flight long enough to turn and fire. Though men fell around Lem, the protective shield around him somehow held firm. Jeremiah, too, was unharmed.

The Southerners ran on into another forest into which the Yankees had retreated. Here, huge slabs of rock had heaved up from the earth and lay in regular rows, with deep crevices between them hidden by the engulfing smoke. Glancing around, Lem saw that the soldiers he was now fighting with were strangers. Looking behind him, he was relieved to see that Jeremiah was on his heels. "Poke, where are our boys?" he called.

"I don't know," Jeremiah yelled back.

Preacher suddenly came up beside Lem, rifle held in front of him at the ready. Briefly, he turned his head to give Lem a nod, his keen, pale-gray eyes holding Lem's. Then he refocused his gaze ahead, raised his gun, shot, and reloaded with practiced dexterity.

Lem followed Jeremiah and Preacher up ahead, bounding over the odd, rectangular rocks. Bullets whizzed past him, making a sharp snap as they struck tree trunks. Sheared-off branches cracked and fell with a rustle of leaves and a thud. How was it possible, Lem thought, that none of the bullets or falling limbs were hitting him? Nothing, it seemed, could touch him.

He caught a glimpse of a figure in blue running away. He took aim and shot, but the man did not break stride. Gray daylight appeared through the trees ahead, indicating a clearing. Maybe the Yankees were firing from there.

Suddenly, he heard a shout—Jeremiah's voice. Rushing forward, Lem saw that his friend had fallen and was pulling his leg out of one of the fissures between the rocks.

"Hellfire!" Jeremiah said.

"It's not broke, is it?" Lem drew near, extending his hand and hauling Jeremiah to his feet.

"Nah…" Jeremiah looked up from smoothing down his trouser leg, and his eyes went wide with alarm, fixed on something behind Lem. "Lem! Look out!"

Lem whirled around.

The events of the next few moments unfolded with that same clarity of perception and the sense of time having radically slowed. He saw a Yankee advancing toward the two of them with his bayonet extended. The man was running, and Lem took in every detail of how his shoulders moved forward and backward, and his canteen and cartridge box flopped up and down, and the loose flesh of his thighs quivered beneath his bloodstained trousers with the impact of every step. He saw the soldier's bushy brown whiskers on either side of his inflamed cheeks. The man's mouth was distended into a large open square, with his teeth bared, a wide gap between the two front teeth. He saw the man's eyes—blue eyes, so wide open with murderous rage that the whites were visible all around them. The Yankee's eyes were not fixed on him, however, but on Jeremiah.

There was no time for Lem to reload his gun. "Lord have mercy!" he heard his friend cry as the enemy soldier, some six feet away, drew back his rifle, then with a mighty grunt thrust the bayonet forward with the full force of his body toward Jeremiah's chest.

Lem lunged to the left. The bayonet hit his midsection like a blunt blow.

A humming sound enveloped him as he toppled backward onto one of the rock slabs, his head striking the stone. The deep, sustained chord swelled, drowning out all other sounds, but he dimly perceived violent motion around him. Preacher's face briefly appeared above him. "God bless you, brave son," the older man said, then was gone.

"Lem!" Jeremiah shouted, seemingly from a great distance. "I have to keep on fighting, or I'll get killed. But I'll come back for you. I promise. Wait for me, Lem. Please don't die."

CHAPTER 20

SILENT ANGUISH

HE LAY ON the rock, cold mist sifting down, prickling his face. He could not move, not even to close his eyes, which were open to the gray sky, freezing rain stinging his eyeballs. The furious sounds around him were increasingly muted by the steady deep humming. His thoughts and feelings were muted, too; he knew there was terrible pain somewhere, but it was apart from him, he couldn't feel it now, couldn't feel anything.

A presence enfolded him in a fog that glowed as if burning. The humming intensified, and the deep vibrations gathered and became words heard by Lem's heart rather than his ears: *Be still, be at peace. Come with me now.*

Oh, no, he pleaded wordlessly, desperately, with whoever or whatever it was, *please don't take me yet.* The officer's bones in the Clarksville woods, the men blown to bits—he had to spare his loved ones the agony of uncertainty. He and Jeremiah had their pact, but what if his friend did not survive this hellish slaughter to carry the news to his home?

These thoughts emerged from the gathering darkness in his head; as he tried to grasp them, they slipped away. His vision was failing, the humming growing fainter. With all his strength, he made one last effort to communicate with the luminous presence surrounding him. *Just let*

144

me stay till I'm sure my family—my sweetheart—know what happened to me and where to find me.

The flaming fog dispersed then. He was left alone on the cold rock in the pitiless rain. At last, his spirit disengaged from his body, and he felt nothing more.

JESSIE COULD NOT speak for a long time. Finally, she asked, "Lem, who was that who came to you?"

"I can't rightly say."

"Was it the Lord?"

"I thought it might be. Or maybe one of his angels. Unless I was dreaming. It felt just as real. And so did what happened next. But I can't swear I didn't just imagine it."

"Tell me."

He was silent for a moment. "For a time after that angel or whoever it was left me, I didn't know or feel anything. Then, somehow, I woke up. And I was at my home! It was dark, I was in the side yard of our cabin, near the corncrib. I can't tell you how in the world I got there. Then I saw my dog, Jed. Oh, I was so happy to see him! I loved that dog. I walked toward him. But instead of how he would always run to me and jump up and wag his whole body, he backed away and growled deep in his throat, and the hair was standing up all over his back.

"I tried to say to him, 'Don't you know me, boy? It's Lem.' But no words would come out. He stood his ground and began to bark at me. Then I thought to look down at myself, and I could see what scared him so. All that blood, that terrible wound on my stomach.

"And then, out of the house came Mama. She had a shawl wrapped around her nightdress and a pair of Pa's old shoes a-flopping on her feet. She said, 'Jed, hush! What in the world has got into you?' And then she looked up and saw me.

"She stood still, like she had turned to stone. She stayed that way for

I don't know how long. I couldn't say anything to her. My heart hurt for her, and all I could do was look at her and hope my face showed how much I loved her and how sorry I was to scare her.

"Then she sort of groaned, 'No, no,' and turned right around and hurried back into the house. And I departed from there. I honestly don't know how, only I was home one minute, and back laying on the rock in the woods in the dark the next."

"Who buried you?" Jessie asked, brushing tears from her eyes.

"Jeremiah and some fellows I didn't know," he said. "I think it was the next day. They drug us out of the woods and dug a grave for me and the other boys who got killed. There were about seven of us. One of them was Preacher."

"Oh, no!" Jessie cried, as shocked and saddened as if she had known the older man.

Lem nodded, his expression solemn. "My spirit saw them digging that grave and putting us down in there. Jeremiah had my blanket with him, and he wrapped my body in it. This blanket, here." He touched its edge where it lay over his shoulder. "He sure could have used it himself, to try to keep warm—he had that terrible cough, like I told you. But instead, he rolled me up in it and I heard him crying as he shoveled the dirt over me. I felt so bad for him. I don't know why I couldn't make my spirit appear to him then, but I couldn't."

"So Jeremiah never told your parents what happened to you," Jessie said.

"I reckon not," Lem said. "Nobody ever came here, at least. It made me think something must have happened to him. We made us a solemn vow."

Jessie was struggling with a new thought. "Lem, if you had gone to Heaven with the angel or whoever that was, you would have seen your family and your sweetheart when they passed into the next life. You could have been with them maybe more than a hundred years sooner than waiting all this time."

"That's sure enough true," he acknowledged. "But like I told you when we first met, I didn't have any sense of time passing. And anyway, it wasn't just for my folks that I stayed. How would Preacher's people ever know what happened to him? And the other boys laying here with us? Maybe they'd have a letter or a picture or some piece of paper in their pocket or sewed into their clothes that would tell who they were, so when their bodies got found their kinfolks could know. They could bring them home and bury them proper. It was for them I stayed too."

She looked at him, her throat aching with emotion. "I've been so selfish."

"What do you mean?"

"Here I've been stretching out our times together as long as I can, because I wanted to be with you. But you need me to find your family so you can go to your rest."

"It's not selfish, Jessie. I wanted to be with you too."

"This is no existence for you. Stuck here between the earth and Heaven. I don't want you to have to stay like this anymore. Even though it will mean losing you." She bit her lower lip to keep it from trembling.

"You know," he said, looking off into the distance, "it won't, really. We'll be together again in eternity."

"Eternity is so far away. I can't stand the thought of having to live all that time without you." She put her face in her hands.

A motion of electric warmth eddied around her shoulders, and she knew that he was trying to put his arms around her. Small shocks tingled on her cheek, stirred her hair—his kisses? A vibration, like the lowest bass note of an organ, resonated throughout her body, deeper than mere hearing.

"Stop your crying, darlin'," he said gently. "Hush now."

She drew a deep breath and straightened up, looking into his eyes. His face was very near hers, his gaze tender.

"I don't have to leave you yet, now, do I?" he said, as if soothing a small child.

"No, not just yet." She wiped her eyes with the sleeve of her blouse. They sat for a while, close together, watching the fireflies stitch the darkness with pricks of light.

It was after midnight. With great reluctance she stood up, and he rose too. "I'll go now," she told him.

"Good night, turtle dove."

"Good night, Lem."

"I sure do love you."

"I love you too." It was the first time she had heard those words from a man—or said them herself to anyone except her family. She turned so that he would not see her crying again and walked away without looking back.

HOME IN HER APARTMENT, she took out the tape recorder and rewound the tape. She pushed "Play."

All she heard was her own voice—speaking, singing, laughing—over a low, pulsating drone that sounded like the laboring mechanism of the machine.

She laid her head down on her folded arms.

CHAPTER 21

CONFESSION

JESSIE UNLOCKED THE door to the administrative building of the Pine Bridge Church. It was six-thirty on a Friday evening and the secretary had gone home. The main office and the long hallway that led to Pastor John Brinton's study were dark. She approached the minister's brightly lit doorway and saw him sitting at his computer, his back to her. He hadn't heard her; she could still turn and leave, texting him with an apology about a last-minute conflict.

She forced herself to tap on the doorframe.

He turned in his chair. "Come on in, Jessie." He stood and came around his desk as she entered. A tall man who habitually stooped, seemingly in an effort not to intimidate people shorter than he—which was just about everyone—he had a broad, mild face and thinning brown hair. Sloping shoulders, a slight potbelly, and hands and feet that seemed disproportionately small for his height made him look even more benign.

Jessie had grown up with him as her pastor and had never known him to be anything other than tolerant and kind. What she was about to tell him would surely test that tolerance. Her hands were clammy, and her heart was racing.

"Thanks for seeing me tonight," she began. She had called him that morning and told him she had something urgent that she needed to talk with him about. Now, at his invitation, she sat facing him in one of two armchairs in front of his desk and tried to think of how to begin. Her fingers worried at the brass nailheads around the edge of the leather armrest.

He sat in the other chair, crossed his legs, and rested his clasped hands on his knee. The gold of his wedding band gleamed in the light from the recessed fixtures in the ceiling. "How can I help you?" he asked. "You sounded upset this morning."

"It's going to be hard to explain …"

"Take your time," he said.

She fixed her eyes on the photograph on the bookcase behind his desk, the church directory portrait of himself with his wife and two young sons. So conventional, so thoroughly of this world. "I'm in love with someone I can't have."

He nodded, his receptive expression unchanged. "Someone married?"

"No." She sighed. "It'll be easier, I think, if I tell you the whole story, from the beginning." Drawing a deep breath, she told him about meeting Lem in the woods, the instant rapport she felt with him, her return to see him the following evening.

"On the morning we had to leave, I went to say goodbye to him, hoping he'd want to get together again. It was raining hard. It was the first time I'd seen him in broad daylight and he looked very pale, in fact really sick. Then I noticed something else. The rain was soaking my clothes, but he was staying completely dry.

"I got scared and asked him what was going on. He told me then that he was the spirit of a soldier who was killed in the Battle of Stones River in 1862 and buried right there on that spot, with six other Rebels."

Apprehensive, a little breathless, she glanced up at Pastor John for the first time since she had begun telling her story. "Go on, Jessie," he said in a quiet, encouraging tone. She did notice that a worried-looking crease had appeared between his eyebrows.

"I began to feel faint, and he stepped forward to help me. The blanket he had kept closed around himself fell open and I saw a huge bloody gash in his stomach. I turned and ran away." She paused as the gold clock on the minister's bookshelf chimed the hour with seven melodious dings. "I was terrified," she went on at last. "But something drew me back to him a couple of days later. I felt sorry for him, for one thing. He had to be lonely, waiting there all that time. I wondered why he couldn't just rest in peace, like the other men buried in that place. But mainly, with him I felt something I'd never felt with a man before." Heat rose up her neck and into her cheeks. "I felt admired, and… wanted."

She couldn't meet the pastor's gaze and rushed on. "Lem told me he'd seen or heard about so many soldiers just disappearing in the war, either being blown to bits, or buried in unmarked graves. He couldn't stand to think his family might never know what happened to him. And that the families of the men buried with him would never know, either.

"So he's been waiting for someone who'll find his people and tell them that he died and where he's buried. He was shocked when I told him 144 years have passed, but that didn't—doesn't—make any difference. He also wants the grave to be made known and the men in it given a proper blessing. Then he'll feel free to leave this world and go to… the next."

"Good heavens." Pastor John's face was drawn in a troubled frown.

"I've told him that I'll help him," she said. "As it turns out, he comes from near where my mother's mother lives, up in East Tennessee. So it might not be too hard to track his family down, the way people stay put up there. But everything in me wants not to, because if I do, he'll be gone and I'll be alone again." The tears that she had been fighting spilled from her eyes. "I've been so lonely. My life has felt stuck, musically, romantically. When I met him, it was like a door opening, and I had to go through it."

Pastor John was looking at her, his gaze now compassionate. However, the crease of concern had deepened between his brows.

"Do you believe me?" she asked him.

He replied slowly, obviously choosing his words with care. "I haven't had any experience of such… manifestations myself. It wasn't a subject we covered in seminary." Looking down at a silver pen he was turning in his fingers, he asked, "Has the relationship been physical?"

"No," she said. "The few times we've tried to touch, there's just this strange prickling sensation where his body appears to be and a deep vibration of sound."

Pastor John sat back in his chair, shaking his head. "I'm mystified, Jessie. I honestly don't know what to make of your story. Do you think you could benefit from talking with a good counselor? I know an excellent Christian therapist."

Jessie felt a flash of anger. "Pastor John, I don't need a shrink. I promise you I haven't imagined all this. I'm not having some kind of mental breakdown. I thought you knew me better than that."

He nodded. "Yes, I've always known you to be sensible, well-grounded. But there's another thing. I want to be sure you're not putting yourself in spiritual danger."

"That did occur to me," she admitted. "I read some articles online about what the Bible says about ghosts and spirits, and some of them said they're just tricks of the devil. I promise you, in all the time I've spent with him, Lem has seemed nothing but good, and he's concerned for me. And concerned for his family and for the other men."

Pastor John sat in silence for a moment, looking at the floor, apparently pondering. "Jessie, would you be able to take me to him? I can't feel confident I'm giving you sound advice until I've actually seen him."

She hadn't been prepared for this. Her initial response was to balk, to stall. "When … when would you want to go?"

"As soon as possible. How about right now?"

Jessie was still hesitant, apprehensive—of what, exactly, she couldn't say. She began throwing out objections. "Are you sure you want to? It's raining. And do you have time?"

"Yes, I have time, and yes, I'm sure."

"All right." Her heart felt motionless and heavy.

"Let's pray."

She bowed her head as Pastor John asked God's guidance and protection—she noticed that word—for them both.

A FINE RAIN was sifting down as Jessie and the minister approached the forest clearing. Jessie held her umbrella over herself and Pastor John. She was shaking, fearful of the encounter about to occur, but even more fearful that it might not happen, thus revealing to both her and the pastor that she truly was unhinged.

"Lem?" she called softly.

He emerged from the darkness between the trees. She heard Pastor John draw in his breath.

"Oh!" said Lem, hesitating. "Jessie, I wasn't expecting you to have somebody with you."

"Lem, it's all right," she said, moving nearer to him. "This is my pastor, Reverend John Brinton. I told him about you. He wants to say a prayer with you now."

"Well, thank you, Reverend. That's right kind of you." Lem removed his hat and held it down by his side. Jessie noticed that he had drawn the two sides of his blanket together to conceal from the minister the wound in his abdomen, just as he had in their first times together. As always, even though he stood in the rain, he didn't get wet.

"Lem," said Pastor John, "Jessie has told me your story. I want to do everything I can to help you find peace."

"Thank you, sir." Jessie was struck by the contrast between Lem's present solemn courtesy, the same he had shown to her in their first encounters, and the range of uninhibited emotions—humor, wonder, anger, sorrow, tenderness—that she had been privileged to come to know in him over the past several weeks. At this reminder of how deep their intimacy had grown, she felt both proud and anguished at the thought of having to give it up.

"I'm going away for a time," Jessie told Lem. "To stay with my grandmother in Sevier County and try to find your family. So you won't see me for a while."

"Time doesn't mean much to me," Lem said to her. "I can wait as long as it takes."

"May I say a prayer with you now?" Pastor John asked, taking his Bible out from under his rain jacket. Jessie moved her umbrella over his head. She noticed that the book trembled in his hands.

"I'd be obliged if you would, sir."

The pastor drew a penlight from his pocket and held it in his mouth as he leafed through the Bible until he found the passage he was looking for. Jessie saw Lem glance at the small flashlight with keen interest.

Pastor John took the light in his hand again and shone it on the page. "Hear God's holy word."

Lem and Jessie bowed their heads.

Pastor John read from the book of John, the account of Jesus promising that those who believe in him will have eternal life, and that even the dead will be restored to life. When he finished reading, he closed his Bible and said, "The Word of the Lord," and Jessie and Lem murmured, "Amen."

"Let us pray." Pastor John stepped closer to Lem and moved to put his hand on the young man's shoulder. Jessie glanced up at him and saw the minister flinch a little as he encountered only tingling where substance appeared to be. Lem kept his head bowed.

Pastor John prayed in a quiet voice, asking God to make the search for Lem's family a quick and successful one so that he could go to his eternal reward, and so that his family and those of the men buried with him could have certainty at last. "We ask for your blessing, too, on Jessie," he went on. "Give her the strength to do what needs to be done for this man she loves."

"Amen," Lem and Jessie said again.

"Thank you, Reverend," Lem added.

"God bless you, Lemuel." Pastor John left them, his flashlight bobbing through the darkness.

"You told him you love me," Lem said to Jessie. His eyes seemed to shine with a light brighter than the faint illumination suspended in the damp gray gloom around them.

"Yes," she said. "I always tell him the truth."

"Did you tell him I love you?" His voice was low and tender.

"Yes." Jessie was almost too exhausted to form the word. She could hardly imagine how she would have the strength to walk all the way back to the car.

"Jessie," Lem said, "I like to think that was our wedding, that the parson blessed us as husband and wife."

A low moan tore out of Jessie's throat. She turned and fled through the darkness toward the bobbing gleam of Pastor John's flashlight, hearing Lem calling her name.

SHE CAUGHT UP with the minister.

"Thank you for trusting me enough to share this with me," he said. "I confess I feel shaken, and confused, and a little afraid. But the one thing I'm sure of is that he needs to go home to the Lord."

"So you don't think he's a demonic presence?"

"I didn't get any feeling of evil from him. In fact, he seemed like a good and sincere young man. But I can't be sure of anything, Jessie. As I said, I've never even heard of, much less directly experienced, a situation like this."

She had never seen him so troubled. Anxiety coiled in her chest.

They drove back to the church in silence. Jessie pulled into the parking lot and stopped the van near the pastor's car. A fine mist of rain swirled around the streetlamp above them.

Pastor John didn't move at once to leave the van. Jessie looked at him.

"You've been through a lot recently, haven't you?" he said, meeting her gaze.

"Yes." With that realization, something deep inside her gave way, and tears stung her eyes. For all the joy of her time with Lem, it had been a huge strain too—the late nights, the keeping of such a strange secret.

Pastor John turned his head to look out the front window. "The other day, something reminded me of you when you were little," he said, his tone lighter. "You were maybe age eight. You had those long pigtails bouncing down your back as you walked up the aisle to the piano to play for the congregation for the first time. You sat down with your feet swinging off the bench because you couldn't reach the pedals. And in front of a hundred grown-ups, you started to play, and I was just floored by your focus and the assurance of your playing. How brave you were."

Jessie shook her head. "Thank you for that, but I don't think I'm brave. Lem was. He died protecting his best friend. I hoped some of his courage would rub off on me." She found that she was gripping the steering wheel as though on an icy road. She relaxed her stiff hands and set them in her lap. "But I can't imagine how I'll do what he needs me to do." She gave a short, mirthless laugh, shaking her head. "I can't even figure out how to manage my own life!"

"Don't sell yourself short, Jessie," he said. "You've achieved a lot. And bravery is something we have to work all our lives to develop, as each new test comes along. We build our courage by always trying to do the right thing. I've found that the right things are usually the hardest things, the things we least want to do. But God gives us the strength. And when we are aligned with his will, miraculous things happen. Different, maybe, from what we wanted or expected. But always better."

She drew a deep breath. "I think what you're getting at is that I shouldn't see Lem anymore."

"Yes, I do feel that, very strongly. He needs to go to his rest. And you need to look for the door in *this* world that will lead to your happiness."

She could not speak for a moment.

"Go to the Smokies," he said. "Find his people."

JESSIE WOKE AT DAWN the next morning, still exhausted but unable to prolong the restless sleep she had managed to sustain for a few hours. She got up and padded barefoot into the kitchen, fixed a cup of tea, and carried it through the living room to the doorway that led out onto a small balcony.

She gazed out over the rear of the apartment complex which faced eastward over a grassy lawn and rolling farmland beyond the chain-link fence that marked the boundary of the property. A dense fog from the previous night's rain hung over the pastures. The sun's first rays streamed through a stand of trees. Birds sent up a morning chorus. It was a peaceful view, but there was no peace in her heart or her mind, which roiled with questions.

She knew she had to heed Pastor John's urging to go to East Tennessee as soon as possible to look for Lem's relatives. But if she did manage to find them, what in the world would she say to them? "Hi, you don't know me, but I know where your long-lost relative was killed in the Civil War and buried in an unmarked mass grave. No, I don't have any proof, you'll just have to take my word for it."

They would think she was insane.

She couldn't possibly tell them about her meetings with Lem. And he didn't want her to bring them to see him "all dirty and bloody the way I am."

If she didn't manage to find his family, then what would become of him? She felt sure that he would not abandon the purpose he believed in so strongly, not only for his sake but also for that of the other men. What would that mean for her? How could she go on with her life—much less find love with a living man—knowing that Lem was still, in effect, in the world?

And now her most trusted advisor had just told her, in no uncertain terms, that for Lem's and her own good, she had to give him up.

The sun touched and warmed her closed eyelids. She sat in contemplation that was wordless except for one phrase, repeated over and over.

"God, help me."

PART III

THE SEEKER

CHAPTER 22

DEAD LETTER

JESSIE SAT AT the church piano, playing through the hymns for the following Sunday. The evening was dark and wet; thunder rumbled in the distance. In a moment's pause between pieces, she closed her eyes and heard, through the open window, rain gurgling in the gutters and drumming on the ground. She envisioned the rain splashing on the large stone in the center of the glade in the forest, the heavy drops pattering on the leaves in the woods and passing through or around the ethereal form of the sentinel watching among the trees.

She planned to leave for her grandmother's the following afternoon, after work. Time was growing short; there was only a week left before she had to report to school for faculty meetings, and in two weeks she would be teaching again. She would spend the week in Caton's Forge searching out every possible lead for the Sanders family or people with the other names Lem had given her. Then, when she saw Lem—she had to see him, one last time, to bid him goodbye—she would either have happy news for him or be forced to tell him her best efforts had failed.

Noise and commotion at the front of the church broke her reverie. Ben and Pete DiSpirito came in, Pete carrying a dripping umbrella and Ben wearing a hooded black windbreaker shining with rain, his trumpet case in his hand.

While Ben took his instrument out and went to the front of the sanctuary to warm up, Pete came over to the piano, carrying a worn leather briefcase. He opened it, took out a musical score, and handed it to Jessie. It was the Haydn Trumpet Concerto, arranged for piano. "Ben's trumpet teacher suggested the first movement for the audition," he said.

Jessie leafed through it.

"Seem okay?" Pete asked.

"Fine," she said, "though just a tad more challenging than 'The Bonnie Blue Flag' or 'Lorena.'"

He laughed. "I can imagine. It'll be nice to hear you on a classical piece." He sat down in the front pew.

Ben walked up the aisle, holding his shiny silver trumpet. When Jessie suggested they read through the first movement, Ben nodded and opened his music on the stand that Jessie had set beside the piano. He raised his horn and played a few warm-up notes, then shook his hair out of his eyes and looked at her. He seemed jittery.

"Ready?" She poised her fingers on the keyboard and began to play the introductory bars, taking the tempo a little slower than the score called for because she was sight-reading.

Ben cracked his first notes but gained confidence as he continued. His sound was strong and centered. Pete sat with his eyes closed.

For the next hour and a half, they read through the piece, stopping to go over specific passages. It felt wonderful to collaborate with a talented musician on sophisticated music, something she hadn't had the chance to do since leaving the University of Tennessee.

The time sped by, and when Jessie thought to look at her watch, she was surprised that it was nine o'clock. "I guess we should quit for the night," she said with regret. "I'm really enjoying playing with you."

"Thanks," Ben said. "Same here."

"You both sounded fantastic," Pete said. "A completely unbiased view, of course."

Ben packed up. He thanked Jessie and told his father he would meet him at the car.

Pete handed Jessie three twenties. "I asked Ben's trumpet teacher, Dwayne Stringer, what he gets for a lesson, and this is what he told me."

"Oh, too much!" Jessie said. "He's first trumpet in the Nashville Symphony, and I'm just a church musician."

Pete looked at her with a quizzical smile. "Why do you always put yourself down?"

"Do I?" She waved a hand, making light of it.

"You do. According to you, you never get a date, and you're just a little church mouse."

She gave an embarrassed laugh and looked away.

"Have more confidence, Jess. Anyway, if you don't think this payment is too little, let's make it our rate. Shall we do this again next week, same time, same place?"

Jessie agreed, but added, "I do have to go up to East Tennessee for the next few days to take care of some family business. If it's going to take longer than a week, I'll call you."

"Would it be okay with you if I brought Andie one time?" Pete asked. "I know she'd love to hear you and Ben."

"Of course, Pete. She's welcome anytime. I'd like to get to know her."

He turned abruptly, picked up his briefcase, and snapped it closed. "So! We're off," he said. His eyes met hers and she glimpsed pain in them, momentarily unveiled.

JESSIE WAS AT WORK the next morning when her cell phone rang. "Middle Tenn St," the caller ID read.

"Hello?" She expected to hear Becky DePew's voice, but instead it was an unfamiliar man who asked, "Is this Jessie Gibbs?"

"Yes."

"This is Dr. Philip Goldsmith from Middle Tennessee State University. I'm a colleague of Becky DePew."

"Oh, yes. She's mentioned you to me," Jessie said. "You're writing a book about Stones River, right?"

"That's right. I have something that might interest you. Becky said that you asked her about a certain soldier who fought in that battle. As it happens, I have some documentation, a letter, that refers to that man, Lemuel Sanders."

Jessie squeezed her eyes shut as her heart gave a lurch. "Oh? I'd like to see that. He's the relative of some… friends of my family"—she couldn't exactly remember the details of the story she had told Becky, but pushed on—"and they're trying to find out what happened to him."

"The letter describes his death, on December 31, 1862. I'll be glad to send you a copy."

She wondered who the writer was, and if she could bear to read it. "Dr. Goldsmith, would it be possible for me to get it right away? I'll be seeing his relatives in the next few days." Or so she hoped.

He said he could meet her that evening and give her a copy. She had planned to leave for her grandmother's that afternoon, but this, of course, trumped everything. They arranged to meet at five at a restaurant near the MTSU campus.

PHILIP GOLDSMITH STOOD as she approached his table at Applebee's. He was a stocky man of about fifty, balding, his remaining hair thin and dark brown. He wore black jeans and a denim work shirt with a bolo tie, its clasp a hammered silver arrowhead set with a turquoise stone.

"Dr. Goldsmith?"

"Ms. Gibbs."

"Please, call me Jessie."

He didn't make a reciprocal offer, but she wasn't surprised by that, being so much younger. She saw him swiftly sum her up, head to toe, then he extended his hand and shook hers, his grasp surprisingly limp. She sat down opposite him.

"Thank you for taking the time to meet me," she began. The waitress came over and Jessie ordered a diet soda. Her heart was pounding, and she hoped she was doing a decent job of hiding the agitation that was making her feel almost faint. "How did you find the letter?"

"I was giving a talk last fall at the library in Franklin, on letters of Tennessee's Civil War soldiers." Jessie noticed he had no Southern accent; his flat vowels suggested a Midwestern background. "I have a book coming out on the subject this fall."

She tried to arrange her face to express both interest and calm receptivity. When the waitress set down the drink in front of her, she gratefully lifted the glass and took a sip.

"After the presentation," he continued, "an old gent came up to me carrying an antique-looking black, oiled-canvas haversack. He told me that it had been in his attic ever since he could remember, and he hadn't known what to do with it. He asked me to look it over and let him know if it had any value."

"What was in it?"

"A knife, and a square of nearly decayed cotton—probably a bandanna or handkerchief. It has some dark stains on it that may very well be bloodstains. Some kernels of corn. And an envelope with the letter inside that was apparently never mailed. It was still sealed. I gave the guy a hundred bucks for it all. He was happy with that." He handed her a manila envelope. "Here's the copy."

Jessie thanked him, took the envelope from him, and opened it. She drew out four sheets of paper. The first page was a copy of an envelope addressed in a bold slanting hand to Mr. and Mrs. Horace Walker, Beulah, Tennessee. She let her eyes roam, unseeing, over the pages of close, dark handwriting, trying to control the shaking of her hands. When she got to the signature on the last page, "Your son Jeremiah," she realized with a shock that the writer of this letter was Lem's best friend, Jeremiah Walker.

"Oh!" she cried softly.

"What is it?" Dr. Goldsmith asked.

"Nothing, sorry—I misread his writing." It was useless to try to read the document here, in the professor's presence, with her heart racing so fast she felt faint. She focused on keeping her hands steady as she put the pages back into the manila envelope. "Thank you for this. Lemuel Sanders' relatives will be very happy to get it."

"I went looking for the gravesite, based on Jeremiah's description," he said. "But with nearly a century and a half of overgrowth, I couldn't spot any of the landmarks he mentioned."

As they finished their drinks, they chatted about his research. He was obviously interested in talking about himself. She tried to tell him about her work with the band and as camp cook, but he said dismissively, "It would have been extremely unlikely to find respectable civilian females working as cooks in military camps. By and large, only women of ill repute were camp followers."

"But sometimes officers brought their families along, didn't they?"

"Rarely. But yes, sometimes."

"Well, on that one point maybe we stretch the facts, but we try to be accurate in everything else." She was annoyed by his pedantry, and anxious to get home and read the letter.

Dr. Goldsmith gave a perfunctory nod. Then he sat back, looked around the room, and signaled to the waitress. "Oh, one more thing," he said. "I did some research to try to find out what happened to Jeremiah Walker."

He had her complete attention again. "Did you learn anything?"

"Yes, he was captured at Stones River on January 2 and died of pneumonia in a Yankee prison camp."

"God!" The word burst from her before she could stop herself. "Did *anybody* survive that awful war?" She fought to hide the emotion that this news roused. Lem's stories of his wry, feisty, loyal boyhood friend "Poke" had made her care for him. But even more upsetting was the thought that Lem's self-sacrifice to save his friend had been for nothing.

"More than half the men who fought died," said Dr. Goldsmith, seeming mercifully oblivious to her distress. "Estimates range from

620,000 to 750,000 total on both sides. That was about two percent of the entire population of the country at that time. An equivalent number today would be around six million. One out of every five Confederate soldiers died. More died from disease than in battle." He rattled off these dire statistics matter-of-factly.

When the waitress brought the check, Jessie, having regained her composure, paid for both of them, and asked Goldsmith for his email address. He gave her a business card.

Back at home, she fixed herself a cup of strong tea and lit a candle on the dining table to create a solemn atmosphere. She opened the manila envelope, drew out the sheets, and steeled herself to begin reading:

January 1, 1863

Dear Mother and Father,

I take up my pen to write to you with a hevy heart. We just came through a dredful Battle near the Stone's River in Murfreesboro. I feel bound to write to you about this battle even though it will greve you, because it took the life of my Best friend Lemuel Sanders. Mother and Father, Lem died for me. He stepped rite in front of me and took a Yankee bayanet in his Stomack that was ment for me. I killed that Yankee. I'm not sory about it and may God forgive me.

The fiting was Hot so I had to go on and leave Lem there. We were ordered to go back today to find our dead Rebels and bury them. The Ground was muddy and it was frezing cold but we tried our best to give our Boys a decent berial. I think I was the only one of the Grave diggers who knew one of the dead men, two in fact as a man we called Preacher also died near Lem. There were seven of them alaying in that place. I wrapped Lem up in his blanket and layed him in the Trench with all the others. There arnt words to tell how it felt to do that with Somebody who was like my own Brother.

*I will tell you how to reckonize the Place if you or the Sanders
ever want to try to find it and I am not around to take you there.
It is probly a quarter to a half mile West of the Railroad tracks to
Nashville. I reckon It is about two miles north of the Triune Road
where we started our Attack on Dec 31. It is in a clearing past a
woods with huge flat rocks in reglar rows with big gaps between them.
We dug up a big old Stone and rolled it out of the woods to mark the
Grave in the clearing so it would be easy to find, also to keep animals
away. On one side of that Clearing is a part of a snake rail fence.*

*I wanted to be sure to write down these directions even tho they will
be probly be hard to follow because I promised Lem that I would let
his Peple know if he died where he was beried. We promised each
Other that. You will tell them, I know. I am so tired and cold and
my Chest hurts something terible. I will lay down and hope that sleep
stops these awful Thouts and pictures. Tell Mr and Mrs Sanders that
Lem died a Heros death. Especilly tell Mr Sanders.*

Your son Jeremiah

Jessie held the letter, tears running down her face.

The blood on the bandanna in Jeremiah's haversack—it was possible,
even likely, that it was Lem's blood.

She wondered if, when Jeremiah was captured, some soldier-ancestor
of the old gent at the Franklin library grabbed up his haversack and kept
it. Certainly, Jeremiah's parents never received this letter and so were
never able to tell the Sanderses about their son's fate. And now she knew
that Jeremiah never made it home to tell them himself.

The realization slowly broke upon her that this letter was exactly
what she needed to show Lem's family, if she could ever manage to find
them.

CHAPTER 23

THE INDIFFERENCE OF STRANGERS

JESSIE'S MATERNAL GRANDMOTHER, Constance Garner Marshall—called "Ganny" by her grandchildren—lived in an old cabin made of dark logs unevenly hewn and chinked with crumbling gray cement. The house had been a hunting and fishing retreat for her businessman husband and his friends from Knoxville; Ganny came along on those outings to do the cooking and housekeeping for the men. Jessie knew now how much work that must have been and understood it when her grandmother said that she liked living alone now and "not having to do for anybody." After Papaw died, Ganny sold the Knoxville house and moved down to Caton's Forge full-time.

Ganny had grown up in this town, the youngest child of twelve, her father a doctor. Once, she had taken Jessie to see where the family's old homeplace had stood on a bend in the Little Pigeon River, and Jessie was chagrined to see that the site now held a Hot Rod Museum, and beside it, a shabby white bungalow with a heart-shaped neon sign advertising it as "Chapel of Love Weddings 24 Hours Minister on Call."

Ganny's eleven acres of mountainside property remained unspoiled, far from the amusement parks, outlet malls, motels, and chapels of love that had turned this part of the Smoky Mountains into a garish tourist mecca. The land was wooded and hilly, veined with brooks and streams that ran down from the mountains and fed a large pond where Jessie and her grandmother had often fished. Ganny liked living simply, in harmony with the natural world. She spent much of her time outdoors, tending a vegetable garden, feeding "her birds," and chopping back the vines and bushes that threatened to engulf her small yard.

Jessie often came up to the mountains alone to spend a few days with Ganny, and they were content to pass their time reading, cooking together, and taking drives to marvel at the scenery which never lost its fascination for either of them. Ganny taught Jessie how to knit, crochet, and sew, skills that had saved Jessie a lot of money in being able to make her own Civil War clothing.

Jessie found her grandmother a restful, calm companion, and more than that, she always felt from Ganny a deep understanding that required few words, or none at all. Now more than ever, Jessie needed that.

As she turned into the driveway and approached the house, announcing her arrival with a little beep of her horn, Ganny came out, wearing one of the pastel shirtwaist dresses she favored for most everyday activities. Jessie had never seen her grandmother in pants. Ganny's tanned, shapely, but slightly knock-kneed legs were bare and she wore red, lace-up US Keds, her preferred footwear. Her white hair was restrained, as always, in a net—this one had little multicolored beads woven among its gray strands. Her sun-spotted, wrinkled face was beaming as she came over to the car and grappled Jessie in one of her breath-defying hugs, then held her a little away from her, gripping her shoulders with strong hands.

"A-law, honey, let me look at you," Ganny said. "Why, you just get prettier all the time. I'm so proud of my namesake." Jessie's full name was Jessamyn Constance Gibbs.

"Come on inside," Ganny urged.

Jessie took her bags from the back seat and followed her grandmother into the house. Stepping through the front door, she absorbed the beloved sights familiar to her from childhood: the large central room with its worn, wide-planked floors, wagon-wheel chandeliers, and a huge stone fireplace with iron rods that swung out to support cooking pots back in earlier times. On the mantel sat the old clock from Ganny's childhood home with its painted picture of strawberries on the glass that covered the weights and the pendulum. Ganny had once told Jessie that the clock had been in her parents' bedroom, which Jessie found amusing, since the clock's mechanism and chimes were so old and worn that, when they struck each hour, it sounded like someone banging on a tin pan. The old timepiece had witnessed the coming-into-being of Ganny and her eleven brothers and sisters, but it kept its secrets demurely.

So soothing was this environment that Jessie, suddenly overcome with the emotional stress of the past few days, craved a nap. She asked Ganny if she minded.

"You just go right ahead. You've had a long drive. We'll have plenty of time to visit."

"Thanks." Jessie went to the bedroom she usually occupied and turned back the faded plaid spread. *Nothing ever changes here*, she thought. It was deeply reassuring. She lay down and within moments was sleeping soundly.

She woke as the late-afternoon sunlight was filtering through the leaves of the tree outside her window, dappling the bed. She found Ganny in the kitchen fixing supper—chicken-fried cube steaks with peppery milk gravy, green beans cooked that morning with salt pork and left to stand on the back of the stove all day, and the instant rice that Ganny inexplicably preferred.

"Did you have you a good sleep?"

"Yes, ma'am."

As they ate at the scrubbed wood kitchen table, Jessie said, "Ganny, I know we had relatives who fought in the Civil War, but I don't know much about them."

"Well," said Ganny, "my father's great-uncles Lloyd and Clarence Garner fought for the Confederates, and Papaw's great-grandfather Roy

Marshall fought for the Yankees. It was that way with a lot of folks in East Tennessee. They took different sides, sometimes in the same family."

As Lem had said.

"Did everyone survive?"

"Uncle Joshua lost his leg. Uncle Clarence came home and lived to ninety."

"You knew him, then."

"Oh, yes. But not too well. We saw him and Aunt Fan at Christmas time. They lived over near Asheville."

"How about Roy Marshall?"

"He died before I married Papaw. But I know he did survive the war."

Jessie mused over this, wondering if her great-great-great-uncles Garner, among the rare Rebels from Sevier County, might possibly have served in the same regiment as Lem. She recalled Lem telling her that he thought he had met some Garners and Marshalls but that he didn't know them "to speak to."

She had another question. "Ganny, are any of your birds turtle doves?"

"The old mountain people called the gray doves turtle doves, or turkle doves, but we call them mourning doves nowadays. Mountain folks believed that the turtle dove was a sign of death."

Jessie thought about Lem's story of the mother dove nesting on his windowsill, and she wondered if the bird's trusting attitude toward him had been more ominous than he knew. A huge sorrow for him suddenly filled her chest. She stood abruptly and began to clear the table.

Over dessert of Ganny's homemade peach pie, Jessie asked, "Do you know any people named Sanders around here?"

"I believe there are quite a few," Ganny said. "Though I don't know any myself."

Jessie told Ganny about the letter describing the death of the young soldier named Sanders from Beulah, and how it had come into her possession. "I brought a copy of the letter, and I thought I'd try to find this poor boy's kinfolks. They might want to have it."

"I'm sure they would."

Ganny didn't have a "dishin' machine," so after supper, Jessie washed and dried the dishes, focusing on the rhythm and tactility of the task and letting her eyes rest on Ganny's rosebushes outside the window, glowing red and pink and peach in the mellow evening sunshine.

It was about seven o'clock when she finished. She steeled herself and went into the living room and over to the small table where the old-fashioned black phone rested. Sitting down, she took the phone book from the shelf underneath the table. It listed the residents of all the towns in Sevier County, conveniently sorting all the names alphabetically rather than separating them by towns. There were several Sanderses, three listed in Beulah, some in Bentonville, some in Caton's Forge, two in Brushy Gap. And a number in Sevierville as well, but Jessie thought she would start closer to Lem's home.

She drew a deep breath for courage. Her shyness was most acute on the telephone, which made no allowance for silence; she needed to see people and read their body language so she could know how to take what they said.

But she had a promise to fulfill to Lem, so she dialed the first Sanders in Beulah. The receiver on the other end was lifted with a clatter.

"Hell-o." The first syllable was accented. It was a man's voice. A television blared in the background.

"Hello, Mr. Elvin Sanders?"

"Yes?"

Jessie had prepared herself with a brief little speech. "My name is Jessie Gibbs and I'm from Murfreesboro—"

"Are you selling somethin'?"

"No, sir. I'm looking for the relatives of a Civil War soldier named Lemuel Sanders."

"Oh, I wouldn't know nothin' about that."

Click.

She steeled herself to continue making calls. The next person in Beulah, Mrs. David Sanders, was courteous, but said her husband's family had moved from Alabama only twenty years before.

The last Sanders in Beulah was an Ida Mae. Her telephone rang and rang.

Discouraged, Jessie gave up for the night. It was still too early for bed, so she asked Ganny if she could practice the piano. Ganny had an old upright that hadn't been tuned in years, but it would do for Jessie to train her fingers on the Haydn piece.

Ganny said she'd love to hear some music. As Jessie played through the first movement, her grandmother sat on the old brown corduroy sofa, its back draped with one of her hand-crocheted afghans, nursing her nighttime sleeping aid—a small jelly glass filled with the screw-top muscatel wine that she kept under her bed for medicinal purposes. The old piano gave the music a honky-tonk quality doubtless never heard in classical Vienna. Ganny said it sounded beautiful, just like it was coming from the radio.

Then, after the sun had disappeared behind the mountains, Ganny said good night and went to bed, and Jessie headed outside to sit for a while. The front porch stretched across the length of the house, with a view over the treetops and valley and the mountains beyond. There were six rocking chairs for adults and four little child-size rockers that bore the names of the grandchildren, Jessie, Lou Ann, and their two cousins, Betty's brother's children.

She sat down in one of the weathered rockers, her feet up on the porch railing, watching the last light fade from the sky. The summer was ending; darkness was coming noticeably earlier. Darkness, and winter. Even if she did go against Pastor John's advice and her own reluctant sense of what was right and continue to see Lem, meeting with him in the biting wind and freezing rain of wintertime would be impossible.

"Help me," she whispered to the mountains, whose undulant forms were black against the peach-streaked aqua sky. The same mountains that, such a short time ago in their ancient story, had sheltered and nurtured the man she loved. They had given him their quiet, their strength, their steadfastness. "If his people are still among you," she said to them, "and please, God, let them be, won't you lead me to them?"

As Jessie ate breakfast the next morning, Ganny came in from sweeping the living room and asked her to drive to Brushy Gap, some ten miles away, to pick up a vacuum cleaner that she had left at the hardware store for repair.

Jessie set out at eleven. The road to Brushy Gap followed a stream, just a trickle of water over a bed of rocks now, but undoubtedly in the spring thaw a torrent. The day was blue and beautiful, the mountains stretching off into the distance, their flanks so densely covered with dark green trees that they looked furred. White, puffy clouds, pushed by a strong wind, sailed low in the sky and cast swift-moving shadows over the slopes.

In the little town, Jessie found the hardware store, an old-fashioned establishment with creaky wooden floors. Among the aisles of paints, tools, nails and screws, and fishing equipment was a display of crafts made by local people. Jessie spent a few minutes admiring the quilts, birdhouses, and corncob dolls.

After retrieving the vacuum cleaner and putting it into the van, Jessie realized that she was hungry and began walking down the main street, looking for a place to get an early lunch. The row of storefronts gave way to a park. On one side of the park stood a small, weathered log building. "Brushy Gap Museum," read a sign out front. It closed at noon, in half an hour.

She decided her hunger could wait. She walked over and lifted the iron latch on the rough wooden door.

The inside of the museum was only about the size of her parents' modest living room. Tall, lighted glass display cases occupied most of the wall space except for a spot just inside the door where a desk stood with a silver-haired lady sitting behind it, reading a book. A stuffed bobcat, which Lem would probably have called a "painter," snarled menacingly on a shelf above her head.

"Hello," the woman said with a smile. "Welcome."

"What an interesting building," Jessie said.

The woman explained that it dated from the early nineteenth century; the historical society had taken it over in the 1950s. "We don't charge admission, but we ask visitors to make whatever donation they wish." She pointed to a copper kettle, a remnant possibly of a moonshining operation, that rested on a wooden stand beside the desk.

Jessie put in a few dollars. "I'd just like to look around."

"Feel free, take your time. Let me know if I can answer any questions."

Jessie passed by the glass cases, quickly perusing the displays: photographs of Main Street as it looked at the turn of the twentieth century; old tools and household objects; broadsides advertising circuses and tent revivals and medicinal treatments; and arrowheads and artifacts from the original native inhabitants of the area.

She came to a case dedicated to local Civil War history. There were a Union and a Confederate uniform, and a brown-and-white-striped cotton lady's dress with a fan-pleated bodice and an ivory linen collar with brown splotches like tea stains. Looking at these garments, Jessie marveled at how much smaller people were in the 1860s. These clothes looked like they would fit a small preteen of the current time. The waist on the dress must have measured less than twenty inches.

Lem, at around five-eight, had once described himself as tall, and Jessie supposed that by the standards of his day he had been. She must seem to him, at five-six and 125 pounds, like an Amazon, though he never showed anything but approval of her appearance.

Next to the uniforms was a framed essay about the history of the Civil War in East Tennessee which explained that, as Ganny and Lem had said, sympathies were sharply divided between the Union and the Confederacy. The conflict came to violence in some places. These people had it doubly hard, Jessie thought, not only suffering from the national civil war but from a local one as well, neighbor against neighbor.

She moved slowly past the rest of the display, inspecting swords and muskets and pistols and cartridge cases hung against a background of tan burlap. Someone with fine penmanship had hand-lettered all the cards explaining the purpose, history, and provenance of every item in the museum.

Back at the front desk she wrote her name and hometown in the visitors' book.

"I hope you found it interesting," said the lady.

"Oh, yes, ma'am," Jessie replied. "Especially the Civil War exhibit. I'm here from Murfreesboro on sort of a mission related to the Civil War" She explained her purpose. "I wonder if there might be any documents in your collection that mention that soldier or his family. Lemuel Sanders was his name."

The woman frowned thoughtfully. "I'm sorry, I can't say I know of any. But I'll ask the director when she comes in next Monday. I'm Joy Mayfield, by the way." She extended her hand, and Jessie shook it and introduced herself.

Near the front door, there was a case displaying souvenirs and books of local interest, and Jessie paused to examine the contents. A volume entitled *The Bitter Cup: East Tennessee Confederates, 1860–1870* caught her eye. She asked Joy if she might look at it.

"It was written by one of our local authors," Joy said, taking the book out and handing it to Jessie. "It's quite interesting."

Jessie leafed through it, and although at twenty-six dollars it was expensive, she decided to buy it. Maybe it would help her understand a little more about what Lem and his family went through. It was even possible that his kinfolks or her own forebears might be mentioned in it.

That afternoon, she called a few more Sanderses, keeping a notebook beside her to jot down details about the people she reached.

Joe Bob Sanders, of Sanders and Sons Collision Repair, said, "The what, now?" when Jessie explained that she was looking for the relatives of a soldier from the Civil War. Some machine whined loudly in the background.

"The Civil *War*," Jessie shouted.

Ganny came out of the kitchen. "I don't know what you said, honey."

"I'm on the phone, Ganny," Jessie mouthed to her.

"I can't hardly hear you," said Mr. Sanders. The machine shrieked louder.

"I was saying that I found a letter from a soldier named Sanders in the Civil War," Jessie hollered, starting to perspire from the strain.

"Well, that was a long time ago."

"Yes, sir, it sure was, but I thought this soldier's family might like to have the letter. His name was Lemuel Sanders, and I wondered if he might be kin to you." She found herself slipping into the mountain diction.

"That name don't ring a bell, but if you want to carry that letter over here, I might could show it to my brother. He knows a right smart about our family history."

The next call was to a Raylene Sanders. In the husky voice of a longtime smoker, the woman said, "Yes, ma'am, my family's been here for generations but I don't have any idea what my great-grandfather did in the Civil War. I don't think his name was Lemuel but to tell you the truth I'm not sure. We've never been a close family, to say the least."

After that, Jessie had to take a break. Learning that Lem's family had no interest in his fate would almost be worse than not finding them at all.

She went into the kitchen, where Ganny was stirring cornbread batter for supper. "So many Sanderses," she said, opening the refrigerator.

"Did you find the ones who're kin to your soldier?"

My soldier. The words made her heart give a little leap. "No, ma'am, not yet. I'll keep trying." She poured herself a glass of what her grandmother called "Co-cola," and after asking if Ganny needed help with supper and being told no, she went out onto the front porch to rock and drink and reflect.

With her feet up on the railing again, and the old rocker rhythmically creaking, Jessie thought about her relationship with Lem. What if it could go forward in the real world? What, for instance, would they fight about? Every couple fought, even the most harmonious ones, like her parents. At issue were little irritations, usually on her mother's part: "Frank, how many times do I have to ask you not to track dirt in the front door? Can't you come in the basement when you've been working in the yard?" Jessie had never heard her father raise his voice to her mother; his way of coping with these complaints was to endure, apologize, and then slip away for a long day of fishing.

What would Lem frustrate her with? At present, the newness of their romance and the heroism and tragedy of his situation kept Jessie from seeing any weakness in him. Forcing herself to be objective, she imagined that some of the qualities he said his father had criticized in him: dreaminess—what in modern parlance might be called passive-aggressiveness in resisting doing the work his father asked of him—might well drive her crazy. She was, after all, a focused person, dedicated to a purpose—when she knew what that purpose was.

And what would he do in the modern world to make a living? Though intelligent, he wasn't highly educated; reading Jeremiah's letter, she had wondered if Lem's spelling was as bad as his friend's. He would have to have some sort of menial occupation. Maybe her father would take Lem on in the plumbing supply business; maybe Lem would be one of the good old boys in the warehouse who drove the forklifts, loaded the trucks, made deliveries. How would that fit into the life she wanted to live, a life devoted to classical music and artistic achievement? And, being a traditional man, wouldn't he consider it Jessie's proper role to do all the cooking, housework, and childcare? That could certainly cause conflict.

It was good to think about these things, a useful reality check of the potential difficulties. If she could really believe them, it might make it easier to give him up.

CHAPTER 24

RESTLESS SPIRITS

THAT EVENING AFTER she had washed the dishes, she tried Ida Mae Sanders in Beulah again. The receiver was lifted but it was a second or two before a wavery old voice said, "Hello?"

"Hello, is this Mrs. Ida Mae Sanders?" Jessie took a guess at the woman's marital status.

"Yes, it is."

"My name is Jessie Gibbs, and I'm the granddaughter of Mrs. Constance Marshall. She lives in Caton's Forge."

"Yay-ess," Ida Mae said, the slight lift of a question at the word's end.

Jessie pressed on and told her about the letter.

Ida Mae said, "Well, now, my husband's grandfather was named Lemuel Sanders the second."

Jessie froze, unable for a moment to speak. Her mind raced: Ida Mae sounded like she was quite elderly, maybe in her eighties, which meant that her husband's grandfather might have been born right after the Civil War.

"Are you still there?"

"Yes, yes, ma'am. Do you happen to know what that gentleman's father's name was?"

"Let me think… it began with a C … Calvin?" She paused. "No, it was Caleb, Caleb Sanders."

Lem's brother was named Caleb. Had he named his son after his lost brother?

Jessie was aware that she was gripping the receiver hard. Trying to keep her voice calm, she asked, "Mrs. Sanders, can I come visit you and show you the letter?"

"Why, you sure can. I have to go out to the hair parlor today, but come tomorrow, anytime in the afternoon, I'll be here." She gave Jessie directions.

Jessie thanked her and said she'd be there around three o'clock.

MRS. SANDERS LIVED in a small white cottage on Beulah's sleepy, hilly main street. Ganny had come with Jessie, bringing one of her peach pies. "Do me good to get out of the house, make a new friend," she said. Ganny expected that everyone she met would be a friend, and Jessie had never known this expectation to be disappointed.

Jessie clutched the manila envelope that held Jeremiah Walker's letter as she and Ganny stepped up onto the front porch and rang the bell. After a few moments, a curtain was pulled aside, then the door opened.

Ida Mae Sanders was a small, stooped woman with gray hair, faintly purple and tightly curled, no doubt the result of the previous day's visit to the "hair parlor." Despite the heat of the August day, she wore a pilled pink cardigan sweater over a floral snap-front housecoat. Jessie and Ganny greeted her, and Ganny handed her the pie.

"Why, thank you," said Ida Mae. "Y'all didn't have to do that but I'll sure enjoy it. I'll just put it in the Frigidaire. Make yourselves comfortable in the den."

The den was a dark-paneled room crowded with oversized brown and rust-colored chairs that seemed to suck all available light into their upholstered depths. A game show was blaring on the TV. Framed photographs stood on every tabletop and shelf, and hung on the walls. Jessie studied the people in them, searching for a trace of family likeness. To her panic, she found that she couldn't at that moment call to mind a clear image of Lem's face.

As she and Ganny sat down, Jessie opened the manila envelope and waited for Ida Mae to return from the kitchen. Canned laughter blasted from the television. The old woman came in and settled into a large recliner that nearly swallowed her up. "Just turn off the TV, if you don't mind." She pronounced TV as Ganny did, with the emphasis on the first letter: TEE-vee. Gratefully, Jessie rose and switched off the set, then sat down again in the ringing sudden silence.

Ganny and Ida Mae chatted about people they might know in common, while Jessie took out the papers, unable to do anything but clutch them and wait.

When there was a pause in the conversation, she said, "This is the letter I told you about, Mrs. Sanders. A professor friend of mine at Middle Tennessee State University found it in his research for a book he's writing. Would you like me to read it to you?"

Ida Mae said she would. Jessie began reading Jeremiah's letter aloud. Her voice sounded flat to her ears. She felt as though the young man's anguished words were drifting down in this stale atmosphere like motes of dust. Even though she cut out the long, detailed description of the burial site, reasoning that it would be too hard to follow, the reading seemed to take forever.

"What a pitiful letter," Ganny said when she had finished, shaking her head. "That poor, poor boy. Those poor boys—both of them."

"I wish my husband was here to hear that," said Ida Mae. "He'd know more about whether that young man was kin to us. But he passed away ten years ago."

Jessie murmured condolences. Then she ventured, "Mrs. Sanders, would you by any chance have any old letters, or pictures, that you might be willing to let me look at? Maybe there would be some more information about this soldier that I could tell my professor friend about, for his book."

"There is a box in the attic," said Ida Mae. "I can't remember what-all's in it. You're welcome to look through it."

She gave Jessie directions to the attic. The box was cardboard, large and green, Ida Mae said; she last saw it beside a wooden trunk, though it had been years since she'd been up there. "I just can't get up all those stairs anymore," she said.

"I know what you mean," Ganny sympathized, though Jessie knew that Ganny's physical agility and stamina equaled, if not exceeded, her own.

She left her grandmother and Ida Mae talking about a new cafeteria that had recently opened up in town, where the desserts were just out of this world.

In the attic, Jessie found the large green box under a window. She blew off some dust and insect corpses and carried it down the stairs.

Ganny and Ida Mae were still talking away in the den. "I found it," Jessie said, poking her head in. "Would you mind if I looked through it in the kitchen, where the light is brighter?"

"You go right ahead," Ida Mae said.

Jessie set the box on top of the kitchen table and lifted the lid. The jumble of loose photographs, letters, greeting cards, dance cards, and other items inside the box was overwhelming. If there was time, it might be fascinating to read through all these things. What keenness of purpose, discipline, and endurance it would take to be a scholar, a historian, like Philip Goldsmith. Also, it would require the intuition of a detective to home in on the important clues amid the clutter. To say nothing of the diplomatic skills needed to win people's trust in order to gain access to their personal memorabilia, and to persuade them to part with valuable documents.

At the moment, Jessie felt helpless in the face of this welter of material. Ida Mae might be related to Lem by marriage, but she had shown little interest in pursuing the connection. There was no point trying to focus on these documents right now; depression and a sense of futility were clouding Jessie's brain. She went back into the den.

"Did you find anything?" Ida Mae asked, looking at her with faded blue eyes made huge by the thick, convex lenses of her glasses. *She really is a kind lady*, Jessie thought, and felt obscurely guilty, as if she were trying to put something over on her.

"No, ma'am, there's so much to look through. It would take too long to go through it all."

"Well, there's no reason why you can't carry that box with you and bring it back when you've finished with it. I can tell you're a trustworthy girl."

Jessie thanked her and promised to bring the box back the next day.

"No hurry. Like I said, I haven't looked at what's in there for years. I hope you'll find something your friend can use."

Jessie's mind went blank.

"That professor," said Ida Mae.

"Of course." She went back into the kitchen, closed the box, and brought it out to the front door. She and Ganny took their leave, but not before the two ladies had made a promise to each other to have lunch at the new cafeteria sometime real soon.

THAT NIGHT, JESSIE SAT on Ganny's living-room floor with the contents of the box spread out around her, sorting through the various artifacts.

There were photographs of Ida Mae and her husband, Carson, as quaintly dressed children from the 1920s or so. From the absence of birth announcements or pictures of children from the 1940s, Jessie surmised that Ida Mae and Carson were childless. There were letters— several of them written on thin airmail stationery to Ida Mae from Carson, bearing stamps from France, Belgium, and Italy where he must have been serving in World War II. Jessie would have liked to read these out of sheer curiosity, but not wanting to lose her focus or waste time, she set them aside.

She picked up a newspaper clipping. It was an obituary from 1944 of one Grace Sanders, née Loudon, age seventy-four. Jessie's interest quickened as she read that Mrs. Sanders was the widow of Lemuel Sanders the second from Beulah who, Jessie strongly suspected, was the son of Lem's brother. She jotted down these names and relationships in order to keep them straight. Mrs. Sanders, the article went on, was survived by her son, Richard Sanders of Brushy Gap; and her grandchildren, Carson Sanders of Beulah—Ida Mae's late husband—and Julia Sanders Pruett of Sevierville. Jessie wrote down those names too.

As Jessie continued her excavation, Ganny came out in her nightgown and robe, white hair loosed from its net and hanging down to her shoulders, straggly and thin.

"Are you going to stay up all night, honey?"

"No, ma'am, but I told Mrs. Sanders I'd bring these things back to her tomorrow. I thought we could drop by after church."

"Wasn't that nice of her to let you take that box? Are you finding anything?"

"Maybe. There's a newspaper article that's kind of interesting. I hope I'm not keeping you up."

Ganny headed for the kitchen. "Oh, no, I just couldn't get to sleep. I think I'll have me a piece of pie and a glass of milk."

"Sounds like a great idea." Jessie stood up and brushed crumbs of paper off her jeans.

In the kitchen, Ganny turned on a small wall lamp. It cast a warm glow over the table, leaving the shadows undisturbed in the rest of the room.

They sat with their pie at the table. Jessie said, "Ganny, one of the reasons I wanted to come see you is that I've lost somebody I really loved." It was easier to put it in past tense.

Ganny took Jessie's hand in her own firm grasp. "Oh, honey, I'm so sorry. He was your sweetheart?"

Jessie nodded. "You would have liked him. He was from around here. A real East Tennessee country boy."

"And y'all couldn't work things out?"

"It's more like… fate was against us," Jessie said. "What I want to ask you was, how do you go on after you lose someone dear to you? How have you done it, with all the people you've lost?" Three of her four children; a husband; eleven brothers and sisters; parents, of course; numerous friends—her grandmother's list of bereavements was long.

Ganny patted Jessie's hand, considering. "I keep myself busy. And I try to never look back."

"But don't you want to remember the people you've loved?"

"Why, sure I do. You can't help but remember them. But you can't let yourself dwell on the past. I've seen too many folks make themselves miserable and just stop living by always thinking of what's gone and can never come again."

Ganny sat still, continuing to pat Jessie's hand, her cool, dry fingers gently tapping. The old refrigerator whirred, the electric clock on the wall hummed, the logs in the walls creaked as they continued their long process of settling into the earth.

"And I have always put my trust in the Lord," Ganny continued. "We can't see it sometimes, but God has a way of working everything out for the best. Bringing good out of bad. If something's meant to be, it'll be. And if it's not, you'll get over this boy and find somebody else."

"What if I don't *want* to get over him?" Jessie asked, a little defiant.

"Well, now, that's when you just have to be strong," Ganny said. "I know you're hurting now, and I'm just as sorry as I can be." She gave Jessie's hand a final squeeze and released it.

She began to get up, but Jessie said, "Ganny, I know it's late, but I have one more thing to ask you."

"What, sugar?"

"Do you believe in ghosts? Spirits?"

Ganny searched Jessie's face. Uncharacteristically, she said nothing.

"Somebody I trust said they'd seen one," Jessie said. "The spirit of somebody they loved. I just wondered what you thought."

Ganny sighed. "Well, since you asked, I'll tell you. Yes, I do believe some spirits linger, if they have to leave this life too soon, if they haven't had time to make their peace." She paused. Jessie waited anxiously.

"After your Papaw died," Ganny went on, "that first night I spent alone, I was lying in our bed, in the Knoxville house. The door to the hall was open and a gray light was coming in from the hall window. There was nobody else in the house, but all of a sudden, I had the feeling that somebody was moving in the hall, coming closer to the door. There was kind of a swirling in the air and in that dim light. And I was as sure as I could be that the next minute, I'd see Papaw standing in the doorway.

"I wasn't really scared. I knew it wasn't a burglar; a living person would've made noise, the way the floorboards creaked in that old house. I knew it was your papaw's spirit, and I knew why he'd come. So I sat up and said to him, 'Tate, you rest now. I'm all right. The children are going to be fine. We love you so much and just want you to be at peace.' And when I stopped speaking, the air was still, and the light was steady again. That was the closest I ever came to seeing a spirit. But I know in my heart he was there." She looked down and put her fingers over her mouth.

"I've upset you," Jessie said. "I'm so sorry."

"Oh, it's all right. It was a long time ago, and he didn't appear to me again. In a way, do you know, I was glad I could give him peace. The heart attack that took him was so sudden and he suffered so much. And then at the hospital, before they closed the door to the room where they took him, I saw the doctors all crowded around him, pounding on his chest and hollering at each other. It was just a terrible way to leave this world."

They sat quietly for a moment. The refrigerator clicked off, releasing the room to silence. Jessie reflected on how similar Ganny's story was to Lem's memory of visiting his mother the night after his death, another unquiet spirit seeking to reassure, or be reassured by, a loved one left behind. Then the heart-sinking thought occurred to her: If Ruby Sanders had been able to console her dead son and allay his anxiety, he might have been spared his long vigil. He would have been sure, at least, that his family knew what had happened to him.

But Ruby had not had the certainty Ganny did. And so she fled from the truth she could not bear.

Ganny pushed back her chair and rose, bringing Jessie back to the present. "I think I can sleep now."

"I hope so. Thanks for telling me that." Jessie stood up too and hugged her. "I just want you to know that, whenever I wonder how to be strong, it's you I think of."

"Well, thank you, honey. Now you go on to bed and get a good night's sleep, and things'll look brighter in the morning."

"I love you."

"And I sure love my namesake."

CHAPTER 25

THE BITTER CUP

THE NEXT MORNING, Jessie carefully replaced all the contents of the box and put on the dress she had brought to wear to church. She carried the box to the van, holding it away from her to avoid getting dust on her good clothes.

She and Ganny attended the service at the small white-frame Methodist church in Caton's Forge. The congregation was sparse, most of them elderly women. The clear-glass windows were open, letting in a gentle breeze. Jessie was sitting next to one of the windows and from time to time glanced outside at the old graveyard beside the building, its thin, mossy stones leaning every which way, the writing on them eroded.

A little choir made an effort to harmonize on "What a Friend We Have in Jesus," accompanied by a woman on a piano that sounded like Ganny's.

In a silent moment during the service, Jessie closed her eyes and thought about her search. She had hoped that finding Mrs. Sanders might be the breakthrough she sought, but Ida Mae didn't seem to be very knowledgeable or curious about her husband's family's past. Jessie did have the newspaper article; maybe she could track down some of the people named in it, though the idea of more phone calls to strangers made her chest tighten. And what if she did find Lem's family but, like

Raylene Sanders, they didn't care about what had happened to their long-ago relative, much less about identifying his grave and giving him and the other men a proper burial? She slumped against the back of the pew, feeling overwhelmed.

Then she thought, *You call yourself a person of faith. Why do you think this is all up to you?*

Drawing herself up straighter, she made the decision to turn over all her hopes, anxieties, and doubts to a power greater than herself.

AFTER THE SERVICE had ended, Jessie said to her grandmother, "When we bring back the box, should we ask Mrs. Sanders if she'd like to go with us to that new cafeteria?"

"I'm sure she'd love that."

Ida Mae met them at the door, in the same housecoat as the day before, and she seemed delighted by the idea of going out to lunch. "Let me just run and put on something nicer. I didn't feel up to going to church this morning," she said, as if feeling the need to explain why she was at home on Sunday morning. Motioning to the box in Jessie's arms, she asked, "Did you find what you were looking for, young lady?"

"Unfortunately, I didn't find anything about that soldier I mentioned," Jessie said, setting the carton on the floor. "I did find a newspaper article, though. An obituary for a Grace Loudon Sanders, from 1944. She was Lemuel the second's wife. It said that she was survived by her son, Richard, and her grandchildren—your husband, of course, and also a Julia Pruett of Sevierville. I was wondering if Julia Pruett still lives there."

"Oh, no, Cousin Julia passed away a few years ago."

"And her husband?"

"He died before her, around 1986."

"Oh, I'm sorry." Discouragement settled like a stone in Jessie's chest. She made one last effort. "Did you and your husband have children, Mrs. Sanders?"

"No, honey, the Lord blessed us in many ways, but not that one."

"Did the Pruetts?"

"They had one child. My niece, Sarah Gowan."

"Where does Sarah live?" asked Jessie.

"In Sevierville."

"Do you have her phone number?"

"Why, yes."

Buoyed by hope, Jessie followed Ida Mae into the den, secretly smiling at the thought that prying information out of the old lady was like being in one of those fairy tales in which you had to ask the question in exactly the right words to get the secret door in the impenetrable stone cliff to swing open.

Ida Mae took a tattered floral address book from a table and opened it. "Here it is," she said, and Jessie put the number into her phone.

"I'll just carry this box back to the attic," Jessie said. Amazing, how much lighter it felt now that this small victory had given her a new vitality. She hauled it up the two flights of stairs and set it back precisely in the clear rectangle surrounded by the dust of ages.

BACK AT HOME after lunch, Ganny said, "I ate too much! I'm going to lie down for a little nap."

"I'll be quiet," Jessie said. She sat down beside the phone and took a few deep breaths to calm herself. The next call she made would be a decisive one; it seemed that Sarah Gowan was her only hope.

She dialed the number that Ida Mae had given her. A woman's brisk voice answered.

"Is this Sarah Gowan?" Jessie asked.

"Yes," the woman said warily.

"My name is Jessie Gibbs," Jessie pressed on, trying to sound calm and friendly. "My grandmother and I just had lunch today with your Aunt Ida Mae Sanders and she gave me your number."

"Well, hey, Ms. Gibbs." The tone was noticeably warmer.

"Please call me Jessie."

"And I'm Sally. What can I do for you?"

"I have something you may want to see." Jessie related her by now well-practiced story about the letter and its discovery. "Mrs. Sanders thought the soldier who was killed might be related to you. His name was Lemuel Sanders."

"Gosh," Sally said. "Lemuel Sanders the second was my great-grandfather. This Lemuel must have been the generation before him, to have been in the Civil War. I'd have to look at my family tree; I did one a few years ago that went back to the early 1800s. I'd be just fascinated to see that letter. Did Aunt Ida Mae mention to you that history is something of a passion of mine?"

"No, ma'am, she didn't." The wicker chair crackled as Jessie leaned back in relief.

"I work at the Sevier County Historical Society," Sally said. "I'm the educational program director, which I assure you is much less impressive than it sounds."

Jessie tried to keep her voice from betraying her excitement at this news. They made a date to meet at a restaurant in downtown Sevierville two days later.

After Jessie hung up, she sat a moment with her eyes closed. A memory of Lem suddenly came vividly into her mind: his smile with its one deep dimple, his eyes that shone even more brightly amid the soot on his cheeks and brow, the way he cocked his head when he was listening to her, the sinewy strength of his hands, the sound of his voice. She wished she could preserve these memories somehow, now that the time seemed to be drawing near when they would be all she had of him.

She spent the evening practicing the Haydn and then, after Ganny had retired, reading *The Bitter Cup*. It was a drier, more scholarly book than she was accustomed to tackling, but her interest in the subject matter kept her going.

As Lem had said, the East Tennessee Confederates were suspected by their fellow soldiers of not being fully loyal. For this reason, many of their units were sent to the deep South, where the hope was that the East Tennesseans, being surrounded by ardent Secessionists, would be inspired to fully commit themselves to the Southern cause. Instead, these men, used to the fresh mountain air, were sickened by the stifling heat and humidity, and succumbed in great numbers to malaria and other illnesses.

Jessie was surprised to learn that of the nine counties that lay on the easternmost border of Tennessee, Sevier County—Lem's and Jeremiah's home county—was one of the most staunchly Unionist, so much so that it was given the nickname "Little Massachusetts." No wonder Jacob Sanders was so angry about his son's joining the Rebels.

The book's title came from a Col. James G. Rose, commander of the Confederate 61st Tennessee Regiment, who wrote to his lady friend in Virginia: "The war is over now, and we must drink that bitter cup which we have so long striven in vain to dash from our lips." And a galling drink it was—as the book described, the hostility after the war among some of the victorious Unionists, and the punishments they inflicted on the former Rebels, that ranged from stripping them of the vote, to beatings and property destruction, forced a number of East Tennessee's former Confederate sympathizers to seek sanctuary in Georgia and Virginia. "This Country is crowded with Reffugees from Ten[nessee]," one Anderson R. Edwards from Washington County, Virginia, was quoted as saying, "and they are coming Dayly. They Git orders to Leave in So many days or take the consequences."

An extract of a letter followed, from a woman identified only as the mother of a Confederate soldier missing in action. The woman and her family had decided to remain in their home in Sevier County. Their barn had been burned down, by whom she did not know, but she could not rule out neighbors who were angry about her family's presumed allegiance during the war. She wrote to her daughter-in-law: "And now, in defeat, I can't help asking what was all that suffering, what were all those broken hearts for? There's a painful rift, a mistrust, between people here who took different sides. Some have been driven away because of it. But we can't move away, because how would Lemuel know where to find us?"

Jessie stared at the words. The old clock on the mantel whirred to life and struck the hour, eleven dully clanging notes, but she barely heard the sound as she turned to the back of the book and found the notes for the chapter. She located the footnote for the quote: "Mrs. Jacob Sanders to Mrs. Caleb Sanders, July 16, 1865, Special Collections Library, University of Tennessee, Knoxville."

Jessie could hardly believe it. She jumped up from her chair and went out onto the porch. A strong, hot wind had blown up and was thrashing the trees, possibly in advance of a thunderstorm. Lights from the valley twinkled among the moving branches like captured stars. As she rested her hands on the log railing, a rough knot pressed into her palm. The pain seemed somehow to steady her amid the swirling chaos in her brain, so she didn't move her hand. She leaned forward and with wide-open eyes searched the landscape, whose familiarity suddenly seemed to be a mere veil over infinite mystery.

WHEN SHE CALLED the UT Knoxville library the next day and asked for Special Collections, she reached an answering machine. The outgoing message said the archivist was on vacation until the following week and that requests could be sent via email, to be answered on the librarian's return.

At eleven, the hour that the little library in Caton's Forge opened, Jessie drove into town to use one of the library's computers. She sat at a desk that overlooked a sparkling stream and the mountains beyond—a beautiful view, but she hardly took notice of it as she composed an email to the UT librarian mentioning *The Bitter Cup* and requesting a copy of the complete letter from Mrs. Jacob Sanders. She explained that she believed Mrs. Sanders' descendants were unaware of the letter's existence. She would be grateful, she added, if she could receive the document as soon as possible. She hit "Send" and then sat for a long moment, suddenly exhausted.

CHAPTER 26

MOTHERS OF SOLDIERS

THE HOME COOKIN' Luncheonette on Sevierville's main street was doing a brisk business. It was directly across from the courthouse, and every table was occupied by suit-clad attorneys, business-casual court workers, and people in a variety of attire from overalls to Spandex, who, Jessie assumed, were supporters of defendants who had come for their dates with justice.

At a table by the window sat a lone woman whose appearance set her apart from the rest of the crowd. She looked to be in her fifties and had short blond hair, tousled and spiky. Tanned arms were exposed by a black sleeveless top. A choker of gold beads encircled her neck, with matching earrings. White pants and black patent leather sandals completed the impression of an affluent woman of leisure.

She offered a friendly smile as Jessie approached, blue eyes keen over the tops of purple-framed reading glasses.

"Sally?"

"Jessie, hey."

The two women shook hands. Sally's grip was firm.

Jessie felt shy in the face of Sally's age, polished appearance, and obvious wealth, signaled by the large diamond and sapphire ring on her right hand that flashed in the light from the window. She herself wore jeans, a striped t-shirt, and old sandals—the rustic, comfortable clothes she always wore at Ganny's, that seemed inappropriate for the company of such an elegant dining companion.

She opened the manila envelope and took out the pages. "I'm sure you're curious to see this."

"Yes, I admit I am."

She passed the letter across the table and Sally took it, adjusted her glasses, and frowned at the pages thoughtfully. Jessie noticed that Sally's fingernails were bitten down; this little hint of a weakness somehow humanized the older woman. As Sally read, Jessie gazed out the front window at the bronze statue of Dolly Parton, Sevierville's most famous native daughter, sitting with her guitar on a rock in front of the courthouse.

"Good Lord," Sally said. "Oh my, how sad." She looked up at Jessie. "It seems like my relative was quite a hero."

"Yes, it does."

"Do we know what happened to the poor young man who wrote this?" Sally handed the letter back to Jessie, who said it was hers to keep. Sally folded it carefully and put it into her purse.

"He died of pneumonia in a Yankee prison camp," said Jessie. "The professor I told you about did some research and discovered that Jeremiah Walker was captured on the second day of fighting at Stones River. So you see, from the fact that this letter was never mailed, and Jeremiah died soon after writing it, it seems there's a good chance that your ancestors never found out when, where, or even *that* Lemuel was killed."

"How terrible." Sally looked out the window, her expression solemn. The noontime glare illuminated the fine wrinkles etched around her mouth and eyes. She said after a moment, "That would explain a problem I had when I did that family tree I told you about. I looked at it after we spoke the other day. I had found a Lemuel, born in 1840. He had an older brother, Caleb, and a younger sister, Polly. I found spouses for Caleb and Polly, and descendants for Caleb, but no wife or kids for

Lemuel. Which would be the case, if he died in the war. That would make him my great-great uncle, wouldn't it? It seems you may be right, that no one ever found out for certain when and where he was killed. Until now."

"Do you know where the Sanders family lived?"

"In Beulah, I know that much, but when I tried to track down their homeplace I ran into a dead end because the Sevier County Courthouse burned down in 1856 and all the deeds and records from before then were destroyed."

"So how did you find birth records for the three Sanders children?" Jessie asked. "And marriage and birth records for Lemuel's brother and sister?" She had to be careful not to slip and call him "Lem."

"Mama had an old family Bible passed down from her great-grandmother, Ruby Sanders, Lemuel's mother. I have it now. It has birth and wedding and death dates written in it."

"Wow. What a treasure." Jessie would have given a lot to see that Bible but felt it would seem strange to ask. "But nothing for Lemuel, after his birth?"

Sally shook her head. "I guess, when he just never came home, Ruby couldn't bring herself to write anything that would make the loss seem final. How heartbreaking. That poor mother."

The waitress came over and asked for their orders. When she left, Sally said, "You mentioned that Aunt Ida Mae gave you my number. Do you know her?"

"No, ma'am." Jessie told her about calling every Sanders she could find in the phone book and at last locating Ida Mae and borrowing the box of family documents.

"My goodness, you were determined," Sally said, and Jessie was embarrassed, hoping she didn't seem like some kind of stalker.

"I just thought it was so tragic that this soldier's family never knew what happened to him," she said. "And since I come up to see my grandmother pretty often, I thought I'd see if any of them—of *you*—were still around," she finished, feeling awkward.

Sally gave her a smile. "Well, as the mother of a soldier who's serving in Iraq, I can't even conceive of having something happen to my child and never knowing about it. So I surely do appreciate your efforts."

Jessie relaxed. "Speaking of mothers, the most amazing thing happened the night before last." She told Sally about finding the extract from the letter in *The Bitter Cup* from Mrs. Jacob Sanders. "The footnote in the book said that the letter is at the UT library," she said, "so I emailed the librarian and asked for a copy. I'll send you one too, when I get it." She asked Sally for her email address and entered it into her phone, and then the waitress arrived with their food.

"Do send me that letter," Sally said earnestly. "What an amazing coincidence."

"I will, I promise." Jessie thought about something Pastor John often said: "There is no luck and there are no coincidences. It's all God."

"But enough of the past," Sally said. "Tell me about yourself, Jessie."

Jessie told her about her present occupations, and encouraged by Sally's interest, confided her frustration at not being able to do more performing.

"Well, I'm sure you'll succeed at anything you put your mind to," Sally said. "You're obviously a person with initiative."

"Thank you," Jessie said. It was a heartening view; she wished she could entirely believe it.

"I taught school too, when I was first married," Sally said. "Second grade. I always knew that when my babies came, I would want to stay home with them. I never had any big ambition like you have. Or, I'd say, any big talent to justify it."

"I don't know about the big talent," Jessie said. "But the ambition, it's kind of a blessing and a curse." She was suddenly eager to turn the conversation away from herself. "Tell me about your kids."

"Amy's thirty, a part-time real estate agent. She's married and has two little children. And Avery, the one who's in Iraq, in the army, is twenty-seven."

"Is he married?" She took a guess that Avery was a man, though the name was fashionable for girls now.

"Oh, no," Sally said emphatically. "There hasn't been a girl yet who's made him change his wandering ways. Though I keep hoping. As for him being in Iraq, I try to keep myself so busy I don't have time to think about what he's going through. He keeps in touch by email and Skype, thank God. I know he shields me from the details, and I try to stay away from the news."

"I don't blame you. When will he come home?"

"I hope in November."

"What does your husband do?"

"He's a dentist. But we're divorced—no, it's fine," she said, in response to Jessie's murmur of apology for bringing up a sensitive subject. "It's been twelve years, and my life has just been getting better and better. I have a job I love and my two little grandkids to make me feel young."

"Do you have pictures?" Jessie asked, and Sally opened her sleek black purse and took out a wallet.

Jessie admired the photographs of her daughter and her family, and a young soldier in his dress blues standing with his arm around his mother in bright sunshine. It was hard to make out his features beneath the shadow of his cap, but he was tall and trim.

"My father is a Vietnam veteran," said Jessie. "I think his military service in the Marines is the thing he's proudest of. Except for his family."

"Avery's proud too," Sally said. "It's really been the making of him."

The waitress cleared away their empty plates, and they both ordered coffee.

"There's something I haven't told you yet," Jessie began. "From Jeremiah's letter, it sounds like the gravesite is in the area where my Civil War band camps out. Near the Stones River National Battlefield. I've actually seen a place that looks a lot like what he describes."

"Really? That's amazing," Sally said. "I would love to see that place, if you could spare the time to show me."

"I'll be glad to take you there anytime," Jessie said lightly, though her heart was racing.

Sally said she would look at her calendar and email some dates in the near future. She paid for both of them, dismissing Jessie's protests. "Nonsense, after what you've done for our family, it's the least I can do." Then she said, "If you don't have to rush off, would you like a tour of our historical society? It's right around the corner. Definitely a 'loving hands at home' type of operation, but we're proud of it."

"I'd like that," Jessie said.

As she followed Sally into the hot afternoon sunlight, Jessie felt shaky and off balance. She was thrilled to have found Lem's family and seen Sally's eagerness to find out more about him. Yet she dreaded the loss this victory hastened.

CHAPTER 27

SOME LITTLE ROOM FOR HOPE

JESSIE RETURNED HOME from the Smokies on Wednesday night. Early Thursday morning, she headed to school for a full day of faculty meetings, organizing the music room, and a planning session with the head music teacher. It was disheartening to realize how little she was looking forward to the new school year.

When her workday ended at three, she went out to the van and turned on the air conditioner to cool the humid ninety-degree heat as she checked her email. There was a message from the UT library. The Special Collections archivist had attached a copy of the letter.

Jessie clicked on the attachment. A gracefully handwritten document appeared on the screen.

July 16, 1865

My dear daughter Mary,

Thank you for your letter. I was happy for news of you, Caleb and our grandchildren. What a comfort, that you and Caleb named your baby for Lemuel.

It has been way too long since I wrote to you but honestly I have not had the spirit until now. Mary, hardly a single moment goes by that I don't think of my son and wonder about his fate. "Missing, presumed dead" leaves some little room for hope. But I have nightmares that can seem so real they leave me shaking. I can't tell Papa about them, he is grieving terribly. At least he had a last letter from Lemuel, which he wrote on Christmas Eve of 1862. He did not say where he was. It was a loving letter that made Papa cry. That is the last we heard from or of our son.

And now, in defeat, I can't help asking what was all that suffering, what were all those sacrifices and broken hearts for? There's a painful rift, a mistrust, between people here who took different sides. Some have even had to move away because of it. But we can't move away, because how would Lemuel know where to find us?

Our farm was pretty near ruined by the Yankees and the Confederate government confiscating whatever they needed and thefts by just plain robbers. The barn was burned last December. We don't know who did it. I don't want to think it could have been any of our neighbors but feelings do run bitter about Lemuel fighting for the Rebels. We sent Polly to Richmond to live with Papa's sister Jane as it was too dangerous out here in the country for a young girl. Little did we know what would happen to Richmond! Polly wrote to us that after the city fell she escaped with a crowd of refugees and found work as a nurse at a large Confederate Hospital outside the city. I can hardly believe my flighty little Polly doing the difficult work of a nurse but she writes that she loves it. She says she keeps searching all the wards looking for her brother. There are still patients there, and some keep arriving from other hospitals, so God willing we'll have good news in time.

We all live in that hope, Mary. Please keep us in your prayers, as I hold you all in mine.

Your loving mother-in-law

Ruby Sanders

The fourth page was a copy of the envelope, addressed to Mrs. Caleb Sanders in Sacramento, California.

Jessie sat for a while, gazing down at the pages though she could no longer read the writing through her tears. It confirmed her intuition that Lem's mother had tried to convince herself his appearance to her was a nightmare. Poor woman, unable to bear such a dreadful truth. Jessie wondered if Ruby had ever managed to reclaim any joy and peace in her life after such a devastating loss and the treatment as an outcast in her hometown, with her son and daughter and grandchildren living so far away.

Rousing herself, she emailed the UT librarian thanking her for the letter, then forwarded it to Sally and to Philip Goldsmith. To Sally, she reiterated her willingness to show her the possible burial site, and to Philip Goldsmith she said she would call him soon with news about her successful search for the family of the young soldier in the letter he had given her.

Then she called Pastor John at the church. She told him about finding Sally Gowan, discovering the reference to Lem's mother's letter in *The Bitter Cup*, and then getting Ruby Sanders' letter that day from the library.

She went on to tell him that in Sally Gowan she had discovered not only someone who was keenly interested in her deceased relative, but also someone who Jessie sensed could grow to be a trusted older friend. "It was so hard not to slip up and tell her about Lem."

"I can imagine. Especially since you felt such a rapport with her. You wouldn't want to tell her?"

"No," said Jessie. "You're the only one. It's too big a mystery—and too precious a secret to me."

"I'm honored, and I'll keep your trust." A silence stretched between them. Then he said, "Jessie, I've done a lot of praying and thinking since that meeting with Lem. I believe now that you're not in the grip of some delusion. Or being used by evil influences. What, exactly, his nature is, I can't say. I just have to accept that I can't presume to know the mysterious ways God works."

"I'm glad you think that." Jessie took a deep breath and went on. "I wanted to tell you I've taken your advice to heart and not seen Lem since that night you met him. But I do want to go to him, one last time, to tell him about finding his family."

"Would it be easier if I came with you? Or went by myself?"

"No, thank you. I want to say goodbye to him."

"I understand. I pray the Lord will grant you courage and peace. And Lem too."

THAT EVENING, she headed to the church for Ben's second rehearsal. As she pulled into the parking lot, she saw Pete taking a wheelchair out of the back of his Volvo. Andie sat in the passenger seat, turned to face outward, with her feet resting on the pavement. From a distance, she was an elegant figure, wearing a loose white shirt over black pants and a bright scarf on her head. Pete wheeled the chair over, and Ben helped his mother into it. She moved very slowly and seemed to lean all her weight on her son's arm.

Jessie waved to them, then hurried to unlock the front entrance of the church, which had a wheelchair ramp. She propped the door open and went to the piano to warm up with a few fast scales.

In a few minutes, the DiSpiritos came in, Ben first, carrying his trumpet case, and then Pete pushing his wife up the center aisle. Jessie rose from the piano and went to greet them. "Andie, welcome. I'm so glad you could come."

Andie took the hand Jessie extended; hers was thin and cold despite the warmth of the August evening. The contours of her skull were painfully prominent beneath her skin. Even so, it was obvious that she had once been a beautiful woman.

"Jessie, we can't thank you enough for all you're doing for Ben," she said, a smile crinkling the corners of her jade green eyes.

"I just want to be able to say I knew him when." Jessie tried to focus on the smile, on the warmth in the eyes, and not on Andie's shocking thinness and almost luminous pallor. Then, realizing she hadn't yet greeted Pete, she turned to him. "Hey, Pete."

"Hi, Jess." He was making an obvious effort to be cheerful.

Andie said, "I wanted to come tonight because all *I* get to hear are the long tones and mouthpiece buzzing and the endless repetitions. And, of course, an infinite loop of Civil War tunes."

Jessie nodded. "One time, when I was practicing the same passage over and over again, my mother came running out of the kitchen with a cast-iron frying pan and said, 'I'm sorry, honey, but I'm going to have to hit you over the head with this if you play that one more time.'"

Ben made a kazoo-like noise with his mouthpiece, and they all laughed.

Because of her hours of practice at Ganny's house, Jessie was able to accelerate the tempo close to what it should be. They ran through a good portion of the movement, stopping occasionally to discuss dynamics, and once for Jessie to advise Ben to take care to neither speed up the easier parts nor slow down the harder ones. When he got frustrated after multiple repetitions of a troublesome passage, she suggested some playful mental tricks that had often helped her break free from her own musical impasses.

Jessie suggested that they try reading through the second movement. They began to play the lyrical andante. At first, Ben was tentative. Jessie followed his tempo. Glancing at him midway through, she could tell that he had moved beyond his earlier tension. His tone grew increasingly confident. After a while, he was swaying as he played, completely under the spell of the music.

When they finished, everyone sat still, savoring the last echoes of the music's resonance. Jessie looked over at Ben's parents. They were holding hands, and Andie was beaming. Pete's eyes looked bright, rimmed with red.

She quickly turned her attention back to Ben. "Let's meet again next week, and if you get stuck again, think about trying some of those techniques. Or better still, invent some of your own."

He thanked her. They packed up their music and Ben shook the condensation out of his horn and put it in its case. Jessie went over to Pete and Andie while Ben walked a little way down the aisle to make a phone call.

"It was great, the way you helped him break down that trouble spot," Andie said. "Those were creative suggestions."

Finished with his call, Ben came back to join them. Jessie said, "I think we should start recording next time and see how we sound. Do you think you might be able to figure out the church's recording equipment?" she asked Ben.

"No problem," he said with teenage male assurance.

"Want to take a look at it?"

"I'll come too," Pete said. The two of them followed Jessie to the room where the computer and recording controls were located. Jessie unlocked the door.

"There it is, you're on your own. I can't tell you a thing about it. I'm going to keep Andie company."

She went back to sit in the pew beside Andie's chair. "You have a very talented son," Jessie said. "It's a gift for me to see someone who's so passionate about his music. He reminds me of myself at his age."

"'At his age'… you make it sound like it was so long ago. What are you, in your mid-twenties?" Andie asked, teasing.

"Oh, well—a little more than *mid*."

There was a pop, and the speakers hummed loudly all around the church. Both women started.

"Technological genius at work," Andie said, and they laughed. Andie leaned forward and adjusted a soft pillow behind her back. A fleeting wince tightened her features, then was gone. "Do you have private piano students, Jessie?"

"No, not yet."

"Well, it seems like you're a natural teacher. Patient and knowledgeable and supportive. With a spirit of fun too. That's what young performers need."

Before Jessie could reply, Andie went on. "I don't know if Pete told you, but I'm a teacher. I was a dancer in New York, and when we moved down here, my friend and I opened our own studio."

"Pete didn't tell me," Jessie said. "But I'm not surprised. You look like a dancer."

"Ah, well…" Andie gave a little shrug, and a wistful smile. "Do you play anything other than classical music?"

"Oh, sure. I can play just about anything. But classical is my first love."

"Like ballet is mine."

There was a silence. More humming from the speakers. Then a blast of very loud organ music.

"Why don't we go out to the reception room and sit there?" Jessie said. "Then we won't risk having our eardrums blown out."

"Good idea."

"Can I give you a push?"

"Sure, thanks."

Jessie maneuvered Andie's chair through the hallway to the large room behind the sanctuary. It was furnished with hand-me-downs from church members over the years. She pulled the wheelchair up beside a brocade wing chair with a cat-scratched arm and sat down. There was still enough of the waning daylight that she didn't need to turn on a lamp.

Andie seemed at ease with silence. Sitting with her there in the twilight, Jessie had the strange thought that there was a quality about her that reminded her of Lem. A transparency of the physical form that let a spiritual radiance shine through.

"I'd give anything to go to one of your Civil War events," Andie said. "The scene at Gettysburg sounded really cool. Thank you for that video."

"I thought you'd enjoy seeing how Ben was the star of the cornet section."

"He was obviously loving it. And playing on the field just thrilled him. Pete got a kick out of it too." She looked down at her long, pale fingers as they smoothed the black material of her pants over her thin thighs. "You know," she said in a musing tone, "we've been so busy raising our boy and both of us working that we haven't really had much chance to make many friends here or develop any hobbies. We've spent whatever free time we have together, doing things as a family. The band and all the events have been good for my guys. Ben has his school friends, but Pete really values the social outlet."

Jessie sensed a deeper significance to her words—that she didn't want her husband to be lonely after she was gone. "Everybody loves him," she said. "He tells great jokes around the campfire. And he's one of the few people I can always count on to help me with the kitchen work."

"Where'd you ladies go?" Pete's voice called out from the sanctuary.

Jessie got up and went to the door. "Hiding out in here."

Pete and Ben entered the room.

"Did you figure it out?" Jessie asked.

Ben shrugged. "I could if I had some more time."

"I decided to stop before I blew anything up," Pete said.

"I'll ask the guy who does recordings for the church if he can come next Tuesday," Jessie said.

They thanked her. "I enjoyed our chat," Andie said.

"Me too."

When they had gone, Jessie moved slowly around the church, shutting off the lights, turning off the organ, putting away her music. She felt pensive, melancholy, thinking of how close the DiSpirito family seemed and how great a grief awaited them.

She herself would face loss soon. Tomorrow, in fact. She would see Lem then and tell him goodbye. Her heart was caught between two conflicting impulses: soaring at the thought of being with him again, plunging at the prospect of parting from him forever. It seemed to lie in her chest like a stone.

CHAPTER 28

PORTAL TO PARADISE

THE WHITE MOONLIGHT flooding the path along the edge of the cornfield made a lantern unnecessary. Jessie was carrying a lot this evening; one arm was draped with the double-wedding-ring quilt that Ganny had given her when Jessie first got her own apartment. She had brought the quilt instead of the usual rough, scratchy blanket in honor of this occasion. A basket of treasures to share with Lem dangled over her other arm.

She was wearing her best Civil War dress, a polished-cotton gown she had made for special concerts and the fancy-dress balls at re-enactments. The neckline, trimmed with lace, bared her collarbone; puffed sleeves, also lace-trimmed, began at the tops of her shoulders and ended halfway down her upper arms.

She had taken care with her hair, pinning it up into a soft roll in back. Crystal earrings dangled from thin gold wires looped through her earlobes. They brushed her neck as she walked.

Lord, she thought, *just don't let me run into a stranger in this getup.*

She entered the clearing, stopped, and looked around. The night was still. She could feel, and in the silence could hear, the thudding of her heart. "Lem?" she called softly.

Then she noticed the stakes of bright new wood driven into the ground, trailing streamers of plastic ribbon that even in the moonlight she could see were neon pink. The stakes marked out huge squares within the clearing. Some trees at the edge of the forest, not far from the rock on which Lem had died, had been cut down.

"Lem!" she called again, hearing the edge of desperation in her voice.

And there he was, emerging from the forest darkness.

"Oh, thank God," she said, rushing to him. "I saw all this here and thought you were gone, that somebody drove you away. When did these stakes get put here?"

"Some fellows came with big sheets of paper and some kind of long metal ribbons they stretched out to make measurements. They were here a long time, marking out these squares and driving in the stakes. They were talking about building houses, I could hear that much. I took care for them not to see me."

"Houses?" she exclaimed. "This is sacred ground. They'd better not try to build houses here." Then she reminded herself that in actuality no one else knew that this was indeed sacred ground, the resting place of seven soldiers. There would need to be some evidence to block the development. And it would have to be found fast.

But now was not the time to think about that.

"I missed you, Lem. All those days away from you."

"I'm so glad to see you. That's the prettiest dress I ever saw."

She stepped back and twirled, making her hoop swing. "I wanted to wear my best dress for you."

"It's mighty nice. But you'd look pretty wearing a croker sack."

As he spoke, she searched his face, wanting to imprint its every feature on her memory: the changing expressions, the way his lips moved, the tilt of his head as he looked at her. Her throat ached at the thought of how this night had to end.

She busied herself with spreading out the quilt on the ground and arranging the various items. "Come, sit with me. I have so much to tell you."

"You brought your fancy quilt."

"I did. My grandmother made it."

"Too nice for this rough place."

"No, Lem. Nothing's too nice for our special night together." *Our last night together.* She thrust the thought away.

She lowered herself, corset creaking, to sit with her legs to one side, the hoop spreading out around her. Lem sat down too, crossing his long legs, facing her. She reached into her basket and took out Jeremiah Walker's letter.

"I met a man who teaches at a university here in Murfreesboro. He collects letters of Tennessee soldiers who fought in the Civil War. He gave me this." She held out the letter and Lem reached for it. His fingers closed on the envelope, but it fell to the ground.

"Sometimes I misremember," he said with an apologetic shrug.

"Me too." She picked it up so he could see it. "It's from Jeremiah, to his parents."

"Oh, my Lord."

"I'll read it to you."

"Poor old Poke," Lem said when she had finished. His face looked weary, older than she'd ever seen it. "I think I almost had it easier than him, being the one killed and not the one having to watch it, or bury his dead friends. Wasn't that something, for him to say I died a hero's death?"

"But you did, Lem," Jessie said. "You sacrificed yourself to save your friend's life."

He shrugged. "He would have done the same for me. How came that man to find this letter?"

Jessie told him about the old gentleman in Franklin, and Jeremiah's haversack. "I don't know who originally found the haversack, or where. The old man said it had been in his attic for as long as he could remember." She paused, and then decided not to tell Lem about Jeremiah's death in the Yankee prison camp. The next thing she had to show him would be upsetting enough.

She reached into her basket. "I found another letter, from your mother to your brother Caleb's wife."

"From my mama?" His face lit up, then immediately grew serious as he saw her expression.

"It's sad," she said. "Will you be all right?"

He nodded, his hands steepled as if in prayer, pressed to his mouth and chin. He closed his eyes tightly like someone bracing himself against imminent pain.

Jessie read his mother's words. By the time she finished, she was crying.

Lem stood and walked a little distance from her and turned away, pressing his hand to his eyes. She saw his back and shoulders move in spasms of grief.

She rose and went to him, reached out, and touched the stirring, prickling nothingness that to her eyes appeared to be his solid, blanket-draped shoulder. "Oh, honey," she said. It was the first time she had called him that. "I'm sorry to make you cry. But I thought you'd want to hear it."

"I did, Jessie. It's just that it hurts my very soul to think of them all so sad. Even my pa." He sighed deeply and turned to her, and she saw the streaks of his tears carving pale runnels through the black-powder soot on his cheeks, shining in the moonlight. This must be the first time he had cried in 144 years. Her heart constricted.

"Seems like Mama didn't believe it was really me, my spirit, that came to her that night after I died," Lem said.

"I think she talked herself into believing it was a nightmare so she could hold on to hope," Jessie said. "It's good that you wrote that letter to your father. Maybe it helped him find some peace, in time."

She sat again and patted the quilt beside her. "Come sit with me, I have something else to tell you. Something happy this time."

He sat and passed his hand quickly over his eyes, then looked at her expectantly.

"I found your family."

He drew himself up straight and looked at her in amazement. "You did? You really and truly found them? How? What are they like?" It seemed he could not get the questions out fast enough.

"There's a book that lists every family in Sevier County, and I spoke to every Sanders. There were probably about fifteen of them." She told him about finally meeting Ida Mae. "Her husband's grandfather was named Lemuel Sanders the second. I was so excited to hear that. He was your brother's son."

"Lemuel Sanders the second. You don't say." He shook his head in wonder.

She told him how she had tracked down Sarah Gowan. "She's your brother Caleb's great-great granddaughter, your great-great niece." She paused for a breath, then continued. "Sarah—she calls herself Sally—and I got together."

"Did you tell her about me?"

"No, I thought it might seem too strange to her, at least at first. If we get to know each other better, I might tell her sometime."

Lem nodded.

"I showed her Jeremiah's letter," Jessie went on. "It meant a lot to her. She has a son who's a soldier. There's a war going on now, in a country far away, in a land the Bible talks about. Her son is fighting there."

"Seems like folks'll never stop killing each other, will they?" Lem said with bitter resignation.

"No, seems like they won't. Sally thought you were very brave. She wants me to show her this place. I know she'll do everything she can to see that you're given a proper burial."

"And the others here?" He gestured to the ground they sat on.

"The man I mentioned, who teaches at the university—if those other soldiers have any identification on them, I'm sure he'll try to find their families. And I know my pastor, who you met, will give you all a blessing, here at the grave. He said he thinks you're good and sincere. And that you need to go home to the Lord."

"Oh, Jessie," he said in a low tone, looking down, and at first she thought she had upset him. But then he raised his eyes to hers and she saw an overflowing gratitude in them. "How can I ever thank you for all you've done for me?"

"I would do anything for you." She drew a deep breath to steady herself for the next thing she had to say. "But what I have to do now is the hardest thing. I have to say goodbye to you. Pastor John says I need to find my happiness in this world. But if you only knew how much I don't want to."

He was looking at her tenderly. "I do know. And it's for the best. Your pastor is right."

"Lem, promise me one thing. Send me a sign when you get to Heaven, so I'll know you're finally at peace."

"You have my word."

The night went still. Even the crickets seemed to suspend their abrasive music. She had never seen anyone look at her with the intense love that was radiating from his expression. She was finding it hard to breathe.

"I don't know what's possible for us," she said, "but I want to love you, however we can." She held out her arms to him.

WHENEVER THEY'D TRIED to touch before, she'd drawn back quickly, unnerved by the electric tingling and the way her hand or her lips passed through his seemingly solid form. But now, as they embraced fully, she did not draw back.

The sensations were indescribable, engulfing—shimmering light, vibrating energy that made the hairs stand up all over her body. The ever-present humming was now inside her head, and revealed itself to be composed of different strains of music, emerging and subsiding before her mind could grasp anything beyond an unearthly beauty. Overwhelmed, she went limp but did not fall, held by him. Consciousness slipped away.

When she regained awareness, and her surroundings began to come into focus, her first impression was that she was in a bed. She felt a roughness beneath her, heard a rustling, and realized that the mattress must be an old-fashioned one, filled with corn husks. It was covered with a rough cotton ticking and a homespun top sheet that rasped against her skin. Her naked skin.

Fully alert now, and a little alarmed, she raised herself up on one elbow. And there was Lem, lying on his side with his head propped on one hand, gazing at her. He was smiling at her, a tender, wondering smile. His shoulders and chest were bare above the bedclothes that covered the two of them. A gilding of pale hair on his chest shone in the dazzling white light that flooded through the uncurtained windows.

He wasn't pallid and soot-stained but ruddy with health, and clean, his wavy dark-blond hair appearing freshly washed. She dwelt on every detail, noticing the pink, raised, shiny scar on the right underside of his chin where he had fallen on the shovel as a little boy, and the way the hair on his head grew darker and coarser where it shaded into the stubble of his beard.

Tentatively, she extended her hand to his neck where she could see the pulsing of a vein. Her fingertips encountered warm, solid flesh. Pressing them to that place, she felt the throb of life within him.

"Oh, Lem," she breathed, awestruck. "I can *touch* you."

She moved close to him. The cornhusk mattress crackled softly. It was a rope bed that needed tightening; it sagged in the middle so that its occupants couldn't help being thrown together, but that was exactly what she wanted. She put her arms around his neck, and they kissed. It was a miracle to feel his warm lips and the beard-roughened skin of his face, to inhale his breath that smelled fresh and sweet. She pressed the length of her naked body against his and gasped at the smoothness and heat of his skin, the hardness of him against her lower abdomen.

Then, perplexed, she tore her gaze away from him and looked around. The bed was a four-poster in a white room filled with the brightest sunlight she had ever seen. The walls were of rough-hewn boards, whitewashed. There were two small windows with wavy glass set in their mullions. On the wall across from the bed was a stone fireplace blackened with use but now fireless; higher up beside it were pegs from which clothes hung—his dark trousers and white shirt, her calico dress, but not one she had ever seen before. There was a partially burned candle in a metal candlestick on the table beside the bed, and a white stoneware pitcher and basin on a dresser under a window. A blue and white quilt covered her and Lem.

Nothing was visible through the window glass, nothing except a blinding white glare, as if the brightest sunlight was trying to penetrate a wall of dense fog.

"Lem, where are we?"

"I think we're in my old home place." His expression was wondering. "This looks like Mama and Pa's room."

"How did we get here?"

"I don't rightly know."

"Could this be Heaven?"

"I reckon maybe *our* Heaven. It sure feels like it." He pulled her close.

"Did I die?"

"Oh, no, darlin', I'm sure you're not dead."

"I don't care if I am, as long as I'm with you." Her belly pressed against his and she felt his desire. "Can we do this in Heaven?"

"'Course we can. You're my wife." He lifted her left hand and kissed the ring there. A wooden, hand-carved ring with a delicate pattern of vines and flowers.

"This is one of the rings you carved," she said with wonder.

"Yes. Your wedding ring. Till I can get you a gold one."

"I don't want a gold one. Nothing could be more precious to me than this, that you made with your own hands."

He kissed her lips. For a long moment they lost themselves in the kiss, then she drew back again.

"But Lem …"

"Yes, turtle dove?" His smile showed amusement and an effortful patience with the interruption.

"You're different. You're healthy and strong, and so clean."

He laughed. "You prob'ly can't even recognize me."

"And…" She placed the flat of her hand on his taut abdomen. "You aren't hurt," she marveled. "The war…"

"There's no war here," he said. "There never was and never will be. We're safe here together."

She didn't understand, but all questions ceased as he drew her to him and covered her face with kisses, then gently turned her onto her back and moved on top of her.

When their bodies joined, they were momentarily awed into stillness by the sense of completion, of homecoming in each other. They looked at each other and laughed softly, overwhelmed by so much happiness.

Desire reawakened and intensified. An urgency built within her, to take him ever deeper inside her and clasp him ever closer. She pressed her lips against the base of his throat to feel the heat of his skin and to taste the salt of his sweat, intoxicated by every aspect of his physical being.

At last he cried out her name and pushed so deeply inside her that he reached the as-yet-untouched place at her center, causing an inburst of sensation so powerful that only his arms tight around her seemed to keep her from flying apart.

When she came back to herself, his weight was pressing her down into a white cotton canyon that smelled of soap and sunlit fields and rustled when she stirred. He raised his head to smile dazedly down at her, then he withdrew to lie beside her. Their uncoupling made Jessie whimper with loss. He pulled her onto his damp breast and stroked her hair. She lay in his arms, hearing and feeling the strong pulse of his heart, resting in the deepest peace she had ever known.

When words returned, she murmured, "Lem, I want to stay here forever with you. Don't make me go back."

His embrace tightened around her. "It's not me making you stay or go. You have so much ahead of you. Go on and live your life, Jessie darlin'. Live some life for me."

She sighed in resignation. "I told you I'd do anything for you." Clasped in his arms, she fell asleep.

Jessie woke to a chorus of birdsong. Startled, she sat up quickly and looked around. First light was beginning to spread over the fields and steal into the woods. She was fully clothed; her dress was damp with dew, clammy and clinging to her skin. She glanced at her hand. The wooden ring was gone. She raised her eyes to take in the unaccustomed view, in full light, of the cornfield, the woods, the blue sky above her, the quiet clearing with those sacrilegious stakes and their garish streamers, the pale hacked-off trunks of the trees that bordered the glade.

It was Saturday, so possibly the building planners would not be working; still, if they were, they'd be arriving soon and would find her a very strange sight. Nevertheless, she allowed herself to sit quietly for some time longer.

Memories of the night before rose up, that white room and the lovemaking that she and Lem had shared there—so real in every detail. What was that? A dream, born of her longing and sorrow? A vision of the life they might have had? A foretaste of eternal bliss given to her as consolation for her imminent loss?

She did not know, but something within her was definitely different. The anxiety of the previous days and weeks had given way to a calmness, no longer the stunned stasis of conflicting emotions, but the serenity of something momentous having been fulfilled. The leaden weight in her chest had been replaced by warmth and light.

"Lem?" she called quietly.

The woods and fields and sky were still. She could sense that his presence was no longer in this place.

Weeping, as much from joy as from sorrow, she collected everything she'd brought. As the sunlight streamed full across the field, the warmth within her answered it. Walking away from their meeting place, she heard again in her mind his parting words: *Live some life for me.*

PART IV

IMMORTAL HOME

CHAPTER 29

LOOMING SHADOW

"Jessie, I got the letter," Philip Goldsmith said. "Thank you for it. How'd you find it?"

It was three o'clock on a muggy Monday afternoon, the end of the school day. Jessie was juggling her cell phone, car keys, and purse, and feeling a finger of sweat tracing down her back as she walked across the school parking lot to her van.

She told him about reading *The Bitter Cup* and subsequently contacting the UT librarian.

"You have the makings of a good researcher," he said.

"Thank you. And, Dr. Goldsmith, something else. When I was visiting my grandmother in Sevier County, I managed to track down Lemuel Sanders' great-great-niece and gave her Jeremiah Walker's letter."

"Now I really am impressed."

"It took some doing, but I knew that lots of families, like mine, have deep roots in the Smokies, so I thought there was a good chance some of the Sanderses might still be around. Sally Gowan—that's the Sanders relative—wants to come down here sometime soon, and we're going to see if we can find the burial site from Jeremiah's description. Would you like to come—"

"Definitely," he said, before she had even finished. "Any idea when?"

"She wants to do it as soon as possible. I'll let you know when we get our plans set. Are you around in the next few weeks?"

"My sabbatical's over and I'm back in harness again for the long haul." He didn't sound pleased. She could sympathize.

She promised to be in touch.

When she got back to her apartment, she fixed herself a cup of tea and called Sally at work.

"Jessie, how nice to hear from you," Sally said, then added, "I got that letter. Thank you for sending it, but it about broke my heart as a mother."

"It broke mine too." Then, trying to keep her tone casual, she said, "Sally, I'm wondering if you'd like to come down here sometime soon. We could try to find the burial site and I could introduce you to Dr. Goldsmith, the professor who found Jeremiah's letter."

"I'd love that. When would be good?"

It turned out that the following weekend, the long Labor Day holiday, would work out well for both of them. Sally said she would get a motel room, and they agreed to meet at Jessie's apartment building at three-thirty on Friday.

After they ended their call, Jessie phoned Philip Goldsmith and arranged to meet him at the university on Friday afternoon at around five.

He said, "If the site is on the property of the national park, we'll be in luck. If it's on private property, we have to be careful about trespassing."

"A friend of mine has an uncle who owns a farm next to the battlefield," Jessie told him. "He lets our band use it for campouts. We can park there and then go exploring. If anyone stops us, we can just plead ignorance."

"Works for me," he said. "I've always operated on the assumption that it's better to ask for forgiveness than permission."

After she hung up, Jessie sat for a moment, spent. It was hard work keeping her story straight, not letting slip the true extent of her knowledge. *I'd better remember to always lead an honest life*, she thought. *I'm pretty bad at deception.*

Most exhausting of all was having to pretend calm, dispassionate interest and patiently wait for events to unfold, when in fact she was frantic at the idea that the desecration of that sacred ground by the developers could happen at any time and might even be happening now. She had searched for the website of the real estate developer, the Glenwood Construction Company. It showed a map of the proposed new development, "Two Flags Estates," and Jessie's heart sank to see that a shaded area indicating the dimensions of the construction spread like a menacing shadow over the grave and the stone in the woods where Lem had died.

THAT EVENING, as she was cleaning her apartment in anticipation of Sally's visit, her phone rang. It was Pete DiSpirito.

"Hi, Jess," he said, and she could instantly hear that his voice was subdued.

"Pete? How are you? Are we on for tomorrow night?"

"That's what I'm calling about. Andie's had to be hospitalized, so I won't be able to make it."

"Oh, I'm so sorry. I hope it's…" She hesitated, not wanting to say something tactless. She finally settled on, "I hope she'll get better soon."

"Thank you. I'm actually calling for two reasons. One, Andie wanted me to be sure to tell you this. I hope she'll be able to discuss it with you herself, but she didn't want to wait. She said that she and her partner at the dance studio, Vicky Lang, have been talking for a while about hiring a pianist for rehearsals and recitals, and Andie thinks you'd be great for the job. She said if you're interested, you should give Vicky a call."

Jessie, amazed, began to stammer out her thanks.

"Andie was really impressed by your playing, and we're both so grateful for all you've done for Ben," Pete said. He gave her Vicky Lang's work number, then he continued, "The recording session tomorrow night is the second reason I'm calling. I have to go to the hospital straight from the office, and I wondered if you could pick Ben up from school and take him to the church. It's a lot to ask, I know …"

"I'll be glad to. We'll get some supper on the way."

"Bless you." He gave her directions to their house. "I'll come to the church at eight-thirty."

"Don't hurry. If you're later than that, I'll bring him back home."

"You're an angel."

RALPH TYREE, the church's audiovisual specialist, was waiting for her and Ben when they arrived for their recording session. He greeted her with his usual shy courtesy and shook Ben's hand. Ralph was probably seventy, but his hair was shoe-polish black and combed into a small pompadour in front, like an old-time Grand Ole Opry star. Instead of the one suit he had worn every Sunday she'd known him, on this evening he was dressed in green work pants and a short-sleeved white shirt with a pen protector in the breast pocket that bore the logo of his store, Tyree Feed and Grain.

While Ben played scales to warm up, Ralph set up the microphone and positioned a second mike near the piano. Then he went back to the control room and adjusted the levels as Ben and Jessie played a few measures.

When they were ready, she called to Ralph to start recording, then launched into the opening bars of the first movement. Ben raised the trumpet to his lips and began to play. He hardly looked at his music at all. They kept going even when Jessie stumbled over a short run of notes and Ben cracked one of his entrances. The passage that had given him such trouble in the previous rehearsal flowed flawlessly this time. There was an energy that both of them seemed to feel; they were not just playing the notes but were communicating with each other, collaborating to create something new and entirely their own from this two-century-old composition.

Jessie paused for Ben to play his cadenza. He didn't rush. He played confidently, his notes ringing out through the sanctuary. As he neared the end of the solo passage with a bugle-like fanfare that seemed like a nod to his re-enacting role, he raised his eyebrows to Jessie, and she resumed playing along with him to the end of the piece.

"That's it, Ralph," Jessie called after their last notes had faded away. She and Ben smiled at each other. He looked elated. "Ben, that was incredible."

From the rear of the church came soft clapping. Pete had come in unnoticed and was sitting in a pew near the back doors. He stood, and as he walked up the aisle, Ralph began playing back the recording over the PA system. Pete stopped in his tracks, then sat down in the nearest pew and closed his eyes to listen. He looked exhausted and almost appeared to be asleep. At the end, he opened his eyes and breathed, "Beautiful."

He rose and came to the front of the church.

"How's Mom?" Ben asked.

Pete rested his hand on his son's shoulder. "She seemed more comfortable tonight," he said, obviously measuring his words. "She sends you her love. We'll go visit her tomorrow. I'll see if I can bring her a CD of your performance tonight—that'll make her happy."

"Let's ask Ralph," Jessie said. "Come, I'll introduce you."

Ben began packing up his trumpet and disassembling his music stand as Jessie and Pete headed back to the control room. She introduced Pete and Ralph to each other. Ralph shook Pete's hand and accepted his thanks.

"Here you go," Ralph said several minutes later, giving a CD to each of them. "Just let me know if I can do anything else for y'all."

"I'll need a few more copies of this," Pete said, "but I can get those made. I don't think we'll need to impose on you for more recording."

"I agree," Jessie said. "I think he nailed it in one take."

"You both did," Pete said.

"That boy of yours is really talented," Ralph said. "And of course, I never get enough of hearing you play, Miss Jessie." She never could get him to drop the "Miss."

They both thanked him. Ralph shut down all the systems and bid them good night.

Standing there alone with Pete in the small room illuminated only by the rosy rays of the setting sun, Jessie said, "How are you holding up?"

"I was trying to put on a good face for Ben, but tonight was tough. The priest came. Andie asked for him, to receive the sacrament of the sick. It's only given at critical times, and that's what we're facing right now. But …" He sighed. "We've had crises before and she's pulled through, so I'm praying. Where there's life, there's hope, as the saying goes." He looked drawn; there was a furrow of sadness and worry between his brows, and the hollows around his eyes were shadowed with fatigue.

"She's so lovely, Pete," Jessie said. "I was really happy that she came the other night. We had a good talk. She has such sparkle and warmth. And she's so proud of Ben."

Abruptly, Pete seemed to fall rather than sit on the chair beside the computer. It rolled backward on its casters and struck the edge of the computer desk as he covered his face with his hands. Jessie stared at him, shocked, as a few harsh sobs escaped him.

Hastily, she closed the door to keep Ben from hearing. She moved beside Pete and rested a hand on his shoulder, feeling it shake with the effort of suppressing his grief.

Then he jumped up, startling her again. "I'm so goddamn mad at God!" he said, walking over to the window. "What kind of sense does it make to take a young wife and mother and teacher and dancer in the prime of her life, someone with so much to give to the world—someone so *needed*? When there are all these people who want to die, or maybe even *deserve* to die." He drew in a few deep breaths.

Jessie just stood quietly, feeling helpless.

He sat back down and again stared out the window, his profile outlined in red-gold light. After a few moments, he said, "You go along, trying to lead a good life, and it's like the old cartoons when a little guy is walking along the street and an anvil falls on his head. That's the way we felt when Andie was first diagnosed in 2003. She went through the chemo without complaining, she kept on working and taking care of us and encouraging her students, and we had two wonderful years when we thought she was cured. Then the cancer came back with a vengeance. She let them poison her, mutilate her, take out her bone marrow and put some stranger's in—she tried it all because she loves life, and loves *us* so much." He paused, breathing deeply. "All that suffering for nothing."

Jessie felt tears spring to her eyes. "It's terribly unfair, I'm so sorry."

"Thank you." After a few more moments, he stood and turned to her. "Forgive me for dumping all this on you."

"Don't apologize. I want to help you, however I can."

"Thank you. You have." He passed his shirt sleeve over his face. "I'd better go out and see Ben. He'll be wondering." Then he looked at her. "What you did tonight was truly above and beyond. Thank you so much. You're a good friend." He stepped forward and gave her a quick, strong hug. She felt his tight muscles and smelled the scent of him—a whiff of the hospital, the memory of the morning's aftershave or deodorant, a faint hint of acrid sweat from a long, exhausting, emotionally stressful day.

As they left the control room and Jessie pulled the door shut behind them, Ben looked up from the pew where he had been sitting, oiling his valves. "What kept you guys?"

"We were discussing the next step," Jessie said. "We agreed that we'd all listen to the CD and see if it sounds like a keeper."

Pete darted her a grateful look. The two of them got ready to leave. "Are you coming, Jess?" Pete asked.

"I have to be sure everything's closed up. Y'all go ahead."

They walked together out the back door, Pete's arm around Ben's shoulders.

As Jessie gathered up her music and shut off the lights, she thought about the encounter with Pete. She was moved that he had let her see his unguarded grief, and glad that she seemed to have been able to offer him some consolation. The memory of his embrace, feeling his taut muscles and smelling his masculine scent, lingered like a question in her mind.

But she pushed it away—on the brink of losing the love of his life, he needed consolation, that was all. And, having just lost the love of her own life, she was far from ready to think about a new attachment.

She felt that the time was soon coming when she would tell Pete all she had learned about how love, and those we have loved, live on. That they endure, not just in our hearts, but in a realm of actual existence that, though beyond the grasp of our limited senses, is always near.

CHAPTER 30

A LAND FULL OF GRAVES

THE BROADWAY LIGHTS Dance Studio was located in a shopping mall in the western part of town. Vicky Lang met Jessie in the reception area at five p.m. the following day. She was a tall, willow-thin blonde in her mid-thirties, Jessie guessed. She wore a black nylon wraparound skirt tied over a black leotard. Black tights ended at her ankles and her feet were bare.

"Jessie, come in," she said. Her close-set hazel eyes and long nose gave her face a birdlike quality that was emphasized by a long neck. "The next class isn't till six-thirty, so why don't we start with you playing something for me while I improvise? Then we can talk in my office."

Jessie followed her down a hallway lined with photographs into the dance studio, a large room with mirrored walls and barres at waist-height, and a polished wooden floor. Several young women in leotards were sitting in chairs around the room, putting on street shoes and packing up their dance bags. The room smelled like perfume, sweat, and feet.

There was an upright piano against one wall, and Jessie sat down on the bench and took out an assortment of music, pieces in a variety of musical idioms that she thought would lend themselves to dance interpretations.

When the students had left, Vicky asked her to play something classical, and Jessie chose Tchaikovsky's "Waltz of the Flowers" from *The Nutcracker*. As she played, with her back to the studio, from time to time she watched Vicky's reflection in the mirror, moving lithely to the music. As Vicky changed the tempo of her movements, Jessie kept time with her. At UT, she had been the accompanist for the vocal program, and then there were her Civil War performances with soprano Becky DePew, so she knew how to adapt her style to a soloist's artistic interpretation.

"Very nice," Vicky said. "You just can't get that with recordings. Dancers need to both respond to and influence the flow of the music. That's why Andie and I were committed to having a live accompanist as soon as we could find the right person. She recommended you highly." She picked up a towel from a stack on a shelf and wiped her face and throat with it. "What else have you got?"

Jessie played short extracts from a Scott Joplin rag, a jazzy piece from the Vince Guaraldi Charlie Brown Christmas suite, and the exuberant, Latin-accented "America" from *West Side Story*. Vicky stood listening, the towel draped around her neck.

"That was great," Vicky said, when Jessie had finished. "Come into my office and let's talk about the job."

Sitting at a desk and eating an apple that she had sliced into precise wedges, Vicky told Jessie about the schedule, which worked out well with Jessie's own, since the classes were held after school and on weekends. They discussed payment, an hourly rate that Jessie found generous. She would start the following week.

They shook hands and Jessie stood up to go, delighted to have finally succeeded in getting her first paying job solely on the strength of her playing.

As they walked down the hallway to the front door, Jessie paused to look at photos of Vicky onstage in a billowing tutu, standing on pointe.

"That was *Sleeping Beauty*," Vicky said. "When I was a member of the Houston Dance Company."

Jessie made an admiring sound.

"As I moved into my thirties, my body became a little less flexible, and I also wanted to have a family," Vicky went on. "So my husband and I moved here, and I met Andie, and we went into business back in 2003." Moving on, Vicky stopped in front of a series of dramatic black-and-white photographs of a woman in a clinging white dress, captured in a sequence of graceful poses. "Andie in her prime, in New York."

Looking at the photographs, Jessie felt the presence of shared emotions too large and weighty for words. After a moment, Vicky broke the silence, saying in a brighter tone, "I'll be so happy to tell her that you and I will be working together. And hopefully she'll get better and come back to be with us."

SALLY GOWAN ARRIVED at Jessie's apartment building on the Friday afternoon of the Labor Day weekend in a red Honda Civic with a bumper sticker that proclaimed, "Proud Army Mom." Jessie was sitting on a bench outside the front door.

Sally looked younger than her fifty-plus years, dressed more casually than the last time Jessie had seen her, in a yellow tank top with a white sweater tied around her shoulders, a knee-length denim skirt, and white sandals. With a pair of sunglasses atop her head, the overall impression she gave was attractive, energetic, and capable, with a hint of mischief.

"Dr. Goldsmith got called into a last-minute meeting this afternoon, so we arranged to meet tomorrow morning," Jessie said.

"That's all right," Sally said. "I bet the two of us can come up with some trouble to get into."

Jessie had wondered whether they would be formal with each other, given their roughly twenty-five-year age difference. But Sally's playful tone put her at ease. "I thought we could go out to the Visitor Center at Stones River, if you want," she said. "They might have records of your relative and Jeremiah Walker."

"Great idea."

Jessie hadn't had many visitors to her apartment, just family and Abby, her fellow camp cook. It was gratifying when Sally walked in and said, "Oh, how pretty." As Jessie showed her around the three rooms, Sally complimented details. "I love the color of your kitchen." (Jessie had painted it a dusty coral color with bright white trim.) "What a lovely living room. The piano looks so nice there." She gestured to the electronic piano in its faux mahogany case, a graduation present from Jessie's parents.

"I can play it at all hours using headphones, without disturbing the neighbors," Jessie said.

In the bedroom, as Sally admired the quilt on the bed and the ball gown on its dressmaker's form, Jessie felt her face flush, thinking, *If you only knew*, recalling Lem sitting on that quilt, moving to embrace her in that dress.

AT THE STONES RIVER Visitor Center, a man in a green uniform greeted them, wearing a tag that identified him as "John Lester, Volunteer."

"Welcome, ladies." He was about sixty, with friendly eyes behind his steel-rimmed glasses. "If you have any questions, just ask away."

Sally said, "Actually, I had a great-great uncle who fought at Stones River. He was killed here."

Mr. Lester nodded with respectful gravity. "What regiment was he with?"

Jessie had to bite her tongue.

"I don't know," Sally said. "His name was Lemuel Sanders. He was from Sevier County. His friend Jeremiah Walker also served in the same regiment. We have a letter from Jeremiah describing Lemuel's death."

Jessie chided herself for not having thought to bring her copy of the letter.

"A Union man?" asked Mr. Lester. He pulled a large black binder from underneath the reception desk.

"No, a Confederate."

"Ah. That would make him something of a rarity, from that part of the state. It was quite a bastion of Unionism." Re-shelving the book, he brought out another black binder.

Sally said, "There were also some Rebels, too, right?"

"Oh, yes, indeed," said Mr. Lester, opening the book and leafing through it. It appeared to contain long lists of names. "If we can say anything about the Civil War, it's that it was messy. Alliances and loyalties crossed borders, divided families—there were Confederate sympathizers in the North and men who fought for the Union in the South. There were even a few Black Confederates—yes," he said to their incredulous response. "Some were probably enslaved men brought along by white soldiers. But some might have seen the military as a way out of servitude." He continued paging through the book, then turned it toward Sally. "Here is your relative. Private Lemuel Sanders, Company I, 37th Tennessee Infantry Regiment." On the facing page he found Jeremiah's name. "And here's Private Walker. I'll make you a copy of these pages." He took the book into an office and soon returned, handing Sally the papers.

"Do you know the date of his death, whether it was in the first or the second battle?" he asked.

"December 31," Jessie said. "Sometime in the afternoon, according to the letter." Actually, she recalled with a little pang of chagrin, the letter made no reference to the exact date or time of Lem's death, but she hoped Sally wouldn't register her words or focus on that detail.

Mr. Lester took a map from under the desk and spread it out to face Jessie and Sally. "This shows the troop movements, hour by hour, in that battle."

"How amazing!" Jessie was impressed by such exact documentation.

"Here's the 37th, right over here," Mr. Lester said. The regiments were represented in little blocks, red for Confederate, blue for Union. "This is where they started out, at dawn that morning." There was a little block marked "37 Tenn," just to the west of Cason Lane and to the south of Franklin Pike—in his letter, Jeremiah called the latter road by its old name, the Triune Road. Jessie knew that intersection well. Her father's business was located not far from it; today, the site was covered over by a shopping center and parking lots.

Mr. Lester turned the map over to show Lem's regiment's whereabouts by noon; they had advanced further to the north, across Wilkinson Pike and to the westernmost edge of the conflict.

"What's the terrain like there?" Jessie asked.

"Fields, mostly. Farmland," Mr. Lester replied.

Jessie told him, "The letter we have says that these two men got separated from their unit and fought in a forest where there were large flat boulders. Sanders was killed there." Once again, she was nervous about quoting facts that weren't exactly stated outright in the letter, but she pushed on. "The next day, his friend Walker came back with a burial party and dragged his body and the bodies of six other Confederate soldiers out of the woods and buried them in a clearing."

"Unfortunately, the countryside around here is just full of graves," Mr. Lester said. "Nearly every time there's new construction, they dig up remains that turn out to be Civil War soldiers."

"What happens to those remains?" Sally asked.

"Well, first the police have to make sure they're not the bodies of modern crime victims. Then the Park Service gets involved. If they're identified as Union soldiers, they're buried in the National Cemetery across the street. Confederates are buried in Evergreen Cemetery, downtown."

He took out a glossy brochure, a guide to the national park. On the back was a smaller, simpler map showing the shaded area of the park. "Here's a wooded section that might fit the description of where your relative fell." He pointed to a place just to the west of the boundary of the national battlefield. The location was definitely near the farm where the band camped, Jessie thought.

"My family would love to find that burial site," Sally said.

Mr. Lester looked regretful. "That's private land, and we have to discourage people from trespassing. It's also possible the site was excavated sometime earlier, and your family member is buried at Evergreen Cemetery, in the Confederate Circle. Two thousand men were removed from the battlefield in 1891 by a Confederate ladies' association and buried there. Sadly, though, the identities of only about 150 of those soldiers are known."

Jessie bought a copy of the troop movement map and put it into her purse. She and Sally thanked Mr. Lester.

"My pleasure," he said.

The two women stepped out onto a terrace and stood for a moment, gazing at the peaceful scene of gently rolling fields bounded by snake-rail fences stretching out under a hazy blue sky.

Sally said, "I have to admit I was a little discouraged by two things Mr. Lester said."

"What?"

"The bit about not trespassing on private land …"

"We can get access through my friend's uncle's farm, and we won't stay long or do any harm. And if we're caught, like I said to Dr. Goldsmith, we can just plead ignorance."

"Sounds like a plan," Sally said. "But if we do find the site, how will we know the body—or bodies—are still there? What if he was dug up, like Mr. Lester said, and moved to that cemetery with all the other unknown soldiers?"

Jessie felt the strain of having to stifle the truth she alone knew. Watching clouds of tiny insects wheeling in the air above the field, she realized with a pang of apprehension that, although they had come this far, success was not yet certain. "Maybe we'll find some kind of evidence," she said.

Please, Lord, she silently prayed, *let there be some evidence*. Without it, no one would have any reason to believe her claim that the unremarkable spot in the woods was a historical burial site, or have any motivation to protect it from the encroaching development.

OVER DINNER in a barbecue restaurant, Jessie told Sally about her new job at the dance studio, and Sally said, "That's wonderful! You said you wanted more playing opportunities and now you have them."

Jessie was warmed by Sally's enthusiasm for her small success and couldn't help contrasting it with her mother's tepid, distracted response: *Well, that's good, sugar, if that's something you want to do.* Further signs that Betty Gibbs would never truly understand her daughter.

"How's your family?" she asked Sally.

"My grandkids are doing great. They're the lights of my life," Sally said. "And Amy and her husband are fine." She picked up a straw wrapper and pleated it, frowning with concentration. "It's Avery I worry about. In our Skype conversations, I see something in his face that wasn't there before. A worry, or a strain. He looks thinner. He won't tell me anything, though. Everything's always fine. Bless his heart."

Watching Sally's hands at work, Jessie noticed again her bitten fingernails. Now she felt she knew the reason for them. "He'll be coming home soon, won't he?"

"I sure hope so. But I've heard of soldiers thinking they're all finished with their twelve-month tour, and then they get another six months tacked on. I think that would do me in. I'm just praying my way through this last stretch."

JESSIE LAY AWAKE that night and wondered if Sally was also sleepless, worrying about her son half a world away. And she thought of Ruby Sanders, her agonizing suspense and refusal to abandon hope even after her dead son had appeared to her.

She turned over in bed yet again, feeling like a puppet suspended from taut strings, twitching and tense. Her mind went over the conversation with Mr. Lester. What kind of evidence would prove that the burial site was indeed a Civil War grave? Who would have the interest and the power to order an inspection of the site and halt the development? Would the huge task of finding and persuading such authorities be up to her, God forbid? And if the building went ahead, and the remains were desecrated, what would it mean for Lem, having half of his mission left forever unfulfilled? And what would it mean for her?

She flopped onto her other side, bunched up the pillow, and thought about going to the gravesite the following day. She wondered if there would be any sense of Lem's presence. That, she could not bear.

CHAPTER 31

PAY DIRT

JESSIE ROSE THE next morning at eight, bleary and unrested. After a breakfast of strong coffee and toast, she headed over to Sally's motel to pick her up for their appointment with Philip Goldsmith.

The day was clear, hot already. The professor was waiting in his sports car, a red convertible with the top down, at the front gate of the university. He wore a brimmed leather hat and sunglasses, and had one denim-shirted arm resting on the door.

They all exchanged a wave, and then he followed Jessie's van out along the Wilkinson Pike. "Not the musty historian I was expecting," Sally observed.

"No," Jessie said, "I think he's playing the Hollywood version of the role. Indiana Goldsmith." She was pleased when Sally laughed at the joke.

Parked near the band's campsite, Jessie made the introductions. "Sally Gowan is Lemuel Sanders' great-great niece. She works at the Sevier County Historical Society." To Sally she said, "Dr. Philip Goldsmith is a professor of history at MTSU, specializing in the Civil War in Tennessee."

"That's just fascinating," said Sally.

Dr. Goldsmith nodded slightly, as if accepting his due. "I have a book coming out this fall, a collection of letters of Tennessee Civil War soldiers."

"Will the letter about Lemuel be in it?"

"No, I found it too late. I'm working on a book about the Battle of Stones River and will include it in that."

"I'll be sure to get a copy of both books," Sally said.

As they entered the campsite, Jessie told the professor, "We went to the Visitor Center yesterday and talked with a volunteer about the possible location of the grave, based on Jeremiah's description."

She took out the troop movement map and opened it. Her heart was pounding with anticipation, and she saw that her hands were shaking, so she walked over to a neatly stacked woodpile, and spread out the map on top of it. Sally came up behind and looked over her shoulder.

Jessie showed Dr. Goldsmith the location of the 37th Tennessee in the fighting on the afternoon of December 31. Then she pointed out the area that Mr. Lester had identified as the possible site of Lemuel Sanders' death.

The professor replaced his trendy wraparound sunglasses with reading glasses more suitable for a musty historian.

"I think we're about here." Jessie put a finger on the map.

"And we came in from Wilkinson Pike. So that means …" Dr. Goldsmith looked up and around. "We should walk in that direction." He motioned to the north. He folded the map and handed it to Jessie, preoccupied. Like a hound on the scent, he began heading rapidly in the direction Jessie knew so well.

They passed along the edge of the cornfield and walked through the stand of trees. "Interesting," Dr. Goldsmith said. "There seems to be a pretty well-worn path here."

Jessie kept mum. As they approached the clearing, she braced herself.

When they entered the glade, all was still and empty. Only birdsong and the distant rush of traffic and brake-juddering of trucks on I-24 disturbed the silence.

They paused. Dr. Goldsmith looked around at the stakes and

frowned. "What the hell is this? Another historic site getting raped in the name of commerce?"

"Dr. Goldsmith… Sally…" Jessie looked around, her voice hushed. She was trying her hardest to give a convincing portrayal of someone experiencing a great realization. "Could this possibly be the spot?" She pointed. "Look, there's the remains of an old snake-rail fence."

"And this big boulder," Sally said. "Maybe it's the one Lemuel's friend and the others rolled out of the woods to protect the grave."

Dr. Goldsmith was turning around in a slow circle, taking in the surroundings. He stopped, pulled some papers out of his pocket, and studied them, looking up from time to time. Jessie recognized the close, dark handwriting of Jeremiah Walker's letter.

He strode across the clearing and entered the forest on the eastern edge. Sally said, "I get a feeling from this place, Jessie, I really do."

Jessie only nodded, not trusting herself to speak.

Dr. Goldsmith came back. Still saying nothing, he squatted down and took out a pocketknife. He began probing the earth.

Sally and Jessie walked into the woods, and Sally marveled at the rock formations, how flat and even they were, how treacherous the deep cracks between them. "It would be hard enough making your way over these in clear daylight. Imagine trying to do it in the smoke of battle while being shot at." She gave a shudder.

Jessie moved a little further into the woods and sat on the stone that she alone knew the significance of, placing the flats of her hands on its surface as she remembered.

"Show me the place … where you died. If you can. If it doesn't upset you."

"I'll show you." He rose and walked among the trees. She followed him, holding the candle-lantern, its wavering glow revealing that the grass did not bend under his steps, branches did not move as he passed between them. Some, actually, seemed to pass through him.

He turned to her in front of two huge, flat stones. An eight-inch fissure divided them. The enormous rectangular forms looked as though they could not be products of nature but had to have been shaped by some purposeful, if crude, artisan. "Here," he said. "Jeremiah's foot got stuck in that crack there. The Yankee came from over yonder." He gestured toward the northwest. "I fell back, onto this rock here." He touched the one nearest to where he stood.

Jessie knelt, set down the lantern, laid her hands on the boulder, and lowered herself to rest her cheek on its cool, rough surface. She closed her eyes. After a long moment, she looked up at him and said, "I'll come here every year on the day you died. I'll put flowers here and sit and say a prayer for you."

His eyes shone bright in the dim light. "I'll see you, from wherever I am. And I'll bless you for not forgetting about me."

The professor's urgent voice brought her back to the present. "Ladies, come look at this." Jessie stood and, behind Sally's retreating back, quickly wiped away tears.

Dr. Goldsmith had turned up the soil in a few different spots with his knife, excavating down a few inches. He rose and held up a small black circular object. Gently, he brushed away the encrusted mud and blew on it. A serpentine "I" embossed on its tarnished brass surface could just be seen under the residual dirt.

"This is a Confederate button," he said. "The 'I' means infantry."

Jessie and Sally moved closer to inspect it, awed.

"The volunteer at the Visitor Center yesterday told us that most of the gravesites around the battlefield have been dug up and the bodies relocated," Jessie said. "But could that button mean this place might still be untouched?"

"Definitely," he agreed. "If something this size is still here, and so close to the surface, you can be pretty sure this is virgin ground." He stood and surveyed the rows of stakes. "We have to stop this."

"How?" Jessie asked.

"I have some ideas. Since Civil War soldiers may be buried here, I would think the Federal government might want to get involved. Of course, the Park Service as well, and the Rutherford County historical society—and the city government. I think we should go at this from all directions."

"Can we do anything? Sally and me, I mean?"

"I'll let you know." He pocketed the button. "I'm willing to take the lead on this, and I'll certainly keep you both in the loop."

Jessie looked at Sally.

Sally said, "Fine with me. Please call on me if there's anything I can do—phone calls, letter writing. If our Historical Society can help in any way …"

"I'll be sure to let you know," he said, dismissive.

They walked back to the cars. The sorrow that Jessie had felt at Lem's death-place had lifted. She felt buoyed by what had been achieved today. "Have you told your kids about all this?" she asked Sally, as they made their way through the campsite.

"I told Amy. She was fascinated. Avery must be busy. He didn't reply to my email." To Philip Goldsmith, Sally said, "I have a son who's an army sergeant serving in Iraq."

"Mmm," he said. "And how do you feel about that?"

"Constantly terrified. But I'm very proud of him." Sally stiffened at the obvious disapproval emanating from the professor. "He may not agree with everything about this war, but he's doing his duty. The same way Lemuel Sanders did."

They had reached the cars, and they said goodbye to Dr. Goldsmith. He and Sally shook hands, formally, coolly.

As Jessie and Sally drove away, Sally said, "Thinks a lot of himself, doesn't he?"

Jessie nodded. "I think he'll make this happen. It could be a real boost for his career."

"Yes, he did seem excited."

They were silent for a moment. Jessie pondered the discovery of the button. Could it be the sign Lem had promised her? She thought not. There was nothing about it of personal significance to her, or that suggested that he was finally at rest.

It was still a momentous find. And Dr. Goldsmith was in a position to persuade authorities to halt the development and explore the grave. She felt an enormous relief at the thought that she wouldn't have to do it.

She roused herself and looked over at Sally, who smiled at her, hair blowing in the hot breeze from the open window, blue eyes bright. Jessie said, "So, what are your plans? Do you have to go right back to Sevierville?"

"Honestly, I don't. If you're not busy, I'd love to see a little bit of Nashville and treat you to a nice dinner. And then I could go to church with you tomorrow morning and hear you play."

Once again, Jessie was struck by the fact that this relative stranger showed more interest in her music than her mother ever had.

IN NASHVILLE, Jessie showed Sally the sights that she thought would interest her: Belle Meade plantation, the Cheekwood estate, Centennial Park, Vanderbilt University. "I'd love to see Opryland and the Country Music Hall of Fame," Sally said, "but it's getting late. We can do those another time, maybe with the grandkids." Jessie was warmed by the implication that Sally wanted to include her in her family outing.

That evening, back in Murfreesboro, over dinner in an Italian restaurant, Sally asked more about Jessie's job at the dance studio and how it had come about.

Jessie explained about working with Ben on his audition tape and meeting Andie. "She had been a dancer in New York, and after she and her family moved down here, she and a partner opened up this studio." She paused. "It's so sad, though, she's very sick with breast cancer. It seems like the end isn't far off."

Sally shook her head. "When I hear stories like that, it reminds me how lucky I am. I just passed my five-year survival mark. Mine was colon cancer, not breast, but the five-year milestone is just as important. So I'm calling myself cured."

"Oh, Sally, I had no idea, I'm sorry."

"Not at all, you didn't know." Sally idly swirled a finger in a drop of spilled red wine. "It'll probably sound really strange to you, but the experience changed my life in a positive way. It made me realize how relationships—family and friends—are the most important things in the world. It brought me back to church, which constantly reminds me that we should always try to treat other people with kindness and forgiveness. Forgiveness was a tough one for me. I spent years being bitter toward my ex-husband. I believe it poisoned me and contributed to my getting sick."

"But you have forgiven him?"

"Yes, I've come to recognize the part I played in the failure of our marriage. It was so easy to blame him because he was unfaithful to me. But when you really own up to your own faults and shortcomings, you can let other people off the hook for theirs. And I did love him once. I still do, though in a different, more detached way. We'll always be bound together by our children and grandchildren."

The server cleared their plates. Sally sat back in her chair. "What about you, Jessie? You're so pretty and talented, is there someone special in your life?"

Jessie hesitated. "I'm getting over someone. We really loved each other, and we only had a short time together."

"Oh," Sally said. The candle between them illuminated the concern—and the curiosity—in her eyes. "I'm sorry. What happened, if you don't mind my asking?"

"There were too many obstacles … time, distance. It just could never have worked out."

"What was he like?"

Oh God, Jessie thought. "Kind. Sensitive. Not formally educated, but intelligent and perceptive. A sense of humor—we loved to laugh together. And sing together—he loved music. He was brave. Very spiritual. And so handsome. We were from different worlds, but the understanding, and the love, grew very fast between us." That was all she could think of to say. She sat in silence, twisting the stem of her glass.

Sally was watching her closely. "You really *were* in love with him."

Jessie nodded.

"I can see that it's hard for you to talk about it."

"I'm sorry, Sally," Jessie said. "I haven't talked about it with anybody. The loss is still pretty fresh."

Sally smiled, put her hand on Jessie's, and squeezed. "I hope we have a long friendship ahead. Maybe someday you'll feel ready to tell me about him."

"I hope so too."

They sat quietly, listening to three men at the next table laughing and talking loudly about football over the thumping bass of otherwise indistinguishable music.

"When you lose someone you've loved so much," Sally said at last, "you can feel so hopeless. There's the grief, of course, but you also feel like you've been thrown back to your old self, your old life."

"Yes, that's how I feel."

"But love changes you," Sally went on. "It enlarges your capacity for loving. It gives you a magnetism that attracts other people. It makes you ready for an even greater love."

"Do you think so?"

Sally said emphatically, "Well, I sure hope so, for myself. And in *your* case, I'm positive."

CHAPTER 32

WITHOUT HONOR

Now that darkness had fallen, there was nothing to see outside the car windows but other cars and the black expanse of the passing landscape, at present as devoid of any lights as an ocean or a desert. Jessie figured that, having left Murfreesboro some four hours earlier, they must be somewhere in Virginia.

She pushed the seat back and put her feet up on the dashboard.

"You go to sleep if you want, sugar," her father said, steering the van through the night.

"No, I'm wide awake." Jessie looked over at him. At fifty-seven, he was still a strong man, kept trim by all his outdoor work. His brown hair was graying and receding, but otherwise he looked very much as he had when she was little and thought him the handsomest man in the world with his gray eyes crinkled at the corners, lean cheeks, and prominent nose that the family always teased him about, calling it his "eagle beak."

He glanced over at her. "What?" he asked with a smile.

"Just thinking how glad I am that you came."

"Me, too. Been too long since we did something together, just you and me."

They were on their way to the commemoration of the 145th anniversary of the Battle of Antietam—or Sharpsburg, as the Confederates called it—to be held in Boonsboro, Maryland on the weekend of September 14. Most of the other members of the band would be there, with two disappointing exceptions.

Jessie had been in the kitchen two evenings before, making a huge pot of soup to freeze and take to the event, when her cell phone rang. It was Pete DiSpirito.

"The good news first," he said after they exchanged greetings. "I think the CD is perfect. I'm getting it copied to send off with Ben's applications."

Ben had appointments in the next month to visit music schools— Juilliard, Manhattan School of Music, Brooklyn College. "My alma mater," Pete said. "For English, though, not for music."

"All New York schools."

"Yes, near family. I think that's going to be important to him in the foreseeable future. He's staying with my brother and sister-in-law on Long Island. My brother's taking him to his interviews and auditions so I can be here with Andie."

Then, knowing that she had to ask, but not wanting to upset him, Jessie said, "How's she doing?"

"She has some good days, when she can get up and go sit on the front porch and enjoy some of this beautiful weather we've been having. A nurse is coming in every other day. We set up a den downstairs as a bedroom. We're doing everything we can to keep her at home. Thank God on the bad days her pain is being managed pretty well." What he didn't mention came through as clearly as what he did say.

"Please tell her I'm praying for her."

"I will, thank you. But Jess, the reason I'm calling is that Ben and I are going to have to skip Antietam. I'm really sorry. I'm planning to call Jim myself, but I wanted to let you know we won't be able to share the drive with you this time."

"I understand, Pete. I'll miss you both." She hesitated. "I'll have my cell phone with me, so if you want to talk, or there's... any news, please feel free to call."

"Thanks." Then in a brighter voice he said, "Tell you what I'll really miss. The sounds of 'Sweet Home Alabama' at two in the morning. I may call you up and ask you to hold the phone outside your tent, just for old times' sake."

"If you call me at two in the morning, you're sure going to hear more than 'Sweet Home Alabama.'"

Laughing, they said goodbye.

She went back to stirring the soup. She was sorry Pete wouldn't be there. His presence always added so much to the group, and she had to admit, an extra zest to her own enjoyment. And she had hoped for his help. As she had told Andie, he always pitched in with the kitchen chores that most other people avoided.

That was when inspiration had suddenly struck. She hit the number on speed dial and when the phone was answered, Jessie said without preamble, "Hey, Daddy, want to come to the Civil War this weekend?"

And now here they were, rolling along with some two hours to go before the halfway point of the 650-plus-mile trip, where they had agreed they would find a motel for the night, somewhere in southwestern Virginia.

The quiet and intimacy of the car's dark interior, the late hour, and the seemingly endless unspooling of the miles, seemed to encourage confidences. "Daddy, can I ask you something?"

"Shoot."

"About Vietnam. I've always wondered. What was it like? What did you do there?"

"Hoo-eee, honey. Why do you want to hear about all that old business?"

"Because I want to know more about that part of your life. Why did you go?"

He hesitated. She kept her eyes fixed on his face, illuminated in flashes by the lights of oncoming cars and the steady green glow of the dashboard. She wondered if he was going to avoid the subject, as he had always done before.

"Well, I didn't rightly have a choice," he said at last. "My draft lottery number was sixteen."

"Would you have gone anyway?"

"Yes, I reckon I would have," he said without hesitation. "Your grandfather did his duty in the Second World War. I wouldn't have felt right setting by when my country needed me."

"Did you agree with the war?"

He gave a short, derisive laugh. "I was eighteen! I didn't hardly know what it was all about, except that we were fighting the Communists."

"But the fact that our government told you it was the right thing to do was enough for you?"

He shrugged. "Call me a simple man, but I love this country, and I know that Americans have always had to fight to preserve our freedom. Why should I be excused from that? Things have gotten more complicated since then, but I still believe in duty, and patriotism."

Jessie asked tentatively, "Did you ever have to kill anybody?"

He paused again, and again she wondered if he was going to answer. "I did, and I saw my buddies killed." His expression was grave. "I don't know if I ever told you how Cleotis and I got to be good friends."

"I knew you served together, that's all. You never told me anything about it." *Not because I haven't asked*, she thought.

"Well, he was my sergeant in charge of our platoon. I was just a dumb hick kid. Not used to taking orders from a Black guy. I'm not proud of it, but that's the truth. I gave him kind of a hard time.

"One day, we were humping between two villages. I was the point man. Before I knew what hit me, I was down, shot in the shoulder. It hurt so bad, and I was in so much shock I couldn't move. There I was, lying in the middle of this clearing completely exposed. The rest of our guys had ducked for cover in the jungle behind us when the VC started shooting.

"Cle crawled out on his belly faster than I ever knew a human being could crawl. Bullets were making little explosions in the dust all around us, and Cle rolled on his back and threw a grenade where the shots were coming from. It didn't stop all the firing, but it gave us a chance. Somehow, he managed to drag me back into the bushes without either of us getting killed. He did take a bad hit, though. Right in his butt."

"Oh, poor Uncle Cle." Jessie gave a rueful laugh. "I guess that's why he still walks kind of stiff."

Frank nodded. "Even though he was hurt, he fought till the VC stopped shooting. We lost two men, but we would have lost a lot more—including me—if it hadn't been for him."

Jessie didn't say anything, fearing it might stop this flow of memories.

"The radioman called for a bird, and Cle and I got flown to a hospital ship. We were in beds next to each other in the ward there. We both got Purple Hearts, but I felt like he should have gotten something more for risking his life to save me. Anyway, they brought the medals to us and Cle asked if the official records could, you know, not mention the exact place where he was wounded. He asked if they could say he was shot in the hip." He gave a chuckle. "The answer was no. You don't fool with the official records. Being right next to him I heard everything, and I ribbed him a little about it. It broke the ice between us.

"We spent two weeks there in the hospital with nothing else to do, so we talked. I had the chance to thank him for saving my hide. We got to be buddies, and when he was healed up, they sent him back into combat, of course, and a few weeks later back I went too. We served together another seven months or so, then he was sent home. I stayed a little longer."

Yellow light from the garish sign of a truck stop washed across his face. He went on, "We lost track for a couple of years, then he looked me up. He was living in Virginia then, back in his hometown, managing an auto parts store and not too happy with his life. He didn't whine about it or anything, but he did say he was having kind of a hard time readjusting to being back after all we'd been through. I later pieced together that he was drinking pretty heavy at the time. Anyway, I told him my business was growing, and I needed somebody to manage the warehouse. I asked him if he could stand to wear the shoe on the other foot and take orders from me. He said he'd give it a try, and he and Martha Jane and the two kids moved down here. He bought half of the business in '81. That was a good year for all of us."

Jessie smiled at him. Both she and the Thompsons' youngest child, Denise, had been born in 1981. "Thank you for telling me all that, Daddy."

He gave a noncommittal nod, his eyes straight ahead on the road.

She thought of Lem saying that he hadn't told his mother or Louisa about the things he experienced as a soldier, that war wasn't "something ladies and gals can understand." She imagined that there was much that her father wasn't telling, things he would always keep secret, not only because he didn't want to burden those he loved, but also probably because he himself didn't want to face those dark memories.

FRANK ENTERED into the spirit of the weekend wholeheartedly. He readily volunteered for the heavy work of getting firewood and water, and he made friends with the rest of the band. Stirring beef stew on the fire at midday on Saturday, Jessie looked over at him as he sat on an upended segment of thick log, talking and laughing with the guys, and she smiled at what an authentic yokel he appeared in the clothes he'd borrowed from Jim Bryce; too-short, too-big rough gray wool pants held up by white canvas suspenders, a checkered broadcloth, band-collared shirt with wooden buttons, lace-up rough leather brogans, and to top it all off, a wide-brimmed brown felt hat that looked like something people would cut holes in and put on a mule at a country fair.

She had to remind him to take off his modern watch and keep his sleeve rolled down over his Marine Corps tattoo.

In the mid-afternoon, they walked over to watch the re-enactment of the battle. They stopped beside a fence that bordered the field and surveyed the lines of blue and gray forming on either side of the expanse of pastureland, horse-drawn canvas wagons and mounted soldiers moving into position, cannons gleaming in the hazy sunshine.

The sound of drums beating a cadence heralded the approach of the band. As the musicians came marching out of a barn near the battlefield, the brass players raised their horns and began playing.

Frank watched them, fascinated. "You don't mean to tell me they played music in the battles?"

"Believe it or not, they sometimes did," she said, and he shook his head in wonder.

The battle began with a deafening roar from the cannons. Watching intently, Frank leaned over and asked, "Are they copying the actual movements from back then?"

"Yes, as near as possible."

"Lord God, the way they all marched in a line like that, they were just sitting ducks."

"I've heard some of my bandmates talking about how this kind of battle formation went back to the time of Napoleon," Jessie said. "But the Civil War guns were much more accurate and deadly. The military strategy lagged behind the technology, and that's why the casualties were so high. They say Antietam was the bloodiest day in American history."

"Y'all sure study a lot about this stuff. How many were lost?"

"Some 23,000 killed, injured, or missing."

"Shee-ee. Twenty-three thousand." He didn't take his eyes from the field. Thick smoke enshrouded the soldiers. The throats of the cannons spewed flames, and the booming concussion took a few moments to arrive on the air. Cavalrymen galloped to and fro, some of the horses skittish from the noise. The grass behind the advancing lines was strewn with bodies, some of the fallen incongruously leaning up on their elbows to chat with neighbors or watch the proceedings.

"I wonder who first got the idea to do this, acting out the battles," Frank mused. "I heard they do it for the Revolutionary War, too. One thing's for sure, I don't think anybody'd ever do anything like this for my war. People'd just as soon forget it ever happened. Most of all, the guys who were there."

Jessie looked at him. "You never felt like you got any honor for what you did?"

"Honor? We stopped expecting honor after we heard about all the protests back home, people calling us baby killers. We just hoped nobody'd spit on us or call us names when we walked through the airport in our uniforms."

It was, she realized with a start, the first time she had ever seen her father anything but good-humored, uncomplaining. His mask had slipped, and she glimpsed the pain and confusion and bitterness of the young man he had been. The hurt was obviously still unhealed.

She took his arm. "I'm sorry, Daddy."

He gave her a quick smile. The mask was back in place. "That's okay, it was a long time ago." He took off his hat and pushed back his hair, dark with sweat from the afternoon heat. "Say, how 'bout we walk back to camp? I saw some beer in one of those coolers and I'm hearing it calling my name."

CHAPTER 33

BELLE OF THE REBEL BALL

THAT NIGHT, AFTER all the dishes had been washed and the food put away, Jessie said to her father, "Feel like going dancing?"

"Dancin'? Where?"

"There's a ball tonight, in a tent over by the parking area. Our band's playing for part of it."

"Are you playing?"

"No, there's no piano. I thought we could stroll over and just watch, even if you don't feel like dancing. It's something to see."

"The only kind of dance I ever learned how to do right was the Twist. I stepped on your mama's feet trying to dance to 'The Tennessee Waltz' at our wedding. But, sure, I'll walk over with you."

"Let me put on my good dress." Jessie lit the candle-lantern and carried it into her tent, where she slipped off her work dress and took her ball gown out of its protective calico bag.

She hugged it to her and pressed her face into it, remembering the last time she had worn it, with Lem. She thought of the mysterious, white-lit room, the ecstasy they had shared there—or that she had dreamed or somehow hallucinated they had shared.

She sighed deeply. These memories were all she had, and she dreaded losing them, forgetting the sound of Lem's voice, the way his face changed from solemn to radiant when he smiled, the grace of his strong hands that had fashioned the delicate design on the ring she had worn in that vision or dream.

Jessie roused herself, exchanged her corded petticoat for a hoop, slipped the ball gown on, pulled the laces tight in back and tied them. Then she stepped out of the tent.

"Answer me something," Frank asked as they walked along the rutted dirt road surrounded by the procession of other ball-goers. Jessie held the candle-lantern in one hand and looped her other arm through her father's. "How come a girl who looks like you doesn't have fellows swarming around her? How come you have to go to the ball with your old daddy?" He darted an anxious glance at her. "I hope you don't mind me asking. Your mama and I just want you to be happy."

"I am happy," she said. "And especially now, having you for my date." She squeezed his arm. "I'll be with the handsomest man there."

"And the only one doing the Twist."

She nudged him with an elbow. "You better not! They'll kick us out."

THE DANCE WAS HELD in a large canvas tent, hot despite the flaps tied up all around. An old-time string band was playing the first half of the evening; the Murfreesboro band would take over for the second half. The musicians occupied a platform at one end that was decorated with wildflower garlands. The dancers were in the middle of the tent, following the dance master's instructions for the line dances. Their feet swished over the mown grass, and the ladies' hoops swayed. Soldiers and ladies stood around the perimeter, many of the women cooling themselves with lace or bone fans.

The women's attire ranged from lavish reproductions straight out of *Godey's Lady's Book* that must have cost their wearers hundreds of dollars, to garish and inaccurate concoctions of synthetic silk and nylon lace, to simple homemade calico frocks. The men, as usual, represented a narrower range of styles: plain gray or butternut military wear, civilian sack coats and trousers, and the occasional magnificently tailored officer's uniform. People approached this pastime with various motivations, some to re-create history as faithfully as possible, others just to have an entertaining costume party and maybe learn something in the process.

Frank stood on the sidelines, watching, occasionally chatting with some of the other onlookers as Jessie accepted invitations to dance from a succession of strangers—a forty-ish doctor from Georgia who said he'd be giving demonstrations of Civil War surgical techniques the next day and asked her, with a wink, if she wanted to be his volunteer patient; a young artilleryman from North Carolina who was re-creating his great-great-great grandfather's military role; and a period photographer.

Jim Bryce came up next and asked Jessie for a waltz.

"Your dad seems to be enjoying himself," he said. "He fits right in."

"Thanks for making him so welcome. And for lending him your clothes."

"You do this long enough and you accumulate quite a collection of outfits," Jim said. "Of varying sizes that don't exactly get smaller over the years, at least for me. And you ladies! Danielle had to get a whole closet built for her re-enacting wardrobe."

They both looked over at Danielle, glamorous as always, this evening wearing a pale green silk off-the-shoulder ball gown, her blond hair swept up and anchored by a pearl comb inlaid with small sparkly gems. She was waltzing nearby with a handsome officer with long, curly brown hair and a full beard and mustache. Unfortunately, at that moment, Danielle was laughing and looking up into her partner's face as if utterly captivated by him, and Jessie felt a pang of sympathy for Jim. She had suspected on other occasions that all was not entirely well between the gentlemanly lawyer and his showy wife.

When the dance ended, Jessie went over to her father. "You holding up?"

"Uh huh. I'm glad to see you having such a good time. See, I knew the fellows would be all over you like ducks on a June bug."

Jessie shrugged. "It was never this way before." She waved a hand in front of her face to cool off.

The string band was leaving the stage, and the Murfreesboro musicians took their place, setting up the wooden folding chairs and music stands.

"Let me get us some of that punch." Frank crossed the tent to a white-draped table where two older women, their ample forms corseted tightly and stuffed like sausages into dark silk gowns, were ladling out punch from a crystal bowl into plain paper cups that were at least a little less anachronistic than plastic. Jessie saw the women smile as her father chatted with them with his usual easygoing charm. He returned and handed her a cup and she drank gratefully.

The band began to play. Halfway through their second number, Frank said under his breath, "Here comes another duck."

A stocky young man in butternut breeches, tall black leather boots, and a white homespun shirt approached, bowed, and asked Jessie for the next dance. He introduced himself as Henry Wilkins from the 11th Virginia Cavalry Regiment. The dance was another reel, so there wasn't much opportunity for conversation until after it had ended, when he said, "If you're not doing anything after this, I'd be pleased if you'd walk with me back to our camp and enjoy some songs and maybe some spirits around our campfire." He smiled and winked. "We brought an authentic Civil War beer keg."

"Thanks," she said, returning his smile. "Sounds like fun. But I'm here with my father."

"He's welcome, too."

"Well, tell us how to find your campsite and if we can, we'll stop by." It was a white lie; she was getting tired and thinking of sleep.

He gave her directions. She rejoined her father and told him about the invitation, but he reckoned he was ready to call it a night too. So they walked back through the warm darkness, passing the campfires where men were sitting around talking softly, the sound of a fife occasionally piercing the quiet, and the horses and mules whickering and stomping their hooves.

"I declare, this is really something to see," said Frank.

"I thought you'd like it."

As they strolled along, he hummed softly, tunelessly, as he often did when occupied in thought. Jessie was absorbed in recalling the unusual amount of male attention she had attracted that evening. It had been exciting and fun, and also somewhat surprising.

She wondered if what Sally had said might be true—that a great love changed you, gave you a magnetism that ultimately would draw to you the next great love. If so, that person hadn't been among her dance partners this evening, she felt sure. When, or from where he would come, remained to be seen.

She was in no hurry. It would take time to be able to open herself to another man as she had to Lem. If she ever could.

Inside her tent, she put on her nightgown and was about to blow out the candle-lantern when her cell phone vibrated on the wooden chest. The time read 11:13, and the caller ID said "P DiSpirito." She was instantly alert, alarmed.

"Pete? Is everything okay?"

"Yes, fine—God, I'm sorry, I just realized how late it is. I hope I didn't wake you up."

"No, it's all right. In fact, I just got back from the ball."

"Ah, the ball, that's right."

"The cornet section really missed Ben."

"I'm sure the tenor horns had a rough time without me."

"Yes, they really struggled," Jessie said, and they shared a laugh.

"You must have been the belle of the ball."

"Oh, I had a very strict chaperone. My father came along this weekend. He's really been enjoying it. I have, too."

"That's terrific," Pete said warmly.

"Yes, he told me some things for the first time, about his experiences in Vietnam. Nothing like ten hours of driving on boring interstates to get people to bare their souls."

"That's great, Jess. And I'm glad to hear that Cinderella finally had a chance to go to the ball."

"Cinderella was worried she wouldn't have any help this weekend without you around, but Daddy has pitched right in."

"I really miss being there." She heard the sound of ice rattling in a glass. "Andie's been asleep since eight, so I was reading manuscripts for work. Now I'm just sitting here on the front porch swing in the dark. Ben's out with friends. There's no point trying to go to bed before he gets home. I can't sleep till I know he's safe in his bed. So I thought I'd give you a call and see how things are going. I honestly didn't realize it was this late."

"It's okay."

"Your father's not sharing your tent, I take it?"

"No, there's no room with all the coolers and kitchen gear. He has his own tent. Good thing it's on the other side of our campsite because he snores like a bear."

"Well," Pete said, and she heard the ice again, and the creaking of the chains of the porch swing. "I'll let you get some sleep. I know you have to be up early tomorrow to feed the multitudes. Just wanted you to know I was thinking of you."

"Thanks," she said, a little uncertain how to take that statement. "You're in my thoughts too. You and Andie—and Ben," she added quickly. "Give Andie my best."

She lay awake for a while, musing. Pete was lonely, lonely and hurting. Maybe a little under the influence, too, judging from the clinking of ice cubes—anesthesia to dull the pain of having the woman he loved slip away from him, degree by agonizing degree.

CHAPTER 34

A TIME TO MOURN

THE WEEKEND WITH her father had been a good distraction. Now, back to her ordinary life, Jessie had to resume the task of learning to be alone again, and to find ways to be content with it.

It wasn't as if there was nothing to occupy her; in addition to the mundane chores required to keep body and soul together, she had piano practice, three sessions a week at the ballet school, and school-related tasks to take care of after hours. There was preparation for church, choosing each week's hymns, prelude and postlude, and writing a column for the weekly bulletin giving some background on the music and why she had picked it—a small attempt to stretch her fellow parishioners' musical interests beyond the old standard Southern hymns.

Yet there was again an emptiness at the core of her life. It was likely that many people felt that way at one time or another, and the ways they sought to fill that void no doubt ranged from the worthwhile, to the meaningless, to the downright destructive. Jessie tried to avoid things that she knew were bad for her, mentally or physically. Foremost among these was, she knew, a tendency to endlessly obsess about Lem, to dwell on her memories of their times together and the sadness of having to go on without him.

Since those late nights with him had ceased, she could tell that her health was improving. She was sleeping more, and rather than grabbing fast food or whatever was on hand in the refrigerator in the evenings to save time, she was cooking again. In the early evenings before supper, she would often take a long walk along the road that ran behind the apartment building and after a mile turned into a peaceful and little-traveled country lane. And she tried to end each day on a spiritual note; reading the Psalms or some other inspirational material, praying before sleep.

She was attempting to construct, as if stacking block-on-block, a life that she could inhabit comfortably, not only for as long as she might remain alone, but also when, God willing, she found someone. Recent experience had taught Jessie that loss could happen anytime, and it was never too soon to begin building inner resources to protect against complete devastation.

October 10, 2007

Dear Sally,

Thought you'd like to see this article. Professor Goldsmith is basking in the limelight. Fine with me, just as long as those soldiers, if it turns out there are soldiers buried there, find a peaceful and honorable final resting place soon.

Jessie

HISTORICAL CLAIMS AT PROPOSED DEVELOPMENT SITE

October 8, 2007
Special to the Rutherford County Press-Register
By Sherrill Glassman

On the site of a proposed new housing development, evidence of a previously unknown burial ground for soldiers who fought in the Civil War Battle of Stones River has been discovered by Dr. Philip S. Goldsmith.

Dr. Goldsmith is a professor of American history at Middle Tennessee State University in Murfreesboro and the editor of a forthcoming book of Tennessee Civil War soldiers' letters.

He was led to the site by a description in a letter he discovered in his research for the book. It was written by Jeremiah Walker, a young soldier from East Tennessee who fought in the battle on December 31, 1862, and saw his best friend, Lemuel Sanders, killed. The following day, Walker was ordered back to the site for burial detail.

"He described the grave as being near woods. There were unusual rock formations in the woods and some other landmarks that he described in accurate enough detail to enable me to identify the site," said Dr. Goldsmith. "Then I found an antique Confederate infantryman's button there. This leads me to believe that this may be an as-yet-unexplored place of historical significance, and also a sacred place that must be respected. Far too many Civil War battlefields have been desecrated by thoughtless development. We're very cavalier in America about how we plow under our history for the sake of commerce."

Dr. Goldsmith is currently in discussions with the Rutherford County Society for Historical Preservation and the National Park Service, which administers the Stones River Battleground and Visitor Center, to explore the site further. In the meantime, he has succeeded in obtaining from the city a moratorium on further construction by the Glenwood Building Company until the site's historical significance can be assessed.

To: jcgibbs2560@tnnet.com

Oct 28 12:30 p.m.

Subject: Groundbreaking

Jessie,

Big news! After you sent me the article I contacted Dr. G. and told him that I wanted to be part of any official excavation or exploration of the site, as the only known relative of someone who might be buried there. He just told me that there's going to be a preliminary archaeological excavation on the 15th of November—a Thursday—and (not too enthusiastically) invited me to be present. I wonder if he would have told me if I hadn't asked him?

If you're free that evening I'd like to see you and tell you all about it. I'm sure it will be fascinating, gruesome and disturbing all at once.

xxo,

Sally

To: salgow@shc.org

Oct 28, 3:30 p.m.

Subject: Re: Groundbreaking

Dear Sally,

I would love to see you and will be burning with curiosity to hear about what goes on at the site. Plan on staying with me, and come Wednesday night, if that would make it easier.

Jessie

To: jcgibbs2560@tnnet.com

Nov 2 11:47 p.m.

Subject: Re: Re: Groundbreaking

I should have asked before, want to come to the excavation? You'd be more than welcome; after all it probably wouldn't be taking place—at least not now—without you.

xxo,

S

To: salgow@shc.org

Nov 3 6:30 a.m.

Subject: Re: Re: Re: Groundbreaking

Thanks for the thought, but I'll be glad just to let you tell me about it.

J

Rehearsals were underway at the Broadway Lights Dance Studio for the winter recital to be held in early December. On this Thursday afternoon, Jessie was accompanying the advanced ballet class, taught by "Miss Vicky," as the students referred to her. The piece was Tchaikovsky's "Waltz of the Flowers," and as Jessie played, she looked up now and then from the music and into the mirror to see the movements of the graceful girls behind her. Their toe shoes swished and thumped on the wooden floor. Even though the studio had no windows, the presence of the early darkness outside seemed to make the fluorescent lights harsher and brighter.

The door opened and Laurie Reinhart, another of the teachers, stepped into the room and approached Vicky, who motioned for the dancers and Jessie to stop. Laurie spoke to Vicky in a low tone, her face serious, and Vicky's hand flew to her mouth. Jessie watched, a knot of anxiety tightening in her chest.

"Class, excuse me," Vicky said. "Jessie, would you just run through the piece a few more times, and girls, follow Michaela's lead."

Vicky didn't return before the end of the class at five o'clock. The students departed. Jessie was gathering up her music when Vicky came in, her eyes red.

"Andie died this afternoon," she said, and her chin crumpled as her eyes filled with tears.

"Oh, no," Jessie said, stunned. Though not unexpected, the news was still a shock.

Vicky dried her eyes with the sleeve of her leotard and gave a deep sigh. After standing a moment longer in helpless silence, Jessie gave Vicky an awkward hug.

"I'm so sorry," she murmured. She picked up her music bag and quietly left the studio.

THE DISPIRITOS' VISITING HOURS were held the following Monday. At three-thirty that afternoon, Jessie came home from school and changed into a black dress. She drove across town to the funeral home.

In the entryway of the brick, Georgian-style mansion she was greeted by a solemn man in a dark suit who directed her to the appropriate room. It was crowded. *That must be some comfort for Pete*, she thought.

The burnished wooden casket was closed, to her relief. A prayer kneeler stood in front of it; a large blanket of pink and white roses rested on its lid. Jessie paused in the doorway to sign the visitors' book.

There were a number of members of the band present. It was strange to see some of them for the first time in modern clothes.

Across the room, Vicky Lang stood beside an elaborate flower arrangement, surrounded by some of the older students who had probably worked with Andie for years. The dancers resembled a flock of shorebirds, tall and slender, long-necked and graceful. Many were crying and embracing.

Jessie greeted her bandmates and then went over to Ben and Pete, somber and stiff in their suits. They were standing next to a computer monitor flanked by flowers and displaying a succession of family photographs. Ben saw her first and nudged his father. Pete stepped forward as she came near, and they gave each other a hug.

"I'm so sorry, Pete," Jessie said.

"We're glad you came."

She turned to Ben and hugged him. "Bless your heart, kiddo."

"Thanks." When they separated, he flung his head to the side to get his bangs out of his eyes. He looked at the floor, scowling against tears.

A girl Ben's age, accompanied by her parents, touched him on the shoulder and he turned to her to give and receive a long hug.

"I hope the end was peaceful," Jessie murmured to Pete.

"Yes," Pete said. "We were both with her. Her parents were too. She knew us, and she wasn't in pain. The priest was there." He sounded as if the effort of forming and uttering sentences was like moving heavy rocks.

"How are you?"

"Exhausted. Numb."

"Can I do anything for you?"

"Nothing now, Jess. Except pray for us. My family and Andie's are all here, but I have a feeling that when everybody's gone back home, things'll get tough."

"I'm around. Call anytime if I can help in any way."

Some people came over to speak to him. "I'm going to look at those beautiful pictures," Jessie said.

"Ben spent all yesterday putting that slideshow together. I think it helped him. I can't look at it—not right now, anyway."

She excused herself and went to the table, watching the images change on the screen every few seconds. What a striking family they had been. Slender Andie, with her dazzling smile and strawberry-blond hair, worn long in most of the pictures; dark-eyed, dark-haired Pete, heavier in earlier years than he was now and with a shaggy '80s hairstyle in some pictures, but still strikingly handsome; and Ben through all his ages. There were some professional shots of Andie in black tights and leotard, in graceful dance positions.

As Jessie drove home, heavy drops fell from a leaden sky. She felt the gloom inside her, weighing on her heart. She spent much of the rest of the day at the piano, wearing headphones so she wouldn't disturb the neighbors as, for hours, she meditated and prayed in the way that was most meaningful to her, through her music.

CHAPTER 35

UNEARTHING

November 16, 2007
REMAINS AND ARTIFACTS FOUND IN CIVIL WAR GRAVE
By Sherrill Glassman
Special to the Rutherford County Press-Register

The remains of several Civil War soldiers were exhumed yesterday near the Stones River National Battlefield. The disinterment was performed under the supervision of National Park Service representatives, members of the Rutherford County Society for Historical Preservation, and Chief Arvin Hayes of the Murfreesboro police department.

The burial site was in an area on the western edge of the Stones River National Battlefield, just outside the boundary of the national park. The land surrounding the mass grave has already been broken for a new housing development by the Glenwood Building Company.

Also present at the exhumation was Dr. Philip Goldsmith, a professor of history at Middle Tennessee State University, whose research first suggested the historical significance of the site. A description in a letter from a Confederate soldier enabled Dr. Goldsmith to identify the overgrown woodland grave.

Mrs. Sarah Pruett Gowan of Sevierville also observed the excavation. The remains of her great-great-uncle, Private Lemuel Sanders of the 37th Tennessee Infantry (Confederate) Regiment, are believed to be among the bodies buried in this mass grave.

Preliminary examination of the excavated soil revealed, in addition to an undetermined number of bodies, several artifacts: buttons, belt buckles, canteens and the like, apparently both Union and Confederate. Dr. Goldsmith pointed out that the presence of Union artifacts does not necessarily mean that Union soldiers are buried there. It was common for Confederates to compensate for shortages of uniforms and equipment by salvaging them from fallen Federals.

The soil was carefully replaced to cover the remains and the artifacts until a decision can be made about their final resting place. A protective fence has been erected around the site and the Glenwood Building Company has agreed to suspend construction in that area for the time being.

Sally looked tired as she leaned back against the cushions of Jessie's sofa.

"Put your feet up," Jessie urged.

"Thanks." Sally slipped off her flats and rested stockinged feet on top of the glass coffee table. Jessie had bought a bottle of white wine and chilled it, thinking that Sally might appreciate it after an emotionally demanding day. She opened it and poured them both a glass.

"So what was it like?" she asked, settling herself in a chair across from Sally. She braced herself for the answer.

Sally took a sip of wine. "Oh, so sad. Not as grisly as I expected. There were laborers with shovels, the nicest guys, and when they knew I was a relative they seemed to work extra carefully and delicately. There was no smell, thank God. It was just very, very tragic to see those skulls and all those jumbled bones and bits of cloth and metal. And to think of those mothers who never knew what happened to their precious sons."

Jessie gave an inward shudder at the idea of seeing a vacant-eyed, grinning skull and thinking it might be Lem's. She wondered if his spirit was observing the excavation from wherever he had gone. *If* he had gone. The absence of the promised sign from him troubled her.

"Anyway," Sally said. "Now we know it's a grave. But whether it's Lemuel's …"

Jessie fought the impulse to spill the truth. "I guess we have to rely on Jeremiah Walker's description. He was pretty specific about the location."

"Yes." Sally nodded.

"What'll happen to the bodies?"

"Dr. Goldsmith said they'll probably be moved together to another burial site. Maybe Evergreen Cemetery, like that nice man at the Visitor Center said, if they all turn out to be Confederates." She leaned her head back against the sofa, briefly closing her eyes. "I'm exhausted. Didn't have any lunch, for one thing."

"And here I've kept you talking." Jessie stood. "Everything's ready, let's eat."

Over the meal, Jessie asked, "Is your son still set to come home soon?"

Sally brightened. "Yes, he thinks he'll be home for Christmas. I'm so excited!"

"Will that be the end of his time in the army?"

"Yes, thank God. He's been a soldier since he was eighteen. He's served two tours in Iraq. He told me he's ready to do something else with his life."

"Does he know what that is?"

"Get his college degree, for one thing. He was all set to go to UT in September of '98, but instead, right after his high school graduation, he joined the military. I pitched a fit back then, but now I realize that it was the best thing for him." Sally sighed. "My Amy was a model child, so easy and eager to please. Even as a teenager. Avery—well, the gray hair that's hiding under this bottle blond is mostly due to his teenage years. He was wild, a daredevil. Drove too fast, wrecked a few cars, drank and did drugs—nothing really bad, like heavy drugs, thank God, at least none that I knew of. What I did know about worried me to death."

Jessie thought that Avery sounded like the kind of boy she had avoided in high school. All about hard partying, reckless behavior, and flashy girls, dismissive of a serious introvert like herself. More her sister Lou Ann's type.

SALLY WENT TO CHURCH with Jessie the next day. She sat in the front pew, and glancing over at her as she played, Jessie saw that Sally's eyes were closed and her head moved slightly to the rhythm of the music. During the hymns, Sally sang with enthusiasm.

When the service ended, Sally gave her a hug. "Your playing took me to another place. I wanted to stay there, it was so peaceful and beautiful."

"Thank you," Jessie said, gratified by the sincere appreciation.

During the coffee hour, Jessie introduced Sally to Pastor John. "Do you remember the letter I showed you, from the young Civil War soldier?" Jessie said to him. "The man referred to in that letter, the one who was killed, was actually Sally's great-great uncle, Lemuel Sanders."

"How fascinating." Pastor John was doing a good job of feigning ignorance. "I read about the excavation of the gravesite and the discovery of the Civil War remains. You and your relative were mentioned in that article. What's going to happen now, do you know?"

Sally told him about the idea of relocating the bodies to Evergreen Cemetery.

Pastor John sipped his coffee, frowning in thought. "That could take quite a while, couldn't it?"

"Oh, heavens, yes," Sally agreed. "From my experience with the Sevier County Historical Society, I know that even getting a house or a site designated as a historical landmark takes an eternity of wrangling and paperwork."

"And in the meantime," Pastor John went on, "your relative never had a funeral, just a battlefield burial. At least, that's what I understand from the letter Jessie showed me. If you and your family would like to have a small, private memorial service in the near future, I would be honored to perform it."

"That's a beautiful idea," Sally said, linking her arm through Jessie's. "Honorary family will be welcome, too. Thank you for suggesting it, Reverend Brinton."

Pastor John said, "When would you like to do it?"

Sally told him about Avery's projected homecoming from Iraq in late November. "So, maybe sometime in December?"

Gooseflesh tightened the skin on Jessie's arms. "How about on December 31?" she said. "That would be the 145th anniversary of when Lemuel Sanders died."

"Oh, wouldn't that be perfect?" Sally said.

"I'll get in touch with the professor who arranged the excavation," Jessie told Pastor John. "I'll ask him to help us get access to the gravesite. The article said they've put up a fence around it."

"Let me know when it's confirmed," the minister said. "For now, I'll put the date as a placeholder on my calendar."

Sally glanced at her watch and said she'd better be heading home. She and Pastor John said goodbye, then she hugged Jessie and left.

"Thank you so much for that kind offer," Jessie said to her minister. "I remember that was part of Lemuel's last wish."

"It was." She frowned. "But Pastor John, one thing's been bothering me since my last meeting with Lem, when I told him about finding his family and we said goodbye. He promised he'd send me a sign when he reached his final rest. I've been to the gravesite with Sally and the professor, and there's no trace of his presence there, but so far, I haven't seen anything like a sign. What could that mean? It worries me that he might not be at peace yet."

The minister shook his head. "I honestly don't know, Jessie. This is new territory for me, as I've told you. All I can advise is, keep praying and watching. Trust that God has Lemuel in his care."

CHAPTER 36

GIFT OF COMFORT

PETE CALLED AT the beginning of December. "Are you free to have coffee or a drink with me this evening? There's something I want to tell you."

"Sure." She felt both curious and slightly apprehensive.

They met at a vintage-style diner in a nearby shopping mall, furnished with springy benches upholstered in metallic red, like old car seats, and Formica tables. Colored Christmas lights winked in the window beside them and a soundtrack of holiday songs played over the loudspeakers. The inescapable sparkle and cheer of the season must seem intolerable to someone with a broken heart, she thought, looking at Pete's drawn face.

She ordered a soda and Pete a cup of coffee.

"Jess," he said, cradling the mug in both hands as if needing its warmth, "what I wanted to tell you is, when I was up in New York over Thanksgiving, I had a meeting with the parent company of the publisher I work for. There was an opening there for an executive editor in their trade book department. It's for general fiction and nonfiction, not religious books. I told them I was interested. They called two days ago and made me an offer, and I accepted. So Ben and I will be moving back to New York. I'll go in January, and he'll stay with friends here and finish out the school year, and then he'll join me." His dark eyes on hers were dulled by pain.

"I'll be so sorry to see you go," she said. "But you need your family. Especially now. And it sounds like a great job opportunity."

"It is, for a number of reasons," he said. "For one, it's really been tough lately to work on all these faith-based books when my own faith has been shaken. You might even say shattered. I just can't believe that a merciful God would inflict such agony on someone as good as Andie. Or that he would take her from the family who loves and needs her so."

Jessie was silent a moment, wanting to choose her words carefully. "Pete, I don't think God made your wife get sick and die. I don't know why terrible things like that happen, but I don't believe they come from a loving God."

"But all those promises in the Bible?" Pete went on bitterly. "Saying what you pray for with your whole heart, God will grant you, and you can move mountains? We couldn't have prayed harder, along with a huge network of people in our church and our families' churches. I don't mean to sound naive or simple-minded, but the Bible says it in no uncertain terms: 'If you believe, you will receive whatever you ask for in prayer.' Was there a catch I missed in the fine print? Did none of us, including the best and holiest people I know, believe enough?"

Jessie spoke from her heart. "I can't answer that. I do believe that God shares our grief and pain. And that he comforts us. And takes us and the ones we love into Heaven with him, and we'll see them again there."

"I'd give anything to have such certainty."

The anguish in his gaze was so naked that Jessie could hardly bear to see it. The time had come to tell him her secret, to offer him that consolation.

The diner was quiet, sparsely populated; the music was soft now, some soulful male vocalist crooning "Have Yourself a Merry Little Christmas."

"There's something I've been meaning to tell you," she began. "Do you remember when we were in Gettysburg, and you told me about that book you were editing, about the people who had died and gone to Heaven? And we both agreed we wished we could have some proof that Heaven was real and that we'd see our loved ones there?"

"Yes…"

"Well, I've had that proof."

He stared at her for a long moment. "Tell me."

And so she did, the whole story—from meeting Lem on that mid-June weekend and falling in love with him over the course of the summer, to finding his people and bidding him goodbye, to helping to fight the desecration of his grave by developers. The only part she left out was their mystical encounter the last time she and Lem were together. That was too intimate to share with anyone.

"Oh my God, Jessie," Pete said in a low tone when she had finished. "He's the one you're in love with? That's… amazing. Please forgive me, but what you've told me sounds crazy. But I know you're not crazy."

"My pastor thought I was, at first," she said. "He's the only other person I've told. He wanted to send me to a shrink. Then I took him to meet Lem."

"You did? And he saw him? And he believed that he really was a spirit?"

She nodded.

"That's incredible. I can hardly take it in." He was quiet for a moment, frowning. "And you haven't told the soldier's relative? His great-great niece?"

She shook her head. "It would be too strange, too hard for normal people to accept. I wanted to tell you, because I've been so sad for you. I hope my story gives you some comfort."

He gazed out the window beside him. The blinking Christmas lights cast shifting colors on his pale face. He seemed to be struggling with something. "I'm sure it will, when I can take it in. One thing, Jess. I'm not sure I could handle it if Andie came back to me as a ghost. I think I would lose my last fragile hold on sanity."

"I believe," Jessie said slowly, "that most of the time, spirits or angels won't appear to us. I think God knows it would be too much for us to bear, to see them. I was terrified of Lem at first." She traced with her fingertip a ridge in the metal rim around the tabletop, briefly transported back to that time, seemingly so long ago, when she had fled in horror from the spectral young man in the clearing, but then had been compelled to return, drawn by his gentleness, the aura of goodness that he radiated, and compassion for his lonely plight. How unthinkably diminished her life would have been if she had given in to her fear and never gone back.

She went on, "I also believe those we have loved and lost are always near. Protecting us. Comforting us. Loving us."

He closed his eyes tight and drew deep breaths.

She turned her gaze to the night outside the window. Sleeting rain had begun to fall, ticking on the glass. The lights from the passing cars and from the shopping mall's signs and Christmas decorations made bright smears on the slick pavement.

"I do think God sends angels to us in human form," Pete said softly. "You've been one to me. You have helped me so much during this whole awful time."

"And y'all helped me, you and Ben and Andie," she said. "You got me back into my music again. I needed something in the real world—to make up for what I was losing when I said goodbye to Lem."

"I know the feeling." He said nothing for a while, then with an obvious effort at lightening the mood, he looked up at her with a smile. "So what's next for you, Jess?"

"Six months ago, I would have said that I wanted to be a professional pianist, and I was beating myself up for not putting in four or five hours of practice every day."

"That wouldn't give you much chance to do much else, on top of working full-time."

"No, and it would also be a very lonely life. I've found that I really like sharing my music with other people. Like doing the Civil War concerts with Becky and playing for Vicky and the ballet students. I loved working with Ben too."

"The feeling was mutual."

"Andie suggested that I teach private lessons. I'm going to try to do that."

"Great idea."

"Another thing," Jessie said thoughtfully, looking down at the abstract shapes printed on the Formica tabletop. "I've been acting like it's somehow beneath me to teach elementary school kids. But I'm going to look for the ones who're like I was, and like Ben was too. The ones who fall in love with music early on. I'll encourage them."

"That's wonderful, Jessie," Pete said. "Those kids will be lucky to have you share your passion with them."

"Thanks." Looking up at him, she saw the sincere warmth in his expression.

"Speaking of Ben, and the work you did with him," Pete said, "I should have told you this before, but you know, my brain hasn't exactly been firing on all cylinders lately. Ben's trumpet teacher, Dr. Dwayne Stringer, is head of the brass department at MTSU and he was very complimentary about your playing on the CD. He said he might have other students who need an accompanist. I'll give you his contact information."

"Thanks, I'll call him." It was a mark of how she had changed, Jessie noted, that the idea of phoning a stranger no longer caused a shiver of dread.

"I'm happy for you, Jess," Pete said. "It sounds like you've got yourself on a good path."

Gratitude swelled in her at his genuine concern for her, despite his huge, consuming grief. "Thanks, Pete. I think so. I'm giving up a dream, in a way. But friendship and relationships are more important to me than trying to be a superstar performer."

"Speaking of friendship, let's not lose touch, okay?"

"No way," she said. "And I'll look out for Ben while you're in New York."

"Thank you." He spread his fingers on the table and looked down at them. The gleam from the pendant lamp above them was reflected on his gold wedding ring. "And who knows? Maybe sometime in the future, when I'm whole and sane again, and if you want it, our friendship might develop into something more? I've always thought you're a very special person." With a visible effort, he raised his eyes to meet hers.

For a moment, confusion rendered her speechless. She felt pleasure at this proof that the attraction she'd felt for him had not been one-sided, but it was tinged with uncertainty—was he just, in his grief and loneliness, reaching out for the closest consolation?

"I'm not exactly whole or sane myself at the moment," she said at last. "Even so, that a man like you could think of me that way, it gives me hope."

This time his smile eased his entire face, giving a welcome glimpse of the old Pete. "Oh, there you go again, Little Miss Cinderella church mouse, never-gets-a-date. Think about everything you've managed to do in the past half year." He ticked off her achievements: finding Lem's relatives, getting the gravesite identified, helping to block a real estate development. "I see a brave, determined, capable woman, with talent to burn. And a tremendous capacity for love."

"Thank you," she said, feeling heat rise up her neck into her cheeks.

"And I also see someone who makes a hoop skirt look more… *interesting* than a bikini," he added with a wink.

She laughed at the memory of the old joke. Flooded with emotion, she dropped her gaze.

"Seriously, Jessie," Pete said gently. "Isn't it time to bid that old self goodbye?"

"Yes," she said, and found that she believed it. "Yes, it is."

CHAPTER 37

LOVE TOKEN

JESSIE STEERED THE van along the road that led past the band's campsite. It was greatly altered from the rutted dirt lane she had driven on throughout the summer. In the months since she had last been here, the Glenwood Building Company had widened and smoothed it and put down gravel. They had also extended it past the cornfield so that she could drive right up to the clearing where the gravesite lay, now surrounded by a chain-link fence to protect it until the remains could be removed.

She pulled into the parking area beside Sally's red car. Pastor John's white Taurus was parked nearby, and a gray car she didn't recognize, along with some trucks. Back on the job now that the gravesite had been explored and protected, men were working on the pale skeletons of four large houses that had risen up where the stakes had been the previous summer, just a few hundred feet away. The sounds of their power saws and nail guns and shouts to one another would be a jarring accompaniment to the solemn service.

The day was gray and chill, with a brisk wind blowing. The dark tracery of the bare tree branches was starkly etched against the cloudy sky; the cornstalks had been cut down close to the ground. The balmy summer nights she had spent here seemed to have taken place in a distant past, or even in another reality.

Sally had called the previous week to let Jessie know the plans for the funeral service, and to tell her that Professor Goldsmith had confirmed that the location and contents of the grave matched the description in Jeremiah Walker's letter. There was no doubt that it was Lemuel's resting place.

"I can finally update my family tree," Sally said.

Now Jessie shut off the van and said a quick prayer for strength during the next hour. She was nervous and afraid that she would break down in tears that no one would understand except for Pastor John.

She took a deep, steadying breath, then climbed out of the van and picked up a paper-wrapped bunch of flowers from the passenger seat; red and white carnations set off by sprigs of holly, their bright berries like drops of blood. She hurried toward the chain-link enclosure that contained the landmarks she knew so well, that either had been left undisturbed during the excavation or had been replaced just as they had been before—the snake-rail fence, the large, flat boulder. The only visible difference was that the ground within the enclosure where she had so often spread her blanket and sat with Lem was churned up from the burial excavation.

Thankfully, the construction sounds had ceased; maybe Sally or Pastor John had asked the workers to allow some quiet time, and the men respected that. Inside the fence, a small group stood: Sally, a woman Jessie presumed was her daughter Amy with her two small children, and Avery, a tall, upright figure in his army dress blues, the shiny black brim of his cap shadowing his face. Pastor John was talking with a lean, salt-and-pepper-bearded man in the green uniform and tan hat of a national park ranger. The park superintendent, no doubt.

Jessie hurried in through the open gate. She greeted Pastor John and shook hands with the ranger, who introduced himself as Paul Talcott, superintendent of the Stones River National Battlefield.

Sally came forward and gave her a hug. She was dressed all in black. Only a shocking-pink wool scarf wrapped around her neck and a matching hat broke the funereal monochrome. Then she turned to the family beside her. "I'm so happy to introduce you, Jessie. This is my daughter, Amy Peck, and her children Julia and Billy." Jessie shook hands with Amy, who looked to be in her mid-thirties and had her mother's keen blue eyes and wide smile.

"It's awesome what you did, Jessie," Amy said. "Thank you."

"You're welcome," Jessie said, then bent to greet the children.

"And this," Sally said proudly, "is my Avery, home at last, safe and sound."

Jessie turned to the young sergeant, and as she looked up into his face, the ground jolted beneath her feet. The eyes that met hers were large and serious and of an amber-brown color she had seen only once before. When he smiled at her, she almost gasped to see a dimple in his left cheek.

"Mama's told me so much about you, Jessie," he said, pulling off his white cotton glove to enfold her hand in his strong grasp. "It's because of you that we're here today. Thank you for everything."

"Oh … you're welcome, I was glad to do it." In her agitation, Jessie hardly knew what she was saying. She couldn't keep from searching his features, so startlingly familiar and yet different too—tenser, leaner, more guarded. As their gazes held, a slight question entered his expression, and with an effort, Jessie looked away.

"I don't mean to rush you good folks," said Pastor John. "But it is a little cold out here, especially for some of us who are wearing pretty party shoes." He smiled at Julia, whose small patent-leather Mary Janes were buckled over white tights through which her skin showed pink from the chill. "Shall we get started, Mrs. Gowan?"

"Yes, Reverend, let's do," Sally agreed.

"Let us pray," Pastor John began. "We gather here today to remember Private Lemuel Sanders, who died here 145 years ago today. In his self-sacrificing death, he exemplified our Lord's teaching that 'greater love has no man than this, than to lay down one's life for his friends.'"

Jessie clasped the flowers to her, breathing in the cinnamon scent of the carnations, as the prayer went on.

Then Pastor John opened his Bible and read from the eleventh chapter of John, the story of Jesus raising Lazarus from the dead. When he had finished reading, he closed his Bible and looked down at the ground for a moment.

He began to speak about death, what an incomprehensible waste it seemed when it claimed someone young with all his life ahead of him. How the pain of loss was made even more excruciating when the person just disappeared, denying the survivors certainty and the ability to move on. With the earnest and simple eloquence Jessie had always appreciated in his homilies, the minister went on to talk about death not as an extinction, but a transformation. "It is not an end, it is a beginning," he said. "We will change from corporeal to spiritual, mortal to immortal, from finite to infinite, from temporal to eternal."

Jessie glanced around the circle. Sally stood with her head bowed, gloved hands pressed to her mouth as if in prayer. Avery was gazing up at the sky, eyes narrowed. She was once again startled, not only by the familiarity of his features but also by the grim, defensive set of them, unlike any expression she had ever seen on his great-great-great uncle's open, gentle face. *Haunted*, was the word that came to her mind.

"Dear friends, in closing," Pastor John was saying, "I want to share with you the last words of Lemuel Sanders' fellow soldier, General Thomas 'Stonewall' Jackson. With his dying breath, he said, 'Let us cross over the river and sit in the shade of the trees.' I believe that he was granted a beautiful vision of the tranquility, rest, and renewal that awaited him, that awaits all of us, in the next world.

"On this date 145 years ago, Lemuel Sanders crossed over that river, and now sits with his Lord in the shade of the trees. He waits for us there, along with everyone else we have known and loved and parted from in this life. Let's share a moment of silence in his, and their, honor."

Jessie could not suppress a small sob. She bowed her head, fighting for composure.

Wind rushed over the stiff grasses of the clearing and made the branches of the trees sway. Weak shafts of sunlight penetrated the overcast, touching the landscape with brightness, then disappearing as the clouds closed again.

The minister concluded the service with the Lord's Prayer, and gave a final benediction to Lem and the men buried with him.

Then he stepped forward and extended his hand to Sally. She was holding Avery's arm; her eyes were red. She thanked the minister warmly, and then said, "Jessie, Reverend Brinton, we're having lunch before we head back up to Sevierville. Paul has said he'll join us. Won't you come too?"

Jessie thanked her and said she would. She wondered when Sally and Paul Talcott had progressed to a first-name basis; it made Jessie smile to hear it.

Pastor John regretfully said that he had to visit some parishioners in the hospital.

"Well, thank you again for a beautiful service," Sally said again. "We really appreciate it."

After Avery and Amy had expressed their gratitude, Jessie said to Sally, "I just want to speak to Pastor John for a minute. Y'all go get warm in your car."

"Where should we go for lunch?" Sally asked.

Jessie thought for a moment. "Do you know the Star-lite Café?" she asked Paul, and he said it was his favorite place.

"Go on ahead and I'll meet you there in just a few minutes," she said.

Paul escorted Sally and her family along the path to the parking lot, Avery resting a protective, white-gloved hand on his mother's back.

"Thank you, Pastor John. Thank you so much."

He patted her arm. "I hope this brings you peace, Jessie."

"It will. Your words were beautiful."

"Thank you. They were heartfelt."

"Pastor John, did you notice how much Avery looks like Lem?"

"I did notice. The family resemblance is very striking."

She struggled to choose the words that would express the fullness in her heart. Pastor John waited patiently.

"I just wanted to thank you for seeing me through this," she said. "I think ninety-nine ministers out of a hundred would think anyone who came to them with a story like mine was crazy, or blasphemous. But you listened, and then you said, 'Well, let's go out right now in the pouring rain at night and hike through a rough, deserted field to see this spirit.' Then you were so kind to Lem. I will always be grateful to you for that."

"It was a gift for me too, Jessie," he said. "It gave my complacency, my sense of the settled order of things, a healthy jolt. That's always a good thing for one's faith."

She nodded. "I won't keep you. I'll see you Sunday."

"Aren't you going to lunch with the others?"

"Yes, I just want to stay here one more minute."

She walked into the woods, which were thankfully untouched by development—at least for now. Beside the stone slab where Lem's life had ended, a squirrel was digging energetically. He kept on until Jessie was quite near, and she smiled in wonder at his boldness, his purposefulness. Holding something in his mouth—round and brown, a nut, probably—he hopped up onto the stone and jumped off the other side to bound off into the woods, dropping the nut onto the stone in his haste.

All was still and silent. Jessie sat on the rough cold surface. She spoke aloud softly. "Lem, you see I brought you your family. And Sally and Pastor John gave you that beautiful funeral." Tears came. "Oh, sweetheart, if you sent me a sign, I missed it. I guess I just have to pray you've found peace at last."

She wiped her eyes. Then, conscious that the others were waiting for her, she stood, took the wrapping from the bouquet, and began spreading the flowers over the surface of the rock.

Something caught her eye on the edge of the stone, the round brown object the squirrel had left behind. She picked it up and turned it over in her fingers, looking with wonder at a wooden ring, its delicately carved vines and flowers crusted with mud.

Hardly daring to breathe, she slipped it onto the fourth finger of her left hand. It was a perfect fit—as it had been that night in the white room, lying in Lem's arms. Her wedding ring.

With her hands pressed to her chest, the ring over her heart, she turned her eyes to the sky. "Thank you, my love."

THE END

Acknowledgments

My deepest gratitude to:

My editorial, design, and production team: Graeme Hague, Stephanie Parent, Mark Swift, and Damonza Studio;

The members of my wise and generous Radish Farm Writers' Group: Dana Shavin, Linda Voychehovski, and Kris Whorton;

Sam Mentzer, audio engineer, who helped me produce the audiobook in the Chattanooga Public Library recording studio;

Editors, friends, and fellow writers who helped make this a better book: Penelope J. Stokes, Sally Arteseros, Susan White, Eleanor McCallie Cooper, Carol Hardy White, Kathy Sagan;

Cassandra Barboe for her graphic design guidance;

Gail Hochman, whose early encouragement meant everything;

And most of all, to Douglas Hedwig, who supported and shaped this project in so many ways, and who brings music to my life.

An excerpt from

SOLDIER'S JOY

Book II of
The Sentinel Heart Trilogy

"For he shall give his angels charge over thee, to keep thee in all thy ways. They shall bear thee up in their hands, lest thou dash thy foot against a stone."
- Psalm 91

PART I

THE GUARDIAN

Chapter One

Avery Gowan woke to the sound of his own shout fading in the stillness of the room. He lay for a moment, heart galloping, eyes darting around in the dim light, until he made out the models suspended from the ceiling—Deep Space Nine, the USS *Enterprise*, a Klingon bird of prey. Okay, okay, he was home, in his boyhood room. The models rotated in the draft from his air conditioner fan which, despite the chill winter air outside, he had to run in order to be able to sleep in the disquieting silence of the Tennessee night.

Thank God his mother was not home to hear him yell. She was at his sister's house babysitting his niece and nephew while Amy and her husband were vacationing in the Caribbean, normal people with normal lives and carefree enjoyments.

In his dream, his buddies Hunter Trask and Nelson Estrada had been running across a bridge toward him, laughing as they raced to beat each other. With the sun full on their faces, and the bridge arching steeply so that they couldn't see its center, they didn't realize the structure was unfinished. A huge gap yawned between their side and the one Avery was on. He frantically waved and shouted to them to stop, but they neither saw nor heard him as they rushed to the edge, halted too late, teetered, and fell 200 feet to the water below.

That was when he woke himself up with a yell, the first time that had ever happened. He lay, panting.

It was weird the way the mind combined images from so many different parts of his memory. His family used to vacation on an island in south coastal Georgia. When Avery was about six, his father had taken him to see a new drawbridge under construction, spanning a broad, swift tidal river that flowed through the inland marshes. As he and his father approached the edge, holding hands, Avery had flung himself down on his stomach, clutching the concrete, frightened by the huge drop. Only his father's strong hands on his shoulders gave him the courage to get up.

How had that half-finished drawbridge over the rushing brown Georgia tide, and his friends from Iraq, been linked in his unconscious? If only it could have been water that took them, a quiet death by drowning. Wasn't that supposed to be a peaceful way to go? Instead of the explosion—the inferno—the terrible screams of men being incinerated inside an inescapable metal shell.

Clammy with sweat, his mouth dry, he sat up and swung his legs over the side of the bed—and then let out another shout. Across the room, next to the door that led to the hallway, stood a figure: the form of a man, but glowing in the dark, his outlines and features pulsing and shimmering.

Cold spider legs stampeded up the back of Avery's neck. He jumped to his feet and grabbed the first thing he saw to use as a weapon—his seventh-grade soccer trophy with its heavy marble base. He stood, poised to strike, feeling vulnerable in his boxer shorts and t-shirt.

"Don't be scared," the man said. "I don't mean you any harm."

And, in fact, he looked too unsteady to be a threat. He was leaning back against the wall, his hands behind him, his expression dazed. He was wearing loose white pajama-like things—a pullover shirt, baggy pants—and he was barefoot. He had long wavy hair. Some kind of hippie? But there was that strange, shifting light emanating from him.

Avery could make no sense of any of it. "Who the hell are you?" he demanded. "How'd you get in here?"

"I… I came to help you when I heard you holler."

"Help me? You break into my house and say you want to help me?" Avery gripped the little brass soccer player hard, resting the cold marble base in his left hand.

"I didn't break in."

"The doors were locked. I checked them before bed."

"I don't need doors or keys."

"You came through the wall, huh?"

"I think it was through the roof," the intruder said in a tone of apology, as if obliged to state an unwelcome fact.

Avery shook his head, muttering to himself, "I'm still sleeping. This is a dream. How do I wake up?"

"It's not a dream," the figure said. He straightened up and seemed to gather his strength. "I'm really here. Don't worry. I only want to help you," he said again.

There was nothing aggressive about his demeanor. He moved closer and Avery saw his face clearly for the first time. He sucked in a startled breath. He might be looking at his twin, except that the man was shorter than he, maybe five-eight to Avery's five-eleven, and considerably thinner—judging from what Avery could see of his body in its loose white clothing. But the two of them shared the same large eyes, dark eyebrows, lean cheeks, full mouth. Avery's hair had been just like the other man's, before his military scalping.

"Who are you?" Avery said again, his voice husky.

"You might could think of me like your guardian." The intruder spoke in the accent of rural Eastern Tennessee, the same accent that had always conveyed comfort and ease to Avery in the voices of his late grandparents, both of them born and raised in a small town in the Smoky Mountains.

"A guardian *angel*?" Avery said, incredulity making his tone contemptuous.

The man shrugged. "Well, I don't rightly know about the angel part…"

"Whoever or whatever you are, I'd like you just to go back where you came from and stay there. This is way too freaky."

"Well, all right then, Avery."

Avery felt himself gaping. "You know my name!"

"I do. And the names of all your kin. Your mama's Sarah. You have a sister, Amy, with two young'uns…"

"And how about you? Do you have a name?" Avery demanded.

The man hesitated. Then he said, "You could just call me Comrade."

"Comrade?" Avery snorted. "What are you, Russian or Chinese? You don't look or sound like it."

"No… I just thought, what soldiers call each other."

"We sure don't call each other Comrade. Buddy's more like it." But Buddy was way too warm and friendly. Impatient, agitated, Avery brushed off the name issue. "How did you know I was a soldier?"

"I know you just came home from a war in a place far away. Bad things happened there, and you see 'em over and over in dreams that make you wake up a-hollering. Like you just did."

He paused and his eyes met and held Avery's. "You shouldn't blame yourself."

"What the hell do you know about it?"

"I know bad things happen in war that aren't anybody's fault."

"Well, thank you. That really makes things better, to know that you excuse me."

The figure nodded, seeming unaware of the sarcasm. "Oh, and one more thing," he said. "That gal you just met? You ought to get to know her. She can help you."

Avery tossed the trophy onto his bed with a thud. "That's it! That's enough. Listen, Bud, Comrade, whoever you are, go guard somebody else. Quit prying into my business. I didn't ask for you. I don't need you."

"All right, like I said, I don't mean any harm. I'll go now. But if you need me anytime, you can just holler and I'll come."

"I won't need you, so go on now. I mean it. Go away and stay away. Now!"

"If that's what you want." He turned, and, like water soaking into sand, his luminous form faded into the wall, leaving Avery staring, stunned.

Going back to sleep was impossible. Avery went down to the kitchen and turned on the lights to banish hallucinations and nightmares.

He ate some leftover cold meatloaf right out of the Tupperware container, staring at the bulletin board beside the kitchen table. On the calendar, in the square for December 19, two weeks ago, his mother had written: "AVERY HOME!!!!!!" He recalled her joyful, tear-stained face as he came through the arrival gate at the Johnson City airport. "Oh, honey," she had cried, throwing her arms around him as passersby smiled at the sight of a mother welcoming her returning soldier. "At last, I can stop worrying."

He wished he could say the same. For the first time, he wondered if he really was more unhinged than he knew. The Army shrink at his discharge evaluation before leaving Iraq had said he should seriously consider getting counseling when he got home, after what had happened, and Avery had put him off by saying he probably would. But he had lied. He wanted to leave the events of the past year behind, bury them deep, not endlessly dwell on them and pick them apart.

Now, however, he wondered if he did need some help. It was much more plausible—and easier to take—to think that he was crazy than that he had actually been visited by a spirit. Or a guardian angel, for God's sake.

Finished eating, he shut off the light but then stood for a moment looking out at the night, the black, bare trees in the front yard swaying in a strong wind against the brightening sky. He wondered if the stresses of the past few days, the emotions and memories roused by the funeral he had just attended, had overloaded his nervous system, causing him to see things that weren't there. And hear things, crazy things.

Like, *That gal you just met? You ought to get to know her. She can help you.*

Dear Reader:

Soldier's Joy will be published in 2026. To be notified of the release date and promotional discount, please join my (low-frequency, spam-free) email list. You'll also find out about additional titles coming from Fieldwood Books, as well as other discounts and giveaways, book club discussion topics, author interviews, and more. Please sign up using the contact form at www.mfjoneswriter.com.

If you have enjoyed *Stones River*, kindly leave a rating/review on Amazon or Goodreads. Positive reader responses are the fuel that launches indie authors. Thank you for reading my work!

Mimi

M. F. Jones

About the Author

Before turning to writing full-time in 2008, M. F. (Mimi) Jones worked in publishing. She got her start at Viking Press where, as an editorial assistant, she discovered the bestseller *Ordinary People* by Judith Guest in the slush pile, and became its editor. She then moved to magazines and was a fiction editor at *Redbook* and a senior editor at *Family Circle* and *Reader's Digest*. Her feature articles and columns have been published in those and other magazines. When not writing, she can be found reading, knitting (while listening to audiobooks), singing in a choir, or hiking with her rescue dog. She lives in Tennessee with her husband, composer Douglas Hedwig. *Stones River* is her first novel, and the first book of *The Sentinel Heart Trilogy*. Connect with her at www.mfjoneswriter.com.

www.ingramcontent.com/pod-product-compliance
Lightning Source LLC
Chambersburg PA
CBHW032346310726
48973CB00007B/1870